01/02

An
Enduring
Love

OTHER BOOKS BY MICHELE ASHMAN BELL

An Unexpected Love

An Enduring Love

A Novel

Michele Ashman Bell

Covenant Communications, Inc.

Covenant ®

Published by Covenant Communications, Inc.
American Fork, Utah

Printed in the United States of America
First Printing: October 1998

05 04 03 02 01 00 99   10 9 8 7 6 5 4 3 2

ISBN 1-57734-333-6

Library of Congress Cataloging-in-Publication Data

Bell, Michele Ashman, 1959-
      An enduring love / Michele Ashman Bell.
          p.   cm.
      Sequel to: An unexpected love.
      ISBN 1-57734-333-6
      I. Title
      PS3552.E5217 L68 1998
      813'.54--dc21   98-41059
                                               CIP

This book is dedicated to
my father,
who taught me how to dream and blessed me with
his gift of creativity,
and to my mother,
for her testimony, strength, endurance, sacrifice,
and example of diligence and hard work.
I want to be just like you when I grow up.

Acknowledgments

Special thanks to my two truly "grand" mothers,
Viola Bauer and Norene Ashman, who shaped my life.

I'd also like to thank to those who helped in the research
and development of this story—
Diane Morrison, for her knowledge of art,
Evie Morton, Joan Whicker, Nicole Hill,
and my brother-in-law, attorney Matt Miller,
for helping me understand the special
circumstances and laws surrounding adoption.

Thanks to Julie Christensen, Barb Dutson,
Detra Soto, Lynelle Spencer, Amy Bell,
Peggy Schwendiman, and Caren and Brittany Tucker
for their time, input, and encouragement.

Thanks to my husband, Gary,
for being able to see things I can't, and
for helping me research Europe and making
it a second honeymoon.

And a special thanks to the wonderful people at Covenant,
JoAnne Jolley for her kindness and encouragement, and
especially to my friend and valued editor, Valerie Holladay.
Thank you just isn't enough.

When Alex McCarty visited her sister and brother-in-law in Island Park, Idaho, she didn't plan on learning anything more about the strange religion her sister belonged to. She only came because her sister, Jamie, was on the verge of yet another miscarriage and desperately needed some support.

Both sisters knew their mother would never come to see Jamie, even during this difficult time. Judith McCarty, like Alex, had avoided Jamie ever since her baptism into the Mormon church. It wasn't that they didn't love her; they just felt uncomfortable around her.

But Alex didn't expect to meet Rich Greenwood, the kindest, most handsome man she'd ever met. Both the gospel and Rich touched Alex's heart in ways she never imagined, and before long she'd accepted both into her life.

Alex's newfound faith and knowledge of the gospel also supplied the key to overcoming the eating disorder that had haunted her for years, despite her own training as a national fitness consultant and aerobics instructor.

Although Jamie ultimately miscarried yet a third time, she was comforted by Alex's recognition of the true gospel and her reconciliation with her mother, who did finally come to visit after all.

Now, as Alex looks forward to baptism into the true church of Jesus Christ, she feels a happiness she has never known. With her family and the man of her dreams beside her, Alex feels life is as perfect as it can be.

But when has true love ever been that easy?

Chapter 1

Alex McCarty was beginning to think Rich's great idea wasn't so great after all. Her back ached, her neck muscles cramped, and her arm felt as though it weighed a ton.

"Alex, can you hold that hat just a little higher?"

"Higher? Rich, I've been sitting here over an hour," she complained. But even though she was exhausted, he could have asked her to stand on her head and she would have said yes. Because the handsome man behind the easel was the love of her life, and she would do anything for him.

"Alex, please, I'm almost done." He looked around the canvas at her and grinned, and she was completely unable to resist his broad white smile and wonderfully warm molasses-colored eyes.

"Oh, all right." With a deep breath she tilted the straw hat a little higher. After all, this was for the man she loved.

Besides being part owner of an outdoor recreation rental business with her brother-in-law, Rich was an artist. He painted colorful, sweeping landscapes of Yellowstone National Park, the Grand Tetons, and the surrounding area. Island Park, Idaho, where they lived just outside of West Yellowstone was a gold mine of opportunity for an artist who loved the outdoors as much as Rich.

But he had decided to try something new. He wanted to paint a portrait. Of her. Something soft and romantic.

Alex had first met Rich Greenwood three months before, when her car had slid off an icy road as she was traveling to visit her sister, Jamie, and her husband, Steve, in Island Park, Idaho. Fortunately Rich had been there to rescue her. Alex had been surprised to learn that Rich was her brother-in-law's best friend, and Rich had been equally surprised to learn that she was Jamie's sister. And from that moment on, the magic had just happened.

Coincidence? Alex didn't think so. Even when she had struggled with the knowledge that she was falling in love with a man she could have no future with, she knew their paths hadn't crossed by accident. They couldn't help falling in love because they were made for each other. They both felt that way.

Rich had been Steve's mission companion, best friend, and business partner for seven years. Jamie loved him like a brother. It seemed only natural for Alex to join them and complete the picture. A picture made perfect by Alex's decision to join the Church.

How grateful she was that she'd finally put aside her pride and stubbornness long enough to let the Spirit touch her life. Both she and Rich had fought their attraction for each other, knowing that their love was doomed because she wasn't a Mormon and had no intention of becoming one. But the Spirit had taken care of that, just as the Lord had guided their paths to collide straight into each other. Alex would be eternally grateful that she had come to Island Park and met Rich and learned the truthfulness of the gospel.

"Alex?" Rich's voice broke into her thoughts. "You're not falling asleep again, are you?"

She focused back on the present. "Sorry, I was just thinking."

"Okay. I'm almost there. Tilt your head toward me just a bit more."

With all the patience she could muster, she tilted her head and tried to keep her expression pleasant. When he'd first come to her with this idea a few weeks ago, she'd asked him, "Why can't you just take a picture of me and paint from that?"

"Because," he'd said, running his fingers through her nutmeg-colored hair and kissing her softly, "you are my inspiration. With you there it will be a masterpiece."

"If this is how Mona Lisa felt when Leonardo da Vinci painted her portrait, no wonder she was smiling," she'd whispered.

"Have I told you how happy I've been these last three months?" he'd replied, as she had melted beneath his tender touch.

"Yes, but tell me again."

"I don't know what I did to deserve you, Alex, but I have never known such happiness and contentment in my entire life."

She never knew how to reply when he said things like that. Each day, each week, they grew closer, their love became stronger, and their lives became better.

"To be able to baptize you," he'd said softly, his voice full of emotion, "will be the best day of my life."

"And mine, too, Rich."

And so, dressed in a filmy white dress that swayed gently in the breeze and with her hair hanging in soft curls around her shoulders, Alex had sat for hours on a white wrought-iron garden bench in the shade of a glorious weeping willow whose branches dusted the ground. She was surrounded by fragrant flowers of every kind—rose bushes, poppies, and hanging baskets with geranium ivy lazing down the sides. It was a setting that brought forth images of the Garden of Eden.

And she was getting sick and tired of it.

Over the last two weeks she'd spent twenty hours or more, sitting in one position, on the bench with one knee up, her arm draped over her knee, while she held a stupid straw hat that Rich called a focal point. She'd had to sit extremely still, holding her head in one position, not looking directly at Rich, but not completely looking away either. She was sure rigor mortis was starting to set in.

After another minute her tolerance gave out.

"Rich, my arm's asleep. I need to take a break."

He didn't answer for a moment. The easel hid him from her view.

"Rich, can I move now?"

"Hold on," he said.

He hadn't let her see the painting yet. Of course, she knew it would be wonderful. But part of her couldn't help but worry. What if it wasn't? What if she hated how she looked in it? She was a bit nervous for the time Rich would let her see it. What would she say if she didn't like it?

"And . . . finished!" he said with a flourish and a sweep of his arm. "Alex, it's magnificent."

"Really? It's that good?" She moved slowly as her complaining muscles relaxed. Pushing herself to her feet, she tossed the large-brimmed hat onto the grass, resisted the urge to stomp it to pieces, and started for the easel.

"Wait, I want you to cover your eyes."

She could barely lift her arm to her shoulder, let alone to her eyes. "I won't peek, I promise."

"Here, let me guide you." He rushed to her side and carefully steered her around to stand in front of the painting.

"Okay, you can look now."

Slowly she opened her eyes.

"Oh, Rich," she whispered as unexpected tears stung her eyes. "It's beautiful." She meant it, too. The color, the shadows, the angles, everything, was in perfect balance. She loved it immediately.

Turning to him, blinking away the tears, she said, "It's more beautiful than I could have ever imagined." She threw her arms around his neck and hugged him.

"I'm so glad you like it." He lifted her off her feet and swung her around. "I knew it would be good, but it turned out even better than I could have imagined." He lowered her gently to the ground. "I don't know how you do it, Alex, but I feel inspired just being around you."

"You do the same for me," she said sincerely. He'd been the one who'd challenged her to read the Book of Mormon and find out for herself if it was true. His example, the way he relied on the Spirit and showed such a Christlike love for others, had touched her life in a way she'd never thought possible.

They kissed briefly, then Alex turned to look at the painting. She thought it would be strange to see herself in the portrait, but Rich had done an incredible job of capturing her expression, of somehow showing the love she felt for him, on her face.

"How did you do that?" she asked.

"Do what?"

"Make me look light, almost glowing."

"Shadows, contrasts. But mostly, I painted you the way I saw you—I painted you from my heart."

She didn't know why tears kept coming, but the moment was so beautiful, the tribute so moving, she couldn't help it.

She dabbed at her eyes with a lace handkerchief she'd been holding, until finally she was able to speak. "It's really breathtaking,

Rich. The more I study it, the more I love it. The whole feeling of the painting is so . . . peaceful. Reverent, even."

"That's how I feel when I look at it."

"Thank you," she said.

"For what?"

"For letting me be a part of the painting and a part of your life. I love you."

"And I love you, Alex."

Alex melted in his arms, marveling at the love she felt for this man. From the first time they had confessed their love for each other, barely a month ago, up to now, the word seemed to take on a stronger, deeper meaning. And even though that one word didn't seem to describe what they felt, it was the only one that came close.

As they held each other closely, the birds sang in the trees, the fragrant flowers swirled the air with their intoxicating perfume, and the breeze played the branches of the willow tree like a harp.

Everything was perfect. Alex wondered if heaven itself could be any better than life was right at that very moment.

* * *

That night everyone gathered at Jamie and Steve's house to welcome Judith McCarty back from New York where she lived in Manhattan and worked for a glitzy women's magazine. Alex knew it had nearly broken her mother's heart when she, like Jamie years before, had announced she was going to be baptized. Judith had never completely stopped blaming the Church for her husband's death; he had been killed on the way home from a church meeting not long after his own baptism into the church. Like her mother, Alex had also blamed the Church. But the last few months had changed that. And Alex thought her mother was beginning to change her mind as well. It meant a lot to Alex that her mother had wanted to be there for Alex's baptism, despite her own ambivalent feelings about the Church.

Judith had come to Island Park to visit her daughters around the same time Alex had come to take care of Jamie. Although Judith had been reluctant to come for a visit, she had enjoyed spending time with both her daughters. She'd also felt surprisingly comfortable exchanging her New York life for the relaxed pace of Island Park. Her editor-in-chief had allowed her to bring some work from the office, which meant she could stay on for several weeks, even months if she wanted. Alex had laughed when her mother, who had once pooh-poohed fax machines and the Internet, *now* admitted how wonderful it was to do her work just about anywhere in the world.

Alex looked around the room at the people she loved most in the world. Rich, her rock of strength to lean on, sat next to her, caressing her hand lovingly. Her brother-in-law sat in the wing chair, with Jamie sitting next to him on the floor, her head resting against her husband's thigh. Alex and Jamie exchanged amused glances as they watched Judith flirting lightly with Dr. Rawlins, the family doctor and treasured friend, whispering and laughing privately. Alex could tell the two needed some time alone to catch up on the weeks they'd been apart.

Jamie and Alex secretly wished, hoped, and prayed that their mother and Dr. Rawlins would find a way to be together. Neither he nor Judith had realized it yet, but they were perfect for each other, and the girls aimed to find a way to make the situation permanent.

Over the last few months, the two sisters and their mother had been through some rough times as they had worked through hurt feelings and painful emotions from their shared pasts. But they'd managed to forgive and forget, and had become even closer to each other than ever before.

Yes, these last few months had been difficult ones. Alex had taken a leave of absence from her job as a national fitness consultant, canceling lectures and presentations at fitness conventions. She had decided to extend her stay with her sister and brother-in-law when she finally realized it was time to face the biggest challenge of her life–the eating disorder she'd developed as a teenager and never fully overcome.

Jamie and Steve had been a great support to her through this emotional time in her life even though both were facing challenges of their own. Jamie had miscarried three pregnancies in two years and had become consumed with the desire to have a child. This obsession, as noble and righteous as it was, was beginning to drive a wedge between Jamie and Steve.

So, as Alex grew stronger, gaining understanding about her eating disorder and freeing herself from it, Jamie, who'd always been the stronger sister, was slowly crumbling. This created a dilemma for Alex, who was ready to resume her career, now that she was feeling better and in control of her life. The problem was, she didn't want to leave Rich, Jamie and Steve, or her new home and go back to California.

Alex loved living in Island Park. She looked forward to getting up with the sun every morning and hiking in the hills behind the house, or jogging the trails through quaking aspen and lodgepole pines, meeting deer, squirrels and even moose along the way. Or, going for picnics with Rich, sitting near crystal-clear creeks, in meadows of larkspur, monkshoods, asters and glacier lilies.

She never wanted anything to change. Life couldn't get any better than it was right now.

"So," Judith said, interrupting Alex's thoughts, "enough about New York. Let's talk about your baptism, Alex. I think I've got the food figured out for the dinner after the baptism. How many people do you expect to have there?"

Alex looked up. She had heard her mother's voice, but hadn't heard the question.

"It could be close to forty," Jamie said, "A lot of branch members have told me that they're planning on coming."

"Forty!" Alex couldn't believe that many people would take time to come to her baptism. "Are you sure?"

"You may even have a few more than that," Dr. Rawlins said, "This is one of the most exciting events our branch has had in a long time. I'm sure we'll get a big turn-out. Especially with Judith doing the cooking. After that gourmet cooking class she gave at home-making meeting, you may have people show up just for the food."

When Judith dipped her chin shyly and smiled, Alex tried to hide her own smile. Her mother was actually blushing. Judith McCarty was a strong-willed, independent woman, especially when it came to men, but Dr. Rawlins had exposed her vulnerable, sensitive, feminine side. A side Alex was thrilled to see her mother still had.

"Well, if I know Mom there's always plenty of food," Alex said. "But I'm more worried about Rich getting back in time."

"Isn't there any way you two can find someone else to go on this river trip?" Jamie said.

Steve let out an exasperated sigh, before he answered. "Jamie, we've been through this before. We don't feel comfortable hiring someone new until we've spent time with them ourselves to make sure they're qualified. Too many things can happen on the river." He got out of the chair and walked over to the fireplace, resting his arm on the mantel.

"But what about that guy from Jackson Hole? He's been a river guide for ten years," Jamie persisted.

Steve lifted his hand, emphasizing his words. "I've told you twice already. He's decided to go to Alaska for the summer."

Normally, a conversation like this would never take on an unpleasant tone, but Alex had observed Steve and Jamie's growing frustration with their situation and with each other. Jamie couldn't talk or think about anything but having a child. Steve felt like if the Lord wanted them to have a baby of their own they would; since they couldn't, they should adopt. For him, it was that easy. But for Jamie, it wasn't. And Alex knew it was tearing them apart.

Luckily Rich came to the rescue. "Jamie, I don't want you to worry about anything," he said, pulling a tube of Carmex from his shirt pocket. Rich had developed a healthy addiction to Carmex from all the time he spent out of doors. "If I have to swim upstream all the way, I'll be here." He applied some of the salve to his lips, then screwed the lid back on and returned the tube to his pocket. "I'm not about to miss Alex's baptism." Reaching for Alex's hand, he said thoughtfully, "You know, I haven't been in a baptismal font since Steve and I were mission companions."

"That would have been Rosa Jaramillo," Steve said.

"That was the highlight of my mission—baptizing her," Rich said. "Then Steve stayed in the area after I left and baptized Rosa's husband and their two sons."

"They've been through the temple, and their boys plan on serving missions," Steve told the others proudly.

Tightening his grip on her hand, Rich looked at Alex tenderly. "I'll be back in time for your baptism, Alex," he said with conviction. "I wouldn't miss it for anything in the world."

"You promise?" she asked.

"I promise, Alex. You can count on me."

Her heart grew warm as she dwelled for a moment on his words. While the others finished talking about the program and which songs should be sung, Alex thought about Rich.

He'd had a rough time with relationships in the past. Sometimes Alex still couldn't believe he'd been engaged to three different girls and broken the engagements every time.

But their relationship was different. There was something special between them—a deep, spiritual bond. His commitment meant everything to her and being able to count on him was important to her. After her father died when she was eight years old, she hadn't known what it was like to have a protector, someone to lean on and shelter her. Judith had been a wonderful mother, but Alex had missed having a father. She loved the idea of knowing Rich was there for her, always.

This was something she'd wanted for a long time, and finally, with Rich, she would have it.

Chapter 2

Dressed in her baptismal gown, Alex paced back and forth in the dressing room. Steve was still gone, looking for Rich. Everyone else waited in the Relief Society room for the service to start.

Something terrible had to have happened to make Rich so late.

The level of worry rose inside Alex like the evening tide, steadily consuming her, until she felt like she was drowning. She prayed constantly for Rich in her heart and, at times, on her knees.

The dressing room door burst open, and Jamie rushed inside. "Rich is here!"

Alex shut her eyes with relief and silently offered a prayer of thanks. After a shaky breath, she asked, "Is he okay? What happened?"

"I don't know, but he's all right. How about you? You doing okay?"

Her mind had painted awful, tragic pictures of the disasters she'd imagined might have happened to Rich. Thank goodness he was safe.

"I'm fine, now that Rich is here."

"You look pale."

Alex wiped at her eyes. "I'm okay."

"Bishop Miles said they're ready to start."

It was time. There was no turning back now. Not that she wanted to. She had received confirmations and promptings over and over, telling her without a doubt, this was the next step for her. And she was eager to do it. Baptism brought closure to a lifetime of questions and three months of the hardest time of her life. It also opened a door to a future full of promise and blessings.

"I'll be right out. I just need a minute."

Jamie hugged her sister, squeezing her tightly. "I'm so proud of you, Alex. I love you."

"I love you, too."

Alone in the dressing room Alex took the opportunity to kneel one last time before the meeting started. She expressed sincere thanks for Rich's safe return and for her family. Then she thanked the Lord for his spirit in her life and for all the blessings he'd given her. She was also grateful for the chance to have all her sins washed away, to truly stand blameless before him.

She added one last thought before she closed her prayer. *"Dad, if you're up there watching, I'm sorry it took me so long to accept the gospel. Thank you for showing me the way."*

Feeling peaceful and reassured she left the dressing room, following the sound of the music to the Relief Society room.

All heads turned her direction when she entered the room. She felt like a bride, dressed in white, walking down the aisle. Nervously, she smiled at the faces of family, friends, and branch members who'd come to witness this great event.

But the sight that warmed her entire soul was seeing Rich, also clothed in white, standing at the front of the room, waiting for her to take her place beside him.

He looked so handsome in his baptismal clothing, his skin richly tanned from the hours spent outdoors, his dark brown hair waving loosely across his left brow.

Walking towards him, she marveled at the joyous expression on Rich's face, the warmth and love in his eyes, the laughter in his smile. He was everything she could ever want in a man, and more. She loved him with all her heart.

He clasped her hand firmly in his and together they sat on the front row as Bishop Miles took his place at the podium.

"Are you okay?" he whispered in her ear, his warm breath sending shivers down her spine.

"I am now that you're here."

"I'm sorry I worried you. I'll explain what happened later."

She saw the bishop's mouth moving but didn't hear a single word he said. Rich had tenderly placed his arm around her, and there, tucked beneath his broad shoulder, she felt her mind ping-ponging from one thought to another. Would the water be warm? Would her big toe poke up so she'd have to get baptized again? Why had Rich been late? Was everything okay? And her biggest question—would the next year go as slowly as she dreaded, until they could get married in the temple?

Her thoughts flitted back for a moment to the first time Rich had brought up the subject of marriage. She had been lying in a hospital bed, still recovering from getting lost in a snowstorm, and had awakened to find Rich there beside her. That was when she had announced she wanted to be baptized and have Rich baptize her. And that was when he had said he wanted to spend the rest of eternity with her. But the year they had to wait until they could go through the temple together was what seemed like an eternity to Alex.

Rich leaned down to pick up a hymnbook off the floor, breaking her train of thought. Reverently they sang together, their voices blending in perfect harmony, his deep and full, hers soft and clear.

Each phrase created strong emotion inside Alex, building to a crescendo of feeling. By the last line she could no longer sing. Through blurred vision she read the words as Rich continued, *"His Spirit guides, His love assures, that fear departs when faith endures."*

How clearly, how beautifully, the words of the song expressed what was in Alex's heart. With Rich by her side, the two of them together, committed to the gospel and each other, fear did indeed depart. With all they'd been through together, they had witnessed this truth. She felt strong in her faith, a faith that would endure.

Somehow she made it through Steve's talk on baptism, but anticipation for the big moment grew inside until she thought she would explode right there.

"Are you ready?" Rich said, taking her hand to lead her to the water. It was time.

They stood, facing each other on opposite platforms of the font. With wide grins on their faces, they entered the warm water where they stopped in the middle.

The missionaries who'd taught her the discussions, Elder Tinefa and his new companion, Elder Dunston, fresh from Ireland, acted as witnesses. Steve and Jamie sat on the front row. Next to them, dabbing at her eyes, sat her mother and next to her, Dr. Rawlins. Beside them were the Becksteads, who were close friends and members of the ward. Colleen, Donald, and little Sarah had come to mean so much to Alex and her family. How astonished she'd been to learn that it had been Donald Beckstead—the father of sweet Sarah Beckstead, the young girl Alex had met at church—who, as a missionary, had brought the gospel to her father nineteen years before.

And now, after years of being away from the Church and the truths of the gospel, Donald was preparing himself to come back into the fold. His baptism was scheduled for the next month. What a faith-promoting experience it had been for Alex to see the change in the man and his family as the gospel once again became the center of his life. Donald himself had found his faith renewed by meeting the family of the man he had baptized so many years before his own faith had been challenged.

Behind them sat the bishop and his wife, Norene, with their son and daughter-in-law and new baby.

Many other branch members had assembled, all who had opened their arms and hearts to Alex in the past three months. She felt a strong spirit of love and support in that room, especially from Rich, who had been a mountain of strength to her. How grateful she was for the strong, broad shoulders she'd leaned on and cried on so many times during the months she had battled her eating disorder. But that was in the past. She felt cleansed and healed emotionally, and now she would receive that same cleansing and healing spiritually.

He looked down at her, raising his eyebrows as if to ask, "Are you ready?"

She smiled and nodded.

He raised his right arm, and just as they'd rehearsed, he performed the baptism, his voice carrying with it the priesthood power he proclaimed.

As she emerged from the water, she felt a release, a purging of sin as it was literally washed away. She was pure, clean, reborn. Tears of joy filled her eyes.

"Congratulations. I'm so proud of you." Rich pulled her into a hug. "I love you," he whispered in her ear.

Dripping, grinning, and crying, Alex looked at all the smiling, loving faces surrounding her and felt a flood of warmth within her chest.

How could she ever thank Heavenly Father for this glorious experience?

She stole one last look at Rich before leaving the font. Never before had she felt such love for a person. With him she felt complete. They were a matched set, like salt and pepper, the stars and the moon, hot chocolate and marshmallows.

With all her heart she prayed nothing would happen before their year was up and they could be sealed together for eternity.

But a year still seemed like an awfully long time.

* * *

"I'm so proud of you, Alex," Jamie said as she helped her sister get changed for the confirmation. "Look at all you've been through and now, here you are, a member of the church."

"I don't think I could've made any changes in my life without the gospel. Somehow I know, with the Lord's help, I can do anything."

Facing her eating disorder and making the necessary adjustments had seemed impossible. But her whole perspective on life had shifted as she gained an understanding of the plan of salvation and gained a testimony that God was truly her Father in Heaven. She treasured the comforting knowledge that even though she didn't have a father here on the earth, her Heavenly Father was only a thought or a prayer away.

Before she had the gospel in her life, Alex now realized, she had felt like she was trying to fit a square peg into a round hole, thinking she was happy, but never feeling quite content. The process of gaining a testimony and making changes was like shaving the corners off the peg, slowly, painfully, making it round and smooth, until it finally fit into the hole. That's exactly how it felt. The gospel fit perfectly into her life and she was ready and eager to embrace it completely.

"Jamie, can I ask you kind of a weird question?" Alex struggled to straighten one leg on her pantyhose.

"This isn't about polygamy again, is it?"

"No, I wanted to ask you what you think Dad's doing right now."

A wistful smile played on Jamie's lips. She paused a moment before she answered. "I know he is aware of what you did today. In fact," Jamie's eyes filled with tears, "I've felt his presence so strongly today. Just like I did at my own baptism." She wiped her eyes and nose on a tissue, then straightened the waistband on her skirt. "I haven't told many people about this, but right before I got baptized I asked one of the missionaries to give me a blessing. I was so scared because I knew you and Mom were completely against my decision. I mean, Dad joined the Church when he knew Mom didn't want him to; and when he died, she made extra sure we didn't have anything to do with the Church. I guess I needed a little extra assurance I was doing the right thing."

Alex nodded, painfully aware that she had not given her sister any support in her difficult decision to join the Church. Only recently had she gained a greater appreciation and respect for her sister's courage to get baptized, especially when her family had been so adamantly opposed.

Jamie continued, "Do you remember how Dad always taught us to trust our instincts, to listen with our hearts and not always with our heads?"

Remembering, Alex smiled. "Sure, he told us that all the time."

"Alex, we didn't know it at the time, but Dad was teaching us gospel principles. I never understood what he meant when he said, 'Girls, you are never alone,' until I had the missionary discussions. All the things he used to tell us came from the gospel—like remembering that God is always with us and learning to trust that inner voice that speaks to our hearts and minds. He never told us it was the Holy Ghost, but he wanted to teach us the things he knew. Mom would have had a fit if she had known what he was doing, so he had to choose his words very carefully. But his teachings prepared us to receive the gospel."

"How come it took me so much longer than it took you?" Alex turned so her sister could zip up her dress.

"Because you're more stubborn than I am."

Alex whirled around. "Thanks a lot."

Jamie laughed. "Do you mind? I'm not through with my story."

"Sorry. But that stubborn crack really hurt."

"You say it yourself all the time."

"Yeah, but it's different when someone else calls you stubborn."

"Okay, I'm sorry. I'll never say it again. Now, can I go on?"

Alex nodded.

"I'd been thinking a lot about Dad and wondering if he knew I was getting baptized. I missed him so much that day." Jamie tucked a strand of hair behind one ear and went on, her voice growing more quiet. "The elders gave me a priesthood blessing and told me that Dad was aware of my baptism and that he, along with the angels in heaven and those in my family who had gone before me, were singing praises for the decision I'd made.

"But that's not all they said." Jamie looked Alex straight in the eyes. "They said I would witness and rejoice in the day that my sister and mother also joined the Church."

"You're kidding." Alex stared at her sister in disbelief.

"Alex, I swear it's the truth. And believe me, I've wondered these past six years what kind of miracle it would take to convert you two, because frankly you and Mom were the last people I would've expected to see join the Church."

"Because I'm so stubborn?"

"It's not like you clapped for joy whenever I tried to talk to you about the Church," Jamie said quietly.

Alex felt terrible for the way she'd acted all those years. "I guess I do have a pretty hard head, don't I?"

The look in her sister's eyes answered her question.

"But I made it," Alex said proudly. And Jamie was right, it had taken a miracle, in fact, many sweet, small, miraculous experiences to bring her to accept the truth. "What about Mom, though?" she asked her sister, "I can't see her giving up her coffee and paying tithing. It will take a miracle for sure to convert her." She leaned closer to the mirror and checked her lipstick.

"I think her miracle is Dr. Rawlins."

"She won't join the Church just for him," Alex protested.

"No, but she might let down her guard enough so the Spirit can get inside. Haven't you noticed she never misses church when she's here?"

Alex had to admit, her mother seemed to enjoy going to church.

"And what about teaching at homemaking and all those comments she makes in Sunday School? She grew up going to a Methodist Sunday School. She knows the stories in the Bible better than most people. She would love the Book of Mormon if she'd just give it a chance."

Alex nodded. Everything Jamie said was true. How wonderful that would be. Then they could all be sealed together in the temple to her father.

Maybe it wasn't so outrageous after all to think of her mother joining the Church. The thought gave her goose bumps.

Chapter 3

"Steve and I are leaving." Jamie slid her purse strap over her shoulder.

"Why so soon? Is something wrong?" Steve had just blessed the food and everyone was filing through the buffet. But from the puffy redness of her sister's eyes, Alex could tell Jamie was in no mood for socializing.

"I just have to get out of here."

Jamie didn't need to say more. As soon as Alex heard Bishop Miles' granddaughter start to cry, she knew exactly what was going on. As the two-month-old wailed, her mother and father attempted to calm her with cooing, kissing, and cuddling. Using a binky, they managed to soothe the infant, then smiled satisfactorily at their triumph.

Alex turned to talk to Jamie but she was gone.

Feeling helpless, Alex wished she knew some way to give Jamie hope that she, too, would be a mother one day. Looking for Rich, Alex searched the roomful of people who were milling around the refreshment tables.

Just then Judith hurried by on her way to the kitchen. She was managing the food beautifully.

"Mom—" Alex stopped her.

"Yes, dear," Judith said breathlessly, her face beaming with the pleasure she got from keeping a crowd entertained and well fed. "I'm out of cream puffs."

"Have you seen Rich?"

"Not lately. But when you find him, tell him I made his favorite chicken salad croissant sandwiches. But they're going fast."

"I will."

Where was he?

Accepting congratulations and a dozen handshakes as she worked her way from the room, Alex finally emerged into the hallway and breathed a sigh of relief. Receiving an outpouring of love was exhausting.

Voices from down the hallway caught her attention.

Sitting in the foyer on the couch were Rich and Donald Beckstead.

"Well, if it isn't Sister McCarty." Rich closed his planner and set it aside.

Donald jumped up. "Here, take my seat. I was just leaving. I promised Sarah a closer look at the font."

"I'd like to see her before you go so I can thank her for the gift," Alex said. Earlier, six-year-old Sarah had presented Alex with a small gift from the Beckstead family, a beautiful gold CTR ring with a tiny diamond in it.

"I'll tell her." Donald turned back to Rich. "I'll see you after work around six thirty on Tuesday. I'm sure we can get that boat engine started."

Rich chuckled. "If Steve and I haven't made it worse trying to fix it ourselves."

"I'm sure we can figure it out," Donald said, before taking Alex's hand in his and shaking it enthusiastically. "Congratulations again. That was a very nice service."

"Thanks. I'm looking forward to your baptism," Alex said warmly.

"Yeah," he nodded his head, "I'm still amazed at how quickly things can change."

Alex noticed the brightness in his eyes, the pure joy that shone on his face. Since making the gospel the center of his life, Donald had completely changed. Especially considering that only a few months earlier there had been talk of divorce and of separating their family. Now Donald, Colleen, and Sarah were looking forward to the day they would go to the temple and be sealed for eternity.

"Well," he said with a smile, "I'd better go find Sarah. I'll see you both later."

Alex joined Rich on the couch and pulling her close, he took her hand in his.

"I've been looking all over for you," she said. "I missed you." She leaned her head on his shoulder.

He kissed the top of her head.

"Sorry. Don and I got talking about some trouble we had with that boat engine on the river today. That's why I was late; it broke down on us twenty miles downstream. I thought we were sunk until a ranger happened to come by just as I was ready to hitchhike back for help. "

"You made it back, though. Just like you promised." She snuggled closer. "I knew you'd be here, Rich."

"I was prepared to do anything to get back," he said. "I pictured you, standing here in your white dress, waiting for me to baptize you and I knew I had to be here." He wrapped his arms around her, kissing her lightly on the neck. "So, you're not mad at me for being late? Because if you are, I'll do anything to make it up to you." He snuggled closer to her.

"Anything?"

"Your wish," he kissed her again, making her heart rate speed up, "is my command."

"Mmmmmm," she sighed, "Well, okay, I wasn't even mad, and you're forgiven for making me worry so much. But I think I'll hold on to that wish anyway. I may need it sometime." She turned to face him and looked up into his eyes. "I'll never forget how it felt to have you baptize me today."

"I'll never forget it either."

They hugged each other tightly, merging their joy, joining their love, bonding their experience.

The patter of feet and peals of laughter echoed through the hallway. A pack of young children ran around the corner, saw Rich and Alex, and stopped dead in their tracks.

"Oops," a little girl with a mass of red curls said, "We're not supposed to be running. Sorry."

"I'll tell you what," Rich said, standing up. "How about if I give each of you a piece of gum, and you can go outside and run if you want to?"

"Okay," the group chorused.

Fishing a pack of gum out of his jacket pocket, Rich gave each of the four children a stick of chewing gum. Alex enjoyed watching him interact with the children, teasing one of the boys about his missing front two teeth, and the curly red-haired girl about how many boyfriends she had.

Laughing and waving, the children went outside to carry on their game. Alex couldn't help but imagine what a wonderful father Rich would be to their children.

"I forgot to tell you," he said as he sat down again, "an old friend from Sun Valley called. His name's Colt Bywater and he's coming through town in a few days. He wondered if I was still painting."

"Really? What did he want?" Alex had hoped that Rich would one day pursue his painting professionally. He'd given dozens of his landscapes to friends and family, even giving her his favorite painting, a beautiful scenic view of Hayden Valley. It was time for him to get something back for all his hard work.

"There's a woman at a gallery in Utah—up in Park City, near Salt Lake—who is looking for new talent. She wants to sponsor a show in January and expose new artists. Colt told her about my work and said she's interested in seeing it. Isn't that great?"

Alex turned, wrapped her arms around his neck, and hugged him. "I'm so happy for you. I'm sure she'll love your paintings, Rich."

"I'd like you to meet Colt when he comes. He's going to take a look at what I've got, then he'll set up an appointment for me to meet her."

"That's great!"

"I feel really good about this, Alex. I'm ready to take my painting seriously, to give it my all and see if there really is something there. I think working on that portrait reminded me how much I love to paint. It was so rewarding, so fulfilling, when it was completed."

"You have talent, Rich, a real gift. It would be a shame if you didn't try."

"You make me feel like I can do anything," he whispered tenderly.

"I believe you can," Alex responded honestly, "if you want it badly enough."

"You certainly have proven that." He stroked her cheek with his finger.

Alex didn't quite understand what he was getting at. "What do you mean?"

"Look at all you've been through these past three months. You never gave up. I'm so proud of you. Especially for getting baptized."

"This has been one of the best days of my life." She cuddled against him, laying her hand on his chest. "Nothing could top today, except for maybe our wedding day." She ran her finger down the outline of his lapel and felt his heart beating beneath his shirt, its rhythm matching the pulse within her own chest. That day seemed so far away. How she wished she could fast forward the next year to the time when they could kneel together at the altar and get married.

She pushed away the fleeting thoughts and doubts that streaked across her mind. Nothing would happen before then. The year would go by quickly and everything would be okay, she told herself.

* * *

The house was dark and quiet when Alex and her mother returned that evening. Both were exhausted from cleaning up after the baptism and mingling with branch members.

"I think I'll go soak in a hot tub before I go to bed," Judith said, setting her purse on the seat of the hall tree in the entry.

Alex deposited her purse beside her mother's and set her wet baptismal clothes on the stairs so she could wash them later. "Good idea, Mom. You really outdid yourself tonight.

Judith kissed Alex on the cheek. "This was a big day for you. I wanted it to be special, honey. I couldn't believe how many showed up for the service. I'm glad we had enough food for everyone."

"Everything was wonderful, Mom. Thanks for all you did." Alex hugged her mother just a moment longer. "I'm so glad you could be here."

Judith stepped back and looked her daughter straight in the eye. "Honey, I wouldn't have missed it for anything. I'm happy for you. And to be honest," Judith gave her a nervous smile, "I really felt something today, kind of warm inside. Of course, I cry watching Kodak commercials, but it was very emotional watching you coming out of the water like that. It made me wish I would've gone to your father's baptism. And Jamie's. I regret that, you know."

"I know, Mom. They understand." Alex hugged her mother. Maybe Jamie wasn't so far off in her prediction. Her mother had been touched by the Spirit today. And she'd even recognized it.

Judith gave a deep sigh. "Well, I'm bushed."

"I'll be up in a bit," Alex said, watching as her mother climbed the stairs to the guest bedroom they shared.

She turned on a few lights as she wandered through the living room then down the hallway to the family room. Where was everyone? Maybe Steve and Jamie had gone somewhere.

She decided to change her clothes and spend some time reading. There were dozens of church books she wanted to dive into.

Once upstairs, Alex noticed a light under Jamie's bedroom door. She walked to the end of the hall and listened at the door, but couldn't hear anything. She knocked. "Jamie?"

She thought she heard a reply.

"Jamie, are you in there?"

"Yes."

She opened the door and found Jamie slumped onto an over-stuffed chair, still in her church clothes.

"What are you doing?" Alex said. "Where's Steve?"

"He had some work to do."

"Have you been sitting here since you got home?"

Jamie nodded, her bottom lip trembled. Something big was up.

Kneeling down beside her, Alex patted her sister's hand and said, "Jamie, what's wrong? Did something happen?"

"No," she sniffed, as two big tears overflowed onto her cheeks.

In the past two months Alex felt like she'd grown stronger—emotionally, spiritually, even physically. Ironically, her sister seemed to be on a downhill slide, and picking up speed. Lately, Jamie was spending more and more time alone up in her room and Steve was spending more time at work. Something was wrong.

"Talk to me, Jamie. I want to help."

"Nothing will help. I could talk until my hair turns gray, and it won't change anything." Jamie didn't even bother wiping at her eyes and nose. "I can't help but feel like the Lord has completely abandoned me. Why won't he let me have a child? Doesn't he think I'll be a good mother?"

"Of course not. Don't be silly."

"Seeing that baby today, listening to her cry, then watching her mother hold her and comfort her, I felt like my heart was being ripped from my chest," Jamie choked out. "I can't take it. I want a baby more than I've wanted anything in my whole life. Nothing matters to me anymore if I can't be a mother. I just don't care about anything else."

Alex could see that this was discouragement talking. Jamie was down and vulnerable, a perfect target for the adversary.

"Listen to me, Jamie. Someday you will have a child, I'm sure of it. You can't give up. You have to have—"

"What, Alex? What do I have to have?" Jamie bolted to her feet. Her eyes sparked. "Faith? Hope?" She gulped as a sob tore from her throat. "You don't know what it's like to lose a child, let alone three. With the loss of each baby, a piece of me dies. My body is alive on the outside, but I feel dead on the inside. I don't know how to cope anymore."

Alex was scared. She was beginning to realize this wasn't something that would pass on its own. Jamie needed some help, someone to throw her a lifeline.

"Jamie, you have to hold on. I know it will get better."

"How? I feel like I've lost my whole purpose in life. What do I do now? How do I go on?"

"I'll help you find your answers. But please don't give up."

Alex led Jamie to her bed and coaxed her into laying down. After holding her sister tenderly for a few moments, Alex removed Jamie's shoes and covered her with a blanket.

Within minutes Jamie had settled down and fallen into an exhausted slumber. Alex watched her sister rest, hoping she at least found some peace in her dreams.

Her heart ached for Jamie's pain. She didn't know why Jamie had been given such awful challenges, but she knew the Lord hadn't abandoned her. Somehow she had to help Jamie understand that.

Chapter 4

Bishop Miles asked to speak with Alex for a few minutes after church on Sunday.

With the door to his office shut, he offered a prayer, then told her why he'd called her in.

"I spent some time with Jamie during Sunday School today," he said. "She's carrying an awfully heavy load right now."

"I'm glad you spoke with her," Alex said gratefully.

He shook his head. "I tried to help her understand that with a little faith, she could hand her burden over to the Lord, but she seems determined to carry it alone."

"I'm afraid for her. She's been saying some drastic things lately." Alex searched the bishop's face, looking for some indication that he had the right answer.

"You have every right to be concerned," he said soberly. "She's been strong for a long time now, but she's losing her strength. Right now she needs a lot of support."

"What can we do?"

"I'm calling Steve in to talk. I know this has been hard on him, too. Jamie's agreed to come tonight for a priesthood blessing."

"That's good," Alex said hopefully.

"And as you know, Jamie's been organist for sacrament meeting for quite a few years. But as we spoke I got the feeling she could use a little break. I don't know your schedule or plans, but I wondered if it would be too much to ask if you'd serve as accompanist for the time being."

Alex sat forward in her chair, eager to do something to help. "I'd like to, but I don't play the organ."

"Not a problem. We functioned for years with a piano."

"I would love to help out any way I can."

The bishop's shoulders relaxed along with his expression. "Wonderful. I'll have Sister Dalby contact you. She's the chorister."

Alex stood up proudly. Her first calling.

"Thank you, Bishop." She held out her hand to him.

Taking her outstretched hand and shaking it firmly, the bishop smiled. "No, Sister McCarty, thank *you*."

* * *

Very early the next morning the phone rang.

Alex answered it. She was up getting ready to go fishing with Rich. "Alex, is that you?"

It was her business manager and good friend, Sandy Dalebout. "Hi, Sandy. What are you doing up so early?"

"I'm about to make your day. I have some big news for you. Remember Rhonda Ferrier from *Today's Fitness* magazine?"

"Sure, she printed my article on boosting metabolic rate with short bouts of interval training. Didn't she call it "Bouts That Boost" or something corny like that?"

"That's the one. She called this morning and wants to do a feature article on you."

"ME!" Alex was stunned. "Why?"

"Even though you haven't been able to spend time promoting your video, sales are skyrocketing. I know you weren't happy about your eating disorder treatment getting mentioned in the *National Fitness Newsletter*, but all that exposure seemed to boost sales."

Alex had, in fact, been furious. While she wanted to tell others about her illness in her own words, the newsletter had somehow managed to find out about her treatment, expose her eating disorder, and blow her struggles way out of proportion. Following the release of the newsletter, her manager had been contacted by every major health and fitness publication and reporter in the business. A few had even managed to track her down at her sister's.

"Anyway," Sandy continued, "I told Rhonda about the chapters you wrote in the cookbook about your battle with anorexia, and she thinks your story would be wonderful to include as an article in their magazine."

Today's Fitness was a leader in their class. Their magazine was popular, informative, and highly respected by fitness professionals. Alex realized this was the perfect opportunity to tell her story in her own words.

"I think this would be a wise move, Alex," Sandy encouraged her. "You've managed to overcome something that thousands of people are struggling with. And Rhonda's willing to pay a pretty high price for your exclusive story. She wants to know by tomorrow so she can set up the interview for next week."

"That doesn't give me much time to think about it."

"What's to think about? We're talking big bucks and great promotion."

Trust Sandy to think only in terms of dollars.

"Plus, it would give you a chance to tell your story in your own words."

Alex had to agree with Sandy on that point.

"She wants to do the interview here in Palo Alto, with a photo shoot of you at the gym and at your office. But wait, that's not all."

Alex wasn't sure she wanted to hear the rest.

"You're never going to believe this. Do you remember that guy, Nickolas Diamante, from Italy?"

"Italy?" The switch in topics was too much for Alex. What did Italy have to do with anything?

"C'mon, Alex, remember the fitness conference in Manhattan a few years ago and especially last year in San Diego? He seemed to be everywhere we were."

Manhattan. San Diego. Nickolas! She hadn't thought about him in months. Of course she remembered Nickolas—all six-foot-three tall, dark, and handsome inches of him. "Oh, *that* Nickolas."

"*That* Nickolas," Sandy mimicked. "I thought you'd remember him."

"What about him?" Alex had been flattered by his attention, and his good looks and charm hadn't gone unnoticed. But she had just ended one relationship, and Jordan, her possessive, controlling ex-boyfriend, had managed to kill any desire for another relationship. That is, until she had met Rich.

"His office in Rome mailed an invitation for you to participate in a European fitness tour for two months."

"No way. Are you kidding me?"

"Nickolas is no joke. You are one of the six instructors he's chosen from around the world to participate in this European tour. I told you he 'liked' you."

"He doesn't 'like' me," Alex protested, but she liked knowing he could've chosen any one of hundreds of professionals—and he chose her.

"Alex, don't be stupid," Sandy argued. "How else do you explain his presence at every meal we ate, every lecture and demo you gave, and even running into us at the airport like he did?"

"Coincidences," Alex explained. "That's all." But she smiled as she spoke. Both she and Sandy knew that Nickolas had intentionally planned his "chance meetings" with Alex; but he had done so with such winning grace and charm, she might have actually fallen for him if circumstances had been different.

"Coincidences? You've been up in those mountains way too long. All that lack of oxygen must be killing brain cells. He's invited you on a first-class tour to sixteen cities in Europe—Rome, Barcelona, Monte Carlo, Salzburg. There's even a big convention at EuroDisney in France. If that's not 'like,' I don't know what is. And they've assured me in this letter that you will have plenty of free time to sightsee on your own."

"I can't believe it. Europe." Alex was stunned. She'd been to England once before, but that was as far into Europe as she'd gotten. This was incredible news.

"I'll fax you a copy of the letter so you can read the details. But will you do me one favor?"

"Sure."

"When you call to accept, will you ask him for an autographed picture of himself for my wall?"

Alex's voice was hesitant. "I don't even know that I'll go on the tour."

"You don't have long to decide," Sandy said firmly. "They're kicking this off in three weeks."

"Three weeks!" Alex was horrified. "There's no way I can go in three weeks. Why didn't they give us more notice?"

There was silence on the other end.

"Sandy? Are you there?"

Still silence.

"Sandy, you haven't let the mail pile up again since I've been gone, have you?"

"Alex, I'm sorry. I've been busy with the cookbook and video, and I do represent other clients."

"But three weeks! How can I possibly be ready that soon?"

"What are you doing that you can't get away from?"

How could Alex explain that her sister was falling apart and she didn't want to leave Rich for two days, let alone two months?

"Alex, you *need* to come to California and do the interview. We could talk more about the tour then. Plus, there's a lot of other business we need to take care of. It's been difficult having you gone so long."

"I know," Alex agreed. Expecting Sandy to do everything for her was a lot to ask. "I'm just trying to figure out how I can sneak in a trip to California."

"You only need to be here a few days. Besides, I want to hear about everything you've been doing, especially about Rich and your baptism."

Talking to Sandy made her realize how much she missed her friend, and Alex felt bad for neglecting her all this time. "Okay, I'll see what I can figure out. Fax all that stuff to me today if you can."

"I will and don't forget you need to call Rhonda tomorrow with an answer. Then we'll set up a time for you to fly out here."

"Okay, okay. Is that all?" Alex shook her head, tiredly. She sure hadn't missed all the stress and headaches of her job.

"I think so. At least for now."

"I'll talk to you soon then, but please make sure you go through my mail each day." She didn't want any more surprises.

"I promise. And don't forget to call Nickolas and ask for my picture."

"Good-bye, Sandy," Alex said with a laugh.

With a sigh she hung up the phone. She'd been thinking about going back to California to check on her apartment and take care of business. But not for another month or so. Now it seemed as though she had no choice. Especially *if* she decided to do the interview and *if* she decided to go to Europe.

Europe! Nickolas Diamante. She had to admit she had thought about him a few times after that conference. But that was months ago. She wasn't interested in him now. This was a business proposition. And besides that, she was in love with Rich.

The doorbell rang.

Pushing her sweatshirt sleeves up to her elbows she went to the door.

Wearing a goofy-looking hat with fish hooks dangling around the brim, a pair of waist-high waders, and a plaid shirt that made him look like a Brawny ad, Rich stood in front of her, smiling from ear to ear. Alex felt suddenly breathless at the sight of him.

"Hi. I'm not quite ready," she stammered.

"That's okay," he said easily. "I'll wait in the truck."

She was glad they were going to have some time alone. Maybe he could give her some helpful input about this European tour.

She raced up the stairs, stumbled into her room where her mother slept, and quickly changed into jeans, a t-shirt, and tennis shoes. Pulling a ball cap onto her head, she ran to the bathroom, brushed the front side of her teeth without toothpaste, then flew back down the stairs.

Remembering she hadn't eaten breakfast, she hurried to the kitchen, grabbed two bagels and two apples, threw them into a bag, and headed for the front door. She'd committed to her treatment counselor to eating at least twelve hundred calories a day. Most days she was lucky to eat one thousand. But the important things was, she wasn't losing weight.

Even though she felt like she had conquered her disorder, it was still a conscious effort to eat enough each day. Especially when she got busy or upset or distracted or worried or . . . Okay. So she wasn't cured, but she was getting better.

Gulping for air, she climbed into the truck. "Sorry I wasn't ready."

"No problem. I've been sitting here making a list of the paintings I want to show Colt when he gets here."

"When is he coming to town?"

"Wednesday sometime. Are you going to be around?"

"I don't have any plans."

"Good. I want to show him that landscape I gave you."

For a moment she was afraid to agree. What if Colt loved it as much as she did, and wanted it for himself, or the show? She wasn't about to part with the painting. *That's silly*, she told herself. *Rich gave you that picture. He's not going to ask for it back.*

"Sure, it's hanging in my room."

"Good. I think he'll like it. And I want to show him your portrait. I'd like to see if he loves it as much as I do."

Alex hoped her portrait wouldn't end up in some display.

"I still can't believe this, Alex. The more I think about the chance of actually having a show in a gallery, displaying and selling my work for people to hang in their homes, the more I know this is right. Especially since I've been so distracted at work lately. It's just not the same for me as it used to be. I'm ready for a change. And right now what I want to do is paint."

Rich reached over to the compartment beneath the stereo and rummaged around until he located a tube of Carmex. After Rich had smeared his lips with it, he returned the tube to its spot, then exited off the highway taking the road leading to Henry's Lake. As they made their way over the bumpy road, the little trailer carrying the trolling boat bounced along behind them. Dust from the unpaved road rose in clouds as they followed the winding road through tall evergreens and wildflowers.

At the parking lot, Rich pulled around to the ramp and backed the trailer into the water. He put on the parking brake and hopped out. Unhitching the boat, he whistled to Alex, her signal to drive the truck back up the ramp and find a parking spot. When she had done so, she locked the truck and hurried back to the shore.

The sun was above the horizon now, with no other boats or fishermen in sight. Wispy, magenta-colored clouds feathered across an azure sky. The air was fragrant with the mixture of peppermint, wildflowers, and morning dew. Alex filled her lungs and marveled at the beauty she'd grown to love. Island Park was a milestone in her life. She would never forget the time she spent here. It had become a healing place, a place she'd faced her greatest challenges and experienced her greatest triumphs. And the place she'd found the love of her life.

Taking her arm, Rich helped her into the boat. With the low engine humming, they made their way toward the center of the lake, gentle waves lapping at the side of the boat. The engine gurgled and hissed, then stopped when they reached their destination.

The reflection of the rising sun turned the water to glass, showing a mirror image of the shoreline in the silver lake. Not a breeze or a ripple broke the surface, as if the moment were frozen in time.

"It's so beautiful," Alex whispered.

Rich nodded. "I wish I had my camera."

"Maybe you could paint it."

"Yes, it would be perfect on canvas."

They fell silent again as the trill of a bird echoed through the trees.

Then, from a distance they heard an engine and a vehicle rumbling toward the lake. Within minutes voices and children's laughter filled the air. The tail lights of a trailer appeared, then a station wagon backed a worn boat with chipped, peeling paint down the ramp. Two youngsters scampered to the lake edge, dipping bare toes in the water, then squealing at the nipping cold.

"You two get back here and get some shoes on," a woman called, "I don't want you catching your death of cold. "

Rich and Alex looked at each other, disappointed that the enchanted moment had ended so abruptly.

The next hour was a futile attempt for them to snag some trout for dinner. Several boats and wave runners had joined them, making it impossible for Rich and Alex to find a quiet place on the lake. Finally, after slapping at mosquitos and reeling in empty hooks, Rich and Alex decided to pack it in.

"We're going to have to get out here earlier next time if we want any peace and quiet," Rich said.

"And if we want any fish," Alex added.

Slowly, they trolled their way back to the dock, hanging on as speed boats whipped by, chopping up the water.

Rich shook his head, a look of impatience on his face.

"What's the matter?" Alex asked, not used to seeing him so easily annoyed.

He sighed. "Nothing. It's just that lately I've started feeling irritated by all the tourists. The lakes and streams are overrun with them, the mountains are crawling with them, and the campgrounds and picnic areas are jam-packed with them. I feel like they expect Steve and me to keep them entertained all the time, to get this tent repaired before this group comes, to replace that engine before the next river run . . . It never ends."

Alex was surprised to hear Rich speak like this. She'd never heard him complain about his job or the tourists before.

Just then another truck hauling more wave runners pulled up to the dock, and a load of teenagers jumped out of the back. Sacks of garbage from a fast-food restaurant spilled out with the bodies, littering the ground. Instead of following the dirt paths, the kids spread out over the grass and flowers, running, jumping, and tromping the growth, leaving a trail of destruction in their wake.

Alex watched Rich stiffen as he observed the teens. They were just being kids, just having fun, but their actions punctuated his complaint.

Not much was said as they loaded the boat and drove home, but Alex's gut tightened with worry. Rich seemed preoccupied and distracted.

With their fishing trip cut short, they ended up over at Rich's house. Alex helped him plant some rose bushes and several flats of bright-colored petunias in his front yard. She enjoyed working at Rich's side, talking with him about everything from movies to gospel topics.

This was the kind of relationship she'd always dreamed of, one in which the man not only was her sweetheart, and could make her heart beat at warp speed, but where he was also her best friend, someone she admired, respected, and loved.

Sipping tall glasses of ice water in the shade on his front lawn, Rich and Alex eyed their work and talked about other ways to beautify the landscape. He liked Alex's suggestion of clearing out some scrubby bushes that had overgrown the side of the house and putting in a trellis covered with ivy.

Setting their empty glasses off to the side, Alex leaned back on her elbows, letting the breeze tickle her brow and tug at strands of hair. Rich rested back on the trunk of the tree chewing the stem of a piece of grass, his eyes closed.

"I never knew you were such a landscaper," he said.

"I've always wanted a place of my own to decorate and a yard to grow flowers and vegetables. But I've never lived in anything but an apartment or a condo," she said with a slight frown. "I hope that wherever we live after we get married, we'll be able to have a yard." His eyes still closed, Rich seemed to be listening but he didn't respond.

Alex had a perfect visual image in her mind of the home they would share, a cozy cape cod, with dormers and window boxes, surrounded by huge trees and flower beds. She could see Rich in his upstairs studio, with a view of their backyard overlooking a small duck pond and gazebo, painting at an easel. She would come into the room, holding a basket full of flowers and fresh-picked vegetables from their garden. They would spend the afternoon walking along forested paths and picnicking at their own secret spot near a rushing stream beneath a canopy of trees.

"You know, we haven't ever talked about where we'll live after we get married," she said thoughtfully. "I need to be near an airport, but you need to be here in Island Park for the business. Of course, you and Steve have talked about hiring someone to manage the rental business so that would free you up a bit, then you could have more time to paint." She paused, waiting for his answer, but he still didn't speak.

"What do you think, Rich? Have you thought about where you would like to live? I mean, not that I don't want to live in this house. I love your log cabin. I just wondered if you'd thought about us living somewhere else. And you know," she continued, "we really haven't talked much about a date. Now that I'm baptized and it's just a matter of waiting out the year, we could actually set a wedding date. Have you thought about a date yet? Rich?"

She watched him, breathing evenly, his head tilted slightly to one side. Had he fallen asleep on her?

"Rich?" she leaned forward, getting a closer look.

"Yes," he said, opening his eyes.

"Did you hear anything I said?"

"Of course I did."

"Well, what do you think?"

"I think . . ." he looked at her with a gleam in his eyes, ". . . I think it's been a long time since I've tickled you."

He lunged at her. Alex screamed and rolled out of his way. She hated being tickled. She was ticklish everywhere, even on her elbows.

"Rich, no!"

But before she knew it, Rich had her curled up, laughing until her ribs ached.

Chapter 5

Tuesday night Steve decided to make his famous mission food. Slimers!

Not sure she liked the sound of "slimers," Judith barbecued kabobs—marinated beef and chicken kabobs with potato chunks and green peppers, and Alex's favorite, bacon-wrapped shrimp kabobs with mushrooms, grilled on the barbecue. Just in case Steve created a culinary disaster.

Alex, Jamie, and Judith sat outside on the patio, enjoying the refreshing canyon breeze and the delightful smell of the sizzling kabobs. Inside, Rich and Steve put finishing touches on their masterpiece.

Alex was happy to see Jamie showing a little more life and enthusiasm. She'd actually done her hair and put on makeup for the evening meal. Lately she'd been spending most of her days in an old purple robe with her hair pulled back into a clip on her head.

While they waited for the men to serve the meal, Alex brought up the subject of Dr. Rawlins.

"Mom, are you sure you don't have a medical condition you're not telling us about?"

Alex raised a teasing eyebrow at Jamie, hoping Jamie would help her expose the blossoming relationship between her mother and the good doctor.

"Heavens no, Alex," Judith said, turning the meat on the grill. "Why would you ask such a thing?"

"You're spending so much time with the doctor, I was getting a little concerned," Alex smiled mischievously.

Jamie covered her smile with her hand.

"Dave—I mean, Dr. Rawlins—and I just enjoy each other's company, that's all. We don't spend *that* much time together."

"You're gone so much with him, I thought you'd gone back to New York without telling me," Jamie piped in.

"Would you listen to yourselves." Judith waved the tongs at them. "Whatever you two are getting at, well . . . just stop it."

Alex and Jamie giggled at how flustered their mother had become. Judith attempted to put the kabobs on a platter but in the process dropped several on the ground. "Now look what you made me do."

"Sorry." Alex couldn't let the subject drop quite yet, "So you're saying there's nothing going on between you and Dave?" Alex said. "I mean, Dr. Rawlins."

"Dr. Rawlins and I are just friends. Besides, I didn't know I needed my daughters' permission to date somebody."

"Aha!" Jamie clapped her hands together. "So, you are dating him."

"You two stop it now."

The sliding door opened and Steve walked out carrying a casserole dish. Rich followed behind with a large salad bowl in one hand and a basket of garlic bread in the other.

"Thank goodness it's time to eat," Judith said.

With all the food spread on the table, the women were forced to admit how yummy Steve's dish looked, because it truly did look delicious. To their surprise, it even tasted good.

"I have to admit, Steve," Judith said, "I was a bit nervous to try your 'slimers,' but they are quite tasty. You say they're just diced ham, onion, and green pepper rolled in tortillas with mushroom soup and cheese?"

"Yeah, pretty much. These aren't quite authentic, though," Steve said. "In the mission field we didn't use ham."

"We used 'Spam,'" Rich added.

"Ugh. That sounds disgusting." Jamie pulled a face and shivered at the thought.

"It wasn't too bad," Rich explained. "But Steve got a little carried away with the stuff. In fact, Alex, you could write another cookbook with his recipes and call it *One Hundred and One Ways to Cook with Spam*. Steve made everything from Spam stir-fry to Spam lasagne."

"Gee," Alex said, "what a great idea. I'm sure it would be a best-seller. I'll have to call Sandy."

"Speaking of Sandy," Judith said. "Did you tell everyone your exciting news?"

Alex's forkful of slimer froze in mid-air. Nervous about Jamie's reaction, Alex hadn't decided yet how she wanted to tell her sister about her possible European tour. She had definitely not planned on making a group announcement.

"What news?" Jamie asked, sitting up with alarm.

Wishing her mother hadn't said anything, Alex chose her words carefully. "It's nothing really. I talked to an editor at *Today's Fitness* magazine and accepted their offer to do an exclusive story about my life, mostly my struggle with anorexia and my career as a fitness professional."

"That's great," Steve said. "Do you think you could mention Recreation Headquarters in your article? You know, a little free advertising."

"I'll try, Steve." She smiled at her wily brother-in-law and went on, "I need to run to California in a few days to do the interview and take care of some business."

"But that's not all," Judith said. "Tell them the rest of your news, Alexis."

"Mom." Alex tried to inflect a "not now" tone to her voice.

"But you haven't told them the best part," Judith said. "At least, I think it's the best."

"What is it, Alex? Tell us." Jamie sat on the edge of her seat, looking intently at Alex.

"I've been invited to go to Europe for two months with a group of instructors from around the world on a Fitness Tour," she said at last.

Jamie's expression changed from curiosity to outright fear.

"You're leaving?" she said.

Alex was sick. She didn't know what to do or say. Leaving Jamie when she was under such strain felt to Alex like she was betraying her own sister.

"I think it sounds like a great opportunity," Rich said.

Alex looked at him with surprise. She'd expected him to be supportive, he always was. But he spoke so casually, so unemotionally, as if two months meant nothing to him.

She supposed she was just being oversensitive, but the least he could do was show some emotion at the thought of her being gone for such a long time.

"You do?" Alex swallowed hard, waiting for him to add, "But I'll miss you terribly" or "I don't know how I'll survive without you."

Instead he said, "In fact, I understand it's hard to see all of Europe in just two months. You may even want to stay on after and do more traveling while you're there."

Alex's mouth dropped open. Was he actually telling her to stay longer?

Before she could comment, Jamie reached for the salad bowl and leftover garlic bread, knocking over the salt shaker and clanging it into the water pitcher.

"Jamie, I'll do that." Alex jumped to her feet.

"No, it's okay. I can get it." Jamie rushed from the table so fast she tipped her chair over backwards. It clattered into the barbecue, nearly knocking it over. Rich caught it just in time.

Clamoring through the door, Jamie disappeared into the safety of the house.

"I'd better go help." Steve slid his chair back and hurried inside.

"I didn't think Jamie would get so upset," Judith said. "I feel terrible."

"So do I," Alex said.

"I'll go talk to her." Judith picked up the casserole dish and platter containing leftover kabobs and went inside.

Alex and Rich remained in awkward silence. She didn't know what to say or feel. Concern about Jamie filled her mind, but confusion about Rich filled her heart. Maybe she was just being oversensitive, but it seemed like he was anxious to not only see her go to Europe, but to even stay away as long as she could. That didn't make sense. Why would he?

"I hope she's going to be okay," he said, stacking plates and gathering silverware.

"I do too," Alex said. "I wish Mom hadn't said anything. I didn't want to tell Jamie until I'd decided for sure if I was going or not."

"You wouldn't pass up this chance, would you?" he said with some surprise.

"I don't know," Alex said slowly. "I haven't really had time to think it through all the way. I am worried about leaving Jamie, though."

"I hate to see you miss an opportunity like this, Alex," Rich said seriously. "This sounds like the chance of a lifetime."

"It's for two months, Rich," she reminded him. Didn't he realize how long that was?

"I know. But it would go by fast." His tone sounded flat, almost unconcerned.

She tried to read his expression, look into his eyes, but he was too involved in cleaning up dinner. "I'd have to leave in three weeks."

He looked up. Finally she'd jarred him. "Wow. Can you get a passport that fast?"

She looked him dead in the eyes. "I've already got a passport, Rich."

He lifted his eyebrows. "That's great. Then you're all set." He picked up an armful of dishes and turned to take them indoors. "Can you get the door for me?"

"But, Rich . . ." Looking at him, Alex suddenly felt like she was talking to a stranger. What was going on? Why was he acting like it was no big deal that she would be gone so long?

"What, Alex?" His voice held a note of impatience as he took a step closer to the door.

"Doesn't it matter to you that . . . I'll be gone so long?" she asked slowly.

Rich shrugged. "You'll be busy, I'll be busy. Like I said, it'll go fast. Besides, I think it's good for couples to take time away from each other."

She searched his expression, trying to understand. His words didn't make sense. In fact, the whole conversation had gotten off on the wrong exit and she didn't know how to turn it back around.

She said nothing, but simply opened the door so he could go inside. What was wrong with him?

* * *

Steve left early for work the next morning. He didn't stay around the house much anymore. Sometimes he didn't get back home until late in the evening, just to eat a warmed-up dinner and spend the rest of the night in front of the television until he fell asleep on the couch.

His behavior, combined with Jamie's reclusiveness, worried Alex. Ever since the stillbirth of their last baby, they had drifted apart. She could see the pain and longing in their eyes, but their grief had sealed their hearts and mouths. If they would only open up to each other, share their feelings, Alex knew they could rebuild their relationship even stronger than before.

Sitting in the quiet of the living room, Alex mulled over the events of the previous night. Jamie had gone straight to her room and hadn't come out even to say good-night. Steve and Rich found some work related project in the garage to keep them busy, and after cleaning the kitchen, Judith and Alex sat on the porch and wondered what to do for Jamie and Steve.

Alex still wondered what to do.

One thing she had decided, she wasn't going to Europe. Staying with Jamie was her main excuse to stay home, but she knew deep down she was using Jamie's needs as a way to be with Rich. The problem was, he didn't seem to want her here!

She knew she was just being oversensitive, upset that he wasn't pining over her possible absence, but darn it, why wasn't he? She would be overcome with grief if he were leaving her for two months.

Was she just insecure or were the vibes she was picking up from him as strange as they felt?

Maybe Jamie and Steve needed to talk, but so did she and Rich. All his talk about love and needing her, wanting to spend his life with her had given her the impression that he wanted a lasting relationship. Nothing between them had changed, at least in a verbal sense, but Rich did seem preoccupied lately. Restless. Uneasy. And at times, distant. Just like last night.

Yes, they needed to talk.

Alex could hear the printer upstairs in the office. Judith was working on a feature article on Yellowstone National Park and the surrounding area. The required research gave her the perfect opportunity to turn her vacation into a "work" assignment, with minimal "work" required.

Still in her room, Jamie hadn't come downstairs for breakfast or even to see where everyone was.

Maybe Jamie would feel better if Alex told her she wasn't going to Europe. But before she had a chance to find her sister and tell her, the doorbell rang.

Rich and another man stood before her.

"Hi, Alex, we came to see the paintings."

Why hadn't he said something the night before, or called this morning to tell her what time he was coming?

"Oh, hi. This must be your friend."

The man stretched his hand forward, "I'm Colt Bywater, nice to meet you, Alex. Rich has told me a lot about you."

They shook hands and she invited them inside.

She immediately liked Colt. He was Native American and carried himself like a warrior. He stood several inches taller than Rich's six-foot-one frame, with shoulders as wide as the doorway. He wore jeans and a denim shirt, along with some beautiful turquoise and coral jewelry. His hair was pulled back into a braid, tied with a leather cord and hanging between his shoulder blades. He also had a warm, friendly smile that set her immediately at ease.

"Would you both like something to drink?" She wasn't sure what to offer. It was almost eleven in the morning, too late for breakfast, too early for lunch.

"We just came from the diner," Rich said. "Colt got here around nine, so we grabbed a bite to eat before we came over."

"Rich tells me you're getting ready to go to Europe." Colt hooked his thumb through a belt loop and leaned against the newel post.

She knew her face registered shock, but she couldn't hide her surprise. She hadn't even decided yet. Why would Rich say she was going when she herself didn't even know for sure? Quickly she gained her composure and said, "Actually I haven't decided yet. My sister isn't feeling well and needs my help."

"I'm sorry to hear that," Colt said. "I just got back from Paris. The museums and galleries there are unbelievable. If you do go, you should make time to visit some of them."

"You really aren't thinking about staying home, are you, Alex?" Rich seemed awfully disappointed she wasn't already on the plane. "I'm sure your mom would stay with Jamie so you could go."

As before, her mind filled with confusion. What was going on? Why did he seem so anxious to get her gone so quickly? Just the day before, they'd been talking about their dream home.

"We haven't had a chance to discuss it yet," Alex said, feeling the muscles around her heart clench and tighten. *Why are you talking like this, Rich?*

As if the matter wasn't of great importance, which obviously it wasn't, Rich turned to Colt and said, "Let's take a look at the pictures they have hanging here, then I'll take you to my place and show you the rest."

Alex stood back watching the two men study and discuss Rich's painting. One man she'd known for months, the other she'd just met. Both seemed like strangers.

She and Rich had made plans to go out to dinner and maybe to a movie over in West Yellowstone that evening. The way he was acting she wondered, would he say anything? Would he even remember their date?

"Alex, do you think Jamie would mind if we looked at the picture in her bedroom?"

"I don't think so, but I'd better ask first."

Feeling like she was the brunt of a cruel joke, she numbly made her way to Jamie's room. Knocking first, Alex entered and found Jamie, in her purple robe, on the bed, watching television.

"Oh, hi, Al."

"Rich is here. He wants to show his friend the picture on your wall."

"Okay." Jamie just sat there, watching an annoying game show.

Alex didn't have much patience. All her energy was being used to cope with Rich. "Don't you think you ought to at least get dressed and make the bed before they come up?"

Jamie didn't answer.

"Jamie. Will you turn that thing off and get dressed?" She didn't mean for her voice to take on a frustrated tone, but it had and she was.

Without a word, Jamie clicked off the remote and rolled off the bed to her feet, slowly making her way to her closet.

Through stinging tears, Alex made the bed, tearing at the sheets and blankets, nearly ripping them in two. She threw the pillows onto the bed, covered them with the bedspread and slapped at a few wrinkles.

Between Jamie's depression and Rich's unexplainable sudden change of heart, she thought she was going crazy. It seemed like he was getting cold feet and they weren't even engaged!

"Alex," Rich called from the stairway, "is it okay for us to come up?"

She cleared her throat and took several deep breaths. "Just a minute," she hollered back.

Ripping a few tissues from a box, she blew her nose, wiped at her eyes and opened the blinds.

"Jamie, are you dressed?" She kept her voice steady, but felt at any minute it would betray the tornado of emotion building up inside of her.

Stepping out of the bathroom, Jamie appeared, wearing a wrinkled Winnie the Pooh t-shirt and an old baggy pair of Steve's sweats. The straggly purple robe looked better.

Feeling defeated, Alex called Rich and Colt to come upstairs.

Introductions between Jamie and Colt were briefly made, then the men turned their attention to Rich's painting. Judging from Colt's reaction and comments, Rich had a good chance of getting his work in a gallery—if not in Park City, then in one of the many other galleries he was connected with in Vale, Jackson Hole, or Sun Valley.

Gathering from their conversation, Colt was also an artist, working mostly with clay sculpture, wood carvings and metal. With his connections, he couldn't foresee any problems helping Rich launch his artwork.

They were just about to leave when Rich turned. "Jamie, thanks for letting us barge in like this." He looked at Alex, "Can I show Colt your portrait?" He'd let her bring it home so everyone could see it.

Without warning, defensive feelings of protectiveness flared up. Maybe she was overreacting to Rich, misreading his actions, but he was definitely acting different. Instead of being warm, loving and attentive, he was cool, formal and distracted. She was no expert, but something had to explain this El Niño-sized change in him. He'd said he was ready for a change at work. Was that all it was? Or was there more?

Something had happened, but what?

Chapter 6

That evening, Alex and Jamie sat on the porch swing, watching the sunset together. Judith had gone out with Dr. Rawlins for the evening, and the two sisters sat silently in worlds of their own.

Alex was thinking about Rich. Just as she'd expected, he had completely forgotten about their plans for that evening. Colt had spent the day with Rich and Steve at work, and they were still together, somewhere. Jamie didn't even seem to notice Steve hadn't yet come home. But Alex felt a Grand Canyon-sized gap in her life when Rich wasn't with her.

"Alex?"

Jamie's voice startled her.

"Yeah."

"I've been meaning to talk to you about something important," Jamie spoke tentatively.

This is about the trip to Europe.

"Sure, go ahead." They gently started the porch swing in motion.

Jamie was quiet for a moment before beginning. "I've been doing a lot of thinking these past few months since Katelyn died. Mostly I've tried to figure out why the Lord allows me to get so close to having a child, then takes it away."

Alex continued listening. They rocked gently back and forth.

"In the blessing the bishop gave me on Sunday, I was told these trials are to help me grow and to strengthen my faith. Of course, that didn't really make me feel better, but something he said did give me hope."

"What was that?" Alex was grateful something had helped Jamie.

"The bishop promised that I would have a family and that the Lord would help me in my efforts to have a child."

"That's wonderful, Jamie."

"I've been thinking and praying about what the bishop meant by that, and I've decided my children aren't going to come to me the regular way. That perhaps there's going to be some special intervention, heavenly intervention in bringing my children to me."

Adoption. Maybe this meant Jamie was finally considering adopting a baby. Alex felt a thrill of excitement course through her.

Jamie continued. "I want to apologize again for getting so upset when you announced your trip to Europe."

"You don't need to apologize, Jamie. I understand." Alex felt a wave of relief at her sister's words. Jamie finally seemed to be accepting her situation and trying to make the best of it.

"I think you should go on this trip."

"You do?" Alex wasn't prepared for that much acceptance.

"Yes, because I want to ask the biggest favor a person could ask another person." Jamie clasped and unclasped her hands as she shifted nervously.

Alex didn't understand why Jamie was so tense. "Jamie, you know I would do anything for you," she assured her.

"Yes, I know. And that knowledge helps me have the courage to ask you this."

"What is it already?" Alex gave a little laugh to soften her words but she was getting a bit impatient.

Jamie's next words took Alex completely by surprise.

"I want you to be a surrogate mother for me."

Alex burst out laughing. "I'm glad to see you haven't lost your sense of humor."

Jamie didn't say anything.

"That's a good one," Alex said, still giggling at the thought of being pregnant.

Jamie was still silent.

"Jamie, you were joking, right?" Alex looked at her sister and saw the tears in Jamie's eyes. "You're *not* kidding?"

Jamie shook her head. They stopped swinging.

Alex's stomach curdled. A wave of nausea swept over her. Was her sister really asking her to have a baby? Hers and Steve's baby?

"I . . . I . . . I don't know what to say. I mean, pregnant? Me? With your baby?"

Jamie wiped the tears from her eyes. "You'd be what they call a 'gestational surrogate.' I've been learning about it. You wouldn't need to contribute an ovum like most traditional surrogates, because I can provide an egg. I just can't carry a child full term. And that is what I need you for."

Alex was amazed at the amount of thought and research Jamie must have put into this idea. She knew without a doubt that she couldn't possibly go along with Jamie's wishes, but this was a delicate issue and she didn't want to upset her sister any more than she already was.

"I'm honored you would think of me, Jamie, really I am. But you have to understand how unprepared I am for something like this. I mean, I don't even know anything about that kind of procedure."

Seeing that Alex hadn't rejected the idea outright, Jamie suddenly switched into high gear. "But that's the beauty of it. The implantation process is quite involved at first, and it may take a few tries, but after that it's just dealing with the pregnancy. Although there is one complication I should tell you about . . ."

Alex had already heard enough.

". . . There's a high multiple birthrate because they sometimes place three or four embryos in at a time. Steven and I would pay you something since it would take you away from your work."

Before she ran screaming from the porch, Alex drew in several breaths, hoping to remain calm. "Money has nothing to do with this, Jamie. The whole idea is so—I don't know—extreme. Have you talked with Steve about this?"

"Not yet. I wanted to get your reaction first."

Alex sought for the right words. "Jamie, I just don't know if . . . if it's the best alternative for you."

"It's my *only* alternative!" Emotion jumped back into Jamie's throat quicker than a flash flood in spring. "If I want to have a child that is mine and Steve's, you are my *only* hope."

One look at her sister's face and Alex knew she was walking on egg shells. Jamie was clearly near the breaking point.

"I think a decision like this would take a lot of time and thought, and fasting and prayer," she said cautiously.

"Absolutely," Jamie said. "And that's why I think you need to go to Europe. You should get away and have a wonderful couple of months, because you would be committed for the next nine months."

Alex felt like a paper bag in a whirlwind. Maybe she should go to Europe. If anything just to escape.

* * *

"Hi, Alex, are you ready to go?"

She stepped out on the porch with Rich. He'd called that next morning, after Colt left, and apologized for forgetting their date. He wanted to make it up to her.

"There's a wonderful new steak house I've heard about. Does that sound okay?"

"Sure," she tried to sound convincing.

She knew her anorexic days were behind her, but her anorexic tendencies would forever remain. Anticipating a big meal for that evening, Alex hadn't eaten much more than a few bites of toast for breakfast and an apple for lunch. She didn't trust herself completely yet, especially when eating out. At home she could control her food intake—salads, bagels, fruit, vegetables. But out in the real world, she had a more difficult time resisting.

Keeping her weight up to a steady 112 was something she worked on every day. This weight was approved by her treatment counselor and medical doctor with the hopes that she would eventually reach one hundred and twenty pounds. But that wasn't going to happen anytime soon. Especially if she continually worried about what was going on with Jamie and how Rich was acting.

She hoped she and Rich would be able to talk over dinner. She needed to find out what was going on with him. And she wanted to talk to Rich about Jamie. There had to be some church rule that discouraged surrogate parenting. At least she prayed there was.

The steak house turned out to be a cosy country chalet with French decor. Window boxes spilled over with brightly colored geraniums and pansies. Inside, beautiful prints from artists like Monet, Renoir and Matisse lent a European air about the place. The restaurant's name, *Ambiance*, was a perfect description of the place itself.

Their shoes clicked on the rustic tiled floor as the waitress, wearing a peasant blouse and skirt, led them to a table tucked away in the corner, near the fireplace. Overhead, Alex noticed the rafters, adorned with clusters of dried wildflowers and copper pots.

Over a flickering candle, as they waited to be served, Alex studied Rich's handsome, familiar face. A face, she thought she knew so well and had fallen in love with. She found nothing in his expression to explain his distance toward her. In fact, she found quite the opposite. In his eyes she sensed warmth and sincerity. He seemed like the same relaxed, caring person he'd always been. Maybe the crisis, whatever it had been, was over.

They ordered their meal of poached salmon and steamed garden vegetables, and waited as their water glasses were filled. When they were alone again, Rich reached across the table for her hand. Lacing her fingers with his, he smiled that bone-melting smile of his and said, "So how are you doing? We haven't talked for a few days."

Even though she was thrilled he was showing warmth and attention, she couldn't help being a little confused. Had she made it all up? Been oversensitive to his actions? Maybe these yo-yo emotions she had, trying to deal with Jamie and her own personal demands with work, were causing her to blow everything out of proportion. Right now, in front of her, was Rich, her Rich, the same guy she'd known for three months. Acting the same, treating her the same. Nothing seemed different. At least for now.

"How did things go with Colt? He seemed to have good things to say about your artwork."

"He's impressed with my work and thinks I could have a successful show. He's a good friend, so what else can he say? But he's got an eye for art. And he loved the portrait of you. He thinks I should add a few more portraits to my collection."

Alex felt a flicker of fear. "But he knows it's not for sale right? I mean, it's just to show your talent."

"Absolutely. I made it completely clear to him," Rich said soothingly.

"I'm so happy for you, Rich. The first time I saw your paintings I wondered why you didn't display your work. This is really exciting, isn't it?"

He nodded. "The timing couldn't be better. I've grown so restless at work, I can't seem to stay focused or get enthused about anything lately. Sometimes I feel like walls are closing in around me, until I can barely breathe. Like I'm constricted, confined . . . I can't really explain it. But this opportunity to pursue my painting has given me a sense of freedom again."

A flood of relief washed over her. He had been struggling with his job. He admitted it. It didn't have anything to do with her. He'd been overwhelmed with work, had grown tired of being on the trail and dealing with tourists constantly. She didn't blame him.

Rich continued. "He's going to call me in a few days and tell me what the woman in Park City has to say about doing a show in her gallery. If she's interested, I'll need to go to Salt Lake and take some of my paintings."

The waitress brought their food and for the next twenty minutes they ate their meal and shared small talk. The salmon was moist and flaky, the vegetables crisp and flavorful.

Many times throughout the meal Alex was reminded how good it felt to be with Rich again, to have him refill her water glass, flag down the waitress to bring more rolls for the basket, or just gaze at her from across the table.

After a few moments of quiet, Alex decided it was as good a time as any to ask the question she'd been wanting to ask. "Rich, I wondered if I could talk to you about something."

"Absolutely. Alex, you can talk to me about anything." He set down his fork and pushed his plate aside, giving her his full attention.

"I really need your help. It's quite personal and I want to keep it confidential."

He nodded, waiting for her to go on.

Alex sighed wearily and set her napkin beside her plate. "I've been worried about Jamie for a long time. Instead of getting stronger, she seems to be pulling in, closing everything and everyone out."

"I've noticed the same thing."

Resting her elbows on the table, Alex leaned forward so she could keep her tone down. "She wants to have a baby so badly she's completely obsessed with the idea."

Rich nodded knowingly. "Steve's been spending a lot of extra time at work lately. I wondered why, until he finally told me what's been going on. He's really worried about Jamie, too, but he doesn't know what to do. Everything he tries has the wrong effect and seems to make the situation worse. He's decided it works better if he just stays out of the way."

"That's the last thing he should be doing!" Alex said firmly. "He needs to get Jamie to open up and share her feelings with him. I'm afraid of what will happen to them if they don't communicate with each other."

Rich agreed.

"But that's not even the worst part." Alex scooted to the edge of her chair and looked at Rich. "Jamie and I had a very strange conversation yesterday."

"What happened?"

"She talked to me about being a surrogate mother for her," she whispered.

Rich's eyes opened wide. "You? She wants you to have her baby?" He said it loud enough that Alex ducked her head, hoping no one they knew was sitting nearby.

"That was my reaction, too," she said quietly. "I thought she was joking at first, but she's very serious."

"You're not, I mean, you wouldn't—"

"Have their baby?" she finished his sentence. "Not a chance. Don't get me wrong, I love Jamie, and I'd do anything for her, but this is asking just a little too much."

"I'd have to check the Church handbook, but I'm willing to bet this isn't a practice that's encouraged."

"I was hoping you'd say that."

"How come they don't just adopt?"

Alex shrugged, feeling defeated. "She's determined to have a baby of her own, one who is hers and Steve's together. Adoption at this point isn't even an option."

"That's too bad. I know so many people who have had wonderful experiences with adoption."

"She won't even consider it."

The waitress brought their Pot au Creme, a delicious whipped chocolate dessert, and cleared away their dinner dishes. Rich and Alex waited for her to leave before resuming their conversation.

"What kind of an answer did you give Jamie?"

"I didn't tell her anything. She's so volatile right now I don't want to do anything to set her off."

"Has she talked to Steve about this?"

"Not yet. I know he won't go for the idea. But she's so convinced it's the perfect solution."

"This must be so hard for you," Rich said softly as he covered her hand with his. It felt good to have his strength and support again. She needed him in her life. With him by her side, she felt as though she could handle any challenge life threw her way.

She was grateful they'd been able to talk. Knowing his frustrations with work helped her understand why he was behaving so strangely.

It just didn't explain why she still didn't feel better.

Chapter 7

Dreams of Rich carried Alex through the night. The next morning, she awoke reluctantly, wishing she didn't have to leave her fantasy world.

Perhaps it was the thought of going to Europe, or the lingering joy she'd felt last night at the restaurant, that had her and Rich strolling down cobblestone streets, stopping at outdoor cafes and hiking in the lush green Alps in her dream.

But as she woke up she realized she would be there alone. She stayed in bed a moment longer, trying to recreate the magic from her sleep, but reality had tromped in and taken over. Europe just didn't sound fun if she couldn't share it with Rich. She knew she needed to call Sandy with her decision, but she was still torn, afraid to leave, wondering what would happen while she was gone.

After making the bed and pulling on her robe, she ventured out into the hallway, wondering where Steve and Jamie were. As she descended the stairway, she heard them back in the family room. Jamie was speaking quickly, her voice filled with emotion.

"Steve, why are you so mad at me? All I did was ask her to think about it. It's not like we made any arrangements or anything."

"But a surrogate mother? I can't believe you'd even consider such an idea."

Uh-oh, it finally came out. It didn't sound like Steve was keen on the idea.

"Why can't you see it from my point of view? Steve, this is one way we can have a child of our own. We could finally have a family."

"Jamie, it's not that easy. You don't just ask people to have your baby."

"Alex seemed a little surprised when I asked her but she didn't flip out like you are."

"You bet I'm flipping out. You come up with this hair-brained scheme, and you don't even discuss it with me first." There was a pause then Steve spoke again, his voice measured and even. "Honey, I know how much you want a baby and I realize how hard this is on you, but if you need to have one so badly, why can't we just adopt like everyone else?"

"Because I want my *own* baby!" Alex could tell Jamie had a harder time keeping her emotions in check. "I want a baby that's part of me and you. And if I can't give you that, then I feel like I've failed you as a wife. In fact . . ."

Alex heard the emotion escalating.

". . . maybe you should just divorce me and marry someone who can give you children."

Jamie was sobbing now. Alex felt tears fill her own eyes.

"Honey, please don't cry. I love you. I don't want anyone else. We just have to have faith that it will work out."

"It's so hard, Steven. I don't think I have any more faith."

"I know it's hard. But you've been promised a family. The bishop even said so in his blessing. Jamie, you can't give up. And you have to talk to me. We have to do this together."

"I know. But it would help if I knew why this was happening to us." Alex heard Jamie sniffing. "I just don't get it. My patriarchal blessing tells me I will have children. This just doesn't make any sense."

"Honey, I know this is hard, but we can get through this."

Jamie didn't respond.

"Com'ere," Steve said. "It's going to be okay."

Alex retreated to her room, her heart filled with anguish for Steve and Jamie's challenge. Even though the discussion she'd overheard had been difficult and emotional, she was grateful Jamie and Steve had talked. For a moment she'd wondered if they would survive the ordeal, but their love had proved stronger than the problem.

She took a moment and knelt by her bed, pouring her heart out in prayer. Right now they all seemed to be in need of help. Heavenly help.

* * *

Later that day Alex got an unexpected phone call from Rich.

"I called to tell you some wonderful news."

"What is it?"

"Colt's friend from Park City, Elena Fewtrell, just called. She's very interested in seeing my work and wants me to come to Park City right away."

"Rich, that's wonderful." Jamie and Steve were in the kitchen with her and stopped their conversation to listen. "When does she want you to come?"

"What's up? Tell us," Steve said.

Alex covered the receiver with her hand. "That woman from Park City called Rich to tell him she wants to see his work right away." Speaking to Rich, she said, "Rich, we're all excited for you."

"Are Jamie and Steve there?"

"Yes."

"I wondered if you three would like to come to Park City with me?"

She covered the phone again. "He wants us to go to Park City with him."

Jamie clapped her hands. "I love Park City!"

Alex felt like turning cartwheels. Spending a whole weekend with Rich sounded heavenly.

"When are you leaving?" she asked.

"This afternoon."

"Today?" It sounded like that art dealer wasn't going to waste any time.

"Sorry it's not much notice," he said. "But it's either this weekend or two weeks from now. She's going out of town."

"Hold on," she said.

"Steve, can we go?" Jamie begged. She turned to Alex. "Remember? We went to Park City on our honeymoon."

Steve thought for a second. "I would have to find someone to cover the Stringhams kayaking trip tomorrow."

"Alex," Rich said over the phone, "if Steve's wondering about the Stringhams, tell him they called to reschedule."

"The Stringhams rescheduled," she relayed the message.

Jamie let out an excited, "All right! We're going."

"Wait a minute." Steve thought a moment longer, then said, "I can't think of any other reason not to."

"We're going with you," Alex told Rich.

* * *

Later that afternoon they arrived in Salt Lake City. Since Alex had never been to Temple Square they decided to spend the evening in downtown Salt Lake before going on up to Park City. Stopping first at the shopping mall across the street from the temple, the two couples talked and laughed nonstop as they scavenged the mall and wandered from store to store. As dinner approached, Alex was surprised when Rich announced he'd made reservations for them at The Roof, a restaurant overlooking Temple Square. They laughed all through dinner and were still joking and laughing when Steve returned to the buffet for a fifth time. Rich was back to his fun, loving self, and Jamie and Steve were attentive and affectionate with each other. This trip seemed to be exactly what both couples needed.

"Did you see the look the waiter gave you when you sat down with that last plate of shrimp?" Jamie said.

"Hey, it's not coming out of his pocket. Besides, I'm making up for what you and Alex didn't eat."

"You know, Dixon," Rich said. "I've never seen anyone start with dessert then move on to the main course."

"I wanted to make sure I got some of that pecan pie."

"Honey, I'm afraid you're going to get sick from all that rich food," Jamie told Steve.

"It takes more than that to get me sick."

"Are you guys about ready to go?" Rich said. Alex noticed he'd been checking his watch off and on for the last half hour.

Reluctantly Steve consented to leave and they stepped out into a warm summer evening. The streets were busy with evening traffic. Horns blasted, and the smell of exhaust mixed with the aroma of hot dogs from a nearby street vendor. After so long in the remote town of Island Park, Alex enjoyed the excitement of being in the city again.

Walking past the line of horse-drawn carriages along the street around Temple Square, Rich stopped at one of the polished buggies and said, "Let's go for a ride."

"If I get in one of those, I'll get sick for sure," Steve said, holding his stomach.

"Oh, come on," Rich said. "Just a short ride."

As the tree branches swayed in a gentle breeze, evening shadows danced about them. Alex thought it was a perfect evening for taking a romantic ride in the carriage.

"I'll go," she said.

"Me too," Jamie added, giving Steve an annoyed look.

"Okay, okay, I'll go. But if I get sick, it's not my fault," he said.

"Wrong," Jamie said. "No one told you to eat like there was no tomorrow."

"I guess it is my fault. But I worked hard eating all that food. I'd hate to waste a perfectly good meal throwing it all up."

"Could we please talk about something else? I'm starting to feel nauseous," Alex said, holding her stomach.

"All right, all right. I'll be fine. Let's just get in already."

When they climbed inside, Alex was alarmed to find a dozen red roses on each of the two seats, along with four long-stemmed, plastic glasses and an ice bucket containing sparkling cider.

"Rich, I think we're in someone else's carriage."

"Uh-oh, let me check." He picked up the card on one of the bouquets and read the name. "No, it says 'Alexis' right here."

"And this one says my name," Jamie said excitedly. "You had this planned all along, didn't you, Rich?"

"Hey, I was in on it too," Steve said. "All that talk about getting sick was just to add a dramatic touch."

"You big romantic kook," Jamie said scooting over so Steve could take a seat next to her. "Come here so I can kiss you."

The carriage shifted as the wheels began to turn, and Rich quickly sat next to Alex. She drew in a long breath of the fragrant flowers then said, "This was so sweet. I wondered why you kept checking your watch."

"I was afraid Steve would keep going back for more and make us miss our reservation."

"Hey," Steve said, "I heard that." He still had his arms wrapped around his wife, but managed to break away momentarily in his defense.

Alex settled back against Rich's chest and blocked out the traffic and tourists and noise of the world.

The horse clip-clopped down the road as the foursome drank a toast to love, laughter, friendship, and, Steve added, all-you-can-eat buffet dinners.

When the ride ended, the driver received a round of applause and a handsome tip. Leaving their carriage behind, the couples strolled hand in hand through the gates onto the temple grounds. Alex was immediately captivated by the lush gardens and groomed lawns. Her breath caught in her throat as her gaze traveled the majestic granite walls of the temple, upward to the heaven-reaching spires and the golden statue of Moroni. Within the temple gates the feeling of tranquility and reverence shut out the selfish worldliness that existed only yards away on the outside.

Organ music drifted on the summer breeze. Alex heard it first. As the others tuned in, they walked toward the tabernacle where a blend of male voices joined the organ.

The hostess near the tabernacle entrance held her finger to her lips as they approached the door behind several other interested parties.

"It's the BYU men's choir concert," she said softly.

"Can we go inside?" Rich asked.

"Up the stairs to your right. The balcony."

Rich nodded, took Alex's hand and led her inside.

Still clutching her bouquet of roses, Alex took a seat next to Rich and marveled at the expansive layout of the building. The dizzying height of the ceiling and the brilliance of the brass organ pipes lent a powerful edge to the songs being sung. Goose bumps tingled her flesh as the choir sang louder and stronger, building to a crescendo of voices in perfect harmony.

The audience sat mesmerized as a few voices in the choir started the next song a capella. The beautiful melody and sweet message stirred Alex's emotions. Her throat tightened and eyes filled with tears as they sang "When Faith Endures," the same song they had sung at her baptism. Memories of that day, such a short time ago, flooded her mind and heart. That gentle, loving spirit which had touched her then, reminded her now of the great love her Heavenly Father had for her.

She looked over at Rich and wondered if he felt the same as she did. She felt within her heart that the Lord had brought them together, and that there was a reason why they'd met and been drawn so quickly to each other. He was the man of her dreams, the man she knew she wanted to spend eternity with.

Tears filled her eyes as this realization expanded in her mind. She could vividly picture herself with Rich, surrounded by the laughter of children, their children. She could see the two of them working side by side, gardening, building a swing set, cuddling on the couch in front of the fire after getting the kids bathed and to bed. She wanted to turn to him right there and tell him of her feelings and those heavenly promptings telling her they were meant for each other, but it was hardly the time or place.

The choir concluded the song with, "*The Spirit guides, His love assures, that fear departs when faith endures,*" and Alex knew again, as she did the day she was baptized, that their hearts were bound together, and that they would rejoice forever in their love for each other and for the Lord. Whatever they went through, whatever challenges or changes they experienced, they could survive. They had to.

Lost in her own thoughts, Alex was startled when the others stood to leave. She turned to Rich, looking at him with a deeper appreciation and understanding. Their gazes locked and she saw in his eyes a reflection of what was in her heart. Without speaking they filed out of the building with the crowd, their hands clamped tightly together so they wouldn't be separated.

Outside, they stepped away from the rush of people, to wait for Steve and Jamie. Taking advantage of the moment, Rich pulled her close, burying his face in her silky hair and kissing her neck softly.

"Rich," she whispered, "I love you."

He pulled her even closer and rocked her gently. "I love you, too."

She wanted to express everything in her heart, the experience she'd had inside the tabernacle, but at that moment Steve and Jamie found them and hustled them toward the visitors' center. The moment was lost, but Alex knew she would find a time to tell him.

They wandered the building and admired paintings. Then they watched a film presentation of "The First Vision," which brought tears to Alex's eyes each time she saw it. Afterwards they joined a group, led by a sister missionary with a cute British accent, up a winding ramp.

As they emerged into an open space, Alex's breath caught in her throat. In front of her was a large, brilliant white statue of the Savior. She noticed nail marks in his extended hands as well as in his feet. She was drawn to him, her eyes riveted to his face. Perhaps it was just a statue, but for her the effect was very real. She felt his presence. His love.

The room grew hushed and reverent, and for a few seconds there wasn't a sound. After a moment, voices from another group approached the landing and the spell was broken. But it was a treasured experience for Alex. Again her testimony was confirmed. The Savior lived.

"Thank you for joining us this evening," the cute little missionary said. "My name is Sister Leighton. If you have questions or need assistance, I'd be happy to help you."

"I know a girl from London whose last name is Leighton. I wonder if they're related," Alex whispered to Rich.

"Go ahead and ask."

Alex waited for the crowd to move on before she approached the young girl. "Hello, my name is Alexis McCarty, I wonder if you know a girl from London named Julianne Leighton."

"Julianne is my cousin!" The sister's already smiling face brightened. "How do you know her?"

"We were guest instructors at a fitness conference together in Manhattan a few years ago."

"What a coincidence."

Alex could see a slight family resemblance between Sister Leighton and her cousin, Julianne. "Do you ever hear from Julianne? Or talk to her?"

"I've written her a few times, but she never writes back. She's very busy. Travels a lot. But you probably already know that."

"I'm afraid I do. If you do write to her or hear from her, will you tell her 'hello' from me?"

"Sure, I'd love to. I tried to talk to her about the Church, but she's not very open to it. Are you a member?"

"Yes," Alex said proudly. "I just got baptized one week ago."

"That's wonderful. I'll be sure to tell her 'hi' from you and that you've joined the Church."

"Please do. I'd love to talk to her about the gospel."

"Your name is Alexis?"

"Right. My last name is McCarty."

They said their good-byes and moved from the room.

"You know what?" Rich said.

"What?"

"You're a natural missionary."

"Do you think so?"

Rich tilted his head as he looked at her. "Yes, I do. I have a feeling, Sister McCarty, that a lot of people are going to learn about the Church from you."

"It's strange you would say that. Now that I know what it's like to have lived without the gospel in my life and how much better my life has become since I've joined the Church, I want to tell everyone about it. I don't think most Mormons realize just what they have. I don't think they understand how powerful the gospel can be in their lives. In a way I feel like I have a responsibility to tell others. I want everyone to know what a difference it has made in my life. I guess if that's being a missionary, then you're right."

It was true. Alex felt as compelled to tell people about the gospel as she did to tell them about healthy eating habits and lifestyles. Even though it was a little scary to approach people about the gospel, her desire was stronger than her fear. How wonderful it would be to help even one person find the great joy and the answers she'd found through the gospel and the Book of Mormon.

Chapter 8

Jamie was quiet the next morning as they traveled from their hotel through Park City toward the gallery. Steve and Rich talked sports. Alex sat next to Rich in the front seat and admired the beautiful scenery from her window.

During a break in Rich and Steve's conversation, Jamie said, without warning, "I have to tell all of you something."

Immediately Alex became alarmed. She could tell something was wrong by the faraway look on her sister's face, the strange tone in her voice. Steve and Rich stopped talking.

"Honey, what is it?" Steve asked.

"I had a dream last night."

Alex wasn't sure that Steve rolled his eyes, but it looked like it.

"What about your dream, Jamie?" It was up to Alex to give Jamie the chance to express her feelings.

"It was a dream, yet it seemed so very real. I felt as though I looked into the future." She rubbed her arms, like she had goose bumps. "I was in a hospital room. You were all there with me, and Mom, too. At first I thought I was in the hospital because something had happened to me, but the next thing I knew, a nurse came into the room, carrying a baby. My baby."

Jamie's voice had dropped to a whisper. "This tiny little girl was so beautiful. She had olive skin and dark curly hair. And when I put my finger on her cheek, she grabbed it with her little hand and held on so tightly. And she was mine. My very own baby."

Steve sighed heavily. Alex sensed his concern and frustration. Did he think his wife was losing her grip on reality? Was Jamie making herself crazy over this baby thing?

Her voice grew stronger. "It was so hard this morning to wake up and realize she wasn't there. It seemed so real. I can still remember how warm she was in my arms, how soft her skin was, how she smelled. She was an angel."

"Uh, I'm sure she was, honey." Steve patted Jamie on the leg. After an uncomfortable pause, he leaned forward from the back seat to ask Rich, "So, what were you saying about the Jazz making a trade with the Lakers?" Rich responded enthusiastically, and the two men continued their conversation, almost completely oblivious to the women present.

Alex didn't know what to say to Jamie, but she knew she needed to say something. She just hoped Jamie's dream didn't put a new wall up where she and Steve had just knocked one down.

"It seemed so real," Jamie said, almost as if she didn't expect anyone to even listen or answer.

But Alex was listening. "Jamie, maybe it's the Lord's way of letting you know it will happen. It just might take some time."

Jamie absorbed Alex's words, then said, "I think you're right about the dream telling me I will have a baby, but I don't think it is going to take a lot of time."

"What do you mean?"

"I don't know, yet. I don't know."

Jamie drifted off into her own thoughts. Alex looked at her sister and the distant expression on her face, then shifted her gaze to the clear sky outside. *Please, Heavenly Father,* she prayed, *help Jamie. And help Steve to be patient. And help me to know what to do about this trip to Europe.*

* * *

Following the directions Colt had given them, they drove directly to the gallery called "Elena's," named after the director, Elena Fewtrell. Rich was scheduled to meet with her at eleven a.m. It was almost that now.

The gallery looked small from the outside, almost unimpressive except for the elaborate sign overhead announcing its name.

"We'll wait out here." Alex said. "Then we can help carry in the pictures when you're ready."

"Okay, but if I don't come back in a few minutes, just come in."

"If I can get Steve to wake up," Jamie said. The truck ride had eventually put Steve to sleep. He was tired since he spent most of the night awake with a bad case of indigestion.

"Good luck." Alex smiled reassuringly at Rich. "She's going to love your work."

"I hope so. " He released his seat belt, then quickly leaned over and kissed Alex. "For luck," he said. Grabbing his planner, he walked into the gallery.

"He's so cute," Jamie said. "I'm glad you two talked." Alex had told Jamie about their last conversation and how concerned she was about Rich. "Steve's said he's noticed how distracted Rich has grown at work. He's been worried about him, too."

"It's helped me a lot to understand what was going on inside of him." Alex leaned back on the headrest. "I'd about decided to go to Europe, but I think I'm changing my mind. I can't stand the thought of being away from him for two months, or from you guys either."

Alex couldn't help but remember Jamie's request about being a surrogate mother. They still hadn't resolved the issue verbally. Rich had checked the handbook and found that the Church strongly opposed surrogacy. She just didn't know how to tell Jamie.

"I need to let Sandy know my decision right away. I've put them off as long as I can."

"Oh, look, here comes Rich already."

Alex rolled down her window. Judging by the smile on his face the news was good.

"She wants to see the paintings. She's really excited. Colt did quite a sales job on her."

"That's great, Rich."

"Honey." Jamie jiggled Steve's shoulder, "Wake up. We need to help Rich."

"Already?"

"Yes, already. Come on."

They each carried a painting to the front door. An older man, very distinguished looking, with neatly groomed hair, gray at the temples, and a double-breasted navy suit, held the door for them.

Once inside, they leaned the pictures against the wall and stepped back while introductions were made. The man introduced himself as James Fewtrell, owner of the gallery. His daughter, Elena, who was in the back taking a call, managed the gallery and arranged for the shows. She had a knack, he said, for spotting talent.

Rich was explaining some of his paintings to Mr. Fewtrell, when Elena walked out from the back room. Alex's mouth nearly dropped to the floor. The woman was gorgeous. Tall—Alex guessed close to five foot ten—curvy and blonde.

Elena wore a trim red suit, the skirt just above the knee to expose shapely calves. Her outfit was perfectly tailored and modest, but for some reason, Elena made it look as sexy as a clingy evening gown.

In the shadow of Elena's radiance, Alex suddenly felt dowdy and uncomfortable. Even though Rich had complimented her earlier on her slim-fitting khaki pants and crisp white blouse, she felt like a dandelion next to this voluptuous rose.

"I'd like you to meet my friends," Rich said. "This is Steve Dixon, my business partner, and his wife, Jamie, and her sister, Alexis."

"Nice to meet you," Elena said, not really looking any of them in the eye. Her manner was businesslike and very curt.

Alex didn't like the fact that she'd been introduced as Jamie's sister.

"Well, well." Elena crossed her arms and studied the paintings. "Colt wasn't lying when he said you were good."

She stopped in front of the portrait of Alex and stroked her chin with one long, red manicured nail. "Outstanding. This is brilliant. You must do more portraits." Alex guessed Elena hadn't recognized the woman in the picture as herself; otherwise, she might not have been so complimentary of it.

"I'm glad you like it," Rich said.

"You say you have more paintings still at home?"

"Yes. Quite a few."

She nodded slowly, her eyes still on the paintings. Without looking away, she said, "Daddy, what do you think?"

"I'm impressed. I think this show could be a great success."

Again, she nodded and studied the pictures. Finally, after a long pause, Elena turned and said, "Do you have lunch plans?" Her question was directed only at Rich.

"Uh, no." His gaze slipped to Alex for a half-second.

"We need to talk more. I'd like to see you add a few pieces to the collection using local landscapes. We need to discuss terms, arrangements, details of the show, and . . . ," her eyes traveled from Rich's head to his feet, ". . . image. You're going to be a famous artist. We want everything to be perfect the first time we present you to the public."

Alex noticed Rich's eyes narrow for a moment. Obviously he wondered why his "image" wasn't fine the way it was.

"We also need to discuss a date and talk about publicity." She walked over to Rich and extended her hand. "Congratulations," she said.

They shook hands.

Mr. Fewtrell also shook Rich's hand, then said, "She's the best in the business, son. You two will make a great team."

"We can walk to the restaurant," Elena said, still ignoring Alex, Jamie, and Steve.

Her father held the door as Rich and Elena stepped out into the sunny day. She looped her arm through his and together they walked out of sight, without a backward glance.

* * *

All through lunch, Jamie wouldn't let the topic of Elena rest.

"Didn't it bug you the way she took over Rich? Like she owns him now. And by the way, do you think she's naturally blonde?"

"I don't know," Alex said. "Besides, what's that got to do with anything, anyway?"

"I bet she's not." Jamie turned to Steve, who was busy finishing his wife's salad. He'd gotten his appetite back. "You didn't think she was that pretty, did you, honey?"

"Who?"

"That Elena woman," Jamie said.

"Pretty?" He looked at his wife, then at Alex. "No, I wouldn't say she was pretty."

Jamie gave Alex a satisfied smile.

"I'd say she's gorgeous."

Jamie smacked him on the shoulder.

"Ow, what was that for? You asked me what I thought."

"How can you think she's beautiful. She's like NutraSweet."

Confused, Steve looked at his wife. "What?"

"Just what I said. At first she's all sweet, but there's a bitter after-taste. I don't trust her."

Alex didn't either. "Do you think they're back from lunch yet?" she asked.

"It's been almost two hours. I'd think they'd be done by now," Jamie said.

"Did Rich tell you she's LDS?" Steve said.

"What?!" Alex and Jamie said in unison.

"I don't believe it," Jamie said.

"It's true. She's even a returned missionary," he said.

Alex was in shock. She had a hard time imagining Elena knocking on doors and bearing her testimony.

"Is she still active?"

"According to Rich's friend, Colt, she is. That's one of the reasons Rich was interested in meeting with the Fewtrells, because they are LDS."

Alex knew all her insecurities were surfacing. She didn't doubt that Rich could handle a woman like Elena, but he'd been so different lately—unpredictable, vulnerable even—she just didn't know what to expect anymore. Even his confession of love for her at Temple Square yesterday didn't convince her that their relationship could withstand a blow from a blonde bombshell named Elena. Especially since Elena was involved in art, just as Rich was; she was a returned missionary, just as Rich was; and she was with Rich right now, just as Alex was not.

Alex was mad at herself for not having more faith in Rich, but she loved him so much. And she was terrified of losing him.

* * *

"I'm sure they'll be back any minute," Mr. Fewtrell said after another hour had passed. "Elena has an appointment at four o'clock she can't miss."

Just then the couple strolled past the window. Elena had one arm entwined around Rich's elbow, and was laughing as they opened the door and stepped inside.

Rich's gaze met Alex's. He smiled and opened his mouth to speak, but Elena beat him to the punch.

"Oh, Daddy, this is going to be our most successful show ever," she said enthusiastically. "And while he's looking for locations to add to the collection, Richard is going to use the private studio and apartment here."

Mr. Fewtrell looked pleased. "Wonderful. You won't have trouble finding scenery in these mountains. We're certainly looking forward to working with you, Mr. Greenwood."

"Thank you," Rich said.

"We had such a wonderful time at lunch, we forgot all about the time, didn't we, Richard?"

He just smiled and let her go on.

"We ironed out most of the details of the showing. We just need to draw up a contract. And I've decided to do all the publicity for the show myself. With Richard's good looks and talent, he needs to be out in public—attending social events, mingling with collectors and other artists. I'll introduce him to all the right people. This will be my finest show yet." Then she laughed, "I guess I should say, *our* finest show."

The phone rang.

"I'll get that." Elena tossed her hair back with a sweep of her hand. "It's probably François in New York."

"Excuse me, Richard."

If she called him "Richard" one more time in that exaggerated "East coast" accent, Alex knew she was going to yank some of that blonde hair out by its dark roots.

Mr. Fewtrell busied himself greeting a customer coming through the door.

Rich walked over to them. "So, have you guys been having fun?"

"Oh, yeah," Jamie said. "Tons."

"I didn't realize we were gone so long. You wouldn't believe how much planning it takes to put on an exhibition like this. Elena . . ."

As Rich rattled on about "Elena this" and "Elena that," carrying on about her extensive art knowledge and connections with galleries around the world, Alex's mind read between the lines. She knew she was being oversensitive, overparanoid and overreactive, but Rich's exuberant tribute to Elena made her very uncomfortable.

". . . and she told me that she'd never had such a good feeling about another artist like she has about me, and that she's rarely wrong when it comes to judging talent."

"That's great, Rich," Steve said.

Alex and Jamie remained silent. By the look on Jamie's face, Alex could tell her sister wanted to slap Rich back into reality, but he was like a kid with a report card full of A-pluses. It didn't seem the right time to burst his bubble.

"So," Jamie finally said, "are we going to hang around here all day, or what?"

"I think we're through for today," Rich said. "I'll go check with Elena."

They watched Rich walk to the back of the gallery, then Jamie came unglued. "That woman is an absolute shark! I can't believe Rich can't see through her."

"Shhh." Steve nodded toward Mr. Fewtrell only a few yards away.

"I don't care if he hears me. She's not only after Rich's artwork, she's after him."

"Jamie, will you stop?" Steve whispered nervously. "We don't even know her."

"Steven Dixon, can you honestly say you don't think she's manipulative and phony?"

Steve frowned. "I think we should have a little faith in Rich's judgement. He wouldn't be so exited about all of this if he didn't feel good about the arrangement. Besides, Rich doesn't get sidetracked with good looks and flattery. This is strictly business."

"Sorry, Steve, but I don't trust her. Don't you agree, Alex?"

Alex tried to swallow the knot in her throat so she could answer. She didn't know what to think. Every fiber in her being told her that Elena was only concerned about herself. She managed to put on quite a show, but Jamie was right. Elena might act sweet, but she had a bitter aftertaste.

"I don't know what to think, yet," Alex managed to say.

Rich came around the hallway and strolled toward them with an enthusiastic bounce to his step. Alex's heart sank just watching him. She wanted to be happy for him, but she couldn't.

"We're all set," he said as he approached them. "I'll talk to her later after she's had a chance to work on some dates." He opened his planner and pointed to a page filled with writing. "Look at all these things I have to do before our next meeting. I'll be lucky to have time to sleep from now on. That Elena sure does know this business. She got her degree at Harvard. Hard to believe someone can be that pretty and that smart, too."

He'd just confirmed Alex's worst fear. Maybe Rich didn't let good looks and flattery get to him, but he'd noticed. Maybe it was her own personal insecurities and fears getting the best of her, but Alex realized that Elena wasn't just a business contact for Rich; she was a "pretty and smart" business contact. And that was the difference that really worried her.

Chapter 9

To Alex's relief, after window-shopping and stopping for ice cream, the day did improve. The foursome wandered through the side streets of Park City, admiring quaint homes and shops. Jamie and Steve lagged behind, drawn to a furniture store's window display.

"This is a beautiful place," Rich said, as he paused to scan the hillside. "Mr. Fewtrell was right. I'm not going to have any trouble finding scenery to paint."

"You're pretty excited about this show, aren't you?" Alex shaded her eyes and followed Rich's gaze.

"I still can't believe it's really happening," he repeated. "Why didn't I do something like this years ago?"

They walked to an intersection, stopping to wait for the light to change.

"The Fewtrells are great, don't you think?" Rich asked Alex.

"Uh," she stammered, "I, uh, they certainly know the art business."

"They've got contacts all over the world."

"You don't feel like you should check out any other galleries just to make sure?" she asked cautiously.

"Not at all. I'm in good hands," he replied confidently.

That's what Alex was afraid of.

The light changed and they crossed the street. "You don't see any reason for concern, do you?" he asked.

"I just wondered, since you're just starting out, maybe you'd want to make sure this was the best place for you to have your first show, that's all," Alex suggested.

Rich was surprised. "But Elena's got great ideas and she really loves my work. In fact, she wants to keep the four paintings I brought, to show to other dealers and collectors. You won't believe it," he said as they stepped up onto the curb, "her favorite picture is the one of you."

Alex felt a twinge in her heart. He wouldn't ask her to put it up for sale, would he?

More than anything Alex wanted to tell Rich again, to force him if she had to, that he should try other galleries, talk to other art dealers, check out his options, but she wasn't sure if this was sound advice coming from her head, or just her insecurities and fears coming from her heart.

They found a bench in the shade and waited for Jamie and Steve to catch up.

"You know," he said, "at first I was concerned they wouldn't like my work. It didn't seem sophisticated enough for a gallery like that. But Elena felt my collection was fresh and alive, and that will make it stand out even more. She has no doubt it will be a success."

"How about you, Rich? Do you have any doubts?" Alex hoped he would at least share some misgivings about Elena and her too-charming veneer. Instead what he said was the complete opposite of what she expected.

"I feel really good about this whole arrangement. The Fewtrells are the best in the area. They know their clientele, they know which other collections are out there, and they have an impeccable success rate. Elena seems to have taken a special interest in my work, and I feel very fortunate that she has," Rich said gratefully.

Again Alex sensed that Elena was after more than just Rich's artwork. Like a balloon with a pin-hole-sized leak, Alex felt that slowly, almost undetectably, her hopes for their future were deflating.

"What kind of a commitment is she expecting out of you?"

"She wants me to add some more portraits and three, maybe four, paintings of local landscapes. She even wants to go with me to locate the right settings for me to paint. You probably heard, but I'll be moving into their private studio for a while so I can get a feel for the atmosphere. To have these pieces ready for a January show, I'll need to get started right away. I still have several paintings at home to finish.

Then there're some other dealers and artists she wants me to meet and dozens of galleries she wants to take me to. The more exposure as an artist I can get, the more successful my show will be—even to the point of eating at the right restaurants and driving the right kind of car. She's going to take me shopping to help me with my wardrobe. I had no idea it was this involved."

"I see," was all Alex said.

Rich angled himself toward Alex and reached for her hand. "The timing is incredible, don't you think?"

She didn't know what to think.

"You want to go to Europe for a couple of months, and I need at least that much time to move down here and get settled. It works out perfectly."

Alex didn't "want" to go to Europe. She would give up the trip, give up her whole career, for their relationship—for their future. Her job, and her work, would always be there. But that was all secondary to preparing to go through the temple with Rich in a year. To building a life with him. To spending eternity together.

It seemed the closer she wanted to get to Rich, the further he pulled away. If things kept up the way they were now, they would never be together.

The ironic part of it was that Rich wasn't even aware of what was going on. Alex believed that *he* believed everything was fine, that everything was falling together as it should. But these sudden turns in their lives were taking their paths in opposite directions.

The worst part was she didn't know how to stop it.

* * *

Early Sunday morning the phone in Alex's hotel room rang. After a fitful night, Alex had finally fallen asleep around three in the morning.

"Alex, is that you?"

Through the thick fog of interrupted sleep, Alex recognized the voice. "Sandy?"

"Sorry to wake you, but I called your sister's house and your mother told me how to reach you."

Alex covered a yawn and forced her eyes to open. "Is something wrong?"

"No, but I need you to be in California by tomorrow morning for your interview."

"Tomorrow!"

"The *Today's Fitness* reporter and crew will be in San Francisco tomorrow. Rhonda said it would work out best if they could do the interview then."

"Sandy, I can't be there by then."

"Why not? You're already in Salt Lake, aren't you? There are two flights leaving this afternoon, one at 3:10 and another at 5:25 for San Francisco. You've got clothes at your apartment, don't you?"

"But—"

Sandy interrupted her. "You could be back in Salt Lake by Monday evening."

Maybe if Alex had been operating on a full night's sleep, her brain would be thinking straighter. She didn't want to go to California, but she couldn't come up with a sensible reason why she couldn't leave that very day. And she was in no frame of mind to spar with Sandy.

"Okay, I guess I can try."

"Alex," Sandy said firmly, "I don't need to remind you that this would be incredibly good for your career. You've got so many hot things happening right now, you've got to take advantage of these kinds of opportunities. It's my obligation as your manager to help you make wise career decisions. And this, Alex, is a wise decision."

"Okay, okay. I'll be on the 5:25 flight."

"I'll pick you up when you get here."

"That would be nice, thank you."

"You won't regret coming, I promise."

"I'll see you tonight, Sandy."

Alex collapsed back onto her pillow after she hung up the phone and tried to go back to sleep, wishing the whole phone conversation had been a dream. But she knew it had really happened. She needed to check on her apartment and take care of business. As willing as she was to give up her career for marriage and a family, that didn't seem to be the direction her life was going. As the saying went, Alex realized she'd better not "burn her bridges behind her." She might need her career for a while yet.

Alex slipped out of bed to get a drink of water. She thought of her conversation with Rich, the reason he'd given her for being preoccupied and distant. She wondered again if his troubles stemmed from dissatisfaction at work, or if there was more to it.

She believed he was losing interest in his work, but she also believed he was losing interest in her. There was something deeper she sensed; she wasn't sure what, but at times being with Rich was like being with a cardboard cutout. His shell was there, but there didn't seem to be anything inside.

Alex sat on the edge of her bed, massaging her temples, wishing she could climb inside Rich's thoughts and see exactly what he was thinking. Even when they talked, she wasn't quite convinced he told her everything. But pressing him didn't seem to produce any answers.

There was only one place to turn.

Kneeling by the side of her bed, Alex rested her head on her clasped hands and wondered how she ever made it through life before she discovered the power of prayer. Even when she was alone, she never felt lonely. She felt the Lord by her side. She had learned that he'd always been there; she'd just never recognized his presence.

Pleading for strength and understanding, she asked the Lord to help her to know what to do. With fresh tears and an aching heart, she prepared herself to receive an answer, hoping it would bring peace of mind and reassurance.

In her mind the solution was clear cut—Rich needed to seek out a different gallery, one focused more on promoting his talent, and she should stay home from Europe to help support Rich and his new venture, and be a strength to Jamie. There were plenty of fitness projects she could start on, and everything would be back to normal. Everyone could be happy again.

But as she listened with her heart, to the promptings and feelings she received, to her disappointment, that wasn't the answer she got.

Chapter 10

Alex, Rich, Steve, and Jamie attended church that morning in Park City. It was a nice, friendly ward and Alex should have enjoyed the gospel doctrine lesson. But her mind was completely out of focus. Her stomach, bunched like a tight fist, was as tense as her frayed nerves. Why was life so complicated, she wondered.

Out of the corner of her eye, she watched Rich as he listened intently to the lesson and followed along in his scriptures. Completely unaware of her frazzled state, Rich never shifted his focus from the discussion. Alex, on the other hand, wondered how she would make it through the last twenty minutes of church.

"That Brother McGavin was a great teacher," Steve said as they exited the building into the warm July day. "He really knew how to keep to the subject. Even when others got off in the weeds, he got right back on the subject."

"That one guy sure was determined to get into some controversial stuff though, wasn't he?" Rich unlocked the truck so they could get inside.

"You mean the one who wanted to talk about the papyrus?"

"What is papyrus?" Alex asked. She'd never heard of it before.

"A man discovered some Egyptian papyri in some old coffins in Egypt and had Joseph Smith translate them for him. That's what the Book of Abraham is in *The Pearl of Great Price.*" Rich started the truck and bumped the air conditioner onto high. It was like an oven inside.

Steve continued. "After Joseph and Emma died, the papyri were given to many different people. But most people believe they were put in the Chicago museum, where they burned in a terrible fire."

Rich drove them through downtown Park City on their way back to the hotel. The sidewalks were already full of Sunday brunchers and shoppers.

Steve went on to explain further. "The problem is, some pieces of papyrus that were part of Joseph Smith's collection were discovered twenty years ago in the Metropolitan museum in New York City."

"Really?" Alex was fascinated with the thought of ancient writings.

"These pieces were identified as part of the "Book of the Dead," which were documents buried with Egyptian mummies. Some people say these papyri were the lost Book of Abraham, but the Church has proved that they aren't."

"I guess I don't understand what the debate is then. Especially if the Church has proven it otherwise." Alex let the fan blow cool air on her face and neck.

"You're going to find, Alex, that there are a lot of people who leave the Church for one reason or another, but they just can't seem to leave the Church alone. They'll try anything to drag others down with them," Rich said.

"But why?"

"That's Satan's plan. He wants to distract us from focusing on the truth. Casting doubts in people's minds is one of his greatest tools in destroying testimonies."

"How do you guys know so much?" Alex asked.

"We got a lot of this on our missions," Rich said. "There are many people out there who are afraid of the truth and fight it with any kind of controversy they can. Missionaries get caught in some pretty strange discussions sometimes. Steve spent a lot of time learning about these kinds of issues and how to defend them. You know, Steve, you shouldn't have given up on law school. You would have been a perfect attorney."

"I didn't get into it all that much," Steve said. "I just wanted to know the answers for myself and for our investigators."

They were almost to the hotel to pick up Alex's bags before taking her to the airport. The other three would spend one more night in Park City; Steve and Jamie to relax and hopefully relive their honeymoon, and Rich to organize and plan his new future.

Before they got to the hotel, Alex asked one more question. "Why can't these people just pray and find out the truth for themselves? Why do they have to go against the Church?"

"Who knows?" Rich said. "It doesn't make sense. They devote their entire lives to tearing down the Church. But there's no way they can win. God's work will go forward no matter what."

Alex appreciated the conviction of Rich's words. She believed what he said was true. She loved the gospel. It brought her great joy and had given her many answers to her prayers. She could never deny that.

* * *

At the hotel, Rich put Alex's bags in the truck, then he and Alex waited outside while Steve made some quick phone calls and Jamie changed her clothes.

Deciding to take a walk, Rich and Alex followed a path up into the hills behind the hotel, looking at flowers, spying a squirrel in a tree. Alex noticed the sharpness of the clear, summer day. The rich blue of the sky was heightened by the deep green of the lofty mountains, which were sprinkled generously with wildflowers, filling the air with their heady fragrance. A breeze rustled the leafy trees and pine branches while choruses of birds chirped and warbled merry tunes. Stopping at a small stream, where large boulders basked in the sun, Alex and Rich rested against the rocks.

"It's hard to believe heaven could be any prettier," Alex said.

"It is perfect, isn't it?"

Rich reached over and tucked a strand of hair behind Alex's ear. He brushed her cheek with his thumb, then leaned toward her. His gentle kiss, as soft as the breeze, stirred her emotions. She loved him so much, yet she was so confused. Why was everything so difficult? Why did relationships have to get so complicated? Only a few days ago they had talked of a future together. Now the subject never came up, and she was uncomfortable even approaching the topic. So much had changed so suddenly. She and Rich were separated by wide chasm filled with questions, doubts, and uncertainty.

He held her for a moment after the kiss ended. His breath warmed her neck, his heart danced in rhythm with hers. Sadness filled her, bringing unwanted tears to her eyes.

Even though she was afraid to bring up the issue of their relation-ship, she was more afraid of what would happen if she didn't. She had no choice. She'd received an answer to her prayers and had gained the understanding she needed. Those realizations forced her to talk to him about her deepest fears.

As one tear rolled down her face, continuing down her chin, it trickled onto Rich's cheek.

"Hey," he lifted his head, felt the moisture with his hand, then looked at her. She turned away, wanting to hide her tears, but he made her look at him. "Alex, what's wrong?"

Alex wiped her eyes on the sleeve of her blouse and pushed away from the rock.

Rich looked intently in her eyes. "Talk to me, Alex. What's wrong?"

All she wanted was for him to hold her, to never let go. But it was now or never. They had to talk. "I'm afraid of how things will change between us these next few months."

"Why is anything going to change?"

"Rich, you don't seem to understand. I'm going to Europe for two months. I know that's not eternity, but it is a long time. And it seems even longer since things between us have been so . . . different."

"What do you mean 'different'?"

She rubbed at the ache between her eyebrows, forcing herself to remain calm. Either he truly *couldn't* see that things between them had changed, or he *didn't* want to see it.

"Up until I got baptized, everything between us was wonderful. We spent every possible moment together, we agreed on most things, enjoyed doing the same things, and could talk about anything. We even talked about getting married in the temple someday."

She dug at a rock with the toe of her boot, pausing to slow the momentum, trying to stay calm.

Looking up at him, hoping to gain answers from his expression, she continued, "It seems like since I've gotten baptized, things have changed. You've distanced yourself from me, physically and emotionally. I know you've said you're struggling with changes in your work and with your career, but I just can't help but think there's something else."

A fly buzzed around her ear. She waved at it, wishing Rich would say something. After an uncomfortable pause, she said, "Haven't you noticed this? Doesn't anything seem different to you?"

He thrust one hand in the pocket of his jeans and dug out a tube of Carmex. Still saying nothing he put some on his lips.

"Rich, please say something." The emotions she'd managed to lock away threatened to burst their confines.

"I don't really know what to say, Alex. Yes, I guess there has been a bit of a change between us."

It was there, in his voice. That edge of defense that sharpened the corners of his words so they nicked and scratched painfully at her heart.

"I'll admit," he continued, "I've felt a little confined lately. I'm not used to having to account for every minute of the day."

Confined! Having to account for every minute of the day! She couldn't believe what he was saying.

"That's how I make you feel? Like you need to account to me for everything you do?" It took a Herculean effort to keep her voice steady.

"Yeah, a little bit."

Obviously he was forgetting about all the times *he* dropped in at Jamie and Steve's unexpectedly. Or how many times *he* was the one who invited her to go places and do things. In fact, now that she thought about it, she could honestly say that *he* was responsible for ninety-percent of the things they did and the time they spent together. She'd always wanted to be with him and was more than thrilled to do things together, but she'd never really been the initiator. She'd never needed to because *he'd* always done it.

She took a deep breath and released it slowly. "I had no idea you felt this way. I'm sorry I didn't figure it out on my own."

"Hey," he said lightly, "I love being with you, Alex. Don't get me wrong. We have a great time together."

Alex tried to keep her voice steady. "What are you trying to say?"

"Nothing. I'm fine with how things are between us. I don't have any complaints. I just need a little more space right now, especially with this chance to have a show at the gallery."

"I guess it's a good thing I'm going to Europe then," Alex said slowly.

Rich looked relieved that their conversation appeared to be resolved. "It's perfect. You'll be busy, I'll be busy. You watch. The time will fly by."

"Yeah," she nodded, realizing he hadn't gotten anything she'd just said. "It'll fly right by."

As she followed him back down the hill to the truck, sparks of anger heightened her pain. Here, all along, she'd imagined herself insecure and unsure, jumping to conclusions about Rich's intentions. But now she realized that she had been right to wonder about Rich's behavior. He was looking for excuses. That way he didn't have to admit he wasn't ready now, maybe ever, to make a commitment to her.

She loved Rich. She would fight for him. But she couldn't hang on forever, and if he wasn't careful, the hurt would turn into anger, which would ignite and burst into flame. Then there would be nothing left. But that was the only way she would be able to survive.

Chapter 11

All the way to California, Alex was haunted by the memory of Rich's apparent apathy toward their relationship. He didn't seem to want any more from her than companionship at his convenience. Companionship without commitment. Alex sighed. She should have expected this. After all, the man had been engaged three times before this. Maybe he wasn't capable of making a commitment.

Leaving Rich, Jamie, and Steve behind at the Salt Lake City airport had given Alex a small taste of what it would be like when she left for Europe. She'd tried to smile and keep the conversation light, but the occasion foreshadowed a much bigger, much more painful farewell.

She didn't know if she could do it.

* * *

"I hope you don't mind," Sandy said. "I invited a few friends over for dinner tonight. I want you to come."

"You don't need to invite me," Alex said, hoping Sandy would notice a speed limit sign soon and slow down. Sandy's Lexus traveled like a dream, but Alex knew her friend's driving record. Sandy was an insurance company's worst nightmare.

"Nonsense, I haven't seen you in three months. The party is in your honor. You won't be in town very long. I'd like to spend a little time with you—catching up on all the fun things you've been doing. Plus we need to discuss a little business and make sure we're set for your interview tomorrow."

"Okay, okay." Alex wasn't in the mood for a party, but Sandy was her friend and she'd gone to the all the work of organizing a dinner. "I appreciate you going to so much trouble."

"It's no trouble at all. It's just so good to see you again."

"It's good to see you. You look great, as usual."

"You're the one who looks wonderful. Especially with a little more flesh on your bones. How did you manage to put it on in all the right places?"

Instead of fighting the compliment, Alex had learned to just say "thank you" and let it go. People seemed to let the issue of her weight, loss or gain, drop more quickly when she did.

It worked. For the next few minutes Sandy busied herself answering a phone call, and Alex had a chance to look out at the beautiful San Mateo bridge stretching across the San Francisco Bay and the tall palm trees shimmering in the evening sun. Except for the traffic, the smog, the high cost of living, the crime, and the earthquakes, Alex loved California.

But it didn't feel like home anymore.

* * *

"Sandy, that stir-fry was wonderful." Alex dabbed at her mouth with her napkin and set it on her plate.

"Are you sure you don't have a little Oriental blood in you, my dear?" Sandy's friend, Barbara said.

"Barb," as she'd asked Alex to call her, was in her fifties. She had a retro seventies look—bleached blonde hair cut short into a bob, bright-pink lipstick, and blue eye shadow. Her conservative clothes were dated and very polyester. Barb's husband, Gerald, was round bellied and wore a very ugly, obvious toupee. Alex immediately pegged him as the kind of guy who liked to tease and make a joke about everything, funny or not. He reminded her of the kind of men who thought horse bites were funny and who liked to pretend they didn't know who you were asking for when you called their house.

The Trumans didn't really seem Sandy's jet-set type, but they were pleasant and very interested in everything Alex had to say. The other fellow who was with them, Thadeus Martin, was much younger and more serious. He made Alex very uncomfortable. He watched her closely, barely said a word, and never laughed at Gerald's jokes— although Alex didn't blame him for that.

After dinner, while they relaxed on the couch eating fresh strawberry pie, Thadeus finally spoke.

"So, Sandy tells us you recently joined the Mormon church."

Alex set her barely eaten piece of pie on the coffee table and cleared her throat with a sip of ice water.

"Yes, I got baptized a week ago yesterday."

He stared at her with an intensity that made her squirm. She decided it was time to confess a headache, which she truly had, and go home.

"Her sister and brother-in-law are Mormons, too," Sandy said.

"Did you talk with the missionaries before you got baptized?" Thadeus asked.

"Yes," she said.

"I guess they told you Joseph Smith wrote the Book of Mormon."

"No, actually he translated it from golden plates. It was written by prophets who lived on the earth six hundred years before Christ."

"Lies," Thadeus said, jumping to his feet. "All lies. That book was written by Samuel Spaulding. The Book of Mormon is fiction."

"No it's not," Alex said, not sure of what was happening.

"I can prove to you that the Book of Mormon is a fraud and that Joseph Smith is, too," he bellowed.

"But it's true. I know it is." She looked to Sandy for support, but Sandy's head was turned, her eyes hidden from Alex's gaze. What was going on? Why was this man upset with her?

Then the other man spoke up. "I was a bishop in the Mormon church," Gerald said. "I went to the Mormon temple. I even filled a mission for your church. You are being taught lies. You are being deceived." His voice elevated to a pitch that hurt Alex's ears. She had to get out of there.

"Alex, dear," Barb said in a childlike tone, "we are here to help you. We want you to see that the Mormon church is based on a false prophet and is filled with lies."

A knot formed in Alex's throat so large she couldn't swallow. Angry, stinging tears burned her eyes.

"Did they talk to you about the temple?" Thadeus bellowed.

"Yes." Alex could barely speak. Where were Steve and Rich? She needed them.

"Did they show you the movie *The Godmakers* and tell you how your church destroys lives and breaks up marriages and families?" Thadeus' voice grew in volume until he was shouting. "Did they tell you that once you go through the temple you must keep the rituals secret or agree to be killed?"

Alex trembled in silence.

"Of course not," he raged on. "They can't tell you these things, because you and every other investigator they brainwash into their cult would run screaming for your lives if you knew the truth. You've been deceived, Alexis. You have been lied to by people you trust, people who themselves have been brainwashed into the Mormon way of thinking. And we are here tonight to help you realize that you can get out of it. You *have* to get out of it."

"You can still be saved," Barb said. "We will help you."

Alex felt an awful heaviness as if the air was thick and closing in around her. She could barely breathe. Her arms and legs trembled. She couldn't speak.

"We will pray for you," Barb said. "We will pray that your eyes will be opened and that you will see the truth. We will pray that you will be free from the evil teachings of that church. That your mind can be cleansed. We will save you."

Pulling Sandy to the floor with them, all four knelt in a circle around Alex. Gerald grabbed one of her hands and Thadeus the other, and they held on tightly, making her wince in pain. Then Barb began her prayer, a wailing, dramatic tirade, pleading for Alex's soul.

Sandy kept her head down, unable to look at Alex.

Alex watched the people kneeling around her, their faces raised to the ceiling, repeating "Amen" and "Hallelujah" as Barb continued her prayer. The thick, pressing feeling surrounding her made Alex feel as though her very bones would crush.

"Stop!"

She broke free of their grip and darted to the other side of the room. "You people are wrong. You are the ones who have been deceived. Satan has a hold on your hearts. I can feel his presence in this very room." She pointed to them, finding miraculously within herself a strong, calming power. "You can't get to me with your twisted, evil ways. I have felt the Holy Ghost with me. I know the Church is true. I know it with every fiber in my being."

Without hesitation she bolted for the door and ran out into the night.

* * *

She didn't know how long or how far she went, but she finally ran out of breath and dropped her pace to a slow walk. Her mind continued racing. Had all of that really happened? The incident in Sandy's living room seemed like a nightmare, unreal and frightening. They were exactly the type of people Steve and Rich had told her about. She shivered as she thought about the horrible feeling that had filled the room and wrapped itself around her like a python, squeezing the very breath out of her.

Her father had told her as a little girl to trust her feelings. The missionaries had told her the same thing—trust her feelings and listen to the still small voice. Her feelings had told her to get out of there tonight.

Standing on the street corner she wondered, what was she supposed to do now? Cars whizzed by, joggers passed, and two doors down, rock music blared from an open window. The night was full of noise and confusion.

She did the only thing she could do; she sought solace in a fervent, pleading prayer. Still upset about the events of the evening and the awful feelings she had felt, Alex asked her Heavenly Father to help settle her nerves and give her peace. Soon her panic subsided, and she received what she needed most—comfort. Even though she still wasn't sure about Barb and Gerald and Thadeus and the things they'd told her, she felt better. The Lord had promised to be with her always. She wasn't alone.

Drawing in a calming breath, she began the walk back to Sandy's. She would get her purse, call a taxi, and go home to her apartment.

Outside Sandy's door she listened for voices. Hearing none, Alex peeked through the window to see if Sandy's "guests" were gone. Then she rang the bell.

The door flew open, and Sandy stood before her, crumpled and sobbing.

"Alex, you came back," she cried and threw her arms around Alex's neck. "I had no idea they would do that to you. They didn't tell me they were going to rip you apart like that. I am so sorry. I don't blame you if you never forgive me."

Sandy sobbed and clung to her until Alex finally pulled away and led her to the couch. Uneaten pieces of pie still littered the coffee table.

"Barb is a friend of my mother's," she began. "I mentioned to Mom that you had joined the Church. She told me Barb and her husband had been Mormons, and they'd left the church. She said Barb and her husband have devoted their lives to helping people see the truth about the Mormons. They spend their time giving lectures and meeting with individuals who are looking into joining the Church."

Sandy found a napkin under one of the plates and wiped at her face, leaving mascara circles beneath her eyes.

"What they do seemed so noble. And to be honest, I was worried about you joining your sister's church. After all, you were the one who told me so many crazy, kooky things about the religion in the first place. Part of me wondered if you had been brainwashed while you were in Idaho."

Alex could see exactly why Sandy had worried. She herself was responsible for Sandy's skeptical attitude toward the Church.

"When you told me you got baptized, I thought the least I could do was make sure you knew what you were getting into. That's why I invited Barb and Gerald over. They brought Thadeus on their own. I had no idea they were going to treat you so horribly." A sob caught in Sandy's throat. "They seemed like such nice people—well, maybe not that Thadeus. What a piece of work he was. But, Alex, believe me, I never ever would have set this up if I had thought something like this would happen."

Alex was still shaken by the event, but she believed Sandy had no motive but Alex's welfare in mind.

"And when they started praying," Sandy shuddered. "You were right, you know, when you said how evil it felt in here. I felt it, too. And the minute they left, that feeling left with them. Alex, they were evil. I'm so sorry."

"I know," Alex assured her. "It's okay. I believe you."

"I would never do anything to ruin our friendship. We've known each other such a long time, I would hate for it to end this way."

Alex gave her friend a hug to prove she held no hard feelings, but she was exhausted and a bit confused. It bothered her that the man had actually been a bishop and had been through the temple. Something terrible must have happened to turn them away from the Church.

"I was so proud of you for standing up to them like you did," Sandy said. "You were so brave and . . . powerful."

Alex looked at her friend and thought about her words. She *had* been brave and she *had* felt powerful. The spirit of the Lord had been with her that night. She was extremely grateful. Without it she wasn't sure she would have had the courage to do what she did.

* * *

Within the safety of her apartment, Alex relaxed although she still didn't understand why those people thought they had the right to talk to her the way they did. She never wanted to go through something like that again, never wanted to have that dark, awful feeling around her ever again.

She wasn't used to facing challenges alone. She'd grown used to having Jamie, Steve, and her mother around her, and of course, Rich. He'd been a great strength to her when she felt weak or needed answers.

If anything, she'd learned something very important from the experience that evening. With the Lord's help and spirit to guide her, she'd had the strength and courage and power to face challenges, even deceived people like Barb, Gerald, and Thadeus.

It was time she learned to stand on her own. She wouldn't always have someone around to help her out. She needed to learn to rely on the Lord, and to strengthen herself and her convictions in the event she ever needed to defend herself and her beliefs again. For a moment her thoughts shifted to the New Testament, where she'd been reading about Jesus and the many confrontations he'd faced. Her trial had been nothing even close to what he'd had to withstand. And what about Joseph Smith? He'd withstood a constant barrage of attacks, both physical and verbal, but had continued to defend his beliefs. The realization humbled her.

But she needed refueling. Tonight's confrontation had drained her.

Dialing the phone, she waited six rings then hung up. Rich wasn't in his hotel room. It was after eleven in Utah. Frustrated, she punched the hotel phone number again, and this time asked for Steve and Jamie's room. Jamie answered after the first ring.

"Hi, it's me."

"You made it. How's California?"

"That's why I called. Something weird happened tonight. Is Steve around?"

"Yeah, he's in the bathroom. He'll be right out."

"I tried Rich's room, he didn't answer."

"Oh, he just left our room. They were watching the sports show after the news. He's probably there by now. Here's Steve. I'll let you talk to him while I go get Rich."

Steve got on the line. "Hey, Alex. What's going on?"

"Steve, I need to talk to you about something that happened tonight."

"Sure, go ahead."

Alex recounted the experience at Sandy's house for him. He listened silently while she explained the things those people had said and the feeling she'd had with them.

"I guess we should have warned you better about all the anti-Mormons who might try and shake you up, now that you've joined the Church," he said apologetically.

"Anti-Mormons. Is that what they're called?"

"Yeah, they're all over. I think I can answer your questions about the things they told you but first, do you remember how you told me about the dark and awful feeling you had while they were talking to you?"

"It was scary and evil."

"Alex, Satan is very clever and very deceptive. He's cunning and has deceived some of the Lord's most elect. He knows if he can get to you, especially while you're just starting out, he'll be able to prevent all the good things you're going to do as a member of the Church and all the people you're going to introduce to the gospel and all the personal growth you'll have. He'll do anything he can to get in your way. But you just remember how you felt when you were talking to them and how you feel when you're with people who have a testimony, or when you're bearing your testimony. You'll always be able to discern which comes from the Lord and which comes from the devil. Hold on a minute. Rich just walked in with Jamie."

She heard Steve give the others a brief explanation. The next voice she heard was Rich's.

"Hey there, are you okay?"

It was so wonderful to hear him. "Yeah, I'm okay."

"Sorry you had to go through that. It must've been awful."

"I was pretty shaken up."

"I wish I could've been there with you."

"Me too." He would never know how much.

"Alex, you're probably going to come up against people like this again sometime. I want to tell you something President Kimball said a long time ago. We used this quote a lot on our missions, because we got hit with anti-Mormon stuff all the time. This isn't the exact quote but he said something like this: 'If this wasn't the Lord's work, the adversary wouldn't pay any attention to us. But because it is the church of Jesus Christ, we shouldn't be surprised when criticisms arise. The truth will prevail because this is his work.'"

"And Alex," Steve was back on the phone, "I found a scripture that will help you. It's from Matthew seven, verses fifteen and sixteen. Listen to this.

"'Beware of false prophets, which come to you in sheep's clothing, but inwardly they are ravening wolves. Ye shall know them by their fruits . . . .'"

Alex marveled at how perfectly the scripture described her experience. Those people had come to her dressed in sheep's clothing, but truly they had been wolves. And she would never forget the evil, contentious feeling that had accompanied them.

"Yes," she answered, "I understand now."

Rich got back on the phone.

"When you get back we'll sit down and answer your questions about Spaulding writing the Book of Mormon and about the movie they were talking about. But, Alex, I want you to know, what you did tonight, bearing your testimony that you knew the Church was true, was the most powerful argument you could have given them. You did the right thing. I'm proud of you."

Tears filled her eyes. "Thanks, Rich." She tilted the phone away so she could clear her throat. "You know what," she said, "In a way I'm kind of glad it happened."

"You are?"

"Yes. I feel a little stronger, and I feel more prepared to face it again if I ever need to."

"You're quite a girl, you know that?" he said.

"Yeah," she said. "And don't you forget it."

Chapter 12

When Sandy picked Alex up at her apartment the next day, she was still full of apologies. Alex was more than happy to put the whole thing in the past.

In hardly any time at all they arrived at the Fitness Academy where Alex's whole career had started; she still had an office there. They learned that the crew from *Today's Fitness* magazine was scheduled to arrive shortly.

Randy Morton, the manager and her long-time friend, was at the front desk when she walked in with Sandy.

"Alex!" He flew around the counter and gave her a hug that nearly crushed her bones. A serious competitive body builder, Randy had enough trophies and titles to fill a room. But even with his pony tail, pierced ears and nose, and Goliath-sized body, he was a wonderful friend and a caring person. Alex had a lot of respect for him.

"You look fantastic," he said, holding her at arm's length. "You really do. And healthy too." He hugged her again. "It's so good to see you."

"You too, Randy."

"And Sandy." He turned and shook her hand. "Nice seeing you again."

"Congratulations on winning the Iron Man competition," Sandy said. "You had some tough competition this year. How's your line of personalized supplements going?"

"Great. I still need an endorsement from Alex, though. It would certainly help boost interest in the female market."

"I'll try and get a few words in today in my interview." She remembered she'd also promised Steve she'd mention Recreation Headquarters also.

"Good idea." He hugged her again. "Man, it's good to have you back. I wish you were staying." He turned to Sandy. "Can't you talk her into staying? I mean, what's Idaho got that we haven't got?"

In her own defense, Alex said, "Try gorgeous snow-capped mountains, clean, breathable air—"

"—and her boyfriend, Rich," Sandy finished for her.

"You broke a lot of hearts when you left, Alex," Randy said.

"I did?" Alex raised her eyebrows. "That's news to me. I wasn't even dating anyone." Some months before she'd gone to Idaho, she'd ended an awful relationship with Jordan, who had been self-serving and possessive, but Alex had had no close male friends after that. Until Rich.

"Jordan still talks about you all the time," Randy said. "Too bad he's out of town. I know he would've wanted to see you again."

Alex was grateful he was both out of town and out of her life. He'd been too possessive and jealous for a healthy relationship.

"I think our appointment just showed up," Sandy said.

Alex suddenly got nervous. "Don't let me say anything stupid, okay?"

"You'll be fine." Sandy fluffed her hair and straightened her jacket.

"You look great," Alex told her. Sandy was in her early forties and obsessed with her looks, especially since her divorce. She had gorgeous wavy red hair, creamy skin, and the most beautiful, thickly lashed, blue eyes Alex had ever seen. But Sandy took seriously the Boy Scout philosophy to always be prepared, since she figured every new man she met could be a future "significant other."

"I know they're here to see *you,*" she said, "but you never know."

Introductions were made, and to Sandy's disappointment a woman named Leigh Stringham was doing the interview.

While the crew found a location in the gym to take pictures after the interview, Alex led the way to her office, hoping it wouldn't be too big of a disaster. To her relief, when she opened the door, her desk was scattered with a few books and papers, but nothing embarrassing. It did have a musty smell from being closed up for so long.

"So," Leigh said, "I understand you've been in Idaho for several months, during which time you participated in an outpatient eating disorder program, your video is on the best-seller list, you've completed work on a cookbook that's currently in production, you're heading to Europe in a few weeks to go on a two-month fitness tour, and . . . ," she glanced down at her notes, then looked up at Alex with an amused smile, "you've just joined the Mormon church?"

Before Alex could answer, Sandy jumped in. "Actually, Leigh, I'm not sure I see what Alex joining the Mormon church, or any church for that matter, has to do with this article."

Alex understood that Sandy was just trying to spare her from another uncomfortable experience. Seeing Leigh's reaction, Alex thought the subject could be easily dropped, but she decided she needed to make a statement. What kind of "Mormon" was she if she couldn't stand up for what she believed in? Especially after last night.

"I would like to answer Leigh's question," she spoke up.

Sandy looked at her like she was crazy, and Leigh's eyebrows arched in surprise.

Alex continued. "For the past three months I've been searching inside of myself for answers: why is food an issue with me, and why do I neglect my health when I know how important good health is? These are questions I wasn't ready to face for a long time because I didn't have the strength to deal with the issues or make the changes I needed to make. That strength finally came when I gained a clear understanding of who I really am and why I'm here on this earth."

If anything, Alex knew she had their attention. Whatever she said next would either make people think she was an absolute kook or give others a reason to search for answers and truth and hope for something better for themselves.

She paused, then said, "Any kind of disorder, whether it's anorexia, bulimia, depression, or addictions, is a symptom of a greater, hidden problem. Until you discover the real, and usually painful, reason for the behavior, you can never resolve it."

The tape recorder caught every word she said. Leigh scribbled notes on her yellow pad of paper and Sandy listened closely.

"My father died when I was eight years old. I turned to food for comfort. Of course, I was covering up the pain I felt from his death, instead of dealing with the problem. Subsequently I gained quite a bit of weight in my youth.

"When I was fifteen years old, I developed pneumonia and was ill for many weeks. During that time I lost some weight, fifteen pounds or so. When I went back to school I was overwhelmed with all the comments about how great I looked. I was finally getting some positive attention, and it felt wonderful. My mother took me shopping and fussed over me, and I loved it. So I kept losing weight, thinking if I lost more I would get even more love and attention, and you know what? I did. People who had never even noticed me before suddenly started being my friend. I was a new person. I had confidence and friends, and I felt loved."

Leigh had stopped writing and was listening intently.

"I struggled for eleven years with anorexia, all because I didn't understand that I needed help. The problem was bigger than me; I couldn't do it myself. No one can. And when I say help, of course I mean from a hospital or some medical facility, but I also mean spiritually. I needed to find a bigger purpose for making myself well. And that came when I realized who the Savior really was and what he meant in my life. Knowing that I was actually a child of God, that I was loved and could turn to him whenever I was in need, gave me incredible courage and strength. I received wonderful treatment at the clinic in Idaho Falls, but the real help, the kind that made a change in me forever, was handing my burden over to the Lord and leaning on him."

Leigh was silent. Sandy looked away, sniffing and clearing her throat.

After taking a long breath, Alex said, "I didn't intend this to turn into a religious interview, but if you're interested in knowing the real reason why I overcame my eating disorder, I had to include the reason I joined The Church of Jesus Christ of Latter-day Saints. I know everything there is to know about nutrition and good health, but all that knowledge still didn't give me the ability to change. The Lord did."

After a few minutes, the interview took on a lighter note, but Alex still felt the great joy and warmth that had filled her as she shared the story of her change and discovery. She also realized that in all her years of working with people, helping them with their goals to become healthier and more fit, her joy was even greater telling them about the Savior. She'd helped many people change how they looked on the outside, but she understood now, it was the change on the inside that really mattered.

* * *

"You handled that interview beautifully," Sandy said as they walked down the concourse at the airport. "Leigh told me how impressed she was with you."

"I'm just glad it's over. I really don't like doing stuff like that. There's a lot of people in the industry much more impressive than I am."

"Don't sell yourself short, Alex. I think this article is going to do a lot of good out there."

Alex shifted her bag into her other hand. The walk to her gate was a long one. "I hope so. I would love to help someone avoid going through what I went through for so many years."

"I learned a lot as I listened to you today."

"You did? But you already know everything about me." They wove their way through a crowd of passengers whose plane had just landed.

"Not so much about you," Sandy said, "but about your church. I didn't realize that Mormons believed in Christ. I thought they were like Moonies or something."

"Moonies! Whatever gave you that idea?"

"I don't know. All that secret temple stuff and all that talk about polygamy and that guy finding gold plates under a rock. I always thought your church revered *him* as your leader. I was glad you cleared up some of my questions."

Alex realized this was an opportunity. She knew she couldn't pass up the chance to share what she knew, but she wanted to handle it right.

"I know how you can get all of your questions answered," she said.

"How?"

"I could have a couple of the missionaries come to your house, then you could ask them anything you want. That's what I did."

"But I don't want to get baptized. I'm just curious, that's all. After last night I wouldn't mind hearing what your side has to say."

"The missionaries would love to help you any way they can. Which reminds me, there's something I'd like to give you." They stepped out of the lane of traffic so Alex could dig through her bag. When she found what she was looking for, she gave it to Sandy. It was the nice leather triple combination Jamie and Steve had given her at her baptism, but she knew they'd understand.

"What's this?"

"It's the Book of Mormon. I want you to have it."

Sandy turned the book over in her hands, examining it. "What are those other titles?"

"There's the Doctrine and Covenants—that's modern-day revelation to the Prophet Joseph Smith—and the Pearl of Great Price, which talks about the creation of the world. It contains revelations that were given to Moses and Abraham. I haven't read it much yet."

"Oh," Sandy said, contemplating Alex's explanation. "So, I guess you guys don't believe in the Bible then."

"Of course we do, Sandy. These other books serve as another testament of Jesus Christ. They go hand in hand."

Sandy was quiet, as if digesting all this new information.

Alex tried to read her friend's face, but without success. "Listen," she said, "I don't know all the answers to your questions. That's why you should talk to the missionaries. That's their whole purpose, to teach people about the gospel."

Sandy shook her head. "I told you, I don't want to get baptized. So don't try to convert me."

"No one can convert you," Alex said. "That part's up to you and the Lord. I just know that I've never been happier and felt more purpose and peace in my life, since I joined the Church."

"Are there many eligible men my age in your Church?" Sandy asked with a teasing lift to her brow.

"Well, I don't have all the statistics, but I met Rich, and my mother met a wonderful man who's a member of the Church. He's a very handsome doctor."

"A doctor, huh?"

They arrived at the gate just as the call came for the passengers to board the plane.

"Guess I'd better go. Thanks for everything, Sandy."

Giving her a quick hug, Sandy said, "I have a feeling I should thank *you*." She pointed to the book in her hand. "Are you sure about this?"

"I've never been more sure of anything."

"Okay. Then call the missionaries for me. But don't go thinking I'm going to get baptized. I look terrible in white."

Alex laughed and took her place in line. As she had reflected on the confrontation she'd had the night before, she realized she was glad it had happened. Not only had it strengthened her testimony, but it had broken through Sandy's protective shell. While trying to tear down the Lord's church, those anti-Mormons had just helped the work go forward.

Chapter 13

Alex was glad to get back to Island Park and to her loved ones, especially Rich, again. This was home for her.

On her way back from California, Alex made a decision about Rich and her relationship with him. After thinking about his comment that he was feeling confined and needed some space, she decided to respect his feelings. She also needed to exercise faith in him that he would get his thoughts and feelings sorted out, especially about this new career opportunity. She knew change was hard and how difficult it was to chart a new course. Right now Rich needed her support and encouragement. She loved him. She was prepared to do anything to help him. Even if it meant leaving him for two months.

* * *

After a long day of housework, laundry, yardwork, and catching up on business, Alex and Jamie relaxed and watched *Jeopardy* while Steve was at a church meeting and Judith was out with Dr. Rawlins. They weren't getting any of the answers on the show.

Alex snorted in disgust. "How do these people know things like 'During the crusades Muslims were called Saracens by the Christians' and 'Giuseppe Garibaldi was the hero of the Italian Risorgimento'?"

"Beats me," Jamie answered. "I was on the dean's list in college, and I only got two answers on the show tonight. But at least one was the Daily Double."

"Yes, but technically you wouldn't get credit for it because you didn't state your answer in the form of a question," Alex argued.

"Oh, so now you're Alex Trebek?" Jamie bantered.

"Hey, I didn't make the rules."

Jamie surfed through the channels one more time before clicking off the TV. "Where's Rich tonight?" she asked.

Alex shrugged. "I dunno."

"Have you talked to him?"

"No."

"Have you seen him?"

"No."

They sat a moment in silence.

"Is it none of my business or do you just not want to talk about it?" Jamie said at last.

"There's nothing to talk about," Alex answered. "He says he feels confined and needs some space. So I'm giving him some space."

"He said that to you?" Jamie's voice rose in surprise.

"Yep" was all Alex said.

"Well, that's stupid."

"Maybe so, but it's how he feels."

"You know," Jamie said thoughtfully, "after a couple gets used to being together so much, it's easy to start taking each other for granted. You weren't pressuring him about things, like, marriage or anything, were you?"

"Are you kidding? Of course, I wasn't pressuring him about marriage. I mean, we talked about it occasionally, but I never pressured him. At least, I didn't think I was."

Jamie looked at her sister compassionately. "You really love him don't you?"

Alex nodded. "I do. I know he's struggling right now, but I truly believe he loves me, too. I just need to be patient and let him work through things on his own."

"He's sure lucky to have someone who's willing to be patient with him," Jamie pronounced.

"I have to be. I have no choice. That is, if I want us to be together. And I feel very strongly that he and I are supposed to be together."

"It's got to be hard though."

"It is hard," Alex folded her legs underneath her and ran her finger down the seam of her jeans. "Things have been so good for us, until lately. I just wish I knew what brought about this sudden change in him."

"I guess we shouldn't be surprised. We both know how hard it is for Rich to make a commitment."

The sisters looked at each other. Then as if two light bulbs switched on simultaneously, they both opened their mouths at their shared realization.

"Oh boy," Alex said. "That word. Commitment. He isn't just frustrated with his job and concerned about a new career. Jamie—"

"Yes."

"Do you think Rich realized when I got baptized that I was getting closer to making him follow through with his commitment. You know, put your money where your mouth is, that kind of a thing."

Jamie stared at Alex, fascinated. "You mean, Rich wasn't afraid to talk to you about marriage or a future, because he knew as long as you weren't a member of the Church, he didn't have to—in fact, *couldn't*—follow through?"

"Exactly. And the moment I became a member, it became a reality that I could actually marry him in the temple."

"He does have a history of avoiding commitment," Jamie said sardonically.

"And he has been very vague whenever I talk to him about our future, like changing the subject and redirecting the conversation." Alex's voice grew louder as her emotions took over. "But, Jamie, what does that mean?"

"What does what mean?"

"Well, does that mean he's not ever going to be able to commit to me?"

"Of course not!" Jamie said matter-of-factly. Then her tone changed and she added, "At least I don't think so."

"You don't think so?"

"Well, how would I know what Rich is thinking?"

"I don't know." Alex shut her eyes, wishing she could understand him, but afraid she had finally figured him out. "I'm so stupid! He's scared. The man's *still* afraid to make a commitment!" She jumped up and walked across the room. "I thought I was different. I thought we had something special."

"You *are* different from the other girls, and you two *do* have something special," Jamie said firmly.

"But, Jamie, he's treating me just like he treated those other three girls he was engaged to. Except he hasn't even gone that far with our relationship. At least he gave them a ring."

As Alex spoke, a flood of pain and frustrations sprang from some hidden well of emotion.

"Alex," Jamie said soothingly, "You can't jump to conclusions. He's just a little gun-shy, that's all. It's nothing to worry about."

"Do you really believe that?" Alex asked, her expression pleading for reassurance.

"Well . . . yeah . . . ," Jamie said unconvincingly. "Rich is acting like an idiot, because he's a little afraid of commitment. But he's not willing to risk letting you get away. You're the best thing that ever happened to him."

Alex nodded, blinking hard to clear a few frustrated tears finding their way to the surface. "He's told me that a dozen times," Alex said. "He's just not acting like it."

"Someone needs to talk some sense into his head. He's just not thinking clearly." Jamie whisked a few strands of hair out of her eyes and tucked them behind her ear. "But I do worry about him spending all that time around 'Elena the Piranha Woman.' He's too sweet and trusting; Elena will have him for lunch."

"I'm afraid for him, too," Alex sniffed, "but he thinks he's got everything under control."

"Then he's fooling himself," Jamie said crisply. "He's going to let you take off to Europe, thinking he's got this wonderful opportunity to get his paintings into a gallery and move to Park City for a while. Then it's going to hit him. His world will grind to a halt, and he'll realize he's made the biggest mistake of his life."

"I hope so," Alex sighed. "I just hope, when he does realize it, if he ever does, that it's not too late. I'll wait for him, but not forever. I'm almost thirty and I'm ready for a permanent relationship. I want to get married and have a family."

For a minute Alex was afraid what she'd said would upset Jamie, but when she looked for a reaction, Jamie was straightening pillows on the couch.

Then Jamie stopped arranging pillows and looked at her sister. "You need to talk to him, Alex. We're sitting here trying to assume what he's thinking and how he's feeling. But you need to ask him straight out."

"I have asked him. He won't talk."

"Then you have to make him. You deserve an explanation and an honest answer."

"I know."

"And you better find out before you go to Europe or things could really get out of control. Oh . . . " Jamie covered a yawn. "Oh, sorry."

"You're right," Alex said. "I'll do it." But she doubted it would get her anywhere.

What would happen if she confronted him? Would he finally open up to her and share his fears? Or would he get upset and end their relationship completely?

Jamie yawned again.

"You tired?" Alex asked.

"I didn't get much sleep last night," Jamie explained.

"How come?"

"I had that dream again. You know, the one about me having a baby."

"Oh." This dream thing was making Alex nervous.

"This is the third time now and it's always the same. I'm at the hospital—we're all there—and the nurse carries a baby into where we are and places it in my arms. I can see her so clearly. I can even smell her and feel her warmth against my chest. It woke me up last night and I couldn't go back to sleep. It seemed so real."

Alex didn't know what to say. More than anything, she wanted her sister to have a baby but Jamie's sense of reality seemed to be slipping out of focus.

"Anyway, I do feel more hopeful that when it's time, the Lord will let me know what I should do. And I guess I should tell you that Steve is totally against having you be a surrogate mother for us, although I appreciate you being so good about it. And after we talked about it, I realized it was a bit extreme. Besides, I'm feeling more positive now, not quite so desperate."

That was the best news Alex had heard for a while. "That's good, Jamie," she said. She supposed that if the dream gave her sister hope, then it was a good thing. Even though it was just a dream. "I wish he'd give me a dream so I'd know what I should do."

"You'll figure it out Alex. You and me, we just have to be patient. The answers will come."

"I hope so, Jamie. I sure hope so."

* * *

That night as Alex knelt down to pray, her heart was heavy. How did she get Rich to open up to her? If he was having a hard time with commitment, could they talk about it? Couldn't they work on solving the challenges together?

She made sure to express her gratitude for her many blessings; even though things between her and Rich were up in the air, she was abundantly blessed. In fact, she felt she was blessed more than she deserved.

"Heavenly Father, it probably isn't normal to ask something like this, but since I have so many blessings and Jamie is struggling with wanting to have a baby so much, could she have some of my blessings? I think she could use a few extra right now and I'll be okay for a while without them. Besides, Rich is being very stubborn and I'm not sure what to do with him yet.

"And one more thing . . . not that I'm doubting really, but I just wanted to check. Am I still supposed to go to Europe?"

She waited, forcing herself to keep her mind and heart open. It would be so easy to stay closed and not receive the inspiration, but again, she felt the same peace and assurance telling her what she already knew.

"Okay, I'll go. But it's taking all the faith I can come up with to do it. I don't know what in the world could be so important over there, when everything that's important to me is here in Idaho. But I'll go." She closed her prayer and crawled into bed.

But I don't want to, she thought as she closed her eyes and went to sleep.

Chapter 14

"Honey, I think you should take my beaded evening dress. The black one."

Judith pulled the glittering gown out of the closet to display it.

Alex shook her head. "Mom, it's just not my style. I'm not glitzy like that. I'd feel like I was playing dress-up or something."

"Alexis, you would look stunning in this dress. I could take it in a little for you in the waist so it would fit better. With black hose and heels and your hair pinned up, you would be ready to attend an elegant dinner, an opera, or even just take an evening stroll down the streets of Paris."

"It would look great on you," Jamie said.

Alex wasn't sure if she appreciated her sister's and mother's help packing. She felt like she was taking much more than she needed.

"It travels like a dream and won't take up much space," her mother continued. "I think you'll be glad you took it along."

"Okay, I'll take it. But I bet I don't use it."

"Do you have a light raincoat to take and a nice umbrella?" Her mother scanned the stacks of clothes folded on the bed.

"I don't. You think I'll need them?"

"Yes. And you could use a new suitcase. As much as you're going to be moving around, wouldn't you rather have one of those kind where the handle pulls out that you can wheel around?"

Alex had been meaning to buy a new suitcase for months; with as much traveling as she did, she needed one.

"You're right, Mom. I think I need to take a trip to Idaho Falls and do some shopping."

"You've only got ten days before you go," Jamie said.

"Why am I doing this?" Alex sat down on the bed in a frustrated huff. "I hate to travel."

"It will be a wonderful experience, dear. And you said the money's good." Her mother added some glittery earrings to the satin bag of jewelry Alex was taking.

"I don't care about the money. They could pay me a million dollars, and I still wouldn't enjoy waiting in airports or eating airplane food."

"Is it too late to change your mind?" Jamie said, her voice raising with hopefulness.

"I'm sure they could get someone else to take my place." Alex grabbed a pair of Nikes and slid them into a plastic bag. "The problem is, I know I'm supposed to go on this trip. I've spent a lot of time thinking and praying about it. I feel certain about it. I wish I didn't, but I do."

"Then you need to go," Jamie said.

"And you don't need to worry about things here," Judith said. "I'm going try and stay most of the time you're gone. I'll need to go back to the office for a week or two, but Jamie will be fine, won't you, dear?"

"Of course I'll be fine." Jamie held her head high, but Alex still didn't believe her.

"Is Dr. Rawlins still planning on going to New York with you sometime?" Alex asked hopefully.

Judith's smile widened. "Actually, he did say he'd enjoy coming back with me for a visit."

"That sounds like it could be fun," Jamie said.

"There're a few new shows on Broadway I'd love to take him to, and it would be nice to show him all the sites around Manhattan. He's never been there."

"You know, Mom," Alex said, shifting her position carefully so she didn't upset all the carefully folded stacks of clothes sitting on the bed, "I think it's great you and Dr. Rawlins have become such good friends. And even though you tell us there's nothing serious going on between you, I just want you to know that if it got serious, I would be all for it."

"Me too," Jamie added.

"Oh, you two." Judith blushed at their encouragement. She fanned herself with a travel brochure Alex had received from the tour coordinator's office in Rome. Then she gave a little smile and said, "He is nice, isn't he?"

"You two make a perfect match," Jamie said.

Judith's eyebrows arched. "You think so?" she asked.

"He's a very classy man, distinguished, intelligent, and handsome," Alex said.

"He is, isn't he?" Judith agreed. "We have such a wonderful time together, and we have so much in common. We both love Chinese food and antiques, and he loves the same old movies I do. We've gotten to be very good friends." Instead of folding the sweatshirt she'd picked up, Judith hugged it to her chest and sighed.

Alex was happy that her mother had finally found someone like Dr. Rawlins. She hoped it was a lasting relationship. Like the one she hoped she and Rich would share again one day.

* * *

Early the next morning, Alex went for her daily jog. Panting steadily, she kept her focus on the trail, forcing one foot in front of the other, striving to reach the summit. Every time she ran this trail and made it to the top, she felt a euphoric flood of accomplishment, as her mind, muscles, and inner being all focused on the same goal. This pure synergy was immediate payback for the grueling work required to get her to the top. The first time she jogged the trail, it had taken close to forty minutes; today she made it in just under thirty.

She loved the demand a strenuous workout like this placed upon her heart and lungs, and her muscles. Gaining strength and endurance, and improving her performance and fitness made all the hard work worth it. And even though it was hard to admit it, she felt healthier and stronger since she'd put on a few pounds and was eating a more balanced diet. She found that it was getting a little easier to stick to her prescribed diet, although it was still a daily effort.

But the part of her workouts that had become more meaningful, more appreciated, was the mind-clearing, thought-cleansing relief she received from exercising. The time she spent outdoors, surrounded by the beauty of nature, breathing the fresh mountain air, was the only time she was able to escape the worrisome thoughts of Rich that ran constantly in her mind.

With her hands on her thighs, she leaned over and pulled in long replenishing breaths. Surrounded by the wildflowers and pine, she allowed their calming influence to replace the turbulent confusion within her caused by her dwindling relationship with Rich.

Swinging her arms front and back to cool herself and let her heart rate slow down, she walked slowly in a circle. Overhead a jet stretched a long white stream of clouds across the sky.

She didn't know how things were going to turn out with Rich, but she did know one thing for sure—she wasn't alone. The Lord was with her, guiding her, directing her. Again she remembered that her father had told her and Jamie as children that they were never alone. He'd tried to teach them the gospel in his own gentle way. And she didn't doubt the Lord was aware of her and her needs. She had no choice but to exercise all her faith. Whatever worked out would be for the best. She just had to stay close to the Lord and stay on course.

But every fiber in her being hoped that somehow she and Rich would be together again, forever.

She loved him. Even though he was hurting her, she still loved him. And in a way she couldn't explain, she knew he loved her, too.

As she made her way back to the house, a refreshing breeze tickling her skin, Alex saw from a distance Rich's truck in Jamie's driveway. Her heart sped up at the sight of his vehicle. Would his visit bring joy or sadness? She never knew anymore.

"Here she is," Judith said as Alex stepped through the front door. Rich looked fabulous in jeans, leather sandals, and a pale yellow polo shirt that showed off his deep tan. He looked like he should have been shopping in Bermuda or sailing in Maine. Her heart ached at the sight of him, at how handsome he was, at how much she loved him and how deeply she wished things were as they had been before.

"Hi, Rich," she said, lifting her foot to untie the lace. Leaving her shoes by the door, she joined the others in the living room.

"How was your run?"

"Great, I saw a few deer on the way back. How are you?" She sat next to Jamie on the couch.

"Fine, fine. I guess Steve told you I took a group kayaking yesterday. I got back this morning."

Alex looked briefly at Jamie. That would explain why he hadn't called or come by. She was going to maim Steve for not telling her. "He must have forgotten."

"So you didn't know I was out of town?"

Alex shook her head.

"Sorry. You've probably wondered where I've been."

It should have helped knowing that he hadn't been home that whole time. But it didn't. Why couldn't he have called her himself and told her he was leaving?

"I was on my way to West Yellowstone to find some fishing supplies and wondered if you wanted to ride over with me."

"I wouldn't want to make you wait while I get cleaned up."

"I'm not in a hurry. If you don't mind me waiting."

"While you're there, Alex, why don't you have Rich help you look for a new suitcase," her mother said.

"Is this for your trip?"

"Yes. And I'm taking a little more than I had planned," she said, looking at her mother and sister with mock appreciation.

"I'll tell you what. Why don't we go to Idaho Falls tomorrow? We can look for your suitcase and anything else you need, and I can get all that fishing stuff there, too."

She loved the idea of spending the day shopping with him.

"Are you sure you don't mind?"

"Not at all. It would be fun."

"Sure, I'd love to."

"I guess I'll run back to the shop then and help Steve with some paperwork. We can leave early in the morning."

"Would you like to join us for dinner, Rich?" Jamie offered. "Mom marinated some chicken breasts and we have fresh vegetables from the garden."

"Sounds delicious. If you're sure it's not too much trouble."

"It never is," Jamie said. "You know you're always welcome here."

Alex walked him to his truck, hoping that being outside would mask the sweaty smell from her jog.

They stood by the passenger door of the truck in silence until

Rich finally said, "Oh, I wanted to tell you. I talked to Colt this morning. Elena called him after we were there this weekend. He said she was so excited she could hardly sleep after we left. She feels really good about my collection."

Obviously he wasn't going to consider approaching any other galleries, Alex thought dismally.

"I can't wait to get started on my new paintings."

"I'm happy for you, Rich." She wondered if she sounded convincing.

"Thanks. That means a lot to me." He fished in his shirt pocket for his keys and found some Carmex instead.

"Thanks for coming over. Tell Steve not to be late for dinner." Her brother-in-law had been a little better at coming home, but there was still a bit of tension between him and Jamie.

"How are Steve and Jamie?"

"They're doing okay. This has really been hard on them."

"I hate to see them struggling like they are. I never thought a marriage as strong as theirs would ever have the problems they're having."

"But they're dealing with it. And they are doing better." The last thing Alex wanted was for Rich to think marriage wasn't worth the work when there were problems.

"I hope so. Those two mean a lot to me. It just goes to show how hard marriage can be, doesn't it?"

Alex hated flies, but at the moment she was grateful for the one buzzing around her head; it gave her an out to not answer Rich's question.

"So," he changed subjects, "when do you leave for Europe?"

"One week from Monday. I fly out of the Salt Lake airport at twelve-thirty." She couldn't even look him in the eye when she said it.

"Are you excited?" he asked casually.

She wished he would show some kind of emotion at the thought of her leaving. "A little. I'm not looking forward to all the traveling."

"But think of all the wonderful places you'll get to see," he reminded her.

It won't be the same without someone to share it with.

"I hope you have a good camera. You'll want to take a lot of pictures," he said.

"I do," she said softly. Her eyes were beginning to sting and her throat felt tight.

"And you'll have to send a postcard from every city so we can keep up on all the fun you're having."

"I will." She kept her head turned away so he couldn't see the well of tears collecting in her eyes.

"Well, I guess I'd better get going. I'll see you a little later." He opened the truck door.

Tilting her head back, she tried to prevent the tears from spilling onto her cheeks. She gave him half a wave.

He pulled the door shut, started the engine, and roared away just moments before the tears fell.

Chapter 15

Saturday morning Alex dragged herself out of bed and lumbered down the stairs to the kitchen. She filled a teapot with water and set it on the stove to make a cup of herb tea.

As the water heated, she looked around the kitchen, which was brightening slowly with the rising sun. Soon she'd be stuck in hotels, eating out for every meal, and living out of a suitcase. The thought did nothing but depress her.

It was starting to hurt too much to be around Rich, but not really *be* with Rich. They used to spend evenings sitting on the porch, talking about anything and everything. She knew every detail of his childhood, every day of his youth, all his hopes and dreams. At least, she'd thought she did. Rich wasn't the same anymore.

The kettle whistled, and she filled her mug with steaming water. Carrying the fragrant, steeping tea into the living room, she sat on the couch, alone in the silence that she somehow found comforting. With only her thoughts to keep her company, she mulled over and over again what to do about Rich.

Did giving him his space mean she wasn't supposed to try to do anything to salvage their relationship?

He dodged her questions, he spent less time with her. They were completely out of sync. With that kind of crumbling foundation, how could they build any understanding between them?

They couldn't.

It took two to tango, and Rich had forgotten how to dance.

The clock on the mantel chimed the time. Rich was picking her up at nine, which gave her an hour to shower and get ready. She almost wished they hadn't planned on spending the day in Idaho Falls together. It was simply too painful to be around him anymore.

A door upstairs creaked open, and footsteps traveled the length of the hallway. She turned to see Steve come down the stairs.

"Morning, Alex." He joined her on the couch.

"You want some tea?"

"No, thanks. I should have been at the office by now, but I didn't sleep very well. I had a tough time getting up."

"Is everything okay?"

He stretched his arms overhead and yawned before he answered. "Jamie had that dream again last night. She just can't get past this." He rested his feet on the edge of the coffee table.

"Don't get me wrong," he said. "I want a baby as much as she does, but she doesn't even value herself as a whole person anymore because she can't have a child."

"That's crazy."

"Well, don't tell her that. She'll fall apart. She just wants to have a baby of her own, and she won't accept any substitutes." He leaned down and pulled up one of his socks. When he sat back up, he said, "I want to apologize to you for Jamie asking you to be a surrogate mother for us. I told her the Church is strongly opposed to such practices, and so was I."

"I know. We talked about it."

"Alex, I am really worried about her. There's a desperation about her that really concerns me. I think she needs some counseling or something."

"Have you talked to Dr. Rawlins?"

"No, not yet. I've been hoping things were finally turning around for her. But they're not. Maybe I'll give him a call when I get to the office."

"I'm sure he'll have some good suggestions."

"I hope so, because I'm out of ideas."

"All you can do is be patient and love her."

"I'm trying, but my patience is wearing thin."

In some ways Alex could relate to what he was saying. She didn't want to give up on Rich, but there was such a hopelessness about their situation.

The clock chimed eight-fifteen.

"Isn't Rich coming over at nine?" Steve asked.

"Holy cow, I'd better get moving." She jumped up.

"Alex . . ."

She looked down at her brother-in-law.

". . . I'm sorry things haven't been so great with Rich lately. Jamie told me how frustrated you are with him. I've been a little frustrated with him myself."

"What do you mean?"

"He's been so distracted at work, I'm almost afraid to send him out with any tour groups anymore. His mind just isn't on what he's supposed to be doing. But worse, his heart doesn't seem to be there either. I don't know what to do. I can't keep covering for him and doing all my work, too."

Poor Steve. Like he didn't have enough to worry about already.

"Do you have any idea what's going on with him, Steve?"

He shook his head, "No, not really. I mean, if he were turning forty and going through some midlife thing, at least his behavior would be understandable."

"Do you think it has anything to do with me?"

"Not really." Steve didn't seem any more convinced than she did. "Yeah, maybe a little."

"Then you tell me, Steve. What do you think is going on?"

"I don't know, for sure. The guy's my best friend, he's like a brother to me, but right now he's acting kind of selfish and, frankly, immature."

Alex had never heard her brother-in-law say a bad thing about Rich before.

Steve must have read her expression because he quickly added, "Don't get me wrong, Alex. I still love the guy, but he's been kind of a pain lately. All he talks about is his painting and his ideas. He isn't a whole lot of help at work." Steve shrugged. "He used to talk to me about you, but he doesn't anymore. If you ask me, I think he's afraid."

"Of what?"

"Of the fact that your baptism was the first step toward marriage. And we both know how he's struggled with commitment. As long as you weren't a member of the Church, he could talk about a future with you all he wanted, because it was just that . . . *talk*. I think he's looking for a good reason to put off making a decision."

Steve had confirmed her suspicions and worst fears.

"Don't get me wrong, Alex. His feelings for you are genuine. I know he loves you, and I honestly think that he feels differently toward you than he did any of the other girls he was engaged to. I just think he's afraid of his feelings, like he doesn't trust himself."

Alex frowned. "That doesn't make sense, though."

"I know. His actions don't make sense at all. He just needs some time to sort through his feelings and realize how much he loves you. In fact, you taking off to Europe may be the thing to bring him around. When you're over there, he'll go nuts without you."

"You really think so?" She remembered the answer to her prayers assuring her she should go on this trip.

"He loves you, Alex. He's told me so many times. He couldn't have just stopped loving you all of a sudden for no reason, even though it seems that way."

That was exactly how it seemed.

"I hope you're right."

"Give him a chance to realize just how much he does love you, to see what it's like not having you around, always being there for him, always being accepting. Give him a chance to appreciate you and miss you. I know him as well as anybody, and I'm telling you, he'll come around."

"Thanks, Steve." Alex leaned over and gave her brother-in-law a hug. "I feel a little better. I just wish he wasn't going to go work with that Elena woman. I don't trust her."

"She's not his type. You don't need to worry."

"I do, though. She seems capable of anything if it profits her."

"He's been so protective of his work, I can't see him placing it in the hands of someone he doesn't believe will do the best job for him."

"But he hasn't even talked to anyone else about it. Maybe there's someone even better than her."

"Not according to Colt. The difference between Elena and most of the other local art dealers is that she not only has connections all over the world, but she loves to discover new talent and launch careers."

For some reason Alex still didn't feel comfortable about the woman. "All I want is what's best for him."

"Me too, Alex. Me too."

* * *

With all her morning's purchases stored in the truck, Alex and Rich found a bustling café with bright, umbrella-covered tables. They located an empty spot and sat down to relax and have lunch.

They placed their order, and the waitress brought them two tall glasses of cold lemonade. As they sipped their drinks, they watched the traffic and shoppers.

Rich was unusually quiet as he concentrated on the condensation collecting on his glass. Alex reached up and smoothed the hair at the back of his neck. Without warning, he caught her hand in his and placed a kiss on her palm.

She sensed a sadness about him. When he looked at her, it was as if her were memorizing her, noting every curve and freckle of her face.

"You okay?" she asked softly.

One corner of his mouth lifted in an attempted smile. "Yeah, I'm okay."

He still held her hand, running his thumb over her knuckles. "I guess you're getting pretty excited for your trip."

His actions puzzled her. She was afraid to guess what his behavior meant, afraid to hope that he was realizing they really would be apart for two months. Maybe he was even wishing she weren't going.

Choosing her words carefully, she said, "I'm excited to be able to see so many wonderful sights in Europe, but I'm not really excited to leave."

"Are you worried about Jamie?"

Not as much as I'm worried about you.

"Your mom is staying with her, isn't she?" he asked.

"For a while. She's supposed to go back to work the first of August, but she's working on a story about Yellowstone National Park and plans on staying a while longer."

The waitress showed up with their food. Alex had ordered a large bowl of colorful sliced and diced vegetables on a bed of salad greens. Rich had a club sandwich that stood nearly four inches thick.

They ate in silence for a few minutes. She wondered why she didn't just come out and ask Rich what he was thinking. She poked at her salad until she finally answered herself honestly —she wanted him to initiate some kind of effort in strengthening their relationship.

He'd been the one turning away, keeping his distance, dodging commitments. Why couldn't he say something from his heart because he wanted to, not because she asked him?

The silence grew awkward.

"I bet you're the one getting excited," she said, dabbing the corners of her mouth with her napkin.

He looked at her, his eyebrows raised questioningly.

"You know," she explained, "to start the new paintings and get ready for your show."

"Oh," he said, his expression relaxing. "Yes, I am."

His tone didn't quite match his words.

"Everything's going well, isn't it?"

"Sure. I've found some beautiful scenery I'm excited to capture on canvas."

"You'll be moving down to Park City for a while?"

"Yeah, I guess so." He picked up his sandwich, looked at it, then set it back down on the plate.

He'd gotten what he wanted, so why was he acting so strangely.

"I'll give you a copy of my itinerary before I go so you can get in touch with me. I'd love to hear from you, Rich."

"And you'll send postcards?" he asked.

"Excuse me," the man sitting at the table next to them said.

"Yes," Rich answered.

"I was wondering if you had the correct time."

Rich checked his watch. "It's 2:15."

The man said something to his wife in a different language. Alex recognized it as German.

"Thank you," the man said. "My watch is in the shop for repairs."

"Excuse me," Alex said. "May I ask where you're from?"

"*Ach ja*, we are from Austria."

"Really? I'm going to Austria soon."

"You must go to Salzburg," the wife said. She had beautiful silver hair, rosy cheeks, and sparkling blue eyes. She looked at her husband lovingly. "It is a beautiful city, full of charm and history. Mozart was born there, you know. And, of course, the movie *The Sound of Music* was filmed there."

"I didn't know that," Alex said.

"It's a wonderful place," the man said, then he leaned closer to them. "But you must be careful."

She'd already been warned about crime in the big cities, in Rome, Frankfurt, and Paris. After all she heard, she wondered if she'd even be safe in her hotel room.

"Careful," he repeated, his accent punctuating his words, "because you can lose your heart in Salzburg."

He took his wife's hand and kissed it. She giggled, her cheeks flushing a brighter pink. The lovable wrinkles on the old man's face seemed to bewitch his words, as if he were casting a spell over them.

The man smiled. "You are going together?"

"Oh, no," Alex said. "Just me."

"*Ach!* Not together?" the gentleman said.

She shook her head.

"Someday then, you will go back and take this fellow with you, eh? It can only be truly enjoyed when you share it with someone you love."

Alex smiled uncomfortably, feeling a tint of red wash across her face. The man assumed exactly what Alex felt, but could never say herself. This trip would mean so much more if Rich could be there with her.

"Make sure when you are in Salzburg you go to Peter's Keller," the wife said. "It is a small restaurant with charming little booths and wonderful food. They even have live music. The owner's name is Peter. Tell him that his brother Rudy and his wife, Marta, sent you. Ask him to sing for you. He has a beautiful voice. He can yodel almost as good as my Rudy. Almost." She patted her husband's hand tenderly.

"It sounds wonderful. I'll make sure to go there," Alex said.

"Please excuse us now," the man said. "We are on our way to visit a new grandchild at the hospital."

"Congratulations," Rich said.

"Thank you," the woman said as her husband helped her from her chair. "Have a wonderful time and don't forget, Peter's Keller. You must try the schnitzel. It's *prima.*"

"Nice meeting you." Alex watched as the husband guided his sweetheart through the tables and onto the sidewalk. Then hand in hand they walked down the street.

After a moment, Alex said, "What a sweet couple. I'm so glad we talked to them."

"Are you sure you're even going to Salzburg?"

"Yes, toward the end of the trip. And I'm definitely going to look up Peter's Keller."

"They made it sound like quite a place, but the name doesn't sound all that special. I'll bet the live music is some guy with an accordion and a kazoo."

Alex laughed. "Tell you what, I'll try it out and let you know. I probably ought to get a travel book or two about Europe so I'll know about all the neat places I'm going to see. I'd hate to walk right past one of Michelangelo's statues and not know it."

"Good idea."

"I guess we're both going to have some interesting experiences these next few months, aren't we?" She picked up her lemonade and said, "I'd like to propose a toast."

He raised his glass to hers.

"To us," she said. "May we learn and grow as we start our new adventures, but never forget those who helped us along the way."

They clinked their glasses together, drank some of the contents, and set them on the table.

Alex took one last bite of her salad and looked up to see Rich staring intently at her. She practically swallowed her food whole as she locked onto his gaze. They didn't have much time left together. She hoped he would open up to her and tell her his feelings. Something was going on inside of him; she just couldn't tell if it would bring her happiness or heartache when she finally found out.

Chapter 16

Sacrament meeting had just ended. Jamie, Steve, Alex, and her mother were in the hall making their way to their gospel doctrine class when Brother Heiner, the branch clerk, stopped them.

"Doctor Rawlins just called from Idaho Falls, Steve. He wants you to call him back right away."

"Did he say why?" Steve asked him.

"No, only that it's urgent."

"I hope he's okay," Judith said, her eyes wide with concern.

"I'd better run home and call." Steve turned to Jamie. "Honey, do you have the car keys?"

"Since this is an emergency, I'm sure you could use the branch telephone," the branch clerk offered.

"Thanks, Brother Heiner, I'll keep it short."

They crowded into the clerk's office while Steve made the call.

"Dr. Rawlins, it's Steve Dixon."

Steve didn't speak for a moment.

"I see," he finally said. "Okay, we'll leave right now."

"What? Leave for where?" Jamie asked impatiently.

Steve held up his hand and turned away as he said, "Thanks, Dr. Rawlins. We'll see you in a little while. Bye."

He hung up the phone and the room exploded with questions. People in the hall shushed them. Rich happened to walk by right at that moment and noticed them.

"Hey, you guys, what are you doing?"

"Come in, Rich." Steve grabbed his arm, pulled him inside, and shut the door.

"Dr. Rawlins needs us to come to Idaho Falls right away."

"Why?" Jamie asked.

"He thought it would be better to explain all of that when we got there. But it's something very important."

"Is Dave okay?" Judith had nearly twisted the button off her vest in her anxiety.

"He's fine. This has nothing to do with Dr. Rawlins."

Judith relaxed slightly. "Thank goodness. I was getting worried."

"So, we're taking off for Idaho Falls right now?" Jamie said. "With no explanation why?"

"Honey," Steve said, taking his wife by her shoulders and looking directly into her eyes, "Dr. Rawlins has been through a great deal with us. He's not just your doctor, he's our friend, and he has never done anything to make us doubt or distrust him."

"So?" Jamie said.

"So, we need to trust him. There's something in Idaho Falls he needs us for, and I see no reason why we should second-guess his motives."

"Jamie," her mother said, putting her arm around her daughter's waist, "I agree with Steven. Dr. Rawlins thinks of you two as his own family."

"Okay, fine," Jamie said. "But this is really weird, don't you think?" She looked at Alex as if to ask for some backup on her position.

Alex nodded. "It is weird, but I'm so curious now you'd have to lock me in a closet to keep me from going." Then she looked at Steve, "I can go, can't I?"

"Of course. Rich, you're welcome to come, too. But we need to get going."

* * *

They exited off the freeway and drove down the streets of Idaho Falls toward the hospital. Alex had traveled this route many times over the last few months to the outpatient clinic for her treatment. As she gazed out the window, she thought of the struggles she had experienced on her way to developing a healthier perspective about food

Her anorexia had given her a false sense of security, of being in control of her life and of what happened to her. She had learned to accept many things that had been out of her control, most importantly, her father's death. She'd also learned that her greatest tool in staying healthy was to talk about things that bothered her, not to hold her emotions and concerns inside. She had had to learn to let things out; otherwise, she ran the risk of falling back into her old habits, which came instinctively. When she was upset or worried, she didn't eat. It was a vicious cycle she fought constantly.

"Okay, I'm getting really nervous here," Jamie said. "I want to know what's going on."

"Honey, nothing is going on." Steve stopped for a red light.

"I know I've been acting strangely lately. You're not . . ." she cleared her throat, ". . . you're not committing me to an institution, are you?"

Steve laughed. "Honey, I can't believe you'd even think something like that." He signaled to change lanes. "You know our insurance doesn't cover that kind of care."

She slugged him in the arm. "Very funny."

Alex didn't blame Jamie for being anxious. She was wondering what was going on herself.

"What's going on?" Jamie chewed her lip nervously.

"We're about to find out." Steve turned the car into the hospital parking lot.

Hand in hand, Steve and Jamie approached the front door of the hospital, with the others following behind.

Inside the foyer a clock chimed three bells. The building seemed unusually quiet. No one else was in sight.

"Where do we go?" Judith asked Steve.

"I don't know. Dr. Rawlins didn't say. I just assumed he'd be here waiting for us. I'll go see if I can find someone to page him."

While they waited, Jamie paced the floor nervously. Occasionally she paused a few moments and cast long wistful looks out the front window at the sky darkening with an afternoon thunderstorm. Judith sat for five minutes, then jumped to her feet and began examining various items in the room—floral arrangements, pictures, brochures about medical conditions, the furniture.

Alex could see from the way Jamie hugged her arms across her chest and her slow, dragging pace as she wore a path in the carpet that she was remembering the last time she'd been a patient at the

hospital. She'd carried this last baby almost long enough for her to
survive on her own. But little Katie hadn't made it.

Voices down the hallway brought everyone to attention. There
was almost a collective sigh of relief as Steve and Dr. Rawlins rounded
the corner.

"Good afternoon, everyone," the doctor said. He shook hands
with Alex and Rich, gave Judith a quick hug, and stopped when he
came to Jamie.

"Hi, Dr. Rawlins," she said, her voice cracking with nervousness.

"Hello, Jamie, how are you?" he asked gently.

She cleared her throat. "Well, as you know, this isn't my favorite place."

"Not a lot of good memories here, are there?" He held one of her
hands in his.

She shook her head, her eyes full of emotion.

"I hope that changes today. I'd like to give you a new memory,
Jamie. A happy one."

"Really, doctor?"

"Really." He patted her hand gently. "Come with me. There's
something I want to show you. All of you."

The group passed the gift shop then continued down the hall,
passing several nurses and a custodian. As they traveled deeper inside
the hospital, they saw more medical personnel, busy with patients
and medical duties.

As they passed through a pair of swinging doors, Jamie stopped in
the middle of the hallway and gasped. They were in the women's
section, specifically, labor and delivery.

"What are we doing here?" she demanded.

"I have something to show you," Dr. Rawlins replied calmly.

"But . . ." she stepped back against the wall.

"Honey," Steve said, sliding an arm around her. "It's okay. Dr.
Rawlins has already talked to me. Trust us, Jamie."

"But Steve . . ." Her voice broke.

"I'm here, we're all with you. It's okay. Really it is."

Jamie allowed Steve to guide her down the hallway, but kept her
head turned into his shoulder. When they passed the nursery, Jamie
buried her head more deeply into Steve's neck. Inside were six bassinets
filled with tiny, bundled newborns. Some wore white stocking caps;

one sported short, spiky black hair, and another was busy crying, his little hands pawing in front of his bunched up, unhappy face.

A nurse inside picked up the crying baby and smiled at the crowd standing outside the window. With bottle in hand, she sat in a rocking chair and began to feed the infant.

"Let's step into this room next door," Dr. Rawlins directed them.

The room was empty, except for a hospital bed, a chair, and a television mounted high on the wall.

"I'll be right back," he promised.

The silence was thick and heavy. Steve held Jamie protectively in his arms, whispering gently to her. Alex looked at her mother, then at Rich, hoping for some idea of what was going on. They both shrugged and shook their heads.

Then, the door creaked open. Jamie looked up, and everyone froze. In walked a nurse with a baby in her arms. She went straight to Jamie and held out the infant, offering to let Jamie hold it. Surprised, Jamie looked down at the tiny face peering back at her from under the hooded blanket.

Glancing quickly at Steve, then back at the nurse, Jamie reached toward the bundle. The nurse placed the baby in Jamie's arms then stepped back. Everyone watched and waited.

At first Jamie held the child stiffly, looking up at the nurse as if to check to see if she were doing everything correctly. Then she pulled the little one in closer to her breast and leaned her head toward the baby's face. With one hand she reached up and drew the blanket back to expose a tiny head of black, curly hair.

"Oh, look," Judith whispered.

Jamie sniffed as tears slipped down her cheeks and fell upon the soft pink blanket. "It's her," she said.

"What, honey?" Steve asked.

"It's her." Tears were coming faster. "The baby from my dream."

Alex was stunned.

"Jamie, what do you mean?" Steve looked down at the baby.

Jamie stroked a soft cheek with her finger. "She's the one I saw in my dream."

With his face full of alarm, Steve looked at Dr. Rawlins for answers. Every head but Jamie's turned to him. But he said nothing.

"She's even more beautiful than in my dream." Jamie wiped the tears from one side of her face with her shoulder. Steve quickly grabbed a tissue out of a box on the wall above the sink and gently dabbed at the other side of his wife's face.

Alex didn't understand what was going on. Whose baby was this, and why was Dr. Rawlins letting Jamie hold her? Didn't he know when Jamie had to give the baby back, it would break her heart?

The baby sneezed a tiny birdlike sneeze, then started to whimper. Almost immediately her whimper turned into unhappy cries. Jamie bounced and cuddled her, talking softly to soothe her. Before even a minute had passed, the newborn settled back into a deep sleep.

Jamie had stopped crying, completely mesmerized by the bundle in her arms. "Don't you think she's beautiful, honey?"

"Yes," Steve said, reaching out to touch the tiny upturned nose.

Rich walked over and stood next to Jamie. He remarked about the baby's hair and beautiful skin, her tiny features, her sweetness. He even leaned over and kissed the sleeping child on the forehead.

In seconds Judith had joined them, cooing and oogling, talking in baby talk, just like the rest of them.

Once more, Alex looked at Dr. Rawlins, hoping to heaven he knew what he was doing. He smiled at her as if to assure her everything was okay, then said, "I think we're missing out on something. Shall we?"

Together they walked over and fussed over the little angel as she slept, her mouth drawn into a rosebud above a tiny chin.

"How old is she?" Jamie asked.

"Born yesterday at 4:55 p.m.," Dr. Rawlins answered.

"How much did she weigh?"

"Seven pounds, six ounces."

"She's perfect." Jamie bent her head even closer to the baby's face.

"Yes, she is."

"Who does she belong to?" she asked without looking up.

As if a volt of electricity had stunned them all at the same time, everyone flinched and looked at Dr. Rawlins.

"Her mother came to the hospital yesterday to deliver. She's a single mom with four other children at home. She's on welfare, has a history of alcohol and drug abuse and lives in a run-down apartment complex. She told us she couldn't afford to feed another child and didn't have time to take care of a baby. She doesn't even know who the baby's father is. I guess she works at a bar outside of town where a lot of truck drivers come through. The bottom line is she doesn't want anything to do with this baby and refuses to take her home."

"Her mother doesn't want her?" Jamie asked with disbelief.

"No, Jamie. This child will end up in a foster home until the state can find her an adoptive family."

"Are you saying what I think you're saying?" She stared at the doctor with tearstained cheeks.

"The baby needs a home, Jamie. She deserves loving parents. Parents like you and Steve could be to her."

"Really, Dr. Rawlins?" Jamie's voice held a note of hope that Alex hadn't heard for a long time.

The doctor nodded and smiled reassuringly. "I wanted you to have a chance to see and hold her before I turned her over to the state."

"I don't know what to say." Jamie looked at her husband. "Steve?"

"I already know my answer, and I think I know yours," he said.

As tears washed over her face, Jamie tried to speak but couldn't; all she could do was nod. As her emotions gripped her, she handed the baby to her mother and fell into Steve's arms. He, too, was overwhelmed, both of them so unprepared, but so ready, to have a child in their lives.

Alex realized that the six adults surrounding the infant in her mother's arms would be bonded together forever, sharing the profound moment when that child became welded forever in their hearts, their souls, their eternal family.

Eternal family. Alex had learned about forever families and longed to be part of one. The feeling in that room, the spirit and power that encircled them, could only indicate even greater love and bonds in heaven.

She looked at Rich, he looked at her. Past the surface, behind the confusion of the world, for a brief moment, she saw deep inside him and knew they had a very strong connection; something bigger than art galleries and European fitness tours, something stronger than they could comprehend . . . something spiritual and eternal.

He pulled her close, kissed the top of her head, and held her as they watched together the forming of a family. Steve and Jamie dried their faces, laughing softly at their abundance of tears, then this time, Steve took the baby in his arms.

Watching his face light up with a joy as pure as the child in his arms, Alex knew that child was his in every way. He would love her, spoil her, protect her, cherish her.

This was one very special baby.

Alex didn't know how it happened, but Jamie's dream had actually come true. And it had happened just as Jamie had described it.

A quiet reverence continued in the room as they each took turns holding the baby, breathing in her newness, cuddling her warmth and softness. They spoke in low tones and whispers as if they were on hallowed ground.

Until her diaper needed to be changed.

A nurse was called to bring in diapering supplies, but as Jamie laid the little one in the bassinet to change her, the child's cries took on a different sound , a high-pitched, agonizing sound. Her tiny body stiffened and trembled.

Jamie attempted to change the diaper but the baby held itself so stiffly she couldn't move its legs. Her face revealing both horror and pain, Jamie stepped back. "What am I doing wrong? Did I hurt her?"

"No, not at all," Dr. Rawlins assured her. "Maybe we should step outside and let the nurse take care of her. There's something I need to explain."

Steve had to coax Jamie from the baby's side, then from the room. Even behind the closed door, the baby's pain-filled cries echoed through the empty hallway.

"I don't know any other way to tell you this, except to be direct. We believe the mother abused illegal substances while she was pregnant. She tested clean here at the hospital, but the baby is showing definite patterns of withdrawal."

Jamie gasped and sought solace in Steve's arms.

"That poor little thing," Judith shook her head sadly. "No wonder she sounds like she's in such excruciating pain."

"The baby's an addict? To what?" Steve asked.

"Cocaine. But it's important for you to understand, this isn't a permanent condition. There are medications like phenobarbital and others we are giving her to help her through this. After a week or so, it should be out of her system."

Jamie wiped at her eyes and looked up. "A week? She's going to be okay then?"

"She'll be fine. This first week is going to be a tough one for her but we can help her through this. We'll keep her here to monitor her progress and give her the medication she needs."

"How could that mother have taken drugs while she was pregnant? What kind of person does that?" Jamie asked. "And how could she give her child away? How could you not love your own child?"

"I think she does love this child," Dr. Rawlins said, "probably more than we will ever understand. She loves this child enough to want to give her something better than she has to offer."

Jamie nodded slowly. She understood.

"Would you like some time to discuss the situation before we make it legal?" the doctor asked them.

"Honey?" Steve asked his wife.

"Well, you'd think we'd need time to discuss it," Jamie said nervously. "But I think we've both already decided in our hearts that, yes, we want to adopt this baby."

"You're sure you're okay with this?" Steve asked her.

"I'm more than okay," Jamie said. "I know that we're supposed to have her. I've known for a long time now."

"Then I guess our answer is yes, Dr. Rawlins," Steve said proudly.

"Wonderful!" the doctor said, shaking Steve's hand. "The birth mother will be released from the hospital today. She needs to sign a Consent to Terminate Parental Rights before she goes. I've got a good friend, John Castleton, who's an attorney here in town. He's handled a lot of private adoptions. He is more than happy to take care of the legal issues for you, unless you have someone else you'd rather use."

"Your friend will be fine," Steve said. "Thank you for taking care of that for us."

"Dr. Rawlins," Jamie said softly. "If you see the mother before she leaves, tell her . . ." Jamie bit her lips as two big tears rolled down her cheeks, ". . . tell her we will love and care for this baby as if she were our own, and that she is wanted more than anything in the world."

"I will." He patted Jamie's hand and nodded.

"I guess that's that," Steve said. "We're adopting a baby."

His words seemed to stir some kind of magical excitement that washed over them all at once. Rich and Alex hugged, Steve and Jamie hugged, Dr. Rawlins and Judith hugged, then they all switched and hugged everyone else.

"You may want to go in with the nurse and have her explain how to take care of the baby once you get her home," Dr. Rawlins said. "There may be a few lingering effects, but nothing you should be concerned about."

Jamie and Steve went immediately back inside the room to the baby. Judith excused herself to the restroom, and Dr. Rawlins went to find a phone to call the attorney, leaving Rich and Alex alone in the hall. Rich slipped his arm around her, hugging her gently. "Hey," he said, "you okay?"

Nodding her head, Alex drew in a deep breath and rested her head on his shoulder, wondering what the future held in store for her. Watching Jamie and Steve and the new depth of their love and sacrifice for the baby and for each other, Alex couldn't help but wonder. Rich obviously wasn't ready for a commitment. Did that mean she waited until he was ready, or did she let go of him and move on with her life?

After what had just happened, she felt a strong need to get going on the important things of life, like marriage and a family. In fact, she almost felt like she was wasting time doing anything else.

It was time for something to change, but part of her was terrified to find out the answer to her question, for fear she would be told to move on.

Chapter 17

With Jamie and Steve gone to the nursery and Dr. Rawlins and Judith off in other directions, Rich and Alex were left standing alone in the quiet hallway.

"Do you feel like getting some fresh air?" Rich asked.

"That would be nice," Alex agreed.

They walked outside to find a cloudy gray sky. A breeze had started up, and it tugged at tree branches and flower stems.

Following a sidewalk around the side of the building, they found a bench surrounded by rosebushes heavy with large blooms. For a moment they sat in silence, listening to the warbling of a sparrow and the swishing of leaves.

"Hey," Rich said, tucking some windblown strands of hair behind Alex's ear. "Are you okay?"

She turned her head to look at him, her eyes focusing on the honest look of concern on his face. With a half-hearted smile, she nodded then scooted into the welcoming arm he wrapped around her shoulder.

"It's amazing how everything else in the world seems so unimportant when you're able to witness something like we've just seen, isn't it?" he said.

Alex couldn't agree more. Being a part of the event they'd just witnessed couldn't help but bring to the front of everyone's mind what was really important.

"Do you remember the day I got baptized?" she asked him.

"Of course I do."

"Do you remember the conversation we had afterwards, out on the couch in the foyer of the church building?"

"Yeah, well, kind of I do."

"You were asking me to forgive you for being late, and you said something like, 'Your wish is my command.'"

"I did?" He thought for a moment. "Oh, yeah, I did."

"I'm ready to cash in on that wish."

"You are, huh? And what would that wish be?"

She was nervous to bring up the subject. He was so convinced Elena was the right one for him, he might get upset with her for even suggesting he give someone else a try, or at least consider looking at other options. But she couldn't sit back and let him get swallowed up whole by the woman.

"I know I haven't got an ounce of knowledge when it comes to art or exhibitions. But, Rich, I really wish you would take some time before you completely commit yourself to Elena and her gallery. Don't you think you should look around at other dealers and galleries?"

She felt him stiffen and pull back slightly. Turning herself to face him to better gauge his reaction, she waited for him to get upset.

She wasn't disappointed.

He jumped from the bench and stood before her with his feet planted and his hands on his hips. "I could tell you had a problem with Elena the first time we met her in Park City. What is it, Alex? Is it her expert knowledge in the field of art that has you so bothered? Or maybe it's the fact that she's almost guaranteed a sell-out show for me. Yes, I can see why you wouldn't like her. Or wait, I know, it just might be the fact that she's intelligent, beautiful, and successful that isn't working for you. Which is it, Alex?"

Proud of herself for holding back tears, Alex maintained her composure and her expression and said, "No, Rich. Actually it's the fact that I don't trust her. Excuse me for being concerned about your welfare, but something tells me she can't be trusted. I wish I could give you something specific to prove it, but I can't. Obviously by your reaction, I'm wrong, so I won't make the mistake of mentioning it again. But then," she rose to her feet as the anger replacing her pain began to boil, "that won't be a problem, will it, since I'll be out of your way for a few months?!"

"Hey, this trip to Europe has nothing to do with me." He raised both hands in his defense.

"No, I guess it doesn't," she cried. "But then, that's the way you wanted it." Her stomach lurched and her knees trembled. "I think I'll go find Mom now."

She took off running. Drops of rain started to fall. Thunder rumbled in the distance.

"Alex, wait a minute."

She kept going, wishing she could just drop into a big black hole, into a peaceful forgetfulness.

* * *

Back inside the hospital, after taking time to rush to the restroom to have a good cry then compose herself, Alex found her family with Dr. Rawlins and his attorney friend, Mr. John Castleton, a friendly, balding, middle-aged man who was as wide as he was tall. Luckily his home was just minutes away from the hospital so he was able to join them quickly.

Rich caught up to them just as they were heading to a conference room to talk. Alex determinedly avoided Rich's persistent glances. There was an ache in her heart that felt like a dagger, but she wasn't about to ruin Jamie and Steve's day, so she kept her chin up and her head turned.

"Well, let me just say that I am very happy for you two," Mr. Castleton said. "Most adoptions are arranged far in advance, but I've had a couple of cases where the birth mother didn't make the decision until the last minute. First, we need to have her sign this consent form terminating her parental rights. Since there is no known father at this time, we will not be able to obtain his signature. It is my duty as legal council to inform you that in the State of Idaho there is a Putative Father Statute, which basically allows the natural birth father the right to come back, at any time, and claim the baby."

"What?!" Jamie jumped to her feet.

"I know it's alarming in a situation like this—"

"You mean, one year, or even five or ten years down the road, some stranger out of the clear blue sky can come and take our child from us, and we can't do anything about it?"

"Honey," Steve coaxed her back to her seat, "let Mr. Castleton explain."

"As I was saying, it is alarming and it doesn't seem fair, Mrs. Dixon, but you have to understand the law is designed to protect the sacredness of parenthood and allow the natural birth parents the right to their own child."

While he spoke, Jamie gnawed her thumbnail.

"If it's any consolation to you," he said, "I've been in this business a long time, and I haven't seen many fathers exercise this right. Since the birth mother doesn't even know who the father of her child is, you have a greater chance of never having to worry about his happening."

"But it *could* happen."

"Yes. There is always a chance. But I would say it's a very slim one."

"What do we do next, Mr. Castleton?" Steve asked.

"The state will need to do a thorough check on you. For instance, they will check for any criminal records, and they'll check your credit status and your income level. They'll also do a family background check, and they'll come to your home and evaluate where you live and what you and your wife are like."

"When will this happen?" Steve spoke before Jamie had a chance.

"Right away, probably within the month."

"Is there anything else we need to know?" Jamie spoke up, her nervousness evidenced by the white-knuckled grip she kept on her husband's hand.

"Not really. Once the state clears you as suitable adoptive parents, we'll set up a court date and finalize the arrangements. Which means a legal termination of parental rights and a completion of the adoption process, where you will be declared legal parents of the adoptive child."

"Unless the father decides to take her," Jamie said.

"Honey—" Steve began.

"I just don't think it's fair," Jamie protested.

"You also have to understand," Mr. Castleton said, "at this hearing, the mother could still contest the adoption."

Jamie opened her mouth to speak but instead let out an exasperated sigh and rested her forehead in her hands.

"This is also a rare and unusual circumstance. In my legal opinion, I see no reason why you shouldn't go ahead with this adoption and even set up a college fund for the child. I would have no reservations if it were me."

Jamie looked up. "You don't think they'll come after her?"

"I wish for your sake I could guarantee one hundred percent that they won't, but I can't. The mother is adamant she doesn't want the child. Frankly, she's relieved to have a good home for her baby, and as I stated before, she doesn't even know who the father is. She spends her time with a lot of different men, some she sees once and never again. Your situation is probably the least likely of any to be contested in court or any other time."

Jamie was silent, digesting everything he said. Finally, she spoke up. "Thank you, Mr. Castleton. It helps to know all of that information."

The lawyer patted her hand. "I know how concerned you are, but I have a good feeling about this arrangement, especially from the wonderful things Dr. Rawlins has said about you."

"We feel good about it, too," Steve said, slipping an arm around his wife's shoulders.

Mr. Castleton rose to his feet. "Then, unless you have any further questions, I'll go get that signature."

* * *

The ride back to Island Park was full of making plans and discussing names. No one even noticed the frigid silence between Rich and Alex.

"I'd like to name her Nicole," Jamie said. "I've always loved that name. What about you, honey?"

"Nicole is pretty, but I like the name Andrea."

"Andrea sounds too grown up for such a little baby," Jamie said "What do you think, Alex? Which name do you like?"

Hearing her name called, Alex put aside her thoughts about her earlier confrontation with Rich and said, "What were the names again?"

"Nicole and Andrea."

"I like them both," she said. "Why don't you name her Andrea Nicole."

"Andrea Nicole." Jamie tested the name over a few times. "You know, I like it. Honey, what do you think?"

"I like it, too."

"Mom, what do you think?"

"It's beautiful, just like she is."

"She is beautiful, isn't she, Mom?"

Jamie and Judith talked nonstop about the baby, making plans and lists of things to buy. Steve smiled proudly as he steered the car home. Alex and Rich remained silent, except when asked a question. The others were too excited to noticed the strain and distance between them.

Rich was leaning his head against the door, with his eyes shut, while Alex stared out the other window, watching as the rain pelted the road. She thought it was ironic that the afternoon storm had broken at roughly the same moment her relationship with Rich had crumbled to pieces. Not wanting to rain on Jamie and Steve's parade, Alex tried to keep up a brave front, hoping it would last until she got home and could find a private place to release the turbulence inside of her.

* * *

During the following days the Dixon household buzzed with excitement. Preparations for the baby and for Alex's upcoming trip kept everyone busy. Alex was grateful to have a lot to do, since Rich had been practically nonexistent.

She realized she was stupid and naive to have assumed things would work out between them without any problems. They had talked about a future and even marriage, but he had never officially proposed to her. They had no obligation to each other.

Somehow during the course of their relationship, things had changed. That was all there was to it.

Judith and Jamie spent most of the time washing blankets and bedding for the crib and folding and stacking jammies and sleepers for Andrea Nicole. Alex tried to do her share, but the world seemed to revolve in a fog-like haze around her.

Steve and Jamie made several trips back to the hospital to check on the baby's progress and strengthen the bond that was just as deep as any biological connection could have been. Jamie stated over and over again that there was such a perfect fit when she held Andrea Nicole that she couldn't imagine not having her in their lives.

One morning while Judith and Jamie were at the store, Alex sat alone in the kitchen wincing at the clash of tart pink grapefruit juice and the handful of Frosted Mini Wheats she was eating.

The phone jingled on the desk. She caught it on the second ring.

"Alex, is that you?"

"Sandy, hi. I was going to call you later. How is everything?"

"Everything's great. I just got a call from *Today's Fitness*. They've already sent a draft of the article for their magazine. She wanted to give me a chance to look it over before they put it in print. It turned out great. They even talked about your conversion to Mormonism."

"They did?"

"It was handled nicely. When Leigh brought up the subject, I wondered if she'd even include it in her article and make you look like a religious kook."

"Sandy!"

"I'm sorry, I was worried. But they worded it well, and I think it actually makes the change with your eating disorder, and with your whole life, seem more believable."

"I'd like to read it."

"I'll send it along with your plane tickets, final itinerary, and files for your lectures. Can you think of anything else I might be forgetting?"

"No, but if I do, I'll call."

"It won't be long now and you'll be in Rome. Mr. Diamante's office notified me that he'll have a driver waiting for you when you get off the plane. I'll send everything to you overnight mail. Let me know if you don't get it tomorrow."

"I will. Anything else?"

"No. Sales are still up and I've got a basket full of fan mail for you. Do you want me to answer it for you or wait until you get home?"

"Go through it and answer the ones just requesting autographed pictures and let them know I'm going on tour. I'll answer the rest when I get back."

"Got it."

"Oh, one more thing." Alex told Sandy about Jamie's baby and how excited they all were.

"Tell your sister congratulations. I'm happy this worked out for her."

"I will."

There was a pause. Alex finally said, "Sandy, is there something else?"

"Well, yes, kind of. The funniest thing happened the other day."

"What?"

"I was home last Wednesday, taking a day off. I'm never home during the week, but for some reason that day I just felt like staying home from work. So I spent the day baking and relaxing, even cleaned out closets. Then just as I was pulling this gorgeous apple pie out of the oven, my doorbell rang. When I answered it, I found two Mormon missionaries standing there."

Alex gasped in surprise. "Sandy, really?"

"They told me no one sent them—they were just in the area—but I had a sneaking suspicion you'd made a phone call."

"Sandy, I promise, I had nothing to do with that. I told you I would call them, but I haven't had a chance to."

"Well, anyway, they were cute little rosy-cheeked boys, very friendly, so I invited them in for a piece of pie."

"What happened?" Alex's fingers and scalp tingled.

"They stayed for over an hour. We had a really nice talk. I'd read some of that Book of Mormon you'd given me, and they answered some of my questions. Pretty smart boys, too. They knew a lot about their religion, but they still seemed to understand the questions and concerns people have who aren't members of your church."

"I'm glad they could help you."

"They want to come back and visit some more."

"Are you going to let them?"

"Maybe. They gave me some pamphlets and some passages in the book to read. They told me to pray about the things I learn."

Neither of them spoke for a moment. Alex felt as though a spiritual current ran along the phone line between them.

"I'm a little afraid," Sandy said softly.

"Of what?"

"I don't know. I get a feeling in my stomach like I'm nervous and excited and scared all at the same time. It feels good, yet it's so unfamiliar and frightening."

"Do you feel it when you read in the Book of Mormon?"

"Yes, and when the missionaries were here. They made me feel so happy. They were so easy to talk to, and so sweet. They ate half of my pie."

"Sandy, you don't need to be frightened of that feeling. It's the spirit of the Lord trying to talk to you. You need to put your fears aside and listen with your heart. He really will guide you and help you. Especially if you pray like the elders told you to."

"I'm still a little afraid, though."

"Of what?"

"I don't know. Of finding out it's true or something. Then I'll have to join your church and act all odd and religious."

Again, Alex regretted painting such an awful picture of Mormons before she'd really understood them herself. "Like me?" she said aloud.

"No. You seem to still be pretty much the same. Only better."

Alex tried to reassure her friend. "Sandy, you don't have to take on a different personality. There will be changes you need to make, and your priorities will change, but these will be things you'll want to do. Things you'll be excited to do."

"I don't know." Sandy paused. "I'm thinking about canceling the appointment."

"Sandy," Alex said patiently, "no one is going to make you do anything you don't want to do. Read and pray and ask for the strength and courage you need. You'll get it. I did. I felt the same as you in the beginning."

"You did?" Sandy's voice reflected both surprise and relief.

"I did."

"That makes me feel better. But still, don't go thinking I'm going to get baptized. My mother would flip her wig after all Barb and Gerald Truman have told her."

"You'll know what you should do, and if I know you, once you set your mind to something, nothing stands in your way." Sandy had a tendency to be close-minded and obstinate once she made a decision. But those same qualities had helped her achieve her success in business.

"Just don't go sending out invitations, yet."

"I won't, but I'll pray for you. And I hope you'll call if you ever need to talk."

"I can't believe we're even having this conversation."

Judith and Jamie burst through the back door talking excitedly.

"Sandy, I've got to run. I'll call you tomorrow when that package arrives."

"Okay, Alex. I hope someday I thank you for all of this. Right now I don't feel that way."

"You will, Sandy. You will." Alex had no doubt in her mind about that.

She couldn't help but tingle with excitement. Sandy had actually talked to the missionaries. The chance of them coming by her place on a day when she wouldn't normally be home seemed awfully coincidental. There wasn't a doubt in Alex's mind; those elders had been sent by the Lord.

Alex helped unload the car, and the three women chattered happily as they carried their purchases into the house, filling the front room with numerous boxes and bags of odds and ends, clothes and toys, a vaporizer and high chair. Alex received a full report of the day's plans. Jamie rattled on and on about the baby; in between explaining the various legal documents and what kind of formula she'd decided to use, she managed to inform Alex that Rich had taken a group of hikers out on the trail for six days.

Alex tried to hide her emotions but nearly buckled from the pain in her heart. Since Steve had hired two new guys to head up river trips and extended backpacking excursions, Rich wasn't needed to go out on the trail anymore. But apparently he had volunteered and wouldn't be home until Sunday. She would leave on Monday.

So much for talking to Rich about what had happened at the hospital. It wouldn't be necessary now. His leaving town said enough.

She didn't matter to him.

The sooner she accepted that fact, the quicker she could get on with her life.

She would have thought by now it wouldn't hurt so much. But with each thoughtless punch, each nonverbal declaration of his complete lack of interest in their relationship, a red-hot, stinging pain streaked through her heart, right to her soul. Even though she'd loved and lost before, it had never hurt this badly. Losing Rich felt like she was losing a part of herself she could never get back.

But she would survive. She knew she would. Her mother had lost the love of her life and had triumphed. Alex would find a way to do the same.

Still, part of her hoped Rich was going through some kind of "phase" or something; he would soon snap out of it and realize that she was important to him. But he needed to be careful. As much as she loved Rich, she wouldn't continue to take this kind of emotional beating. She couldn't.

She just hoped he changed his mind, and that when he did it wouldn't be too late.

Chapter 18

Set up in the living room was a dainty white wicker bassinet, with a white eyelet ruffle that reached the floor. It was dainty and feminine and fit for a princess.

Andrea Nicole hated it.

From the time she arrived in the house she made her presence known. No matter what they did, no matter how they tried, none of them could comfort her. By the evening of Andrea Nicole's first day in her new home, they were all exhausted. Jamie finally managed to keep the baby asleep for half an hour by holding her facing outward, against her chest, and gently bouncing her.

"We're just going to have to take turns with her," Judith said. "Especially if she's up all night."

"Do you think she's okay, Mom? Should I call Dr. Rawlins?" Jamie asked anxiously.

"He warned us she'd have a hard time, dear. We just need to work with her. She'll be fine."

It was decided they would each take a turn, rotating every hour through the night.

Alex had the fourth rotation. Afraid of getting too comfortable and missing her turn, she slept in the recliner in the family room.

Just after midnight she went to Jamie's bedroom to take her turn. Steve looked worn out and completely frazzled. Alex took the whimpering baby from the weary father and with a deep breath braced herself for a long hour.

"Hello, little one," she said to the one-week-old. "You don't feel so good, do you?"

The baby puckered her lips then burst out crying.

Talking in soothing tones, Alex paced the room, bouncing and swaying, trying any movement, any idea that came to her head, to calm the infant.

Spying the boom box on Jamie's dresser, Alex pushed the play button, hoping soft hymns or relaxing classical music would float around the room. Instead it was one of Alex's aerobic tapes Jamie used for walking on the treadmill.

She reached to turn it off then decided to let it play, thinking the music might provide a distraction for the baby. Bouncing to the one, two, cha-cha-cha rhythm, Alex began to move. Holding the baby closely to her chest, one hand carefully supporting her head, Alex did a samba, sashaying smoothly to the low-playing music. Even when the song changed she kept going. She made it through another song, noticing in their reflection on the dresser mirror that Andrea had calmed down considerably and was looking heavy-eyed.

Alex did a little twist to a Beatles song, hustled to a Bee Gees song, and polka'd to a Bavarian waltz. The baby fell asleep and stayed that way the entire time.

Alex didn't dare stop dancing.

The door creaked open right in the middle of her version of the "mashed potato"—a sort of one-legged twist in slow motion. As Jamie looked into the room, her face registered shock at first, before a smile grew on her face with the realization of what Alex was doing. And that it was working.

The song ended abruptly. Immediately Andrea stirred and fussed. "Turn it over," Alex cried. "Quick!"

Fumbling with the buttons and the tape, Jamie flipped the cassette over and the music started.

Alex moved with the music and the baby calmed. Before the song ended, she was back asleep.

Now that she'd started it, Alex wasn't sure she could keep going. She was tired and sleepy. At 1:30 in the morning, she wasn't up to more aerobics. She turned to Jamie who sat in a daze on the edge of her bed. Alex bumped her sister with her foot and indicated that it was her turn.

"I can't dance like that," Jamie said.

"She doesn't care," Alex said. "Just keep moving. But she does seem to like to mambo."

"What's a mambo?"

"Here." Alex gently transferred the baby into Jamie's arms. "Keep moving, I'll teach you."

Andrea cried for a minute until Jamie found the beat and got the footwork. Soon she was gliding around the room and once again the baby calmed down.

Alex watched a few moments longer, then turned to leave. The look on Jamie's face told her she didn't want her to go, but Alex was ready to keel over.

"Maybe she's in a deep enough sleep so you don't need to keep dancing," Alex whispered. She lowered the volume, Jamie slowed her movement, and Andrea remained asleep.

With the volume off, Jamie stood still. Barely breathing, they watched, hoping she was really asleep.

Another minute passed and Andrea Nicole remained still. For the first time since they'd had her, she seemed truly at peace.

Alex gave Jamie a "thumbs up" and slipped out of the room, grateful they were over that hurdle, but wondering how much longer the baby would suffer the after-effects of withdrawal.

Back to the recliner she went, hoping somehow she could get some sleep. Just as she pulled the afghan over her, the crying overhead started again. A minute later she heard the soft beat of music, pulsing through the floorboards.

* * *

After several days, some semblance of a routine evolved. Since Andrea Nicole preferred sleeping during the day to sleeping at night, Judith and Alex resorted to wearing earplugs at night and Steve slept downstairs in the family room. Andrea Nicole gradually adjusted to the rocking chair in Jamie's room, which gave Jamie some relief, although she was nearly always tired. Still, her joy shone through her weariness.

Alex knew she should be packing, but she lacked the enthusiasm or drive to do it. Instead she spent much of her time reading her scriptures and different church books by General Authorities. Somewhere there had to be answers to her questions.

Her prayers were fervent, pleading, and plentiful. Every thought and action was spent in an effort to figure out what she should do about Rich.

Her mother finally convinced her she needed to get her packing done. Between diaper changes and feedings, Jamie and Judith helped with the task of filling Alex's suitcases. Alex felt perfectly comfortable about the things she was taking until her mother got hold of her itinerary. Aside from the black dress she'd altered and insisted Alex take with her, she added several more of her own outfits to her daughter's suitcase.

"Honey, I can take in the waistband on the skirt and these pants; the tops look fine just the way they are. You might need an extra suitcase, though. I'm not going back to New York for a while so you can use one of mine."

"Mother, I don't need all this stuff," Alex protested. "I'm not going to be doing that much socializing. Maybe a reception party or formal dinner occasionally, but other than the conventions, I'll just be kicking around."

"At least take the pantsuit. It looks wonderful on you and can be dressy enough for a dinner or casual enough for shopping. Honey, you don't get to go to Europe every day. I know you'll be glad you took these things. Jamie, you tell her."

Jamie, who held the baby more than she didn't, even when she was sleeping, nodded. "I agree with Mom, Al. Who knows? You may meet someone over there who'll want to take you on his yacht to Monte Carlo or on a romantic Rhine river cruise, and you'll kick yourself for not having that pantsuit. You better take it, and the skirt. It looks so great with Mom's glitzy gold blouse. You know, Mom, I can't believe you have clothes like this. I've never bought anything like this stuff in my life. Where do you wear them?"

"Oh, my goodness, everywhere—to Broadway shows, out to dinner, receptions, business gatherings, socials . . . I get dressed up once a week or more."

"Does Dr. Rawlins like to dress up?" Jamie asked.

"He loves to go out to dinner and dancing and owns his own tuxedo. I think we're going to have a lot of fun when we go to New

York. I've already made arrangements with my friends John and Cynthia Winterwood to let Dave stay with them."

"That sounds great, Mom. You and Dr. Rawlins will have a lot of fun." Alex slid both outfits of her mom's into a garment bag. If she had her way she'd toss her leotards, leggings, sweatshirts, and Nikes in a backpack and be done with the packing. Her mother had her outfitted for tea with the Queen Mother.

"Dr. Rawlins is a such great guy," Jamie said. "I don't think I'll ever be able to repay him for bringing us our daughter."

"He doesn't expect you to, honey. Knowing that everyone's happy is all he cares about. Believe me, he was a little nervous to go through with it."

"He was?"

"He knew how opposed to adoption you were. But he felt so strongly that you and Steve were the right people for the baby, he knew he had to try. He just didn't know what he would've done if you hadn't wanted her."

"I couldn't love her any more if she were my own," Jamie said. "I've learned so much already in these last few days. Being pregnant isn't what makes you a mother. It's taking care of a baby, loving and caring so much for that child you would give your own life for her. That's how I feel about Andrea Nicole. I consider her my own. She is part of me. I would die for her, if I had to."

Jamie laid the baby on the bed and smiled at her. Little Andrea lifted her arms, opened her tiny mouth, and yawned, squeaking and stretching. Then, with a dove-like sigh, she fell back asleep.

"I'm embarrassed now that I was so adamantly opposed to adoption," Jamie said softly. "I can't believe how narrow-minded and stubborn I was. I'm grateful Dr. Rawlins was able to see past all that."

She leaned forward and kissed the baby on the end of her nose.

"You're not worried anymore about the birth parents coming back for her, are you?"

"When we first got her home, I admit I jumped every time the telephone rang or someone unexpectedly came to the door. But I've been able to come to terms with it now. I've spent a lot of time on my knees, and I don't doubt for a minute that she's supposed to be with us."

Looking at mother and daughter pulled strongly on Alex's heart. Sure, Jamie was tired most of the time and barely had time to shower and get dressed each day, but she was the most content Alex had ever seen her. And more importantly Andrea grew more content with each day. There was an obvious bond between the two that Alex envied.

"Enough about that," Jamie said. "We need to get you packed. It's hard to believe you only have two days left. We're sure going to miss you, Alex."

"I wish I wasn't going," Alex said, tossing another pair of socks into her suitcase. "I don't know what I was thinking when I said yes."

"You were thinking it was a great opportunity. And it will be," Judith said. "You can't go to Europe and not have a wonderful time. It's just not possible."

Wanna bet, Alex almost said.

Chapter 19

Church was torture. Rich wasn't there and Alex was so overwhelmed with thoughts of him that it was all she could do to make it through the last two meetings.

As soon as Relief Society ended, she burst out into the clear summer day and rushed to her car. Feeling as though she would blow like a Fourth of July bottle rocket, she vowed she would grab Rich as soon as he got home from the kayaking trip, tie him to a chair if she had to, and get some kind of explanation from him. She was to the point where she didn't even care if he told her their relationship was completely over; she needed to hear him verbally say the words so she could close off her heart for good.

Rich owed her that much, to at least tell her it was over between them.

She threw the car door open, nearly ripping it from its hinges. She should've gotten mad a long time ago. She'd wasted too much time worrying about him when she should have demanded answers and explanations long ago. He'd brought it up first, about their getting married in the temple a year after she got baptized. She didn't dream it or make it up. It was in her journal, the one Rich gave her. Recorded for all of her posterity to read. He'd actually said to her, "Alex, I love you. You're everything I could ever want or dream of having for a wife. Soon you'll be baptized and a year after that we'll be sealed together for eternity. That day will be the happiest of my whole life."

No, he hadn't technically proposed to her, but he'd led her to believe that was his intention. What else was she supposed to think?

Maybe she should take her journal and show him. Show him all the wonderful, sweet, romantic *lies* he'd told her. She had never solicited his promises and confessions of love. It wasn't her style to fish for reassurance. If he wanted to express his feelings for her, she wanted him to do it because he wanted to, not because she asked.

But, boy, that was exactly what she was going to do. Except she wasn't going to ask him to share his feelings. She was going to demand he tell her once and for all what was going on—or off—between them. She couldn't bear the thought of leaving for two months with things hanging out all over the place and loose ends flapping in the breeze. She needed some kind of understanding and agreement—or, at least, some final closure.

Whatever it took, she was on a quest to pin him down once and for all.

Alex had promised to water Rich's flower garden, the one she'd helped him plant, while he was on his trip. As she drove to his house, her mind churned and kneaded thoughts and memories of discussions they'd had, as she tried to figure out once and for all what had gone wrong between them. But the more she thought, the less she came up with. Alex was so frustrated and upset and angry by the time she got to his house, she felt like she had enough pressure inside of her to launch a shuttle to the moon. But since he wasn't home, she couldn't vent her frustrations. So the only thing left to do was cry.

As the colorful blooms soaked in the sprays of water, tears spilled down Alex's cheeks. He'd be home sometime today, but she didn't even know if they'd have any time together before she left. Wishing she could stop her tears as easily as she could turn off the hose, Alex finished her chore and climbed back inside her car and turned the air conditioner on high.

The cold air blasting her in the face was refreshing. It helped dry her tears and snap her out of her pity. Taking one last look at his house and at the cheerful flowers spilling over in the window boxes, she started the car engine.

Darn him!

She pounded the steering wheel with the palm of her hand.

She still loved him. With all her heart she loved him.

But it was time to move on and spend as much time with her family as she could before she left.

* * *

Before going inside the house, she sat in the car sorting her thoughts and praying for help, begging for answers. There was no profound burst of enlightenment that opened her mind to a greater understanding, but she did come to a conclusion, a tiny insight that allowed her to know without a doubt, she would survive, learn, and grow from this experience. More than anything, she wished she knew if their relationship would last, if they would eventually marry and live happily ever after, but she had no such knowledge. One thing she did know, she was doing everything in her power to live her life according to the will of the Lord, to follow his promptings, to be worthy of his guiding spirit in her life. And he would always be there for her and bless her.

It was Rich, not her, who had suddenly changed, suddenly grown as cold toward her as an Arctic blizzard. And try as she might, she wasn't going to fix the problem or help him get past it. This was something he needed to sort out and decide for himself. Right now he needed love, support, and encouragement. And prayers. He needed her prayers to help him receive blessings and inspiration from the Lord.

And if that's what he needed, then that's what she'd do. Because no matter how he was acting and what he was doing, she loved him and she knew the Lord was with her. And for now that was going to have to be enough.

"SURPRISE!"

Alex jumped when she walked into the house. The front room and dining room were filled with people—neighbors, ward members, her family, and right in the middle of everyone, was Rich. He was home.

"What is this?" She laughed, wishing she didn't have stains of mascara around her eyes and hoping the warmth she felt in her face didn't mean it was bright red.

"A farewell party," Jamie said. She walked to the front door where Alex had grown roots and gave her sister a hug. "And kind of a welcome party for Andrea Nicole."

"I didn't notice any cars in the driveway."

"A lot of people walked and everyone else parked at the neighbors or on the street."

Alex looked around at all the familiar faces. "Thank you all for coming." Then her gaze rested on Rich, who smiled broadly in return. She was surprised he'd made it back in time for the party.

Jamie ushered her into the living room where a computer-generated banner read, *Bon Voyage, Alex,* and a gathering of people admired Andrea Nicole sleeping in her bassinet.

Already Judith was encouraging everyone to make their way into the kitchen where Alex was sure a feast was prepared. When had her mother had time to make food for a party?

Alex tired quickly of having to explain her itinerary for her trip to each person who asked her about it. She scanned the room for Rich, hoping he'd make his way her direction, but she didn't catch even a glimpse of him. As the well-wishers and interested parties thinned out and followed the tempting fragrances to the kitchen, Alex found herself able to breathe again and managed to move around the room, hoping to find out where Rich had gone to.

The dining room was full of hearty eaters. More guests with overloaded plates trickled into the family room and living room.

Smiling and greeting as she went, Alex continued her search, running into the Becksteads on her way.

"Thanks for coming, you two," she said to Colleen and Donald. "Where's Sarah?"

"She's with some other children outside playing."

"I feel terrible I'm going to miss your baptism next week."

Donald patted her on the shoulder. "It would be wonderful to have you there, but I understand why you can't be."

"We've already talked to the bishop about working toward going through the temple in a year," Colleen said. "Sarah is so excited to think she can actually go inside the temple. It's all she talks about."

"I'm so happy for you," she said, trying to hide her pain at seeing her own temple dream shattered. "I think I'll go outside and find Sarah so I can tell her good-bye."

"She'll be happy to see you. She wanted to tell you that she's starting ballet."

"I'll bet she's so excited."

"It was all we could do to get her tu-tu off this morning. She couldn't understand why she couldn't wear it to church," Colleen said.

Alex gave Colleen and Donald each a quick hug and exited through the sliding glass door to the deck. A few ward members greeted her and inquired about her trip. Again, she recounted her itinerary. Each time she went through the list she left out more and more details of cities and sights. She was ready to go upstairs to the computer room and print out copies of her itinerary and hand them out. She understood people were just being caring and interested, but Rich had turned her inside out and she wasn't coping well with anything anymore.

Alex worked her way around the side of the house, past a bed of petunias then around to the front, hoping to find a quiet spot. Instead, to her surprise, she found Rich. Alone on the front porch.

"Hey," he said, giving her a smile, "fancy meeting you here." He spoke as if nothing had changed between them, as if they'd never had that last talk. Maybe he thought everything was just fine between them. But she knew better. Still, she managed to keep her response light.

"I escaped out the back door. I couldn't face having to explain where I'm going in Europe one more time."

"By the way," Rich said, "where *are* you going?"

She groaned and rolled her eyes.

"I'm kidding," he said, leaning against a pillar.

"So when did you get back?" she asked, wondering if he knew how much she loved him and missed him when he was gone.

"Just this morning."

"Oh," she said, feeling awkward.

Rich didn't seem eager to offer any more information.

"Would you like to go for a walk?" she asked. "If I stay out here I'm bound to be discovered." She looked in each direction to make sure the coast was clear.

"Sure, let's go."

She was surprised as he took her hand and led her down the driveway and onto the street where she noticed for the first time all the cars belonging to guests.

"So, you leave tomorrow, huh?" he said as he led her down a pathway toward a gathering of pines.

"I need to be at the Salt Lake airport at eleven. My plane leaves at 12:30."

"Why aren't you flying out of Idaho Falls?"

"I'd have to go tonight. There's not a flight out early enough in the morning." She had put off her departure until the last possible moment.

"How are you getting there?"

"I'm driving. I can leave my car in longterm parking."

"For two months?" He stopped walking and looked at her.

"I'm not paying for it," Alex answered, then kept walking.

"Aren't you worried about it getting broken into or damaged?" Rich stepped wide across a tiny stream then held her hand steady while she stepped over it.

"I don't know. Should I be?"

"It just seems like a long time to leave it there."

"I didn't want Steve to have to drive down and back like that."

"How about if I took you?"

She looked at Rich, wondering how she could ever get over those tawny colored eyes of his. Her heart still fluttered when he looked at her.

"You don't have to do that. Besides, if anything happens to my car, Mr. Diamante will just have to pay for it."

"Mr. Diamante? Who's that?"

"He's the guy in Rome who sponsored this tour and put it all together."

"I see." He led her to a fallen log under a canopy of quaking aspen. "I'd still like to take you."

"Rich, you don't have—"

"I know I don't have to, but I want to."

"All right, I guess if you don't mind, that would be nice. I'm sure someone will be able to come and get me. Maybe I could figure out a way to catch a connecting flight to Idaho Falls coming home."

"Thanks, Alexis."

He hardly ever used her full name. He was acting funny, too. Had that prayer she'd offered earlier already taken effect? Was he finally realizing how long she'd be gone and even thinking he would miss her?

"Thanks for what?"

"For letting me take you down. I guess—" he broke a piece of dried bark off a tree branch. He stood with one foot resting on the log while Alex sat on a smooth part of the tree. "—It's just that, well, it's going to be strange having you gone so long."

So, he'd finally realized how long two months was. "I have a hard time thinking about it," she said. "Andrea Nicole is going to change so much while I'm gone. I hate to miss that."

Rich brightened. "She sure is a cute baby. Jamie seems really happy."

"She is. I've never seen a person transform so quickly. I mean, Jamie's tired because she doesn't get a lot of sleep at night, but she never complains. She just goes about her housework with a smile and takes naps during the day when the baby does. I'm amazed at how she seems to know exactly what to do. Like she's had ten kids already. She's a natural."

"Steve and Jamie are wonderful people. They'll be great parents."

"No doubt. But you should see those two. You'd think they were newlyweds. If I didn't love them so much, they'd make me sick the way they kiss and snuggle and ogle each other. Every night they sit on the couch with the baby and just smother her and each other. I have to leave the room when they get like that."

She didn't tell him that she left the room because it was too hard to watch the love being shared, the closeness, the sweetness, and beauty of the little family, a harsh contrast to the love that seemed to be slowly fading between Rich and herself.

"I've seen a big difference in Steve. I used to have to kick him out of the office to go home. Now he's never there, and when he is there, he's on the phone with Jamie. It's a good thing he hired Dax and Justin. Especially for when I leave."

"When are you moving to Park City?"

"In a week or so. I'm not quite finished with the landscapes I'm working on now."

"And you're staying in the Fewtrells' studio apartment?"

"They keep it on hand for occasions like this." He jingled his keys in his pants pocket and remained quiet for a moment, then finally said, "Alex, I know how you feel about Elena. But I can't let this opportunity go by."

"Have you prayed about it, Rich?"

"What?"

"Have you prayed to know if this is the way you should go about starting your art career? I'm not saying you shouldn't pursue getting your art out in public, I'm just saying I don't know if Elena's the right person to help you."

She waited for the reaction, for his defenses to launch their attack, but this time it didn't happen. In fact Rich didn't say anything. He just stared at his shoes.

"Rich," she pressed a little more. "Have you prayed about it?"

"No, I haven't." He finally looked up and their gazes locked for several seconds. "I just feel great about the whole arrangement. She loves my work, she says all the right things. I'm getting what I want out of the deal. I haven't felt a need to pray about it."

"Don't you think this is an important step for you?"

"Of course it is."

"Then I think you should pray about it. And if it is as right as you say it is, you don't have anything to worry about. Right?"

He nodded.

"Rich . . ." She didn't even stop to weigh the risks of what she was about to say. This could be her last chance to tell him how she felt. "I want you to know how much I've enjoyed being with you since we met back in April. It seems like a lifetime ago, not three months."

"It does to me, too."

"You've been so wonderful helping me learn about the gospel and prepare for my baptism. I'll never forget what you've done for me."

Her voice was starting to break up, but she didn't fight for control. For once she was going to let her heart talk and not her head.

"I don't know what's happened between us, or why things are different." Tears formed in her eyes but she didn't let them fall. "I've gone over and over in my mind what I might have done to bring about this change, but I can't seem to come up with anything. All I know is that we used to have something very special between us, and now it's gone." It was hard talking through the emotion that strangled her throat, but she kept going. "All I can come up with is that I misread your actions and your words. Because I thought when you said you loved me, it meant, you *loved* me. I mean—" she paused to wipe her eyes, "—a romantic kind of love, an 'I-want-to-be-with-you-I-want-a-future-with-you-kind-of-love.'"

She looked at him, not caring that her eyes were puffy and red, or that her nose ran, or that she spoke one octave higher. "You used to hold me and kiss me, and tell me you couldn't live without me. And I believed you, Rich." The heat of anger ignited almost immediately, drying her tears. She took a deep, cleansing breath and continued. "You built those dreams for me." She pushed away from the log and took two steps then whirled around. "Why did you do that to me, Rich. Why?"

He looked away from her, saying nothing.

A breeze rustled the leaves overhead and played with the airy fabric of Alex's skirt. She combed her hair back with her fingers and released a frustrated sigh. Her hope faded with the ticking seconds.

Just as she was about to tell him good-bye and walk away forever, he spoke.

Chapter 20

"You're right. I owe you an apology."

She stood with her arms folded, waiting for him to continue.

"I wish I knew why I do what I do. I've tried to analyze myself, figure out what triggers this kind of behavior. And all I can come up with is, I got scared."

She wasn't sure what to say or how to react. She was still angry. He owed her a better explanation than that.

"Before I left on my mission I had a girlfriend. Her name was Kendyl. She was smart and funny and beautiful. Everyone liked her because even though she was a cheerleader and on the student council, she wasn't stuck-up or snooty. She was friendly to everyone and stuck to her standards; she made it seem cool to be religious and go to church. In fact, she made it seem cool to not date before she was sixteen and not go to R-rated movies."

Alex relaxed her stance as she grew interested in his story.

"I wasn't even sure I was going to go on a mission, but I knew she wouldn't have me any other way. She kept after me, reminded me all the time how important it was for me to go. She even said she wanted to go on a mission herself.

"All the guys were jealous of me because they wanted to go out with her. We spent most of our senior year dating, and then a few months before my birthday, I had that 'talk' with my bishop. I told him I wanted to go on a mission. But really, honestly, deep down, I was going for Kendyl, not for me."

He moved pine needles with the toe of his shoe, creating a little pile.

"I got my mission call and she was right there next to me. I was excited because it was the same mission my best friend was in. It felt good that she was so proud of me. She was the best girlfriend a missionary could have. She sent weekly letters that were funny and uplifting, and she sent a package once a month. I kept her picture in the front of my scriptures and showed it to all the other elders. I could tell by the way they reacted, they thought she was as pretty as I did. But as pretty as she was outside, she was even more beautiful inside."

Alex walked back over to her spot on the log and sat down.

"It didn't take long for me to catch the true spirit of a mission, and I realized that I had gone for the wrong reason, but I knew I was staying on that mission because I had a testimony of the gospel and wanted to serve the Lord. Kendyl never skipped a week writing and told me over and over in her letters how proud she was of me. Everything was perfect. I even got to be mission companions with Jeff, my best friend, right before he went home."

Rich brushed at a fly buzzing around his shoulder.

"Jeff and I were great companions. We had fun together, but we worked hard. We had more baptisms than any other companionship in our whole mission two months in a row. Right before he left to go home, I found a beautifully carved wooden jewelry box for Kendyl and asked him to take it to her for me when he got home."

"Did he?"

"Yeah, he took the gift over for me. And they ended up spending time together. To talk about me, of course. But they started spending more and more time together, and the next thing I knew I got a wedding announcement in the mail. *Their* wedding announcement." He kicked his pile of pine needles, scattering them in the breeze.

"Steve was my companion at the time. I don't know how I would've gotten through it without him. I felt so betrayed. I was so full of anger, I just wanted to go home."

Alex's heart recognized the pain in his voice.

"Somehow I managed to survive and get past that. And then I came home and had another bomb dropped in my lap. This one from my parents. They were getting divorced. I'm telling you, Alex, it leveled me. It really did. I had such a numb feeling after that. I even ran into Jeff and Kendyl at a ball game and didn't even care. I felt nothing."

He rubbed his forehead, as if all the memories made his head ache. Alex wanted to reach out and comfort him, but she couldn't. She felt bad he was hurting, but she hurt, too.

"After that I just haven't been the same. Part of me wants to settle down and get married, but I can't seem to go through with a serious relationship. That's why I haven't been able to go through with any of my engagements. I'm over what Kendyl did to me, but I still remember the pain, and I'm afraid of getting hurt like that again. Especially after seeing the pain my parents went through when they got divorced. I'm so afraid the same thing is going to happen to me, and I don't think I could go through it again."

She knew about his parents' divorce and his three broken engagments. But why hadn't Steve ever told her that story about Kendyl? Maybe she would have been more cautious about getting involved with Rich. But then again, maybe she wouldn't have.

"Thank you for talking to me, Rich. It helps, knowing all you've been through." The leaves rustled overhead. A butterfly flitted by, landing briefly on a dainty flower, then flew away.

She continued. "Rich, I don't know all the psychoanalytical reasons behind your behavior based on your past, but it seems reasonable to believe experiences like that would have a huge impact on your life and relationships. I know my father's death has caused me to act out in strange ways that don't seem related. I think I understand what you're saying more than you think I do."

"I haven't told many people that story. It's painful and embarrassing, and I just want to forget it. Even Steve doesn't know the full story. He knows I got a 'Dear John' and that my girlfriend married my best friend, but he doesn't know how badly it hurt. I talked to my mission president about it, and I told my parents, who loved her as much as I did. They expected me to come home and marry her, so I had to tell them. But that's all, except now, for you."

"I'm sorry I got so upset with you," Alex apologized. "I didn't mean to. But, Rich, you have to understand how confusing all of this has been for me. I always thought that the next step for us was going to be marriage. I mean, you talked about it as much as I did for a while. Then you stopped."

He clenched his eyes shut, almost like he was in pain.

"What happened, Rich? Did I do something to change your mind about us?"

His chin dropped forward; she could tell this was hard for him. But she wasn't pulling any punches. She had to know.

"I know this has been hard for you," he said, keeping his chin down. "I haven't really realized I was turning you away, but I see now how badly I've treated you and how confusing this must have been for you."

"Have I been pressuring you?"

"No, Alex. You've been wonderful. I don't deserve someone as wonderful as you." He finally lifted his head and looked her straight in the eye. "It's just that I've started to feel closed in, confined. Maybe because your baptism made me realize that this was really going to happen. And every time you'd bring up the subject of marriage, I'd start feeling that claustrophobic, panicky feeling again. I know it's stupid, but I can't seem to get past it."

An overwhelming sadness filled her. She already knew the answer but she still had to say it. "So, what do we do now? Where does that leave our relationship?"

He shook his head wearily. "I don't know."

"I need more than that, Rich."

"It's like I said before," he answered. "I think the timing for you to go on this trip is good. I need a little space right now to work through some of my feelings, and deal with the pressure and responsibility of making a commitment."

She couldn't help the flare of anger his words ignited. More than anything she wanted to shake some sense into him. "Rich, there are no marriage guarantees."

"I know."

"But if you've felt the same things I've felt, been touched by the Spirit the same way I have . . ." She looked at him, slumped over and defeated, and realized she wasn't going to change anything. "Oh, never mind. Just forget it." She stood to leave.

"Alex, wait." He stood up with her. "I don't want you to ever doubt that I was sincere when I told you how I felt about you."

She turned to him and said, "Thank you for saying that. That helps a little." The anger had died and all that was left was sadness and pity. She actually felt bad for him. She sincerely believed he wanted to go through with a commitment, but was just too afraid.

He just didn't have enough faith, in himself, in her, or in the Lord. She was surprised when his next words vocalized her thoughts exactly.

"I know I just need to exercise more faith, put all my trust in the Lord, and things will work out."

"So, why don't you?"

"I'm trying."

She nearly laughed in his face. "You are?"

"Alex, you don't realize how hard this is. I love you. I'm so afraid of losing you."

"But you're more afraid of making a commitment."

He hung his head.

"Rich, I don't really think there's much more to say. You need time and space to develop the kind of faith you need to let go of your fears and follow your heart. I love you. I am willing to give you anything you need and support you any way I can. But as much as I love you, I don't want you if you're not one hundred percent sure about being with me."

He still didn't look at her.

"It's okay, Rich."

He looked up.

"If things are supposed to work out between us, they will."

"I believe that, too."

"Then we're going to be okay."

He stepped toward her, closing the gap between them. "You are unbelievable. Here you are, a new convert to the Church, and you've got things figured out better than I do."

"Not really," she said. "I have a lot of questions. But at least I know where to go for the answers."

He nodded slowly. "Thanks, Alex. I'm going to miss you."

"I'm going to miss you, too."

They stepped closer to each other.

"Good luck with your painting. I'll be praying for you."

"Thanks. I'll pray for you, too."

She looked up into his eyes. He reached toward her with one hand and pulled her into his arms. He held her for a long time. She wasn't anxious to leave his embrace, for there, with his arms around her, she felt safe and protected. She felt here, in his arms, was where she belonged.

A million thoughts went through her mind, a thousand reasons why they should fight for their relationship, why they were supposed to be together, forever. But she knew it didn't matter. It had to come from his heart, from inside him. She couldn't make him feel or want anything. If it wasn't there, it wasn't there.

She needed to move on. Just like she'd learned in California, it was her and the Lord. Thank goodness he was always there. He would never let her down. He would stand by her and help her. And more than anything, right now, she needed his help.

* * *

When Alex and Rich returned to the house, the party was over and everyone had gone home. Out of energy and too tired to move, Judith and Dr. Rawlins had collapsed onto the love seat. Across from them were Steve and Jamie, slumped onto the couch, with the baby between them. Rich sat in a chair and Alex on the floor, within his reach, but without him touching her.

"I thought they'd never all go home," Jamie said.

"It's all Judith's fault," Steve said.

"My fault?" Judith sat up, then covered a yawn with her hand and fell back into the couch cushion.

"Yeah, if you didn't make such good food, people wouldn't hang around until it was all gone."

"That really was good, Mom," Alex said. "I sure appreciate all the work you went to for me."

"Honey, you know I love to cook and entertain. It's a lot of work but it's fun having everyone over, and besides, you're worth it. We're going to miss you."

"The leaves will be changing by the time you get back," Jamie said. "It's going to be so boring with you gone."

"Gee thanks, honey," Steve said.

"I didn't mean you're boring." Jamie leaned over and kissed her husband on the cheek.

"I'm sure Andrea will keep you plenty busy," Alex said. "You won't even notice I'm gone."

"Maybe by the time you get back we'll have the kitchen cleaned," Judith said. "That is, if we get started today. I sure could use a professional to help me." She leaned toward Dr. Rawlins, who had his head back and his eyes shut.

"In fact," she said, "I set aside a piece of that caramel fudge topped cheesecake just in case I needed a bribe."

"You did?" He opened his eyes and lifted his head.

She laughed. "I remembered how much you like it, so I hid one for you."

"That's worth some kitchen time, I'd say."

They stood up and left the room together.

"Honey," Jamie said, "why don't we go pitch in?"

"Oh," Steve said, faking enthusiasm. "Good idea. Why didn't I think of it?"

"Come on." She pushed herself to her feet. "Mom did most of the work making the food. We can go help clean up the mess."

"I should be the one cleaning the kitchen," Alex said.

"No, no. I need you to watch the baby while Steve and I go help."

Alex moved to the couch and took the baby while Steve and Jamie left for the kitchen. "Did you save me some cheesecake?" Steve asked.

"Honey, I thought the three pieces you ate earlier would have been enough."

Rich took a seat next to Alex. She laid Andrea Nicole on her lap, and they watched her sleeping soundly. Alex was grateful the baby had finally gotten past the withdrawals and appeared much more content. She slept much better at night and was good-natured most of the day.

Lightly, Rich stroked the baby's cheek, bringing a smile to the tiny lips.

"Oh, look, you made her smile," Alex said softly.

Andrea flinched, then dipped her head to one side and hunched up her shoulders, squeaking and stretching. She wiggled her legs and shifted her bottom, getting her blankets bunched and twisted. Alex watched in amazement as she opened her mouth and yawned, scrunching up her little face.

After a long while, the baby grew motionless again but instead of falling back asleep, she lifted one heavy eye lid and then the other. Almost trancelike, Andrea Nicole stared at the pair of faces above her with her big brown eyes.

"What do you think she's thinking?" Alex asked.

"Probably, 'What's my aunt doing with a goofy guy like that?'" He leaned toward the baby and said, "Hey, little sweetie, do you think I'm goofy?"

He stroked her cheek, trying to get her to smile again but the baby turned her head away instead. After a moment, still looking at the baby, Rich said, "I'm going to miss you, Alex."

"I'm going to miss you, too."

In just a few words, he had said volumes to her. There was still no commitment. No "I'll be here when you get home," or "Is it too late for you to change your mind and stay home?" but at least she knew he cared. And maybe for now that was enough. It would have to be enough.

Chapter 21

They were on the road by 5:30 the next morning. Rich loaded her bags in the back of the truck, then joined her in the cab. It was still dark outside and the sky was full of stars.

The only sound was the hum of the engine. They traveled in silence.

Alex couldn't believe she was really leaving for Rome that day and wasn't coming back until the end of September. With their relationship the way it was, she was terrified to leave. But she reflected back on the time she had knelt in prayer and received a strong impression that going on this trip was the right thing to do. That assurance was the only thing that kept her going; otherwise she'd have her bags unpacked and be back in her bed, content to stay in Island Park and wait for Rich to come to his senses.

But that wasn't what the Lord wanted her to do. She just wished she knew if this trip was going to separate her and Rich forever, or bring them closer together. Somehow she doubted it could bring them together. Especially with so much distance between them . . . and with Elena spinning her web around him.

That's what made it so hard to leave. She honestly didn't think things would be the same between them when she got back. Rich would be involved in his art, perhaps making the move to Park City permanent, and she didn't know where that would leave her.

"Tired?" Rich asked, stretching his neck to one side and then the other.

"A little. I didn't get any sleep at all."

"Do you think you'll get some on the plane?"

"I hope so. It helps flying first-class. I can put in my earplugs and pull down the shade, and no one will bother me. But getting comfortable in any airplane seat isn't easy."

"Was it hard saying good-bye?"

"Not as hard as I thought. Of course everyone was in bed when I left; we said our good-byes last night. I feel better leaving Jamie, now that she has the baby."

Alex wanted time to stand still, but the first rays of morning blushed the sky. Wispy clouds ignited with the vivid colors.

As the sun rose higher, traffic grew heavier and by the time they reached Ogden, Utah, forty-five minutes north of the Salt Lake airport, Alex had started to worry about the time. It was past rush hour, but morning traffic was bumper to bumper.

"We'll get you there on time," Rich said.

In a way Alex hoped she missed the plane, then she wouldn't have to say good-bye quite yet. But as soon as they passed the main off-ramps to the city, they picked up speed and were sailing further south.

Before Alex knew it, airport signs appeared and she realized that within minutes she would walk out of Rich's life. She kept her head turned away, because with each new thought, tears gathered in the corners of her eyes.

If only he'd give her something to hold on to. She'd imagined this good-bye scene a thousand times. Half of those times were sweet, romantic scenes, some even with Rich surprising her with an engagement ring. The other half were tense, awkward moments where they ended up not even hugging good-bye. Alex didn't know what to expect.

He'd been unbelievably loving and kind since their talk yesterday, but that could be because he knew she was leaving and the pressure was off of him.

They pulled into the short-term parking lot, only a few minutes behind schedule. As they each grabbed a bag, Alex found that hers was so heavy, she was ready to send it back in the truck with Rich. But it had all her mother's dressy clothes and shoes in it, as well as a dozen copies of the Book of Mormon, which she planned to give away during her stay in Europe.

After she checked herself and her luggage in at the ticket counter, she and Rich went through the security check and made their way to the gate. By that time it was almost eleven o'clock. Neither had eaten breakfast, so they followed their noses to the cinnamon-sweet smell of freshly baked bread, and found a bakery where they both ordered a gooey cinnamon roll and milk. As the two of them sat at a booth, eating and licking their fingers, Alex mentally sifted through the things she wanted to say. She wanted to plead with him to open his eyes and see what he was letting slip through his fingers—and whose claws he was slipping into—but she remembered just in time. She needed to give him space and have faith in him.

So, she sat in silence, watching and studying Rich, memorizing the glossiness of his hair, the smoothness of his freshly shaven face, the width of his jaw line and curve of his lips. She wanted more than anything for him to grab her, swear his undying love for her, and then kidnap her, swearing that he was unable to let her leave him after all.

Instead, he polished off his roll, pulled a few hunks off Alex's barely eaten one, then said, "We'd better get to the gate. You don't want to miss your plane."

Yes I do! she wanted to shout. *And I want you to want me to miss it, too!*

Letting him take her hand, she followed him down the concourse and on toward the gate where the plane waited.

Approaching the ticket counter she asked the desk clerk when they would start boarding. He looked at her ticket, noted her first-class status, then asked her to wait a moment.

He spoke to another worker, who stepped from behind the counter and disappeared.

"I wonder what all of this is about?"

Rich shrugged and looked around.

A moment later they saw the second man come toward them across the concourse, carrying a huge bouquet of deep burgundy-colored roses.

"We were instructed to give you these when you arrived," the man said.

Alex was breathless and speechless. For a minute she suspected, or rather, hoped, they were from Rich. But by the look on his face, she realized that he didn't know anything about them.

"Wow," Rich said, "those are beautiful."

"I wonder who they're from?" Alex stepped out of the way of the other passengers who needed to get to the counter, but who were all looking at her.

"Let's go over there," Rich said.

He led her to a corner of the waiting area where several chairs sat empty. They took a seat, and Alex looked for the card. When she found it, Rich held the roses for her while she opened the envelope.

My dearest Alexis,

Thank you for agreeing to come on the tour. I put it together just to have a chance to see you again. You're in for the time of your life. Have a wonderful flight. I await your arrival. With fondest regards,

Nickolas

She kept the card covered in the palm of her hand. "They're from Nickolas."

"Who's Nickolas?"

"Nickolas Diamante, you know, the tour coordinator."

"The guy in Rome?"

"Yes." She reread the card, put it back in the envelope and tucked it inside the roses, hoping her face wasn't blushing.

"What did he say?"

"Uh," she cleared her throat, "He said . . . 'Thanks for agreeing to come on the tour. Have a wonderful flight.'" She hoped it wasn't considered lying to leave out the rest of the message.

What was Nickolas up to? Certainly he was just trying to flatter her, telling her he put the tour together so he could see her again. That was ridiculous. No one would fund such an enormous and expensive project for that reason. Of course, Nickolas was wealthy enough to afford it. He owned many of the fitness facilities throughout Italy aside from his sportswear line, *ProStar*, and his investments. This was business, not pleasure.

Still, that was quite a message.

"Alex . . . Alex!"

Rich's voice startled her.

"They're calling for first-class passengers to board."

"I'm sorry. I wasn't listening." She looped her purse strap over her shoulder and stood. "Here," she gave him the bouquet of roses, "would you mind taking these to Jamie? I can't take them on the plane with me."

"Sure." He took the bundle.

"Thanks for driving me today, Rich. Take care of yourself while I'm gone. And good luck with your artwork."

"I hope you have a wonderful trip."

"Thanks." She gave him a brave smile. "I'll send you a postcard now and then."

"That would be great."

"Wait," she cried, "where do I send it? I don't have your address or phone number in Park City."

The loudspeaker called one last time for all first-class passengers to board.

"Here," he said, "just send the postcards to this address. I'm sure I'll get it." He gave her Elena's business card.

She wanted to kick him in the shins.

"I have something for you," he said, producing a pale lavender-colored envelope from his shirt pocket. "Open it on the plane."

"Thank you," she said, wondering why she was leaving on this trip when she didn't even want to go.

"Good-bye, Alex."

"Good-bye, Rich."

They hugged tightly. Tears stung her eyes but she refused to let them fall.

"I'll miss you," he said before he let her go.

She appreciated his words, but found it difficult to take them to heart.

"Bye," she said, taking a step backwards. "Thanks again, Rich."

She turned to join the crowd pressing to board the plane.

"Alex!" Rich yelled her name. The passengers swarmed around her. She turned and could barely see his head.

"I love you," she thought she heard him say, but the ticket lady grabbed her boarding pass and ushered her through the door.

* * *

"Excuse me, miss. Would you like some more water?"

"Please." Alex held her glass so the attendant could fill it.

Taking a sip of Evian, she turned to the window, staring blankly at the sea of clouds blocking her view of the Atlantic ocean. From her side of the plane, she couldn't see the sunset, but by the color of the clouds she could tell it was getting toward dusk. Pulling the light airline blanket over her, she shut her eyes, trying to rest. She was exhausted but couldn't seem to sleep. Visions of Rich yelling to her as she was being pushed through the line haunted her. Had he really said he loved her or had she imagined it?

Did it make a difference? To him or to her? It was possible for him to love her, but was it possible for him to commit to her? She doubted it.

She twisted and tried every possible position to help her fall asleep but her mind just wouldn't shut off.

The plane shivered as turbulence shook its metal frame. A bell dinged and the "Fasten Seat Belts" sign came on. Alex stiffened, her nerves tingling, her stomach knotting. For a person who spent as much time on airplanes as she did, she never got used to the shifting air currents and bad weather. Visions of the plane spiraling downward, hurtling toward the water below, filled her mind. Even though she couldn't see the ocean, she knew it was down there. That was the last place she wanted to crash. But then again, she couldn't think of a good place for an airplane to crash either.

Out of the ten other passengers in first class, she was the only one not watching a movie. All the others had settled down after their seven-course gourmet meal of hors d'oeuvres, cream of butternut squash soup, salad, pork medallions with mushrooms, raspberry cheesecake, and finally fruit and cheese, and were engrossed in the small private screens that accompanied each seat. She wasn't in the mood for a movie. She wasn't in the mood for flying. She wasn't in the mood for Europe.

All she wanted was to be back home, fishing with Rich on Henry's Lake, hiking with Rich through tree-lined hills, spotting moose, bison, or an occasional bear, or simply sharing a bowl of popcorn with Rich on the porch swing at Jamie's house.

Instead she had to sit in a luxurious, reclining leather chair, and be catered to by a polite airline attendant from Amsterdam whose every wish was to serve her as she traveled to Rome, where she would be picked up at the airport and driven, by limousine, to her five-star hotel.

Life was so unfair!

With an empty seat next to her, Alex couldn't complain about her accommodations and was grateful for the privacy. But here she was, not even halfway to her destination, and she was already climbing the walls.

Then she remembered Rich's envelope. How could she have forgotten?

She lowered the leg rest, unhooked her seat belt, and grabbed her purse. Tearing through the contents, she located the envelope.

Straightening back in her seat she realized there was something inside, sliding and jingling around. An engagement ring wouldn't jingle, so she sadly crossed it off the list of possibilities.

Ripping the envelope apart, she pulled out the card. Immediately a gold link bracelet fell into her lap. She picked it up. On it were three little charms. One was a tiny snowmobile. The next charm was a book; on it, written in tiny letters, was *The Book of Mormon*. The third charm was a pair of overlapping hearts. On the front of the card was a pitifully sad looking basset hound with big, droopy brown eyes. Inside, the card read, "I miss you already."

Underneath the inscription, Rich had written:

Dear Alex,

I hope the next two months go as fast as the last two weeks. I am finally realizing just how long you're going to be gone.

I've enclosed a little going-away present. I even started it for you and thought you could collect charms as you worked your way through Europe. Hopefully it will always represent happy memories for you.

The snowmobile reminds me of the first time we met. That terrible snowstorm that brought us together and the ride I gave you to Jamie and Steve's that first night. I knew that first night there was something special between us.

Alex put down the card and thought about what she'd just read. He admitted to feeling the same things, remembering the same things about that first night together, as she did. There had been something "special" between them right from the start.

> *Of course, the next charm represents you learning about the gospel and joining the Church. What a small token to represent such a huge impact in your life. But it seemed to be the most significant symbol I could find.*

> *The two joined hearts represent all that we've shared—our love, our laughter, our lives. You've been everything to me—friend, confidante, cheerleader, counselor. I am grateful to have had you in my life. You are and always will be in my heart.*

> *As the card says, "I miss you already." I hope you have a wonderful time. My thoughts and prayers will be with you while you're gone.*

> *With love,*
> *Rich*

Alex stared at the card for two or three minutes, not overjoyed, not disappointed, somewhere in the middle. He hadn't exactly gushed with love and adoration, but he hadn't exactly cemented their relationship. It was just there, without commitment. And he certainly was a pro at dodging that.

But she loved the bracelet and she loved him for being thoughtful. And she was willing to be patient because Rich was worth waiting for. She just wished she knew how long she was going to have to wait.

Chapter 22

Still stuffed from dinner, Alex turned down breakfast and took a chance to freshen up in the bathroom. Putting to use the complimentary travel bag she'd received at the beginning of the flight, Alex brushed and flossed her teeth, swished with mouthwash, washed her face with warm water, then spritzed with a light moisturizing spray. She combed her hair, lotioned her hands, and finished with a coat of lip balm.

The window shades were up when she returned to her seat. Light filled the cabin. On the screen on the wall in front, she noticed the flashing airplane on the map that had charted their path the entire trip and realized they were only minutes from landing.

Rich was an ocean away; there was no turning back now. And even though she was determined to have an enjoyable time she knew he'd always be just a thought away.

The bracelet on her wrist jingled as she fastened her seat belt to prepare for landing. She was excited to shop in each country and find one or two charms representing the experiences she'd had or places she'd seen. When she returned home, she hoped she could share with Rich the significance of each charm. Even though she wasn't exactly sure what else they would be able to share in the future, she thought to herself.

Over the loudspeaker the pilot announced their arrival into Rome. They were twelve minutes past schedule, arriving at 8:42 a.m., but it was a beautiful day in Rome, sunny and warm, about ninety-two degrees. Alex looked out the window at the rolling green hills, lush and thickly forested, with patches of fields and ribbons of roads winding through the countryside. Except for the red clay roofs on creamy white stuccoed houses, Italy didn't look much different than parts of Idaho, she thought.

Carrying a tray of warmed washcloths, the airline attendant came around and offered each passenger one last chance to freshen up before landing. When she got to Alex she said, "I've been given instructions to have you go directly to the front entrance of the airport when you arrive. Your bags will be taken care of for you, and your ride will be waiting."

"Okay, thank you."

"Also, I am supposed to give you this package." The attendant gave her a glossy black shopping bag with the words "European Supertour" in bold, gold lettering, and in smaller letters underneath, "sponsored by Diamante Enterprises and ProStar Fitness Products."

"How much time do we have before we land?" Alex asked.

"Eight minutes or so."

Pulling the tissue from the top of the bag, Alex looked inside and found a beautiful black and white ProStar warm-up jacket. Embroidered on the back were again the words "European Supertour" in the same gold letters. Underneath was her name, "Alexis McCarty."

Also, inside was a thin binder, which held a letter of welcome from Nickolas, a general itinerary, the names and phone numbers of assistants in each city, and a brief outline of each fitness professional who would be in the group.

Alex had either met or knew personally each of the other members of the group. The two other women were both international aerobic champions: Gabriella Guntsmeier, from Germany, and Julianne Leighton, from Great Britain. Alex was surprised to see Julianne's name listed. She and Julianne had spent a whole week together in Manhattan at a convention and had become good friends. Alex was excited to know she would have a friend to spend the next two months with. Remembering that she had met Julianne's cousin at Temple Square, Alex thought it was an interesting coincidence that Julianne was one of the other instructors she would be working with.

One of the men on the tour, J.J. Callahan, had been a presenter with her at many of the national conventions all over the United States. Alex had met the other two, Wes Griffith from Canada and Ricky Ruiz from Venezuela, at an awards banquet in New York, but she had never spent time with them, nor attended either of their presentations.

She did know that all of them were highly qualified and considered the best in their field. She was honored to be named among them and be part of their team. Nickolas had pulled together a dynamite group of presenters.

After flipping through the binder, Alex continued to look through the bag. Underneath the jacket was a white baseball cap with the same European Supertour logo embroidered across the front, in black. There was also a t-shirt with the same logo, and a water bottle.

At the bottom of the bag was a small, silver, gift-wrapped box. On the attached card she read, *My personal thanks for joining the team.* Tearing off the paper she exposed a black velvet box. She opened the lid and her jaw dropped. There was a pair of diamond stud earrings. *Big* diamond stud earrings.

Sandy had always joked that since Nickolas's last name meant "diamond" in Italian, he was probably sitting on a pile of diamonds. Alex wondered how he could afford to give every member of the team diamonds. She wasn't sure she could accept such a gift, but she didn't know if she could turn it down either.

Still they were beautiful; elegantly simple, simply elegant. Impulsively she put them in her ears, wondering what kind of man this Nickolas really was. All she knew of him was that he had been an Olympic skier for his country, actually taking home a bronze medal. She thought back on the first time she'd met Nickolas at the conference in Manhattan as he introduced his new line of fitness gear and athletic shoes to the American public. She remembered how charming and attentive he'd been in San Diego at the biannual fitness convention. When he offered to show her Europe, if she ever came over to visit, she never imagined she would be doing exactly that.

Even though it was costly for him to fund such a first-class tour, she also knew that aerobics and fitness were hot in Europe, and there would be an incredible response to the conferences, workshops, and conventions he had lined up. He would easily make back his investment as well as a huge profit.

A shrewd businessman and promoter of fitness facilities and conventions on the European continent and in Great Britain,

Nickolas ran in circles Alex only read about in *People* magazine or in the entertainment section of the newspaper. Nickolas knew actors, rock stars, and clothing designers. His company, ProStar, was quickly becoming as well-known in Europe as Nike, Reebok, or Adidas.

Alex was aware that Nickolas also had a reputation as a ladies man. He'd been linked with many young American models and actresses, as well as some international celebrities. Alex supposed she should be overwhelmed that he would even notice her, but she wasn't. True, he was extremely good-looking and very classy. He was very Italian with his olive complexion, thick, black hair, and dark eyes. He carried his tall, regal frame with the sophistication of an Italian Cary Grant, and he had a charming, witty sense of humor. But he wasn't her type. Or maybe it was more accurate to say, she wasn't his type. She didn't want to be his type. Life in the fast lane didn't appeal to Alex; she wasn't designed to be a jet-setter. Her mother, on the other hand, would kill for a chance to hobnob with Nickolas and his friends, but not Alex. She was more of a homebody, and she was content with that.

Lost in her thoughts, Alex hardly noticed that the plane was starting its descent. She grasped the arm rests on either side of her and hung on as the plane lowered toward the runway. Clenching her eyes shut, she braced herself for the landing. There was a bump and a jolt, but the plane set down gently on its wheels and slowed rapidly.

When the plane came to a stop, Alex breathed a sigh of relief and realized for the first time that her life was going to be quite different from what she was used to. Two months of being treated like a queen might be interesting, and perhaps even a little fun.

* * *

"Buon giorno, Signorina McCarty." The driver of a gleaming white stretch limousine approached her as she exited the doors of the airport.

"How do you know my name?" she asked, a bit startled the man knew her right off.

"Signor Diamante, he gives me a picture. You see?" The driver held up a glossy publicity photograph of Alex from when she did a Nike ad a year ago.

Alex laughed. "How could you tell that was me? I'm wearing a hat and jogging on the beach."

"Oh, Signor Diamante, he tell me you are the most beautiful woman at the airport. Also," he leaned in closer to her, "I recognize the bag."

Alex lifted the European Supertour bag up for both of them to see, and they laughed.

"*Per favors,*" he said, opening the door to back seat, "I will take you to your hotel now."

"Uh, *gracie,*" she said, proudly remembering the Italian word for "thank you."

She slid into the back of the limousine, sat primly on the edge of the fawn-colored leather bench seat, and looked around her. She saw a TV/VCR on the ceiling, wet bar, telephone, fax machine, laptop-sized computer, and several dozen buttons on a control panel before her.

"Would you like something to drink, Signorina McCarty?" the driver asked over the speaker.

"Thank you, no. I'm fine," she said, trying to see the driver in front. Finally she located part of his reflection in the rearview mirror ahead of her through the privacy glass.

"Then we go. My name is Tony. If you need anything, you push the blue button and talk. I hear you, okay?"

"Okay."

"I show you now our beautiful city on the way. Please put on your seat belt."

No sooner did she have on her seat belt than she was laid back in her seat with all the G-force of a Lear jet. Gripping the arm rests on her seat for dear life, she held her breath, anticipating the jolt of impact with another car and the sound of crashing metal. But the car kept moving, and slowly she dared to open her eyes and look out the windows.

"I give you some nice music," Tony said. As he negotiated a congested intersection, honking and swerving through the traffic that swarmed with motorcycles, mopeds and other scooters, he turned on some instrumental tunes with a rhythmic Mediterranean flare.

As they continued driving, she realized that Tony wasn't going to apologize for the way he was driving, nor the state of the busy roads and chaotic flow of traffic, because this was normal. They flew down open passageways, screeched around corners, and weaved in and out of cars. Tony honked and gestured each time he had to slam on the brakes, and even through the privacy glass, she heard him holler and vent his frustrations.

After twenty minutes had passed, Alex pushed the blue button and said, "Excuse me, Tony, are we in a hurry?"

"Prego?" he said, "In a hurry?"

"Yes, you seem to be driving quite fast."

"Oh, I see. No hurry. This is Roma. Many cars, much speed." Even as he spoke, he blasted the horn and changed lanes. She noticed how he frequently added "a's" to his words and how smoothly he rolled his "r's".

"You would like a drink now?" he said.

Now she understood why he'd offered her one in the first place. Maybe with some alcohol in her system, she'd be so relaxed she wouldn't notice or care how he was driving. She shook her head, declining his offer.

"So," he said, "To the left we pass-a the Palatine. It is the oldest part of the city. There are many imperial palaces built there."

Tony raced toward an intersection, but a small Fiat pulled in front of him and the light changed. With a long blare from his horn and a string of words, the tone of which made Alex grateful she didn't understand Italian, Tony brought the car to a halt. Herds of motorcycles and scooters crowded between the cars, inching their way to the front of the line like racehorses at the starting gate.

As a chorus of car horns joined with Tony's, the phone in front of Alex rang.

After another ring, Tony said, "She's-a for you."

"Oh." Alex picked up the phone. "Hello."

"Alexis, you are here?"

"Nickolas?"

"Yes, it is me. I'm so happy you arrived safely. How was your flight?"

A whole lot smoother than this car ride, she wanted to say. "It was fine."

"Good. Good. You must be exhausted and hungry. Tony will take you to your hotel where you can have some food and rest. Then he will pick you up at thirteen hours—I mean, one o'clock, and bring you to my office."

With the phone pressed to her ear, she felt one of the diamond earrings, which reminded her to thank him. "Nickolas, the earrings are beautiful. And the clothes. How can I thank you?"

"No, Alexis. How can I thank you for coming to Europe? It is my pleasure."

"But *diamonds?*"

"Please," he said, "do not fuss. They are nothing compared to knowing I will see you in a few short hours and we will be able to spend much time together over the next two months."

She wondered why he said things like that. Was that the way all handsome, single, wealthy Italian men were?

"Are the others here?"

"Ricky arrives later this morning, but the others are in Roma."

"I read through the itinerary. Our first convention is in three days?"

"Yes. I hope that is enough time to work off the jet lag and coordinate the presentation."

She heard a short buzz on Nickolas's end, then he said, "Please excuse me. I must take this call. We will talk later, *si?*"

"*Si,*" she echoed.

"*Ciao,* Alexis."

"*Ciao,* Nickolas."

She hadn't noticed the car had started moving again. The whirlwind tour of Rome continued.

"Here," Tony said, "is the famous Colosseum. Signor Diamante has arranged for a private tour tomorrow to take you to some of these sights."

"Are we going to the Vatican City, too?"

"Yes, of course. And many other places."

As they passed the Colosseum, the breathtaking amphitheater with its four stories of archways and crumbling stone, Alex felt an overwhelming sense of wonder that the structure was actually nineteen centuries old. Tony told her it was built in A.D. 72 and was used for gladiatorial combats and fights with wild beasts.

From this point on, her head never stopped turning from side to side. If there wasn't a dome or cathedral on her left, there was a fountain or a statue to her right. Every corner, every building seemed to have some significant structure or masterpiece to its credit. The city was stunning and beautiful, set against a backdrop of lush green grounds and tall palm trees.

Tony sounded the horn, and the car's tires complained as they skidded to a stop. "This road, she's-a very busy. Five streets end up right here. All the cars in hurry," he said. "Here we pass the Piazza Vittorio Emmanuel and Piazza Venezia," Tony announced.

To her left, Alex saw an enormous, white-columned building with a statue of a man on a horse in the front. Even in a New York cab, Alex had never felt such anxiety riding in a car. She bounced around the back seat like a volleyball at a spring break beach party. Then, without further incidence, the car pulled up beside a curb and stopped.

"We are here," he said, "the Ambasciatori Palace."

She leaned toward the window and looked out at the classical styled building, with arched, stone portals and Grecian-type statues along the curb, holding up a canvas awning.

It didn't look like much from the outside, but when she stepped inside, she truly felt she was in a palace. Plush burgundy carpets with green marbled floors spread out before her. Matching drapes trimmed with gold piping and tassels adorned the room. The furniture, in green-palmed print, was sleek and elegant. An enormous, brilliantly lit chandelier hung overhead, crowning the room in regal fashion.

Tony checked her in, paid the bell boy in advance, and tipped his hat as he bid her farewell until one o'clock when he would return to take her to Nickolas's office.

Her hotel room was beautifully decorated, with similar colors and styles to the main lobby, but the most appealing aspect about it was the balcony off the back. She opened the hinged door and stepped outside, and stood in awe at the beauty before her.

From a distance the city seemed suspended in time. Hundreds of domes and arched chapels and basilicas, columned facades and towers, mingled with red clay-roofed buildings. It was a sight only seen on postcards and in movies. And she was there, in real life, breathing the spicy, rich smells, feeling the balmy Mediterranean climate, hearing the sounds of the enormous city, and seeing sights that were a mixture of historical significance and contemporary beauty.

It only took several minutes for the lack of sleep to catch up with her as she basked in the heat and brilliance of the day. Feeling the heaviness of jet lag in her arms and legs, Alex dragged herself back inside, kicked off her shoes, and collapsed in an exhausted heap on the bed.

Sleep was quick in coming, but not before her mind hit rewind, allowing her to view the last scene with Rich—the strange look on his face and the urgency as he tried to yell over the crowd of passengers. But that seemed like forever ago, and she was so, so tired.

* * *

She wanted the ringing to stop. Her cocoon of sleep was too comfy to break out of. But the phone rang on.

Forcing one eye to open, Alex realized she was literally wet with sweat. Her hair was damp, her clothes were laminated to her skin, and her head throbbed.

Knocking the receiver off the hook, Alex finally grasped the phone and said, "H'lo."

"Alexis? Is that you?"

"Yeah." Her eyes had drifted shut again.

"Are you okay? You don't sound well."

"I'm fine, Nickolas," she yawned. "I'm just sleepy."

"Nickolas?! Alex, this is Rich."

His voice and name registered with a zing through the thick fog in her head.

"Rich! What are you doing?"

"We were all wondering if you made it there."

She pushed herself upright and managed to keep her eyes open as she unbuttoned her shirt and peeled it off. It had to be over a hundred degrees inside her room.

"The flight went fine. I was just taking a nap. What time is it?"

"It's almost one in the morning. I'm sorry. Do you want me to call back later?"

"No, of course not." She pulled the phone with her across the room to the balcony door and shut it tightly, then bumped up the air conditioner.

"Why are you up so late?" she asked.

"We've had a bit of a challenge since you left."

"What?" She was awake now. "Is someone sick? Has someone gotten hurt?"

"No, everyone's fine, but there was a fire at Recreation Headquarters. It's a complete loss. No one got hurt, but by the time the fire trucks got there, the whole place was in flames."

Alex was stunned speechless.

"The worst was over by the time I got back from Salt Lake City. Luckily, Steve wasn't at work when the fire broke out."

"Rich, I just can't believe this. Do they know how it started?"

"The detective thought it was electrical, something with the wiring, but they aren't sure yet."

"This is terrible. Was anything left?"

"Nope, not even a pup tent to spare."

"What's going to happen now?"

"We need to meet with the insurance company and check our policy."

"I don't know what to say. I'm so sorry this happened. Are you going to rebuild and start over?"

"We haven't talked about it yet. But you don't need to worry, it will all work out. We just thought you should know."

"I'm so glad you called. I just wish there was something I could do."

"Right now there's nothing. Even if you were here, you couldn't really do much. We all stand around wondering what to do." She could hear the others talking in the background. "So, how's Rome?"

"Beautiful, crazy, hot." A light air current moved across her bare arms.

"I guess you're pretty tired?"

"I didn't sleep much on the plane. It gave me a lot of time to think about you."

"Oh?"

Was that surprise or delight in his voice? "Yes, I love the bracelet you gave me. It's beautiful and so thoughtful. I can't wait to add more charms."

"I didn't know what to get you."

"You didn't need to get me anything."

"I wanted you to know I'd miss you." *Was that actually a hint of caring she detected in his voice?*

"I miss you, too."

"Hey," Rich said, "there's someone else here who wants to talk to you."

"Wait—" She wasn't through talking to him.

"Alex, are you there?" Jamie said anxiously.

"Hi, Jamie," Alex said, still disappointed that Rich disengaged so abruptly.

"Oh, it's so good to hear your voice," Jamie exclaimed.

"It's good to hear yours, too," Alex said, wishing she could fly through the phone cable and be right there beside her. "How are you holding up?"

"Well, we're still pretty shook up about the fire. But we'll manage." Jamie's words were brave, but her voice betrayed her. Alex could tell that her sister was tired and under a lot of stress. "I don't want you worrying about it," she continued. "Steve was just saying maybe this is the Lord's way of telling him it's time to move on to something else. You know how many ideas for new ventures Steve always has."

"Oh, yeah," Alex agreed. "How's Andrea Nicole?"

"She misses you. But she's doing great," Jaime said wistfully.

"I miss her, too. How's Mom?" Alex breathed in some of the fresh, cool air finally circulating through the room.

"She's fine. She's going to Sun Valley tomorrow with Dr. Rawlins."

"Sun Valley?"

"She wanted to see about doing an article for the magazine about it. She's turned herself into their travel correspondent. She's supposed to go back to New York in a few weeks and wants to have the story ready by then."

"I'm glad she's having so much fun."

"Yeah, me too. Keep your fingers crossed for those two. But how are you? What's Rome like?"

"It's interesting. I'll know more tomorrow after we go on a tour of the city. But so far I've noticed that all the drivers act like they're in some kind of Indy 500 without rules, and it's hotter than Steve's homemade ten-pepper salsa. But there are some incredible sights, and I can't believe I'm really here."

"Will you be able to call sometimes?"

"I'll call every chance I get, especially when I reach a new city or anything exciting happens."

"Hold on just a minute . . ." Alex could tell Jamie muted the phone. "Okay, I'm back. I wanted to see if Rich had gone outside with Steve or not."

"Why?"

"What happened at the airport? Rich came home and acts like he can't get back to Utah fast enough."

"Utah? Why, what's he doing?"

"He helped out with the fire and everything, then went home and got packed. He's heading down to Park City first thing in the morning. He came over to tell us good-bye."

Why hadn't he said something to her? "Why so soon? I thought he wasn't leaving for a week."

"That's what I wanted to ask you. Did something happen between you two?"

"No, not really. I don't know. I can't seem to read him anymore. Sometimes I see something in his eyes, like maybe he really does love me. Heck, I don't know. Did he say anything?"

"No, nothing. Just that you seemed excited about the trip and that he needed to get to Park City right away. The way he talks and acts, it's like he's not coming back."

What was going on? "Jamie, will you do me a favor?"

"Sure. Anything."

"Tell him . . ." she stopped and thought about it, "tell him . . . oh never mind. Don't tell him anything."

"Are you sure?"

"I'm sure."

"All right. I'd better go before Steve kills me. He's already worried about the phone bills this trip is going to cost us."

"Thanks for calling."

"Take care, sis. Love you."

"Love you, too."

Alex hung up the phone with a frustrated bang. The man was infuriating. Even if she loved him, she needed to rethink their relationship. Maybe she didn't want to get serious with a guy who couldn't express his feelings. What would he be like after they got married? It would be awful trying to guess how one's spouse felt, what he thought, why he did what he did. It would never work.

The thought came again even stronger. It would never work.

Was this the reality she needed to face? Was it possible to love someone as much as she loved Rich and not be able to have a future with him?

The feelings she had for Rich were too strong for just a casual relationship. She wanted a future, a commitment. He didn't.

It was true. The way things were right now . . . it would never work.

Chapter 23

When Alex was ready, Tony drove her to a building not far from her hotel. Alex stepped out onto the awning-covered curb and was greeted by a doorman. He led her inside the building to the lobby of the office building. The decorations reminded her of a Grecian palace with its gold-leafed picture frames, gilded urns, tall indoor palms, mossy greens, and naked statues.

The elevator dinged and Alex smiled at the elevator operator, a middle-aged man in a bold red jacket, black pants and a pill-box cap on his head. He had salt and pepper sprinkled hair and an olive complexion. He smiled a great deal and spoke in two-word sentences, such as, "Which floor?" and "Very good."

The elevator rose to the twenty-third floor then stopped.

Alex stepped out into another foyer, this one identical to the lobby except for the marble floors and floor-to-ceiling windows. A receptionist stepped from behind her desk and approached Alex.

"You must be Ms. McCarty," she said, repositioning a thick pair of glasses on her nose.

"Yes, I am."

"Signor Diamante is expecting you. Please follow me."

The woman wore a simple gray-knit dress with short sleeves and a black belt. Her hair was pulled back and pinned. She looked like a very professional secretary. Alex had expected a platinum blonde, wearing a short skirt, low-cut blouse, and stiletto heels.

The nerves in her stomach knotted as she followed the woman down a hallway until she stopped and tapped on a door. She hadn't seen Nickolas for a long time.

"Yes," came the reply.

"Ms. McCarty, Signor."

"Come in, *per favors.*"

They stepped through the door into a vast corner office with the same picture windows, a beautiful view of Rome spreading out as far as the eye could see. Right away Alex noticed the Colosseum in the distance. The view took her breath away. And she didn't get it back when she saw Nickolas.

He was just finishing a conversation on the telephone. The receptionist left the room, allowing Alex to drink in her surroundings and calm herself.

Nickolas lifted one finger and mouthed, "Just one moment," then dazzled her with a smile.

Alex had only seen Nickolas at the fitness conventions in New York and San Diego, wearing double-breasted suits, carrying a briefcase. Today he was dressed in a white polo shirt, khaki slacks that hung like they were tailor-made, which they probably were, and soft leather loafers. He looked like he was ready for an afternoon at the country club, taking in a round of golf or sitting on a veranda drinking lemonade.

Nickolas was probably in his mid-thirties, the hair at his temples showing just a hint of gray, but he still had the build of an athlete, tall and lean, toned and muscular. She knew he still skied avidly and biked competitively. The man looked as fit as a twenty-year-old.

"*Si, si,*" he said. "*Arrivederci,* Leonardo." He hung up the phone. Taking a long look at Alex, he smiled and rushed over to her.

"Alexis, you look wonderful." He kissed her on both cheeks, then pulled back and lifted her right hand and kissed her knuckles. "Welcome to Roma."

She liked how he pronounced the city's name so lyrically.

"I've looked forward to seeing you again for a long time," he said.

She couldn't help but smile back at him. The man was pure class, as handsome as one of Michelangelo's statues, and as warm as a Roman summer.

"How long has it been since I've seen you?" he asked, his eyes gazing intensely into hers.

Alex couldn't help feeling flattered by his obviously heartfelt welcome. "A year next month," she replied.

"You look even more beautiful than ever. And I've kept track of you, Alexis." He motioned for her to sit in a white leather armchair. "You've been busy."

"Yes, I have."

"An ESPN series, a best-selling workout video, a soon-to-be-released cookbook, magazine articles. I was flattered you would fit me into your busy schedule."

"Your timing was perfect. I was between projects. And who could resist your offer?"

"Actually, no one," he smiled with assurance. "I only asked a very select few to join the tour, and they all accepted."

"I don't blame them." She crossed her legs and noticed Nickolas watching her. She pulled at the hem of her beige linen walking shorts and continued, "It's a wonderful opportunity. In fact," she sat up straighter and uncrossed her legs, "where are the others?"

"They will be here shortly. I wanted a moment with you to myself before the others joined us."

"Oh?" She raised her eyebrows curiously.

"I want to talk to you about a business proposition, and I'd like to give you plenty of time to think about it."

What kind of business proposition could he want with her?

"I am about to start construction on the biggest, most technologically advanced health club in Manhattan, no, in all of New York—or perhaps even, all of America."

"Really?" Alex asked. *This was interesting.*

"We've located an abandoned warehouse right off Times Square. It's a perfect location and size for our club. It will have the most advanced, state-of-the-art equipment and will cater to the most elite clientele the city has to offer."

"That's wonderful, Nickolas, congratulations. But what has this got to do with me?"

"I am prepared to offer you a position as director of the aerobic program, and I would like to put you under contract as the new spokesperson for ProStar shoes and athletic wear."

"Me? What about that Russian gymnast you had as your spokesperson?"

"Her contract will be up in January, and we want to broaden our market. We've done well here in Europe, but we want to target North America next. We're ready to launch the biggest promotion ever. We have Robbie Tyler, from the Bulls, but we need a female counterpart. Someone the Americans look up to, someone they can relate to, someone they already love."

"You think that's me?" Alex said with a laugh, motioning to herself.

"My research staff has done marketing surveys and dozens of field studies to find out who the hottest new fitness star is in your country. You're in the top ten and, to be honest, the other nine don't interest me."

"Nickolas, I'm flattered but—"

He reached over and placed one of his fingers on her lips. "But nothing. Please do not answer me until you've had plenty of time to think about it. I realize this means you would have to move to New York."

She'd already been considering moving back to New York to be near her mom.

"I also realize this means you would be tied down a little more than usual, but with some good assistants and a top-notch staff, you would be free to travel as much as you'd like."

Actually, she'd been wanting to cut back on her traveling.

"I am prepared to offer you a complete package that would cover all your moving expenses, and also provide you with a company car, a penthouse overlooking Central Park, a sizable signing bonus and a six-figure salary. That's just for your job as director at the new club. There would be a completely different contract with Prostar we would have to negotiate."

Alex was nearly speechless. "I don't know what to say."

"You must take your time and think about it. There is no hurry. But I wanted to talk to you before you renewed your contract with Nike."

Her Nike contract ended in October. Nickolas's research committee had definitely done their homework.

"Having you in New York would keep you much closer to Europe, which I would be very excited about; I want to get you involved in our international business as much as I can. I need someone from the United States to come to my clubs here, as a consultant, and help get our programs together. We're doing quite well but your American gyms are much better."

Alex's hands were tingling, her spine shivered with excitement. With an offer like this, she wouldn't have to work so hard to build her career; he was handing it to her on a silver platter—actually a diamond platter. A "Diamante" diamond platter.

The buzzer on his phone interrupted his sales pitch.

"I will only be a moment." He answered the phone. *"Gracie, Francesca."* He turned to Alex and said, "The others are here. Would you mind if we talk about this later?"

"Not at all."

She remained in her seat as he went to his door to greet the other guests.

What he was offering her was much better than what she was doing now. To run a program and be able to consult with other health clubs on their programs would be a perfect job situation. Was this the reason she needed to come on this trip? To get away from Rich so she could finally open her eyes and see that her love was wasted on him? So she could realize that no matter how much she cared for him, there was no future for them because he didn't want one?

Perhaps this job offer was a blessing in disguise.

* * *

Alex felt immediately comfortable with the two other girls, Gabriella and Julianne. The men, Wes, J.J., and Ricky were going to be fun to work with, too. Ricky was from Venezuela, fun and full of energy. J.J. was totally out of control—funny, crazy, and a riot to be around. He stood out in every crowd, not because of his dark skin color, but because he was so animated. Wes didn't say much, but his presence had a definite impact. He was a big name in Canada, not only for his fitness exposure—he'd won every national body-building competition—but he also acted in popular action movies. Kind of a Canadian Arnold Schwarzenegger, Alex thought to herself. He was handsome, buffed, and very concerned about his image. If there was a mirror in the room, Wes checked his reflection several times.

After the brief meeting, the men and women went to separate rooms where they would receive their "costumes" for the tour. They were excited to get all new workout wear since top European designers had an input on all ProStar creations.

"I've been on vacation for two weeks," Julianne said as they walked off the elevator. "I've put on extra pounds in all the wrong places. I hope they have a lot of black leotards."

"You can afford to put on a few pounds," Gabi replied, then turned to Alex. "So could you. You're both too thin."

Julianne put her arm around Alex and said in her proper English accent, "Alexis looks great just the way she is, Gabi. Besides, we're here, not because of how we look but because of our knowledge."

"*Naja,*" Gabi said, "I suppose so. There's a water fountain. I need a drink. Wait for me."

Gabi crossed the room and Alex seized the opportunity, "Thanks, Julianne. I didn't know what to say."

"I read about your eating disorder in a couple of newsletters," Julianne said. "I hope you're doing okay." Her concern appeared truly sincere.

"Thanks," Alex nodded. "I am. I just wish those publications would have given me a chance to share my story when I was ready. I swear they're as bad as some of those tabloids when it comes to someone's personal life."

"Actually, I was grateful to know that you'd had this problem and have been able to overcome it. You know, I mean," she stammered, "for all those woman out there who have eating disorders. I'm sure it helped them."

Alex shrugged. "I hope so."

"I'm sure Gabi didn't know about your anorexia or she wouldn't have said anything. She really is a nice person," Julianne said in Gabi's behalf.

"I know," Alex said mildly. "I wasn't offended."

"Good. Because I want us to have fun. We're going to be together for a long time."

"So," Gabi said as she rejoined them, "where do we go now?"

"Someone is supposed to meet us here and help with the fittings," Alex said.

"Does Signor Diamante own this whole building?" Julianne asked.

"He probably owns all the buildings on this whole street. He has a huge investment and development corporation besides the family jewelry business he owns. He has fifteen or sixteen health facilities throughout Europe and he's also the owner of ProStar Shoes and Athletic Wear. The man is a billionaire," Gabi told them. "Supposedly he even has Mafia affiliations. He's a very powerful man."

"How do you know all this?" Alex was skeptical.

"Most of the information comes from articles about him in different business magazines. Plus, I am a personal trainer at his gym in Frankfurt, and we hear all about Signor Diamante. He's a very generous man, but . . ." she dropped her voice to a whisper, ". . . I feel I should warn you . . . Signor Diamante is a very big, a— how you say—'ladies' man.' He's made headlines with some very royal women, from Britain and from Monaco. He likes women like you—tall, thin, beautiful—very much. You must be careful. I have seen him with many women and heard about all of his affairs."

"Gabi," Julianne said, "We are professionals, here on business, and he's a very busy man. I doubt we'll be spending much time with him or even see much of the man anyway."

"Perhaps, but I have seen him with the women. He's very . . . uh . . . ," she thought a moment, "persuasive, I think you would say."

Alex didn't see a point to continuing the conversation. Julianne was right. This was a business relationship and they were professionals. Besides, Signor Diamante had been nothing but a complete gentleman when he was around her. Maybe Gabi was a little jealous because she wasn't his type and wanted to be.

Changing the topic, Julianne asked, "Speaking of Signor Diamante, did he give you a pair of earrings just for coming on the tour?" Julianne asked.

Alex opened her mouth to say, "yes," but Gabi jumped in first. "See. I told you, he's very generous. Look," she pulled back her honey blonde hair on one side and exposed a gold stud earring with a small diamond chip in it. "I put them on right away."

"They're just like mine," Julianne said. With her short cropped brown hair, Julianne's earrings were just right. The problem was, Alex didn't get gold and diamond studs. Hers looked liked cubes of ice compared to their tiny diamond chips.

"What about you, Alex?" Julianne asked. "You got some, didn't you?"

"Oh, yes, I got some, too," she said vaguely.

"Thank goodness," Julianne said. "I would have felt terrible if he hadn't given us all a pair."

"*Buon giorno,* ladies." A woman met them at the door. She had on a light blue apron with a measuring tape around her neck, scissors and patterns in her pockets, and straight pins threaded through the apron fabric. "You are here for a fitting, no?"

"We are here for a fitting, yes," Gabi said.

"Good, good. Then follow me please."

She took them to a back room where there was a curtain for them to change behind.

"Gabrielle, these are for you." The woman handed Gabi a pile of sports bras, t-shirts, bike-length shorts, and warm-up clothes.

"And these are for you." She did the same for Julianne.

"And these," she scooped up a pile of clothes off the table for Alex, "are for you."

The girls took their outfits and stepped behind the individual curtains.

Since Gabi's expertise was in the field of exercise physiology and her focus was on personal training and body building, her outfits were more functional, a lot of shorts, tank tops, and jackets. Her style of dress was very athletic and outdoorsy.

Julianne had ensembles of tights—ankle length, biking length, and even shorter. There were matching leotards, all in blacks, heather grays, and navy, as well as some reds and whites. Julianne was a bit more of a refined dresser, lined slacks, silk shirts, light sweaters under blazers—classy but very crisp and fresh. Very British. But when it came to workout gear and working out, she was funky and hip and was responsible for a lot of trendsetting ideas in the fitness industry.

Alex wasn't comfortable with a lot of her outfits. She liked the leggings and leotards in deep purples, forest greens, and charcoal greys, but there were too many short-shorts, bra tops, and midriff-baring ensembles. Never feeling quite comfortable with her body, she had never worn revealing clothes. And now that she'd joined the Church she wanted to be more careful how she presented herself.

"Julianne," she whispered from behind the curtain that separated them.

"Yes." Julianne stepped closer to her.

"I'm not interested in wearing these. Do you want them?"

Julianne peeked her head through the curtain where Alex was holding up an array of colored sports bras.

"Sure. Those colors are great. Hey, I've got a couple of things I know I won't wear." She handed Alex several leotards and said, "I'm glad we're the same size."

"You can wear anything of mine you want."

"Thanks. I just wish we could have some new shoes. The ones I brought are worn out but I didn't have time to buy any before I came," Julianne said. "Maybe we can go shopping while we're here and find some. Would you want to go with me?"

"Are you kidding? Shopping for shoes in Italy?! This is a dream come true. I love Italian shoes. And I have a couple of new pairs of aerobic shoes if you want to try them until you can get some new ones."

"That would be great. Thanks. I never did have a sister to share clothes with."

"Hey, that reminds me." Alex tucked her white silk blouse into her shorts and fastened the belt at her waist. "I met your cousin in Salt Lake City."

"You did?" Julianne slipped over to Alex's side of the curtain when she noticed she was dressed. "Which one?" Julianne held one of the tops up to her chest and looked at her reflection in the mirror.

"The one on a mission for the Mormon church. I didn't catch her first name, but we talked and she said you were related."

"Oh, that's Sydney. Her whole family became Mormons a few years ago. Nearly gave my grandmother a stroke when they did. They aren't as fanatic as I thought they'd be. My mom and dad were really worried when they got baptized. You wouldn't believe some of the crazy things those Mormons believe. Did you know they can have more than one wife?"

Now was her chance to help change a misconception. The experience in California had helped her prepare for opportunities like this.

"Actually, I know for a fact that's not true."

"How do you know?"

"I'm a Mormon."

"What?" Julianne laughed out loud. "You, Alexis?"

Alex looked at her friend directly. "I got baptized three weeks ago," she said proudly.

"Wow!" Julianne stopped laughing, and her forehead creased with curiosity. "Why did you do it?"

"Because I believed its teachings," Alex answered frankly, "and the gospel answered all my questions." Alex paused for a moment then said, "I know it sounds weird, but I just felt like my life was lacking."

"*Your* life was lacking? You have everything you could ever want—you're beautiful, famous, respected . . ."

"And I'm grateful for all the things I have, but it wasn't enough. I don't really know how to explain it except that I just didn't know anymore why I was knocking myself out, day after day. I wasn't sure what the whole point was. I guess I just wasn't fulfilled anymore."

"Yeah, sometimes I feel that way."

"Finding the gospel gave me the strength to face a lot of challenges in my life, mainly my eating disorder. And that's how I know I'll never do that to my body again. Believe me, I still struggle. It's easy to fall back into old habits." As Alex explained, Julianne tilted her head to the side, listening intently. "But I understand the bigger picture now. This life, what we're doing on this earth, isn't all there is. There's so much more."

"You really do believe this, don't you?" Julianne asked, intrigued.

"With all my heart," Alex said fervently. "It's the best thing that's ever happened to me."

"Then I'm very happy for you, and I'm proud of Sydney for going on a mission. I thought she was crazy when she told me she was leaving for eighteen months to teach others about her church, but if she can help people find a purpose in life, then I'm happy she's doing it."

"Ladies, ladies," the clothing coordinator said, "Signor Diamante would like you to join him in his office in fifteen minutes. Does everything fit?"

"Everything's great," Alex said, walking from behind the dressing area with Julianne. She wished she could have continued her conversation with her friend, but they would have other chances to talk about the gospel.

"I have a bag for you to put your things in so you can take them with you."

"Thank you," Julianne said.

They quickly stashed their new workout wardrobe into their bags and headed for the door. "Wait, where's Gabi?" Alex asked.

"She said she didn't need to try on her clothes," the coordinator said. "She's gone to find something to eat. She was hungry."

"I guess we'll see her upstairs then."

"First, you need to go to the room next door. Sergio is waiting to fit you into some shoes."

"We get shoes, too?" Julianne said, nudging Alex with her elbow.

"Certainly. They are waiting for you now."

When the girls stepped outside the fitting room, they dissolved into laughter.

"I love this. Good ol' Nickolas. He's thought of everything, hasn't he?" Julianne said.

"I'm starting to feel a little guilty with all his gifts and things."

"Remember what Gabi said? He's very generous."

"I guess so. But earrings, flowers at the airport—"

"I didn't get flowers at the airport," Julianne said. "Neither did Gabi."

"Oh." Alex wished she hadn't said anything. What was Nickolas up to? Especially his interesting comment on the card. Then she had a thought that sickened her. She'd left the card in the flowers when she gave them to Rich. He wouldn't have read it, would he?

"You got flowers? What kind of flowers?" Julianne was asking.

Alex hesitated before answering, wondering what she could say to play down the issue. "They were roses, but I'm sure it was just an oversight. Perhaps his secretary sent them to the wrong gate, or the people at the airport forgot to give them to you."

"Maybe," Julianne said thoughtfully. "But it's still odd that neither Gabi nor I got them."

Alex's stomach churned at the thought that Rich might have read the card. She tried to reason with herself that he wasn't the nosy, suspicious type. If he did happen to see the card, he probably thought nothing of it, she told herself, and pushed the thought out of her mind. There was nothing she could do about it now.

Refusing to worry about Rich one more instant, Alex turned to Julianne and asked, "What do you think about what Gabi was telling us about Signor Diamante?"

"That he's a ladies' man?"

Alex nodded.

"Is there an Italian man who's not? I think it's a bunch of rot. She's probably just jealous because he hasn't paid her any special attention. Let's face it, she's practically a female version of Hercules. I don't know if I believe all that other stuff. Besides, what difference does it make to us?"

Alex shrugged. It didn't make any difference, really. Alex decided to shift the conversation to a more comfortable topic. "He did a wonderful job pulling our team together, didn't he?"

Julianne agreed. "Gabi is the best in her field at personal training, incorporating resistance and weight training into aerobic classes. But then, one look at those biceps of hers and you know she's doing something right. Of course, everyone knows Wes Griffith, and he and Gabi will work well together. Which I'm glad about," she said. "He's just a bit too much for me. If you know what I mean."

Alex hadn't spent much time around Wes. He seemed nice enough, though the brief time they had spent together in Nickolas's office today told her that his good looks and fame had gone to his head.

"J.J.'s got funk taken care of and a lot of the trendy, new moves like hip-hop and salsa," Julianne continued, "and Ricky's going to be doing boxing and sports moves. I think he's going to cover spinning classes as well. I'm going to present mostly choreography classes. I've been working on methods of starting with simple moves and changing them into higher intensity, more choreographed complex moves. And I was under the impression you're going to work on adding intensity through intervals, and where possible, present water aerobic and nutrition workshops."

Taking a good look at the lineup, Alex relaxed. Nickolas' motive was simply to create a strong group of fitness presenters to represent his European-sponsored tour. Even though his attention seemed a bit slanted in her direction, he was just doing business the only way he knew how. The Italian way. With charm, generosity, and warmth. Why would anyone complain? When they stepped into the next room, Gabi was getting fitted for shoes, and at the same time, eating an Italian calzone, which looked like a pocket of pizza filled with cheese and meat.

After deciding on four pairs of shoes each, they returned to Nickolas's office, where again, they found him on the phone.

He motioned for them to have a seat and continued his conversation.

"I heard he was an Olympic medalist," Julianne whispered to Alex, who nodded.

"He's very handsome, don't you think?" Julianne added. Alex nodded again, then couldn't help but notice how her friend crossed one of her long, shapely legs and angled herself just a little more toward Nickolas's direction. Julianne's background was ballet, and she had the kind of legs that would easily attract any man's attention.

Gabi and Wes were talking weightlifting, Ricky was reading an American sports magazine, and J.J. was slumped down in his chair, his head resting on the back of the seat. If they sat there much longer, Alex was afraid she too would start snoozing.

Nickolas finished his conversation and hung up the phone. "So," he said, "I apologize for the phone calls. I'm trying to clear my schedule so I can make myself available for much of the tour. You've all received your clothing and shoes?"

The group answered enthusiastically.

"Do you have any questions about the convention on Friday?" he asked them.

"How many people you expectin'?" J.J. asked.

"We have over two hundred and fifty registered but expect to see fifty to one hundred more at the door. The convention center is big enough to allow us to run two classes at one time. We will begin promptly at eight o'clock, after registration is completed.

"There will be booths with fitness and nutrition products operating the entire time. We have a special booth set aside for each of your personal fitness products. Gabi, if you have time to go over to the booth and answer questions about your AbMaster and demonstrate it for the participants, I think it will help boost your sales.

"It's almost four o'clock now. There's plenty of time before dinner to rest or shop or even see some of the sights nearby. We have dinner reservations at the Apollo Club at seven. It is a black tie establishment, so I ask that you leave the sneakers in your hotel room. If you haven't anything suitable to wear, my secretary, Francesca, will locate something for you."

Alex thought about Nickolas's job offer and wondered what it would be like to work for such a man. She admired his confidence and no-nonsense authority, and how he still managed to make a person feel needed and important. He was direct, organized, and obviously highly motivated and disciplined. Seeing this side of him made her respect him even more.

"So," he said with a smile and a hint of an accent as he came around to the front of the desk, "is there anything else we can do for you? Are your accommodations acceptable?"

"Yeah, like, this place is dyn-o-mite," J.J. said. "I haven't seen this kind of service in my whole life. One question though, Signor Diamante, my man. Do you care if we eat some of the food out of that little refrigerator in our room?"

The group laughed.

J.J. had grown up in Atlanta. He looked tough on the outside, with his bald head, baggy clothes, and street-slang, but Alex had never met anyone nicer. Everyone knew when J.J. was in "da house" because the whole place came alive.

"Help yourself, J.J., and please, call me Nickolas. Feel free to order room service, or ask Tony, your driver, to take you anywhere in the city. He would be more than happy to do so."

"My driver?" J.J. said. "Man, I love this job."

"You're all staying at the Ambasciatori Palace, so Tony can take you there now, or anywhere else you'd like to go. He'll be outside your hotel at 6:45 to pick you up for dinner. One word of warning. If you do go out into the city, please watch out for pickpockets and gypsies. I would hate to see you lose your wallets and money, or any valuables while in our city. So, if there are no further questions, I will see you all later."

"I'd better get talkin' to that Francesca about some different duds to wear to dinner," J.J. said as they started for the door. "I didn't bring no fancy tux-e-do with me."

Alex laughed at how animatedly J.J. spoke, emphasizing certain words and using his whole body to carry his messages.

"Alexis, do you have a moment?" Nickolas said.

"I'll be right there," she told the others then walked back to the desk where Nickolas waited.

"I took the liberty of having something sent to your room for this evening. Please do not feel obligated to wear it, but I would be honored if you would."

"Nickolas, thank you. You didn't need to do that."

"But you see, my dear Alexis," he said, taking both her hands in his, "I'm trying desperately to persuade you to accept my earlier offers. You will allow me the pleasure of indulging you, no?"

He was almost boyish in his mannerism, yet so completely charming and sophisticated. If charisma had an icon, she thought, it would be Nickolas Diamante.

The intercom on his phone buzzed.

"I look forward to seeing you this evening," he said, lifting her hand and placing a gentle kiss on her knuckles.

Rich or no Rich, she couldn't help being captivated by this man. Never in her life had she ever encountered anyone like Nickolas. She regarded herself as too sensible to be wooed or swept off her feet by this kind of man. Certainly he wasn't the type of man a woman could take seriously. But he was a charmer, and it wasn't hurting her ego any to be on the receiving end of so much attention.

Chapter 24

The large gift-wrapped box on her bed with a single gold ribbon, tied in a bow on top, grabbed her attention immediately. Alex kicked off her shoes and hurried to the package.

Should she or shouldn't she? Nickolas admitted himself that he was indulging her in an effort to persuade her to accept his job offer. There were no strings attached, just a simple bribe; an open and honest bribe. She'd been wined and dined before by big names like Nike, ESPN, Reebok, and others, but nothing like this.

Unable to resist, she untied the bow and lifted the lid. Another black velvet box sat on top of the tissue paper, similar to the one that had held the earrings but larger.

She opened it and gasped. More diamonds. A lot more diamonds. The necklace was delicate and stunning, with eleven diamonds hanging in a wide V-shape. The diamonds were large in the middle and grew smaller in size towards the outside. "Wow!" was all she could say.

Parting the tissue paper, she exposed a black evening dress with a jacket. The dress was knee length, sleeveless and plain, in soft crepe. The bolero jacket was decorated with black glass beadwork that glinted and caught the light in shimmering sparkles.

"Wow!" she said again.

As she sat there, stunned, the telephone began to ring.

"Alexis, this is Julianne down the hall. I'm in a terrible bind."

"Julianne, what's wrong?"

"Drat the airline. One of my bags is missing. I have nothing to wear to dinner tonight."

Alex's mind went immediately to the dress her mother packed for her.

"I have the perfect thing for you to wear. Do you need shoes as well?"

"No, I have everything else. Just none of my dressier clothes. Are you certain it's no trouble?"

"No trouble at all. Come and get it." Then she remembered her gift strewn across the bed. "Better yet, I'll run it down to you."

Just as her mother had promised, the dress had traveled like a dream, with barely a wrinkle in it.

"Alexis, this is gorgeous. Are you sure you don't want to wear it?" Julianne said when she saw the fancy gown.

"I've got something else, so you're welcome to it."

"I don't know how to thank you."

"I'm just glad I had something that worked. You may want to hang it in the bathroom and let it steam for a minute to get any wrinkles out."

"Good idea."

Alex noticed Julianne's room wasn't quite as nice or as big as hers. Hers didn't have a balcony, and the only view out her window was of the building next door.

"I'll ring you when I'm ready," Julianne said, "we can walk downstairs together."

"Don't hurry too fast. I plan on taking a *long* shower."

Alex hurried back to her room, excited to try on the new dress and go out for the evening. Even though she'd been determined not to enjoy this trip, she was already having a wonderful time.

Just as she realized this, she started to feel guilty. Steve and Jamie's life had been turned inside out by the fire, and here she was worrying whether to put her hair up or wear it down. Even though there was nothing she could do from so far away, she still couldn't help feeling guilty for the luxurious room, royal treatment, and generous gifts from Nicko.

In her mind she'd pictured herself spending all her time in an uncomfortable old hotel room with a cement-hard mattress, eating room service and watching television programs in a language she couldn't understand.

No. This trip was nothing like she'd expected. It had been full of pleasant surprises, and she had a feeling there were many more in store.

* * *

Julianne tapped at her door an hour later. Alex glanced at her reflection one more time in the mirror and was forced to admit the dress was like nothing else she had ever worn. After her initial shock had lessened somewhat, she had noticed the label inside the collar on the jacket. It was a Medici original. Movie stars wore Alberto Medici's gowns to the Academy Awards; the first lady had worn a Medici to an inaugural ball. Even the royalty of Monaco wore his creations.

And she actually was wearing one! As she went to answer the door, she reminded herself to be careful not to spill anything down her front; not that she usually did, but she'd never worn a thousand-dollar dress before either. She was afraid she would suddenly become a slob at the dinner table.

Julianne and Alex squealed with delight as they saw each other dressed up for the first time. "You look fabulous," Alex told her friend.

"So do you. No, you look better than fabulous. I love your hair pinned up like that. You look so regal," Julianne said.

"Thanks. I feel like Cinderella going to the ball or something. "

Julianne stepped inside the room while Alex looked for the black-beaded clutch bag her mother had packed for her. The next time she called home, she had to thank her mother for insisting that she take all these fancy clothes and accessories.

"I've never gone anywhere in a limousine before I came on this trip. I can't imagine how fancy this restaurant is going to be," Julianne said surveying the room. "Wow, nice room!"

Finding her bag under a pile of lingerie, Alex slipped her key inside, along with some lipstick, some tissues, and a few thousand Italian lire she'd exchanged from American dollars in the lobby when they'd checked in.

Julianne checked her lipstick in a wall mirror next to the door, then turned to Alex. "I didn't notice your necklace. It's gorgeous. Those diamonds look absolutely real."

Alex fought a smile, still a little uncomfortable that Nickolas had showered her with such extravagance, but amused to think what Julianne's reaction would be if she knew they were real diamonds—from Signor Diamante himself.

"I think we'd better go. Tony should be waiting downstairs," she said.

She had every intention of returning the gift, but she was afraid of insulting Nickolas. And she didn't want to do that.

* * *

The ride to the restaurant was nothing short of a hilarious trip through an obstacle course. The six tour members jounced and jolted around the back of the limo like bowling pins on a strike. But instead of finding it scary and unnerving, they laughed until their sides hurt.

"Man, I've been with some crazy drivers," J.J. said, "but this Tony is driving like some kamikaze pilot."

Even in their seat belts, they were jerked from side to side, back and forth. Alex felt one of her bobby pins fly from her hair when Tony finally brought the car to a screeching halt.

"I think I'm walking back to the hotel," Ricky said. "That Tony, he must be loco."

"Signor Diamante would not give us a negligent driver," Gabi said. "This is just how they drive here in Rome. In fact, if Tony weren't such a good driver, we would probably have been in an accident long before now."

The door opened and Tony's smiling face appeared. "Hello. You are here."

"Great," J.J. said, "I'm getting out of here." He lunged for the exit, anxious for solid ground.

"Signor Diamante, he waits inside," Tony explained as he helped the girls out of the car. "Ooo, your gown," he said to Alex. "She's-a very beautiful."

"Thank you, Tony."

When the car was empty, the six were greeted at the entrance by the doorman and permitted inside.

The lobby left Alex speechless. It looked like something out of a palace. The floor was a deep, eggplant-colored marble. The walls were a matching dark purple but were covered with elegant tapestries of pictures depicting battles and religious settings. Statues and carved pillars, enormous in size and height, filled the lofty, vaulted ceiling. Beautiful gold vases and urns decorated the room with glitz and glamour.

"May I help you?" A gentleman in a black suit with a narrow black mustache and pinched features addressed the group.

"Mr. . . . ," J.J. started, ". . . I mean, Signor Diamante is expecting us."

"Ah, you are Signor Diamante's guests. Please, follow me."

They were led down a dimly lit hallway, through a curtained entrance into a private dining room with a long banquet table and gold-leafed chairs surrounding it. Above the table hung a delicate crystal chandelier, its sparkling lights reflecting in the mirrored walls.

"Please be seated. Your host will join you shortly."

They'd barely sat down when Nickolas entered the room. Shaking hands with the men and kissing the knuckles of the ladies, Nickolas made his way to the far end of the table. He paused a moment longer with Alex, who smiled shyly at him. She couldn't help but wonder how he liked the necklace and the dress now that she was wearing them.

"You look breathtaking, Alexis," he said softly as he brushed her hand with his lips, charmed her with a smile, then went to his seat.

"So," he said, "I assume you are all getting settled in. Is there anything you need? Any questions you have?"

"Signor," Ricky raised his hand, "I've been wondering how we're going to communicate with the participants. I speak pretty good English, but it is much easier if I can do my workshop in Spanish."

"That will not be a problem," Nickolas answered. " I have a staff of interpreters who will be able to help in all languages. Whatever your language, our translators will say it in Italian, French, or German, depending on which country we are in."

"Cool," J.J. said.

The curtain parted and Renardo, the maitre d', announced something about the *primo piatti*. Translating for him, Nickolas announced the first course. In walked three waiters, trays lifted high in the air. To Alex's surprise, a steaming bowl of spaghetti was placed before each person at the table. There was also a salad with a generous dusting of freshly grated Parmesan cheese.

A waiter came around with a wine bottle and began filling one of the several glasses at each plate. When he came to Alex, she told him, "No, *gracie*." The waiter gave her a completely puzzled look, then addressed Nickolas. After a few words, Nickolas said, "Alexis, you do not care for wine?"

"No, thank you," she said, realizing all eyes were on her. "I don't drink alcoholic beverages anymore."

"But this is just wine. Surely you can have a small glass full."

The waiter moved toward her, but Alex stopped him.

"Thank you but no, I wouldn't care for any. I would like some water though, please."

"Water?" the waiter asked.

"Yes, please. Water."

"Water?" the waiter asked Nickolas.

Nickolas spoke to the waiter in Italian. The waiter responded, then Nickolas spoke again, his words taking on a sharper tone. The waiter nodded quickly then disappeared.

With a smile, Nickolas turned to the group and asked, "Anything else for anyone?"

No one said anything.

"Then please, you are welcome to start eating."

Alex hoped she hadn't caused a problem for the waiter and appreciated Nickolas moving the meal forward. She smiled at him, making a mental note to thank him later.

The salad, the spaghetti with its wonderfully rich and spicy sauce, and the toasted cheesy-garlic baguette slices were all incredibly delicious.

Her waiter returned with a tray of bottles. "Water?"

"Yes, thank you."

"With or without glass?"

His accent was so thick, she wasn't sure what he meant. Couldn't he use the wine glasses in front of her for the water?

"Excuse me?"

"With or without glass?" He spoke more slowly.

She turned to Nickolas for help.

"Do you want 'gas' in your water? You know, mineral water?"

"Oh," she exclaimed, he was saying "gas," not "glass." She turned to the waiter. "Without gas, please."

He poured her a tall glass of Evian.

"Excuse me," Julianne said. "I would also like some water without gas."

The waiter ended up pouring glasses of water for everyone at the table.

With that out of the way, they resumed eating. Then to her surprise, before they had even finished, Renardo stepped inside the curtain and announced, the *secondo piatti*.

"Second course," Nickolas translated.

"Whoa," J.J. said. "I thought this was our only course. I think I'm gonna get full."

Platters with different types of food were placed on trays beside the table.

"We have *anguilla al lauro, triglie al forno,* and *branzino in bianco,*" Renardo said.

Again, Nickolas came to their rescue. "The first one is eel with laurel, then baked red mullet, then steamed sea bass."

Alex swallowed a bite of salad and eyed the eel. There was no way she was going to try it although it hadn't looked so disgusting until he told her what it was. She asked for some of the sea bass, as did Julianne and Wes. Gabi and Nickolas and Ricky had the red mullet. J.J. was the only one brave enough to try the eel.

Again the waiter came around with his bottle, this time pouring a different type of wine. He gave Alex a very confused look, almost like he was sorry for her, then continued around the table. The dishes from the first course were removed and they were left to continue eating.

"Hey," J.J. said, "except for being as chewy as an eraser, this stuff is pretty good."

Alex enjoyed a few bites of the moist, flaky fish on her plate then put down her fork. She was stuffed already.

Nickolas took the opportunity to update them on a few date changes, and apologized that he couldn't get away for the tour of the city scheduled for the next day, due to some important business matters he needed to attend to.

"I think I'm going to explode," J.J. said, pushing his plate away from him.

At that moment Renardo stepped through the curtain and announced dessert.

J.J. groaned. "This is worse than Thanksgiving."

Behind him came three waiters with trays filled with confections that were too pretty to eat. They varied between simple dishes of gelatti, which was Italian ice cream, to extravagant plates of cake, sauce, and candied fruits smothered in whipped cream.

"If I'm gonna die," J.J. said, " this is the only way to go."

Alex chose a simple bowl of raspberry *gelatti* and watched the others experiment with the choices. Julianne chose a tall piece of cheesecake with some kind of carmel/chocolate swirled sauce.

Wine glasses were filled again, forks and spoons clinked against the china, then finally with some contented sighs, and painful groans, everyone completed their meal.

"Signor Diamante," J.J. said, "thank you for this wonderful meal. But if I eat like this the whole time, you're going to need to reserve a cargo plane to get me home."

Nickolas laughed. "I hope you all enjoyed yourselves. The chef here is world renowned and has catered parties for celebrities and royalty throughout the world. Now, if you would like to stretch your legs, we will go up to the roof where there is a wonderful view of the city at night, a very nice bar, and dancing."

Nickolas took upon himself the task of helping the ladies out of their chairs and leading the way from the dining room to an elevator around the corner.

Alex caught his eye several times while they rode the twenty-seven floors up to the roof, returning his gaze with a smile. He was a true gentleman in every sense of the word. Classy, dignified, and refined.

A table had been reserved for them on the edge of the dance floor, next to the picture window, which allowed them to look across the rooftops of the city.

J.J. had excused himself to the men's room, while the rest of them admired the view before taking a seat. Alex lingered, marveling at the brilliance of the lights scattered before her. She was able to make out the shapes and forms of several church steeples and domes and was amazed at the traffic on the streets. Rome was a city that never slept. It was easily nine or nine-thirty at night and still the cars were bumper to bumper.

"A beautiful sight, isn't it?"

She turned to find Nickolas next to her.

"Rome is such a beautiful city," she said.

Nickolas nodded appreciatively. "Yes, she is."

"Has this always been your home?"

"Roma?" he asked, rolling his "R" with perfection.

She nodded.

"Actually I was born in Belgium. My family comes from Milano, but we lived for many years in Brussels. This is where my father began his diamond business. We still have a plant there and several retail stores, but I came to Roma to study business and have stayed here ever since."

"Is your family still in Brussels?" He spoke so softly she had to lean in closer to him to hear over the live band.

"No, my father died many years ago, and my mother passed away only last year."

She hadn't known that. "I'm sorry, Nickolas."

"It has been a difficult year for me. But I am doing better and have looked forward to this tour for months. I have been anxious to see you again."

Not knowing how to reply, Alex smiled and looked away.

With his finger, Nickolas turned her face back toward him. "You look very enchanting tonight."

"Thank you. The dress is incredibly beautiful."

"Not as beautiful as you."

"The necklace is exquisite. I love it, really. But, Nickolas, I cannot accept such a gift."

"But that's all it is, a gift. I would not give it to you if I didn't want you to have it."

"I don't know how to thank you. And I have nothing for you."

"My dear, having you here is thanks enough. Let me tell you something. A man in my position has many things—homes all over the world, yachts, airplanes, everything I could ever want. But you see, I have learned one very important lesson: all the money and possessions I have do not bring me joy. And believe me, I have tried to buy happiness."

He turned and leaned against the railing as the warm night breeze carried the scent of tropical flowers and rhythm of the night.

"Perhaps it is that I am growing older and as you Americans say, am suffering from 'mid-life' crisis, or it may be the fact that I have lost both of my parents and am feeling like a ship without an anchor, but right now all I want is to find happiness. True happiness."

Alex didn't know what to say. She was humbled that a man such as Nickolas could make such an honest confession.

"You, Alex, seem happy. There is a serenity about you I crave. Inner peace. It is difficult to explain." He looked away.

Alex knew exactly what would bring Nickolas the greatest joy. And once again her scope of vision broadened to allow her the chance to see that she could actually be the one to offer this man the happiness he longed for.

"Could I ask a favor of you?" he said.

"Of course."

"Would you allow me to dance with you?"

"Dance?"

"I would be honored," he said.

"It would be my pleasure."

He guided her to the dance floor. Even in her heels, she felt short next to his six-foot-three frame.

In his arms she couldn't help but see many of the heads turn their direction to watch them. Nickolas looked dazzling in his black tuxedo and starched white shirt. His dashing good looks and lean but muscular build set him apart from anyone else in the room. Alex couldn't help but feel like a princess in her evening dress, with her hair in curls high on her head, and the sparkle of jewels on her ears and neck.

Gliding and swaying to the music, Alex didn't have to force herself to enjoy dancing with Nickolas. His movements were easy, his steps smooth and graceful. He held her like she was a priceless gem, firmly yet gently.

Alex began to feel a little confused. Leaving Rich had felt like she was leaving part of herself behind, but now, here she was thoroughly enjoying Nickolas's company. In a way, she felt she was being unfaithful to Rich. Was she?

But the bigger question was, did Rich even expect her to be faithful to him?

Her thoughts reached, stretched, and spanned the distance back to Utah where Rich was in Park City, which only caused her to wonder what he was doing. Was he thinking of her? Was he with Elena?

Her stomach knotted as she thought about Rich and she remembered the confirmation she'd received when she'd prayed about coming to Europe. She knew without a doubt she was supposed to be here. The feelings had been strong, too strong to be denied. She'd thought all along it was to help her and Rich and their relationship. Perhaps it didn't have anything to do with Rich. Maybe it was about

Nickolas? Was part of the reason the Lord had wanted her to come to Europe to be with him?

Chapter 25

Between dances, Nickolas and Alex stayed in the center of the dance floor, taking advantage of the breaks by getting to know each other. Alex found out that Nicko, as he'd asked her to call him, had a brother and a sister, both younger. The brother, also a skier, lived in Austria; he didn't wanted anything to do with the family business. The sister, however, was involved in the business and managed the plant in Brussels.

"I'm surprised that a man as busy as you are could find time to spend an evening with all of us," Alex said.

"It is quite refreshing, actually, to eat a relaxing meal instead of trying to lock in a business deal at the same time," Nickolas admitted.

"I understand you have a very busy social calendar," Alex said. Her tone was teasing, but she was curious to learn more about this man she might eventually work for.

He looked at her with amusement. "I suppose you could say that. I spend a great deal of time entertaining and going out to gatherings. But it becomes tiresome. Many women are attracted to me. I know that sounds boastful, but I am a man of great power and wealth. This attention I get from so many people, women especially, is actually one of the biggest challenges I have."

"In what way?"

"You see, Alex, I have many friends and acquaintances, but only a very, very few of them I trust. All of the others are more concerned about my money and status. Except you, Alex. From the moment I met you, I knew you weren't impressed by my wealth or my position. I find your complete lack of interest in these external matters most refreshing. And," he said, taking her into his arms again as the next song started, "very appealing. But enough about me. I want to know all about you and your family. But, first, tell me about this charming little ring you're wearing."

It was the ring Sarah Beckstead had given her when she got baptized.

"What do the initials CTR mean?"

As Alex and Nickolas twirled to the catchy rhythm, Alex caught glimpses of Julianne and Ricky dancing. Wes was also dancing with someone Alex had never seen before.

"It means, 'Choose the right.'"

"Is this a slogan for your nutrition lecture or something?"

"Oh, no," she laughed, "although that might make a nice title for it. This ring is from my church. All the young children wear rings like this to help them make right choices."

"Ahh," he said, "'Choose the right.' I like it. And which church is this?"

"The Church of Jesus Christ of Latter-day Saints—the Mormons."

"You are one of them?" His eyes opened wide with surprise.

"Yes. Do you know about the Mormons?"

"A little bit. One of our employees in Stockholm is Mormon. I remember because he told me about his son going away for two years to do missionary work for his church."

"The missionaries taught me about the gospel. They were young men, just like that man's son. That is why I didn't drink any wine at dinner. We don't believe in drinking alcoholic beverages. I wanted to thank you for your help with the waiter this evening at dinner. I didn't mean for that to be uncomfortable."

"Nonsense. We respect your wishes. But tell me. When did you become 'Mormon'?"

An elderly couple nearby kept staring at them.

Smiling graciously, Nickolas bowed his head to them, then waltzed Alex to a more secluded spot on the dance floor.

"Why do you think they were looking at us?" she asked, remembering Gabi's comments about Nickolas's connections with the Mafia and his affairs with famous women.

"Perhaps they are wondering if you are royalty from a foreign country."

Alex laughed. "Or perhaps they think you, sir, are the royal one," she said.

"No, no. Everyone in my city knows who I am. I am nothing special here. It is you they are watching. But you haven't told me about when you became Mormon."

"Oh, I forgot. I'm sorry. Nickolas, I mean, Nicko." She made sure to pronounce it *Nee-ko*, like he said it. "Do you think we could take a rest; I still have bit of jet lag."

"Of course, *cara mia*, I should have known you would be tired after such a long flight and a busy day. Can I get you anything? Would you like me to take you back to your hotel room?"

"I'm fine. I could use a drink of water though."

"Water, yes. Water would be good. Here . . ." He directed her toward a table, secluded in the corner of the room away from the other guests. "We will rest here."

Motioning to the waiter, Nickolas soon had two glasses of cold Evian with a lemon twist for them. The drink was cool and refreshing.

"The story goes back nineteen years to when my father became a Mormon. It was very difficult when he joined the Church because my mother was opposed to it, but he went ahead and got baptized, hoping, one day, to see us all join the Church. He was killed in an automobile accident a year later and my mother made sure we weren't exposed in any way to the Mormons. Somehow my sister became friends with some kids in Manhattan who were Mormons. When she graduated from high school she went away to college to Brigham Young University in Provo, Utah, and got baptized there."

Nickolas listened intently as she spoke. He was riveted to every word she said.

"She's been after me to take time to learn about the Church for years. This spring when I went to visit her at Easter time, I was able to see what her church was all about and what their teachings were. The more I learned, the more I realized I believed the doctrine. Her church seemed to have all the answers to the questions I found myself asking, and I was able to receive some very strong feelings, for myself, that it was true."

She stirred the lemon in her glass with her straw. "I'm sorry if I'm boring you with my story."

"Not at all, Alexis, it is quite fascinating. That means, then, that you also are a member of this religion?"

"Yes, I was baptized not quite a month ago. And it was the most wonderful day of my life."

"What else does this religion of yours teach you?"

"Something that changed me forever was reading a book that goes along with the Bible. It is a book of scriptures telling about the ancient American inhabitants. It is called the Book of Mormon."

"The Book of Mormon?"

'Yes. It is a wonderful book that has the power to change lives. I know because it altered mine forever. And, Nicko, that is the reason that I am happy. Even when I am dealing with great challenges or overwhelmed by problems. The gospel gives me the strength I need to deal with them."

"You have this book?"

"Yes, actually, I brought one with me. Would you like to read it?"

"Perhaps, sometime." He took a drink of his water. "You continue to amaze me and surprise me. I knew you were different than any of the other women I have met. Now I can see why I am so attracted to you."

"You are?" She swallowed hard.

"I am fascinated by you. You are like no one I've ever known before. Like some rare jewel, some . . ." his hands grasped and gestured, helping him find his words, "priceless work of art. You, my precious Alexis, are extraordinary. And I am a man who recognizes such a valuable piece of work as you are."

"Excuse me, Signor Diamante," a waiter said. Alex hadn't even noticed him approach them. "There is a telephone call for you."

"Alexis, would you excuse me?"

"Certainly." Behind the waiter she saw two men at the doorway. They had been there quite some time. Were they with him? Did Nicko have bodyguards?

"Perhaps I could escort you back to the others so you are not alone in case I am detained for a while."

He transported her over to the table where the others had been sitting. Her mind literally swirled with the wiles of his charms. She knew they were just words, but the way he said them to her, the way he looked at her, made her feel as though she were as treasured by him as he said. She had to be careful. Compared to him and the women he was used to she was as naive as farm girl from Kansas. He seemed so sincere, it was hard not to fall under his spell. But she didn't falter, she knew exactly what she wanted for herself and her future.

She watched Nickolas follow the waiter from the room and just as she'd expected, the two large men disappeared moments afterward.

For a moment she worried about the rest of the group and their reaction to her spending time alone with Nickolas, but the only person sitting at the table was J.J. He wasn't feeling very well.

"I'm never eating eel again," he said, when she joined him. "Believe me, it's not a food you want to see again after you've eaten it."

She couldn't think of *any* food she'd want to see again after she'd eaten it. She had struggled with an eating disorder, but bulimia had never been her problem.

"Why don't I get the others and we can have Tony take us back to the hotel?" she offered. "If we're going to spend the day sightseeing I want to be awake to see the sights."

"I don't think Wes is going to be too excited about leaving his new fan club."

Alex looked out over the dance floor and saw Wes in a corner surrounded by a swarm of beautiful women. It was obvious that they adored him just about as much as he adored himself.

"I'll go tell them you and I are leaving. I'm sure Tony can come back for them if they aren't ready to go."

"But what about Signor Diamante? We don't want him mad at us for leaving early."

"It's after midnight. I'm sure Nicko wouldn't be upset." She clamped her mouth tightly shut in a hurry; she'd meant to use his full name.

"Nicko!" J.J. lifted his head, his dark skin shining from the sheen of cold sweat. "Are you gettin' tight with that dude?"

"No, J.J., we're just friends. I've been acquainted with him for several years."

He rested his head back against the cushioned bench. "Then let's blow this joint, before I blow again."

Alex rushed to the floor to gather the others, hoping they were ready to leave, and that they wouldn't have suspicions about her and Nickolas. She needed to be careful. She didn't want to give the wrong impression to anyone, especially Nickolas.

* * *

Even after nine hours of sleep, Alex felt like she could've slept several more. She wondered how long it would take to adjust to the time change.

After a long shower she felt much better. Francesca, Nickolas's secretary, called at ten o'clock to inform her that Tony would be by to pick them up at eleven.

Dressed in a light, swingy rayon dress, with a colorful print of turquoise and purple flowers on a coral background, Alex stepped into her sandals, slipped her camera into her shoulder strap purse, and left her room a total mess. She hated traveling but she loved hotel maids.

Julianne stepped out of her room at the exact same time.

"Hey, *buon giorno*," she said when she saw Alex.

"How did you sleep?"

"I don't even remember getting undressed I was so tired. How about you?"

"The same."

They rang for the elevator.

"What about Gabi?" Alex said. "Should we get her?"

"She's already gone down. She wanted to eat breakfast."

"Are you having breakfast?" Alex asked, still full from dinner the night before.

"All I want is coffee to wake me up, and some gum to get rid of all that garlic I ate last night. Can you smell it?"

"Don't worry about offending me. I'm sure I ate as much garlic as you did."

They joined the others at the restaurant fifteen minutes before their ride arrived.

"Hey, J.J." Alex noticed he wore an *Atlanta Braves* baseball hat low over his eyes. "How're you feeling this morning?"

"Once I got rid of that eel I was fine, man. But I'm stickin' to McDonald's from now on. They have those here, don't they?"

"I think so," Ricky said, "but they serve 'eelburgers,' not hamburgers."

J.J. groaned while they rest of them laughed.

"Where's Wes?" Alex asked.

"He was out most of the night so he's skipping the sightseeing," Julianne said.

"He saw all the sights he wanted to see last night," J.J. said.

The waitress asked Julianne and Alex if they wanted to order anything. Alex declined and Julianne requested coffee.

"You are not eating?" Gabi said to them. "You are both much too skinny."

"We're still a little full from last night," Alex said. "We'll grab something later."

"Hey! There's Tony already," Ricky said, then quickly drained the last of his coffee from his cup.

In a flash they were out the door and into the limo ready for a day of fun and sightseeing.

* * *

After a busy day of touring Rome, they asked Tony to stop at McDonald's on the way back to the hotel. J.J. actually ran inside the restaurant and kissed the statue of Ronald McDonald.

"That quarter pounder tasted as good as the ones back home in Atlanta," J.J. said, rubbing his full stomach.

"Do you have McDonald's in Venezuela, Ricky?" Julianne asked.

Alex's thoughts drifted from the discussion. She watched out the window as they passed throngs of mopeds and long lanes of traffic. The day had been busy and full with a visit to Vatican City, across the Tiber River, where they saw breathtaking sights of Michelangelo's *Pieta* in St. Peter's basilica, and the amazing Sistine Chapel in the Vatican Museum. They visited the Colosseum, the Forum, the Spanish Steps, and of course, the Fountain of Trevi. Here they stopped and took turns throwing coins in the fountain. Alex knew it was silly, but with each coin she threw she wished with all her heart that Rich would be thinking of her, missing her.

She couldn't help but smile as she remembered the group trying to cross the streets of Rome, and the way J.J. risked his life for them each time he fearlessly led the way through the unyielding traffic. More than once they heard the blast of a horn or the screech of brakes.

But now as the day was slowing, with the fun over and the fatigue of jet lag overtaking her, her thoughts returned home. She needed to call, to hear her family's voices, to know they were all well and surviving the aftermath of the fire. And, of course, she was anxious to find out how Rich was doing. She still didn't have a direct address or phone number for him and hoped that the postcard she'd sent that day from Vatican City would reach him.

How she wished he could be here with her, seeing the incredible sights, especially the history and works of art by the masters themselves. If only they could experience together a Michelangelo, a Leonardo da Vinci, or a Raphael. Rich would be in heaven. The works of art had been more glorious than she could have imagined. But Rich was missing it all, and she was missing him.

Anxious to call home, she was the first one out of the car when Tony pulled up to the curb. Bidding the others good night as she chose the stairs over the elevator, she raced up to her room, ran for the phone, and placed the call.

Bubbles of excitement tickled her stomach as she heard the first and second ring, but as the third ring produced no answer, they started to pop. On the fourth, the answering machine picked up. Taking a deep breath she left a short, cheerful message and told them she'd try back tomorrow. Now she was really getting worried. Where were they?

Maybe it was being so tired, or even a little homesick, or confused about her feelings, but for the first time since she'd arrived, she cried herself to sleep.

Chapter 26

Alex found some relief the next day when they were able to go to the convention center and actually concentrate on the presentations for the conference that would take place the following day. Doing something familiar, something she was comfortable with and used to, helped to curb the homesickness.

She and the other five fitness experts spent most of the morning familiarizing themselves with the sound equipment and interpreters. They also learned some Italian words they could use to greet the participants and help them break the ice at the beginning of their presentations.

The English translator was a nice young Italian man who had spent several summers in America. He talked a lot about Disneyworld and the Grand Canyon and the time he had spent in New York studying English and art at NYU.

His name was Gino and he was very friendly.

"So," he said to both Alex and Julianne, "you girls like to go nightclubbing?"

"Sure," Julianne said. "We have some great clubs in London."

"How about you?" he asked Alex.

"I like to go out dancing, but I'm kind of past the club scene. I'm not exactly into 'Mosh Pits' and the tattooed and pierced crowd. Why?"

"Some friends and I are going out tonight. I thought you two might like to join us. J.J. and Ricky are coming, too."

"I'd love to go," Julianne said.

They both looked at Alex.

"Thanks for asking but I think I'll pass. I need to work on some choreography for tomorrow."

"Come with us, Alexis," Julianne begged. "It will be fun."

"I haven't done a presentation for months," Alex said. "I need the practice. But you go and have fun." She excused herself and went to talk to the sound man about pitch control and microphone feedback.

After a quick lunch break they all took turns rehearsing their presentations and going through sound and lighting checks. Gabi and Wes invited her to spend the rest of the day with them going to see some more of the local sights, and meet up with some of the girls Wes had met, but Alex declined. Braving the streets of Rome and dodging the beggars and gypsies didn't sound fun to her.

So, one by one, after finishing their rehearsals, the rest of the group left the convention center. Alex went through her presentation one more time just to make sure she had it down. Just as she was finishing her step routine and putting all the components together, Nickolas walked in. Cutting her final run-through short, she toweled herself dry then bowed to his applause and climbed down the stairs off the back of the stage.

"You look wonderful up there," he said. "Did everything go well today?"

"I think so. You've got a great crew. They've got everything under control."

"Is there anything else you need?"

"No, nothing, thank you. I've been to hundreds of conventions and this one by far seems to have the most advanced technology being used and the nicest facility."

"Thank you. I'm glad you like it. This building is one of mine."

"It is?" She wasn't surprised he owned something so elaborate. The place was a complete sports and recreation paradise. Anything from ice skating to bullfights could be held in the arena that seated 18,000 fans. There was also a convention center with plenty of small rooms in dozens of hallways leading throughout the building.

"I'm impressed. A facility as nice as this certainly seems like some-thing you would be a part of."

"*Gracie.*" He bowed his head slightly.

Alex took a long drink from her ProStar water bottle and pulled on a light cotton jacket. The gloss of sweat on her skin cooled quickly under the giant refrigeration fans.

"Where are the others?"

"Let's see . . . Gabi and Wes went sightseeing, and Julianne, J.J., and Ricky are off with Gino, one of the interpreters, to a nightclub."

He glanced at his watch. "So early?" It was barely five o'clock. "What about you?" he asked. "Do you have plans?"

"I was just going to go back to the hotel and have some dinner, then polish some routines for tomorrow." She lifted her gym bag to throw it over her shoulder, but Nickolas stopped her.

"Please," he offered, "allow me."

"Thank you," she smiled at him. She'd never known anyone as gentlemanly as Nickolas Diamante.

"And if I may say," he added, "you look 'polished' already."

"I'm a little rusty," she admitted, but she appreciated his compliment.

"You said you are hungry?" He lifted one eyebrow questioningly.

She nodded. "A little."

"What would you like to eat while you're here in Roma?" He gestured as he spoke, giving a wave of his hand as though he were offering her the entire city.

"This sounds crazy, but I am curious to try real Italian pizza."

"Pizza? In Italy?" He tilted his head in mock surprise.

She laughed at his teasing, but couldn't help noticing the bit of boyish charm in him.

"I'll tell you what . . . I'm finished with work for the day and since you are all alone, I would like to invite you to have pizza with me."

She knew in front of her was a very rich, powerful, and important man, but right now he was just a really nice guy, offering to take her for pizza. She couldn't resist.

"I would love to, but I need to freshen up a little." She tried to tuck some loose strands of hair back into her ponytail.

"Do you need to go back to the hotel first?"

"I have extra clothes with me." She motioned toward the bag he held.

"Then I will make some phone calls while I'm waiting. Take your time," he said, handing her bag back to her.

Alex dashed to the ladies dressing room where she plugged in her curling iron, then jumped into the shower.

After a refreshing rinse, she toweled off and dressed in navy shorts and a vest over a silk t-shirt. Placing a few curls in her hair, Alex fluffed

and spritzed, applied a light amount of makeup, then stuffed everything into her bag. Twenty minutes later she went to find Nickolas. He
was talking business with Signet, the producer of the show, making
sure all the players and props were in their places for the big event.

She lingered in the background, waiting for them to finish their
conversation as they talked about the opening of the convention.
Nickolas had told the instructors he wanted to establish a European
Fitness Tour trademark. His plan was to make the introduction of the
six presenters similar to that of an NBA team at the beginning of a
game with a black-out, powerful music, loud announcer, and spotlights. Each member of the "European Fitness Team" would then run
out as his or her name was being introduced, all of the members
dressed in their ProStar fitness attire.

The two men spoke a little in English, but mostly in Italian. She
didn't understand their language and even though she realized that
Italians were emotional, passionate people, it sounded to her like
Nickolas was upset with Signet.

The producer spoke apologetically and nodded many times.

"*Si, signor*," Signet said, many more times, until Nickolas finally
changed his tone and spoke less intensely.

Alex wondered what could have been wrong. Signet seemed very
organized and knowledgeable about running the convention. But
with all the money Nickolas had invested in the tour, she didn't blame
him for wanting to make sure everything was just right.

Nickolas turned as he spoke and stopped talking when he saw her.

"Alexis, you look wonderful." She allowed him to take her hand.
"You are ready, then?"

She nodded and they were off, any concerns or worries to be
forgotten.

* * *

For some reason, driving around the winding streets of Rome, in
Nickolas's Lambourghini convertible was fun and fascinating, not
terrifying like it was in the limo. They traveled past sights she'd toured
and places she'd seen and down winding streets until Nickolas pulled
off into an alleyway and parked.

Always a gentleman, Nickolas helped her out of the car, then hand in hand they strolled down a cobblestone walkway and emerged onto a tiny square. The Piazza della Minerva contained Rome's smallest obelisk, a tall, narrow column surrounded at the bottom by fish and dolphins, carved out of stone and spewing water out of their mouths. At one side of the square was the famous Pantheon; the other held a small, outdoor café.

The Pantheon, Nickolas told Alex, was founded in 17 B.C. as a monument to all the gods. He took her inside the building through the columned portico to see the saucer-shaped dome, where a perfectly round hole opened to the sky. Since rainfall was not abundant in Rome, the hole remained open to honor the seven gods of the planets.

Inside the architecturally stunning building were the tombs of Italian kings Victor Emmanuel II and Umberto I, and the tomb of the great artist Raphael.

Back outside they wandered over to the café through the crowds of people who were sitting on the steps around the obelisk, while others mingled on the street.

"Here is where you can order some of the best pizza in Roma."

Alex scanned the menu and made her choice, pizza with lots of mushrooms, olives, tomatoes, and green peppers. Nickolas also ordered pizza along with two bottles of Fanta, a sparkling orange drink. He probably owned his own winery, but she appreciated him respecting her wishes and drinking soda pop with her.

As they relaxed in the evening shadows of the Pantheon, Nickolas pointed out interesting details of architecture and Roman culture. Alex fell in love with this side of Rome: the couples holding hands, strolling down cobbled streets, church bells ringing in the distance and the sound of soft Italian music playing in the background. It was so very charming and romantic.

Her pizza, though very much different from the Domino's back home, was delicious just the same. The vegetables were crisp and flavorful on a thin, crunchy crust. Instead of a tomato sauce on top, it was more of a creamy, garlic Alfredo sauce. She enjoyed several thin slices of her pizza as well as a few bites of Nickolas's, whose was more like the pizza back home, with sausage, marinara sauce, and cheese.

They ate slowly, leisurely, enjoying the coolness of dusk. After eating their fill, they left their table and meandered back to his car.

Alex was surprised when Nickolas's cell phone rang. She'd forgotten all about the modern world, having spent the last hour transported back in time to a simpler age.

"Pardon me," Nickolas said. "I will only be a moment."

Alex watched a group of children playing soccer around another ornate fountain as they laughed and shouted in Italian. Alex smiled at their fun and antics, especially at the one dark-haired girl doing a respectable job of handling the ball herself. She was smaller than most of the boys, but she was quick as lightening.

She was distracted from the scene when she overheard Nickolas's voice, sharp and agitated. She didn't understand what he was saying but his angered tone was easily understood. Trying to act as though she didn't hear him, but a little embarrassed at his heated conversation, Alex wandered away from him and drew closer to the children playing in the square. She could still hear Nickolas, but his voice blended in with the many other noises in the air.

Only moments later she heard footsteps behind her and turned to see Nickolas approaching.

"Ah," he said, smiling, "such fun the children are having. I remember playing soccer in the square with my friends as a boy."

"Is everything okay?"

"Oh, yes. I am having some trouble with one of my workers. We have had to let him go because of some dishonest dealings. He wasn't happy to be discharged, but I must be able to trust my employees completely. He needed some help understanding my position."

As they started walking again, horns from several automobiles blasted in an intersection and caught Alex's attention. She turned back to see what had happened. Instead she caught sight of the same two men she'd seen the night they went dancing. They looked completely out of place in their black shirts and black suits. She noticed them fade into a crowd, but she recognized them. She couldn't help but wonder who they were exactly and what they did for Nickolas.

"So, how did you like your pizza?" he asked, his tone light and happy.

"I'm so glad you brought me here," she said. "This is the part of Rome I'll remember even more than the Vatican or the Colosseum."

"I am pleased you like my city. She suits you," he said with a nod and flick of his hand.

"*She* does?" Alex laughed.

"Yes, you are very much like Roma—beautiful, mysterious, and full of surprises." Again he waved his hand to emphasize each word.

Alex giggled again. She was nothing like that. But when Nickolas said those words, so dramatically, with that charming accent, she almost believed him.

They walked along the street until they reached the car. He paused by the passenger side, where he reached to open the door, then stopped.

"Alexis, I am happy we could spend some time together. I enjoy your company very much." He reached out and took her hand in his.

"Thank you, Nicko. I enjoy being with you also." She wasn't lying. He was a great conversationalist and lavished her with attention. How could she not like him?

"You are very different from all the other women I know. They try so hard to impress me that I am left very much unimpressed. But you, you are so natural, so honest." He let go of her hand and stroked her cheek.

Alex felt herself blush.

"Thank you again for having dinner with me this evening."

He leaned closer toward her. Her heartbeat quickened. Panic rose inside of her.

A pack of mopeds screeched around the corner and charged recklessly down the alley. Alex let Nickolas put protective arms around her as the gang exited the other side, the alley still echoing its intrusion.

Relieved that they were safe, Alex pulled away from Nickolas and laughed nervously. "I don't think I'll ever get used to those things." She rubbed her bare arms and looked toward the street half expecting another swarm to descend upon them.

But as much as she disliked the noisy little two-wheeled machines, she was grateful for their interruption. She had no intention of kissing Nickolas. But she couldn't deny the tiniest bit of attraction she'd felt. Was it loneliness? The pain of Rich's rejection? Or just Nickolas's incredible charm?

She wasn't sure of the answer. All she did know was that she was grateful to be going back to the safety of her hotel room.

* * *

It was close to eleven o'clock when she got to her room. Nickolas had driven her around the town and shown her some of the buildings he owned and had even offered to show her his villa, which she quickly turned down, saying she was exhausted and needed to get a good night's rest before the conference the next day.

In her room she kicked off her shoes, threw her clothes in a pile on the floor, and pulled on her old oversized t-shirt and baggy boxers to get comfortable.

Without wasting another moment, she placed a phone call to Island Park. To her relief someone answered. It was her sister. "Hello," Jamie said wearily.

Alex wondered if she had wakened her. "Jamie, hi. It's me."

"Alex, how are you. I'm sorry we've missed your calls."

"Where have you been? I've been so worried."

Jamie sighed. "We've had a lot to do since the fire and on top of that the baby got sick."

"Oh, no!" Alex exclaimed. "Is she okay?"

"It was just a cold, but it made her completely miserable. We had to take her to the emergency room because she was having such a hard time. Her ears were infected, both of them. Believe me, things have been awfully hectic since you've been gone."

"How's Andrea doing?" Alex hated being so far away when her family needed help.

"After one day on the antibiotic, she was feeling better."

"I feel so guilty for leaving."

"These things would have happened whether you were home or not," Jamie assured her.

"I know, but I could at least be home to help you."

"We're doing fine. I think the worst is over."

"I'm glad. Are you doing okay?"

Jamie's voice brightened. "I'm fine, just tired, that's all. Tell me what you've been doing in Rome."

"We've stayed pretty busy. We've done a lot of sightseeing and some shopping."

"That sounds fun."

"You'd go nuts over the gorgeous shoes they have over here," Alex laughed, knowing what a shoe fetish her sister had. "Anyway, we've had meetings and spent time getting ready for the conference."

"And how is Nickolas Diamante?" Jamie's voice had a teasing tone in it, which made Alex immediately regret ever telling her sister about him.

"He's keeping us pretty busy."

"Is he still as handsome as you remember?" Jamie prodded for information, but Alex refused to go along.

"I guess so," she answered flatly.

"Alex, is everything okay? You sound funny."

"No I don't."

"This is me you're talking to, Al. What's going on?"

Alex hesitated for a second, then said, "Nothing's going on, really."

"Alex," Jamie persisted.

"Oh, okay. Really, nothing's going on, but I do feel like Nicko's giving me some preferential treatment."

"What kind of 'preferential treatment'?"

"A nicer hotel room than the others, gifts, spending personal time with me . . ."

Jamie was silent for a minute, thinking. "Alex," she said finally, "you're one of the most level-headed people I know."

Alex was bewildered. "What's that got to do with anything?"

"Since I'm the outsider, looking in, let me just give you a word of warning. Right now you're feeling vulnerable, especially after what you and Rich have been going through. And your friend 'Nicko' sounds very charming and charismatic."

Alex didn't admit it out loud but Jamie had described the man completely. What Jamie said next, however, took her completely by surprise.

"I guess what I'm saying is, it is possible to fall in love with a nonmember."

"Jamie, I can't believe you even said that," Alex protested. "You know how I feel about Rich."

"I know, and Rich is being very difficult at the moment. Nickolas Diamante, on the other hand, is not only gorgeous and wealthy, he's treating you like a princess. I'm just saying, be careful. That's all."

"Oh, Jamie!" Alex exploded. "I'm not going to fall in love with him. I love Rich, nothing's changed."

"Good. I'm glad to hear you say that."

"So, what else is going on?" Alex asked, changing the subject.

"Mom's getting ready to go back to New York."

Alex was startled. "What? Why so soon?"

"I'm not really sure. She hasn't said anything, but I think something's happened between her and Dr. Rawlins. He hasn't been over for a few days and she's been very quiet. She spends a lot of time in her room or at the computer."

"I wonder what could've happened?" Alex mused.

"I've been trying to talk to her but she won't say. I'll keep trying," Jamie said.

"How's Steve?"

"He's been under a lot of stress. The insurance company has been giving him a hard time with his claim, and for a few days we wondered if they were going to cover the damage. But the report came back proving it was faulty wiring. It's such a shame they lost everything in the fire."

"What's he going to do now?"

"He's been so upset by this he hasn't had time to make any plans. It would help if Rich were here to share some of the work."

"Why can't he just come up from Park City? It's not *that* far."

"Well, he's . . ."

Alex sensed reluctance in Jamie's voice. "What, Jamie?"

"He's not in Park City right now."

"Oh, he's not? Where is he?"

"I'm sure there's no reason to worry. Rich is an intelligent and responsible adult."

"Jamie, just tell me!"

"He went to Los Angeles with Elena."

Had she been struck by a whole herd of mopeds and run over, Alex wouldn't have felt more pain. He'd actually gone on a trip with Elena, and Alex didn't care if she was LDS or not, Elena was like a poisonous vine who could wrap herself around him and choke out his good sense. Alex hadn't imagined it; Rich had been infatuated by Elena's attention, by her flattering words, and charming wiles. Elena was a vixen with a hidden agenda, at least hidden to the male eye. For some reason, she and Jamie had been able to see through Elena's designs, but Rich was blind. And stubborn. And Alex hadn't been able to open his eyes to the truth. He had to find it out for himself.

The thought of what might happen in the process terrified her.

Chapter 27

She didn't know how long she prayed and cried after she hung up the phone, but a knock on the door brought her from a dazed sleep. Without checking first, she opened the door and found Julianne in front of her.

"Alexis, what's wrong? Are you sick?"

Alex invited her inside. "No," she said plopping down on the bed. "I just received some upsetting news tonight, that's all."

"I'm sorry. Is there anything I can do? Do you want to talk about it?"

Alex didn't reply.

"I brought some chocolate torte from the party and . . . ," she held up two sacks, "I was hoping you would be in the mood for *gelatti*." Julianne kicked off her shoes, tossed her purse into a chair, and joined Alex on the bed.

"Come on, peach, tell me all about it. Only a man could cause tears like this. Here . . . ," she opened one container of the Italian ice cream and handed it with a spoon to Alex, ". . . I actually happen to be an expert on broken hearts. What happened?"

Alex began her story, going back to the first time she ever met Rich, in a snowstorm in Idaho the previous March. How their relationship had developed. How he had practically saved her life. How he had practically proposed. And everything that had happened since then. Even though the clock read twelve, then one, then two, it didn't matter; she needed a friend and she thanked her lucky stars and her Heavenly Father for dear Julianne.

* * *

Somehow Alex made it through the next day. She relied on constant prayer and a lot of luck that she would be able to perform when it came her time. She didn't know if there was such a thing as a chocolate hangover, but she felt like she had one. Julianne ended up spending the night in Alex's room. The seven o'clock wake-up call had seemed to come only one minute after they fell asleep. They both had headaches and stomachaches; neither had enough energy to blink.

The welcome and introduction at the beginning of the conference was a hyped-up, spectacular display that rivaled any Superbowl half-time. Julianne and Alex made their entrance then ran for the restroom, feeling violently ill, while Gabi and Wes started the first presentation.

After a few crackers and some mineral water, they started to feel a little better and were able to catch some rest on the cots in the dressing room. Julianne's presentation was right before lunch. Alex's was after.

Being the professionals that they were, they both managed to pull themselves together for their workshops. Julianne had the crowd whooping and hollering for more as she finished her class. By the time it was Alex's turn, she'd had enough time to get herself back on track and even managed to eat a little soup for lunch to settle her stomach.

She started off shaky, but was determined to give it her best. With the help of motivating music, a great sound system, and all the energy three hundred excited fitness instructors could generate, her work-shop built to a high intensity, and ended up strong and powerful, and a ton of fun to boot. When her segment finished, she received an overwhelming round of applause.

Julianne greeted her when she ran off the stage. "Wow, you oughta get bombed on chocolate every night if you can perform like that."

"I don't think I'll ever eat another bite of chocolate the rest of this trip."

Julianne laughed. "Wait till you get to Switzerland. Then tell me that." She threw a towel over her friend's shoulders and together they walked to the dressing room.

"You saved me last night, you know," Alex told her.

"Pish-tosh. You would've been fine, but it was kind of fun eating all that junk."

"Fun until I woke up this morning." Alex sat on a chair and began unlacing her shoes. "I'm not used to bingeing like that. My stomach was not happy with me."

"I'm afraid I'm the same way. In fact," Julianne checked the back room before she continued, "I wanted to ask you sometime about your eating disorder. One of the articles I read said you'd been through treatment. How did you know you had a problem?"

Alex looked at her friend, her thin, leggy, British friend, who, she'd noticed during the three days they'd been together, drank *a lot* of coffee and only picked at her food. "Why do you ask?" she said carefully.

Julianne shrugged. "I don't know, really. My parents had a long talk with me before I left. They accused me of being anorexic. I admit, I have a problem with food. I don't trust it or myself. I'm very careful of what I eat, and I tend to starve myself a lot. Probably all that pressure from being in ballet for so many years. It's not that I feel like I have to keep losing weight, but I am terrified of gaining weight."

"You don't like to feel full?"

"Not at all."

"You'd rather starve than eat and feel guilty about it?"

"Exactly."

"Are you bulimic?"

Julianne was silent for a moment. "When I overeat I will . . . make myself . . . you know. . . But I'm not a regular binge and purge kind of bulimic."

"Would you be opposed to getting help?"

Julianne pulled a face. "After enough people tell you how bad you look, you can't help but wonder. I don't want to jeopardize my health, but I really don't think I need professional help." She fiddled with the zipper on her warm-up jacket. "When those news articles came out telling about your eating disorder, I wished I could talk to you. I had no idea you'd struggled with anorexia. In fact, I'd always envied how thin you were. I wanted to be skinny, like you."

Alex still felt responsible and guilty for the many women she'd unintentionally misled all those years by her appearance. "But now you realize that I was too thin, don't you, Julianne?"

"Yes, of course I do. And you look wonderful now."

"Listen, Julianne," Alex tried to explain, "I still struggle with how much I weigh and how I look. I'll probably have this challenge my whole life, but I'm at least feeling like my awareness and understanding are greater and my expectations are healthier. I've also learned skills that have helped me cope with my struggles, and I've learned some of the reasons I fall into my old habits, so I can prevent myself from ever getting so thin again. Getting professional help was the only way I could've done it. I kidded myself for a long time and thought I could do it on my own, but it was a problem much bigger than I could handle."

Julianne nodded. Alex could see that the pieces of the puzzle were fitting together for Julianne. "It sounds like you've got a wonderful support system, with your family. That's very important in your treatment," Alex said. "From what you've told me about them, I know they will help you through this, and I will, too."

"Thank you, Alexis. I'm glad I could talk to you about this."

"And I'm glad you were there for me to talk to last night. I really needed a friend."

As Julianne went to change, Alex offered a silent prayer in her heart. She had learned another reason why the Lord had wanted her to come on this trip.

* * *

That night, in her hotel room, Alex packed her bags for Venice and looked forward to getting a long night's sleep.

She was startled when her telephone rang.

"Alexis, you were superb today."

"Nicko, thank you. I didn't see you during my presentation."

"I was there, in the back. Not the whole time but enough to see what a great response you got at the end."

"It was a fun crowd. I really enjoyed it."

"We received a lot of comments on all of you. I'm very pleased. I think we can expect the same type of turnout in Milan and Monte Carlo. But first we'll let you relax and enjoy a few days visiting two of my favorite cities, Firenze and Venezia."

She remembered from her itinerary he meant Florence and Venice.

"I am looking forward to seeing them myself."

"You will love the statue of David, and the Doge's Palace in Venice. I hope to take you there myself. And, since it is your last night in Roma, I called to see if you would be interested in joining me for dinner."

She had anticipated this. She didn't know why, but she had known he would call her for dinner. "It's wonderful of you to ask, but I am completely exhausted. I didn't sleep well at all last night, and after so much excitement today, I'm very tired."

"I understand. Yes, you must get your rest, so you can enjoy the next two days. But promise me a gondola ride in Venice. You must see Venice by gondola."

"Of course," she smiled. "You have my promise."

"Very good. I will say good-night then, *mi bella.* Sleep well."

Why she didn't say no to the gondola ride, she wasn't sure. Maybe it was because she wanted to go on the ride, and maybe it was because she had no reason not to. Rich was with Elena in L.A., so why shouldn't she be with Nicko in Venice?

* * *

From the moment she stepped onto the quaint streets of Florence, Alex felt she was in a fairytale land. This tiny city, with its cozy shops, cobblestoned streets, and rich artistic history held her spellbound. From the breathtaking mauve and green marbled Duomo church, the main cathedral in the city, to its surprisingly numerous museums, she was completely charmed.

The group milled around the tiny streets together at first, but as they explored and discovered different sights of interest, they ended up splitting off in various directions.

Alex found herself alone with Nickolas.

"Come," he said. "I want to take you to my favorite museum."

On the way to the museum they shared a pastry and window shopped. Her mouth watered at the hundreds of shoes that beckoned to her. Sleek, smooth, leather shoes and handbags, crafted by Italy's finest cobblers.

Alex noticed the many heads that turned as they walked down the streets, all of them belonging to women. Not only was Nickolas distinguished and handsome, but, Alex was learning, he was very well-known. Any shop they stepped into brought immediate attention by the owner. And Alex was always aware of the two men who lagged behind, just far enough to give them plenty of privacy, but close enough to be at their side in a matter of seconds if they needed to be.

Alex meant to ask Nickolas about the men who continued to follow him, but it never seemed to be the right moment.

In the line at the museum, they talked and laughed about J.J. and his never-ending antics, from listening to music with headphones on the train and trying to sing the Italian lyrics out loud, to his feeble efforts at speaking the language, while adding a heavy dose of street slang.

Once inside the museum Alex and Nickolas studied the works of art. "I think I would have studied to become a sculptor if I had not taken over my father's business," Nickolas said.

"Really?" Alex looked at him as he examined every detail of the statue before them, his eyes reflecting his deep appreciation and love for the art.

Nickolas nodded. "I came here for the first time when I was a young boy of seven. My mother, who was a beautiful painter, brought me here. Just the two of us. I was young, but I was still able to appreciate the exquisite beauty of this city and the many treasures she holds."

He explained the different artistic periods, and the great artists that lived during them, as they wandered down the long halls of the museum filled with paintings, sculptures and tapestries.

"But this," he said as they rounded a corner, "is what changed me forever."

They entered a long hallway. When Alex looked up, her breath caught in her throat. At the end of the hall, illuminated by spotlights, stood the magnificent sculpture of David.

Looking at such a stunning piece of work, Alex was overcome with a whirlwind of strong and unexpected emotions inside of her. Perhaps it was simply the fact that she'd heard about Michelangelo all her life, or that she'd seen pictures or replicas of his work dozens of times and was finally seeing the statue in real life. Or perhaps it was a sudden and overwhelming appreciation of the great gift God had given to one single man who had used it to portray figures of historical and religious importance, namely David, and the Savior himself.

Held speechless by its height and intricate beauty, Alex admired the sculpture, its detail and perfection, as if the Creator himself had been the artist.

"Can I ask you something, Nicko?"

"Of course, Alexis, anything."

"Why do you think so many of the paintings and statues are naked?"

Nickolas chuckled, then laughed out loud, his laughter echoing through the open hallways.

"I've heard it said that these artists appreciated the beauty and wonder of the human body and considered it the greatest work of art. Perhaps that is why they tried so often to imitate it."

"That was a silly question," she said, "I'm sorry."

"No, Alexis, not silly at all. Just refreshing. I find your questions and everything else about you completely refreshing."

As they finished the tour of the museum and walked back to the train station, Alex said, "In Rome I had such a difficult time believing that I was actually walking streets that were built so close to the time Christ lived upon the earth. But I am continually overwhelmed when I see what incredible creations your country holds. I had no idea it was like this."

"My mother always felt the best education was outside of the school room. Many times she took my brother and sister and me on trips to places all over Europe. She wanted the experience to come to life in front of our eyes, not from a text book. When I learned about the Taj Mahal, it was in Agra, India, standing in front of it, not sitting in a classroom looking at a picture."

"She must have been a wonderful person."

"Yes," he said softly, "she was. I have felt very empty since she passed away."

Alex realized that Nickolas, in his own way, was experiencing a sort of reality check. Perhaps with the passing of his mother, he had learned how delicate and fragile life was, and how family, loved ones, and true happiness were more important than any amount of money or social status a person could ever achieve.

She believed she was seeing a deeper side of Nickolas that he rarely showed anyone else.

Florence was wonderful, but Alex was completely unprepared for their next stop.

Arriving at the Venice train station the group gathered their belongings and followed Nickolas outside.

"Would you look at that?" J.J. said. "My momma would be on her knees in prayer right now if she were here."

Alex could see why. Directly in front of them, not fifty feet from the doors of the train station, lay the glimmering city of Venice. An enormous bridge arched over the canal and was busy with tourists. On the water bobbed large bus-sized boats loaded with more tourists. There were small motorized boats and shiny black gondolas with pointed ends and stripe-shirted gondoliers.

"Take a picture," Julianne thrust her camera into J.J.'s hand. "Alex, Gabi, everyone—stand here so you can be in the picture. Then I'll take one of you, J.J."

The pictures were snapped and the group traveled to their hotel in a small water taxi. Julianne went through a whole roll of film as they floated down the Grand Canal, the main artery of the city. Alex's neck was sore from flipping her head from side to side, as she tried to take in every red and white barber-striped gondola post and every crumbling, ornate building.

"What do you think?" Nickolas asked her.

"It keeps getting better . . . every sight, every city . . . I am completely overwhelmed. It doesn't seem real."

"I've been here many times and am still enchanted by Venice. There isn't another city like it in all the world."

How she wished she could share the sights with Rich. He would never believe the art and beauty in every direction. But he wasn't here to share it with. And it was time she quit dwelling on it. Being here, in Europe like this, was a chance in a lifetime and, she realized, she didn't want anything to ruin it.

* * *

Dinner was at the Danieli Terrace where they could eat outside and enjoy a view of the lagoon. J.J. had been careful to order something safe, but Wes went for the *pasta nera,* which was black noodles with squid. The black color came from the squid's ink. Just the sight of it had Alex's stomach reeling.

Their hotel, the Hotel Rialto, was right next to the famous Rialto bridge. After dinner some of the group opted to go back to their hotel to freshen up and go to one of the coffeehouses that Goethe, Mark Twain, Ernest Hemingway, and Thomas Mann had frequented. Again, as if by design, Alex found herself alone with Nickolas.

They sauntered down to a beautiful square where pigeons were as numerous as the tourists. There was a charm and a beauty about the city Alex had never experienced anywhere else in the world.

Nickolas told her how the city was slowly, but surely, sinking and that one day it would no longer exist. The thought saddened her and she looked around at the great buildings, the ornate palaces and domed cathedrals and hoped that somehow the city could be spared. Her eyes took in the beauty of the buildings, and the way the setting sun reflected crimson and copper off the surface of the water. As she looked around, she caught a glimpse of the two men who had faithfully followed Nickolas wherever he went. Most of the time they were out of sight, but seeing them reminded her that she wanted to know what exactly their purpose was.

Finding a bench near the water's edge, they sat down side by side.

"Nicko."

"Yes, *mi bella.*"

"I have noticed the two men who follow you wherever you go. Who are they?"

"Ahhh," he sighed. "Life is a funny thing, is it not?"

She didn't understand his answer.

"My father spent his entire life working and sacrificing to build his business and become successful. I was given his business when I was only a young man, but I've never forgotten the effort required to achieve what my father accomplished.

"But along with his business came many challenges." He rubbed his hand on his chin as he thought about his words. "I too have made sacrifices to take my father's small business and turn it into one of the continent's largest companies of its kind. But, as I said, that has come from hard work and great sacrifice."

She wondered exactly what kind of sacrifices he'd had to make to achieve his success. What kind of price was Nicko willing to pay for greatness and wealth?

"Money and power bring with it many challenges. But one of the greatest is security. You see, Alexis," he took her hand in his and caressed it softly, "I am not liked by everyone. In fact, there are many who feel threatened by me and even hate me for my wealth and position."

"Have you ever been in danger?" she said with alarm.

"Oh, yes, many, many times. In fact, any time I am outside I am most vulnerable so I am forced to have protection at all times. Guido and Maurice are very devoted, and I trust them with my life."

Then she had a thought that frightened her. If he was in danger when he was outside, being with him made her also vulnerable. A worried look must have crossed her face because Nickolas quickly said, "My sweet Alexis, this has frightened you. I am sorry. Believe me, I would never put you in jeopardy. You mean far too much to me to ever put you in a situation where you could be threatened."

She wanted to believe him, but needed to dispel the rumors she'd heard of his Mafia connections. She also felt that if she were going to work for the man, and have a business relationship with him, she deserved to know the truth.

Without a second thought, she charged ahead before she lost her courage. "I've heard, Nicko, that you have connections with the Mafia."

Nicko started laughing, an innocent boyish laugh that echoed around the square. A few startled pigeons fluttered into flight, then landed and continued pecking for food. "The Mafia, me?" He laughed again. "I am flattered that you think I am important enough for the Mafia to pay any attention to. No, my dear, I am not rich enough, nor am I ruthless enough, to interest them. And even if they did approach me, I am not interested in them. I stay out of their way, and they leave me alone. It is the way I prefer it."

Alex felt silly for asking, but was relieved at his answer. Just then a cool wind swept off the ocean and she shuddered.

"You are cold," he said, removing his jacket. "The air is cool here near the water."

He slipped his sports jacket around her shoulders. The fabric was soft and smooth against her cheek. The musky scent of his cologne filled her head.

"Thank you, Nicko. I was a bit cool."

"So, do you have any more questions, *cara mia?*"

"No," she said. "But thank you for your honesty and openness."

"Ah, my dear," he took her hand and kissed her knuckles, "for you I am an open book."

She smiled at him. If anyone else tried to speak as Nickolas did, it would be corny, but he did it with such charm he was practically irresistible.

"Would you like to take the gondola ride with me now?"

"But it's almost night time."

"It is most beautiful at night."

Somehow that didn't surprise her. Her eyes scanned for Julianne or any of the others to invite along, but they were long gone.

Nickolas located a gondolier who was more than happy to take them on a tour of the city. They boarded the narrow boat and once they were settled, a push from the long oar set them coasting through the water.

Due to the design of the boat, Alex had no choice but to sit right next to Nickolas. With his arm placed comfortably around her shoulders, she relaxed and enjoyed the view. Their gondolier, Enricko, had a beautiful voice and sang "Santa Lucia" as they slipped quietly through the water, past the ornate buildings, crumbling with history.

The canals were dimly lit, aided only by the lantern from the boat, and the disappearing sun. Occasionally laughter and music could be heard as they floated silently beneath arched bridges.

Enricko pointed out various points of interest: an elaborate church, the San Simeone Piccolo, modeled after the Pantheon in Rome; a gothic palace, the Ca' d'Oro, built in 1421; and dozens of other churches, palaces, and bridges.

As they inched their way down a narrow passageway, with the water slapping against the sides of the boat, Nickolas pointed out one more landmark. A tiny enclosed bridge some thirty feet in the air, stretched from one building's top floor, across the ten-foot width of the canal, to the adjacent building.

"This is called the 'Bridge of Sighs,'" he explained. "It connects the Doge's Palace and the state prison. As prisoners were transported from one building to the other, they would look out the window and see a glimpse of the world outside and sigh with sadness and hope that one day they would again be on the outside."

Outlined by a brilliant half moon, Alex studied the bridge as they approached it, then traveled beneath it. At that moment she turned to ask Nickolas a question, and without warning, he kissed her.

She stiffened with surprise. But he was so tender, so gentle, she allowed his kiss to linger a moment longer. Perhaps it was the moonlight, or the water, or Nickolas's romantic charms, that rendered her mind useless, until her good sense finally broke the magic spell.

Placing her hand on his chest, she pushed them apart. "I . . . I . . ." She didn't know what to say.

"*Cara mia,* I am sorry. I could not resist. The night, and you, Alexis, are so beautiful. Please forgive me."

"You don't have to apologize."

"Maybe this will help you forgive me. I have something for your bracelet." Nickolas pulled a box from his pocket, black velvet, of course, and handed it to her.

To her delight she opened it to find, glistening in the lamplight, an adorable solid gold gondola with a tiny diamond on it.

"Oh, Nicko, how wonderful. I love it."

"I'm glad you like it."

"But you didn't have to. In fact, you have to stop. You're starting to embarrass me."

"Alexis, please, don't ever be embarrassed about my affections. I care about you, and this is my way of showing you. I don't mean to make you uncomfortable."

"Nicko, no, I didn't mean that. It's just that you have given me so many expensive gifts and I have nothing to give you in return."

"But I don't need you to give me gifts. I have everything money can buy. What I don't have is a friend, someone to spend time with, to laugh with."

For the first time since she'd met him, Alex felt sorry for him. Here was a man of great wealth and power, who was nevertheless very lonely.

"Then, I thank you, Nicko. For being my friend, and for your kindness and generosity."

"It is my pleasure."

There was such a sweet sincerity in his voice that she couldn't fight her heart's wish to care for him. He was a wonderful, giving, and loving person.

This wasn't about love, or a relationship, or a future, she thought. This was about being friends, sharing kindness, and concern. That was all.

That's all, she told herself one more time.

Chapter 28

The next week flew by. After Venice, Nickolas returned to Rome for business. With the help of Gina Puccoli, a new guide and escort, the group continued on to Milan, where they presented afternoon workshops, speaking to small groups about various fitness topics like diet supplements and weight training, injury prevention, and Alex's area of focus—nutrition.

Then they continued on to Monte Carlo. Aside from outrageous prices on everything, including drinking water and the use of bathroom facilities, there was an unbelievable number of casinos and more nudity on the beaches than Alex ever would have imagined. She wasn't so naive as to have expected otherwise, but still, the open display of unclad bodies made her extremely uncomfortable. Wes was in heaven and headed right to the beach, with the others close behind. Alex opted to spend her time sending postcards and buying souvenirs for the family.

The workshop in Monte Carlo turned out to be great fun and very successful. Participants traveled from the west side of Italy and the south of France to get there. They were the most energetic fitness fanatics Alex had ever encountered. They went wild over every workshop, especially J.J.'s funk and hip-hop.

Thursday Alex and the others were in Barcelona for more of the same, a day workshop with a much smaller group of participants, but with every bit as much of the same enthusiasm.

The next two days were spent working their way northward to Paris. When they finally arrived at the Parc de Bercy hotel in Paris, Alex retreated to her room to finally unwind, relax, and place a much-needed phone call home.

Jamie answered after the first ring.

"Jamie, hi. It's me."

"Alex, how are you?"

"I'm great. Sorry I haven't called for a few days. I've been to so many places, it's all a blur. I hope I can keep track of all the pictures I've taken."

"The last time you called you were in Monte Carlo, right?" Jamie asked.

"Right."

"Now you're in Paris?" Jamie asked. "How is it?"

"Right now it's raining and kind of cold. I haven't really seen much of it yet. But we go to EuroDisney in a few days for a big two-day convention. It's supposed to be huge. There's a big sports convention going on at the same time, promoting fitness equipment and all kinds of booths."

"Are you having fun?" Jamie asked.

"I guess so. Yeah, it's fun, but exhausting. We're on the go constantly. I'm glad I'm in good shape or I would've collapsed in Spain." But she hadn't called to tell them about her trip; they could read that on her post cards. She had more important questions. "So, how is everyone?"

"We're all great," Jamie answered. "You should see the baby. I'm telling you, she is such a doll. When she smiles, her whole face lights up. She's even slept through the night a few times. You won't believe how much she's grown."

Alex hated missing out. "Make sure you videotape her."

"We are. Steve never even puts the camera away. He's got it turned on more than it's off."

"Good. I can hardly wait to see it. I really miss all of you."

"We miss you, too."

"How's Mom? Did she go back to New York?"

"Yeah, she's home, but she calls every day. She finally told me what happened between her and Dr. Rawlins."

"What?"

"He proposed to her."

"He did? Jamie, that's wonderful."

"It would be except she told him she couldn't get married to him until she joined the Church."

"You're kidding!"

"No, I promise. But the problem is, she told him she wasn't ready to join the Church, and she didn't know if she would ever be ready."

"Oh no."

"Yeah, it's pretty sad. She's miserable without him, and he's miserable without her. He comes over all the time, just to see the baby and visit. He's so lonely."

"This is terrible."

"I agree. It's so weird, because he wanted to marry her, without her even being a member. It's Mom who won't go ahead with it. She said she would never again be in a marriage where both people weren't the same religion."

"I hope they can work things out soon."

"Me too, Alex."

"How is Steve?"

"He's actually doing quite well. The insurance is finally straightened out, which is a big relief. It's been so hard not having Rich around. Steve says he talked to him and he doesn't seem to have much interest in the business anymore."

"Did he call from Park City?"

"No, he called from Los Angeles.

Just when she thought she was doing okay, getting stronger, caring less, the old wound opened right back up. Just as deep, just as vulnerable, just as painful. Rich hadn't made any effort to contact her at all. It was as if Alex had gone to Europe, and he'd wiped her out of his mind and heart. It hurt deeply to think Rich didn't care anymore. She was ashamed of herself for doubting, but she'd lost hope in him.

Forcing herself to stay strong, Alex said, "What about Steve? Has he decided what he's going to do now?"

"He's considering reopening the outdoor rental business, but he's been talking about going back to law school."

"Law school?!"

"He's always wanted to be an attorney but got sidetracked when he and Rich started their own business. I know it would be hard to go back to school at twenty-seven, but it's not that unusual. Who knows, maybe this will all turn out to be a blessing in disguise."

Alex appreciated her sister's faith and positive attitude. For their sakes, she hoped it did turn out to be a blessing in disguise. She hated the thought of them having to struggle any more than they needed to.

Faith and a positive attitude. That made all the difference. But Alex was afraid it would take more than faith and a positive attitude to help her.

Fear departs when faith endures. Where did that come from? Was it a scripture? No, it was from a hymn. But Alex didn't know if her faith could endure. She had to give up on Rich. Why shouldn't she? She would love to hold onto him, but there was nothing to hold on to anymore.

* * *

Early the next morning, after a light breakfast of a roll and juice, Alex and Julianne walked out into the streets of Paris alone. Except for a few workers in the tobacco stands and the people at bus stops, the sidewalks were bare. It was Sunday; the whole town was shut down.

"Thanks for coming with me, Julianne."

"Hey, I don't have anything else to do on a Sunday morning," she said. "Besides, it wouldn't hurt me to go into a church once in a while."

They were on their way to find the LDS chapel. The concierge at the hotel had given them directions, and with Julianne's limited knowledge of French they were hopeful they would have some luck.

"Still no word from your boyfriend?" Julianne asked as they waited in line for the number fifty-two bus.

"Not one word. I must have completely misread his actions and words."

"Who knows how a man's mind works? They are a curious lot, never sharing their feelings. And then when they do, in my experience, they lie about it."

Alex wouldn't exactly accuse Rich of lying. If anything he was guilty of not accepting his feelings. His biggest problem was that he listened to his head and not his heart.

* * *

"The building's completely locked." Alex jiggled the door handle one more time. After three wrong bus transfers and a long wait for a subway, they had finally found the building. But it was after one o'clock, church had ended, and everyone was gone.

"I'm sorry. I thought I understood the directions completely."

"That's okay," Alex leaned against the door. "I never would have found this place by myself."

"Hey, someone's coming."

Sure enough, two young men in dark suits and white shirts turned the corner and approached them.

"Good afternoon," Alex said as they drew nearer. "Are you the missionaries?" She knew it was a dumb question since they had name tags on, but it seemed the right thing to ask.

The elders' faces brightened. "Yes," the shorter one answered. He had plump, rosy cheeks and cheerful blue eyes. "I'm Elder Shibler and this is my companion, Elder Maklovich."

"Nice to meet you, elders." Alex shook both of their hands then let Julianne take her turn. "My name is Alexis McCarty and this is my friend Julianne Leighton. We're in town for a couple of days and hoped to make it to church this morning."

"We had a bit of trouble finding our way," Julianne said.

"So, you're members?"

"I am," Alex said. "Julianne's not."

"But I have a cousin on a mission in Salt Lake City, Utah."

"That's great," Elder Shibler said. He turned when voices carried their way. Two young girls and a young man waved when they saw the elders.

Greetings and introductions were made. The youth were members of the ward.

"So, if church is over, why are all of you here?" Alex asked.

"We're having a baptism in half an hour," Elder Maklovich answered. Alex expected him to speak with a Slavik accent but found out he was from Idaho. He told them his ancestors were Czechoslovakian, but he'd been born in the United States.

"Would you like to stay for the service?" Elder Shibler asked.

Alex and Julianne looked at each other and shrugged. "Sure, why not."

The ward mission leader, Brother Marquard, arrived shortly after and let them in the building. He was a friendly man who'd lived in

London for several years. After talking several minutes, he and Julianne discovered they had some mutual acquaintances.

Jean Pierre, the man who was getting baptized, arrived with his girlfriend and several other ward members. He was thirtyish, stood about five feet tall and was very slightly built. They learned he was a jockey. His girlfriend, who stood a good three inches above him, was already LDS.

More members arrived while Jean Pierre and Elder Shibler changed into their baptismal clothing.

"Are you sure you're okay with this?" Alex asked Julianne.

"Sure. I'm kind of curious to see what it's like. I have a question, though. How come they need a font to do the baptism?"

Alex explained the difference between baptism by immersion and the sprinkling method used by most churches. There was even a picture on the wall of the Savior being baptized by John the Baptist. Julianne seemed to accept the explanation without question.

"Mind if I sit next to you?" Brother Marquard asked.

"No, please," Julianne motioned to the seat next to her.

The two picked up their conversation of London and different points of interest, while Alex listened from the sidelines. She noticed that Brother Marquard wasn't wearing a wedding ring. She also noticed that he hadn't taken his eyes off Julianne's face since he sat down.

At first glance he hadn't struck Alex as particularly good-looking, but as she watched him, his animated way of talking, his contagious laugh and broad smile, she'd decided that he was actually quite handsome, and his looks were enhanced by his warm personality.

A young woman played prelude music while the congregation's voices dropped to whispers. Julianne and Brother Marquard continued to speak until a gentleman stood up and addressed the group.

The baptism service was short but very beautiful. Alex marveled at how quickly the Spirit filled her even though she didn't understand a single word of what was being said.

Watching the baptism reminded Alex of her own service barely a month ago, which reminded her of her family and Rich, which brought a feeling of homesickness to her chest. She pushed the feeling deep down inside and forced her mind to focus on the closing hymn.

She and Julianne stayed for a moment after the meeting to congratulate the new member and say good-bye to the elders. As they were about to leave, Brother Marquard met them at the door.

"Thank you for staying, ladies."

"We enjoyed it very much, André," Julianne answered.

Alex looked at her friend with surprise. Obviously they had covered a lot of ground in their brief conversation, especially since they were on a first name basis now.

"I'll call you at your hotel tomorrow evening and perhaps we can get together?" Brother Marquard said, addressing Julianne.

"I'd like that," she said. She turned to Alex, "André says there's a wonderful restaurant overlooking the Seine he'd like to take me to."

"We'd love to have you come with us," he invited Alex.

"I'll have to see. I've made some tentative plans already." She knew she was stretching the truth. She didn't have any plans, but there was a Milky Way of stars in their eyes, and she wasn't about to tag along with them.

Finding their way back to the hotel was much easier than finding the church. Julianne talked of nothing but meeting André. Not only did they have mutual acquaintances, he was actually getting ready to move back to London in a few months and had solicited her input on areas of the city in which to rent a flat.

"Isn't it something?" Julianne said. "Just when you least expect it, someone wonderful steps into your life."

Alex looked at her friend in amazement. She'd really flipped for this guy quickly.

Julianne went on, "I know I just met him, but he was so easy to talk to and so fascinating. He's done so many things in his life—traveled to Africa and throughout the rain forests of South America; he even lived in Tibet for a while. He was a photo journalist for many years, but decided to find a job that doesn't require so much traveling. He's in communications now and is doing quite well."

"He seems like a nice guy," Alex said, not knowing for sure what to say.

"Do you think I'm crazy to go out with him tomorrow night?"

"How do you feel about it?"

"I feel great about it. Excited. I really think I should have at least one date with him. Who knows what could happen?"

"Then you should go. Trust your instincts, listen with your heart. That's what my father always told me. I've learned that it really works."

The bus pulled up to their stop. They stepped out onto the curb.

"Do you think I could borrow one of your books to look at?" Julianne said as she led off down the street. Alex was completely turned around and hoped her friend knew where they were going.

"Sure, which one?"

"The Mormon book. I'd like to take a look at it before tomorrow night. You know, just so I can be more familiar with André's beliefs."

Alex was dumbfounded. She'd been meaning to give a Book of Mormon to Julianne, but had never expected her to ask for one.

"Of course you can borrow it. In fact, you can have it. I've got extra."

"Thanks!"

As many times as Alex questioned the "whys" of the Lord's will, she was glad she had the faith to obey, even when she didn't understand. Going to Europe had seemed like such a big mistake, but moments like this confirmed her promptings to come on this trip.

Still, it was painful to realize Rich was no longer a part of her life. It was hard to let go. She felt like she was hanging on by her pinkies, and knew it wouldn't be long before her strength wore out and the ties would be completely severed.

Again, she relied on her faith in the Lord that he knew what he was doing. She trusted him and knew her life was in his hands. But not knowing what the future would bring nearly drove her crazy!

* * *

"There it is, Disneyland Paris," J.J. shouted when he saw the park's big welcome sign.

"Man, J.J., you'd think you'd never been to Disneyland before," Wes said. He sat next to Gina, their guide who had been with them since Venice. She was a beautiful woman, and Wes hadn't wasted any time getting to know her better.

"I haven't. We were too poor when I was a kid and now I'm too busy."

"I've never been there either," Ricky said. "Venezuela is quite a ways from Disneyland."

"I've never been there," Gabi said. "Have you, Julianne?"

"Actually, I came to Disneyland Paris just last year. And I have been to the park in Florida."

"I'm just glad Nicko—las," Alex added, "allowed us to have a day at the park just for fun. I haven't been to Disneyland since I was in high school."

The shuttle driver dropped them off at the ticket booth in front of the park. J.J. whirled on his heel taking in all the excitement around him.

"Let's go to the Indiana Jones ride first. They have it here, don't they?" J.J. asked.

"Yes, it's called Indiana Jones *et le Temple du Peril,*" Julianne said, "The lines get long so we better hurry."

Alex found that trying to keep up with the boys was a workout in itself. Since there wasn't a crowd at the park yet, there weren't any lines. As soon as they got off the ride, they got right back in line and did it again. And again. And again. After the fifth time Alex couldn't take it any longer.

Julianne and Alex ended up splitting from the group; Gabi opted to stay with the guys. They planned to meet up for lunch in Discoveryland by Space Mountain, or *De la Terre a la Lune,* as it was called.

The crowds grew as the day wore on. The group of fitness friends met for lunch just in time to miss an afternoon thundershower that helped cool off the August heat. Everytime they passed a Disney character, J.J. stopped to get his picture taken and a signature in his autograph book. He had a mouse ears hat made with his initials, and he purchased and immediately changed into a Disneyworld Paris t-shirt with a computer-generated picture of him imprinted on the front.

By the time they finished the park, they'd been on every ride at least once and some of them, like Big Thunder Mountain, Pirates of the Caribbean, and J.J.'s favorite, It's a Small World, two or three times. They were exhausted.

Luckily they'd changed hotels and were staying at the brand new Newport Bay Club Convention Center right there on Disney property. In minutes they were in their hotel rooms recuperating from all the fun.

It took all six of them to carry J.J.'s souvenirs to his room. He'd purchased something for every member of his family. He had eight brothers and sisters.

Alex's phone was ringing when she entered her room.

"Hello," she said breathlessly.

"Alex, darling, how was your day?"

"Nicko, hi. It was great. Where are you?" She sat down on the bed and kicked off her shoes.

"I'm on my way to Paris right now. My plane lands in half an hour."

Alex glanced at the clock. It was almost eight.

"How's the hotel?" he asked.

"Wonderful. We saw the room where the convention is tomorrow. It's unbelievable." When Nicko said first-class, he meant it. Everywhere they went, they received red carpet service. She was surprised he hadn't reserved the whole theme park just for them.

"Did everyone have a good time at the park?"

"We had a ball. Too bad you couldn't go with us," she said, although she had a hard time picturing Nickolas on the rides or stuffing his face with cotton candy.

"Maybe there will be time to pop over tomorrow after the convention."

"That would be fun," Alex said, as she relaxed against the soft pillows—until she felt a hard object underneath her head. Just then, the connection broke up, static charged the line.

"I just wanted to check on you. I'll see you tomorrow then." Alex thought his voice sounded hopeful, full of anticipation. As always, when she was with him, she felt flattered that he so clearly enjoyed her company.

"Uh, thanks for calling, Nicko." *What is this?* She reached around behind her.

"You're welcome. Enjoy your surprise."

"What surprise?"

It was too late; he'd hung up the phone.

"What surprise?" she said again, then looked at the object in her hand. A black, velvet box. Shaking her head in amazement she opened the lid to find a solid gold Mickey Mouse charm. The phone rang again.

"Nicko, I love it."

"Nicko? Who's Nicko? Alex, is that you? This is Rich."

Chapter 29

"Rich!" Alex nearly hyperventilated.

"Who's Nicko?" he asked.

"Oh, I'm sorry. I was just on the phone with our tour coordinator." Even though Rich couldn't see her, Alex felt her face burn. She couldn't believe what she'd just done.

"I see. Is this the guy who sent you the flowers at the airport?" Alex couldn't quite identify the tone in his voice.

"Yes." She felt faint. Why hadn't she kept that stupid card?

"Sounds like I caught you at a bad time." This time Alex couldn't mistake the definite edge of sarcasm in his voice.

"No, not at all," she said quickly. "I'm so happy you called. I've been wondering about you."

"You have?" he said flatly.

"Yes, Rich, I have." His tone puzzled her. He sounded like he didn't believe her. "How are you?"

"I'm fine, and you?"

"I'm fine, too."

An awkward silence stretched across the hundreds of miles of phone cord.

"How's your painting going?"

"Good. I haven't been able to get much done. I was in L.A. for a while."

So, he'd finally said something about the L.A. trip. She'd wondered if he ever would.

"That's what Jamie said. How was it?"

"Good, good."

She felt like she was talking to a complete stranger.

"Are you in Park City?"

"Yes."

"Did you get my postcards?"

"I did. Thanks. Looks like you've been to some interesting places."

"Rich, you would've loved Florence. There were so many museums and so much art. I didn't have time to see hardly any of it. And Rome. You would love Rome."

He didn't say anything.

"There's so much to see. It's incredible . . ." she trailed off.

"I'm glad you're having such a good time."

Had she said she was having a good time? The man had no clue what he was putting her through, how much pain he had caused her.

"Rich, is something wrong? You sound like you're mad or something."

"No," he said quietly. "I'm not mad. I've just been under some stress lately."

"What kind of stress?" She couldn't imagine what.

"You don't want to hear about it."

"Sure I do," she insisted.

"It's nothing. I'm just having some trouble with my painting."

"I'm sorry."

"Yeah, thanks." He didn't sound at all like himself. What was wrong? Something had to be terribly wrong. More than just the note from Nicko.

Again there was silence. She didn't know what to say.

"Well, I'd better let you go. I just wanted to see how you were doing," he said.

Her heart caught in her throat. She wanted to cry out to him to open up to her, to share his feelings. But she couldn't. "I'm glad you called, Rich. I've missed you."

"I've missed you, too," he said.

Tears stung her eyes. "I wish you could be here, seeing all these things."

"Yeah," he mumbled.

"Give me your number," she said. "I'll give you a call soon."

He gave it to her, then said, "Take care, Alex."

"I will. You too."

He hung up first. She burst into tears before her phone made it to the receiver.

* * *

Leaving Paris behind, they went on to Brussels, then up into Holland where they did a convention in Amsterdam. Alex had heard complaints that the city was dirty and it had a seedy side, but she loved Amsterdam. The canals, the feeling, the whole look of the city, reminded her a lot of Venice. Gina explained to the group as they traveled down the Prinsen canal to their hotel that at the end of the war, nearly 1,400 buildings in the city were demolished and over 2,000 were left uninhabitable.

Alex was amazed at the determination and drive the people in Europe had, as city after city was destroyed and those who had survived were left to rebuild. If anything, this trip had brought to life everything she'd learned in school in her world history classes. She gained a whole new appreciation for the European people.

Alex tried to call Rich several times, but he was never home. She left messages on his answering machine, but they went unanswered. Luckily she was able to lose herself in the hectic pace of the Supertour and didn't let her concerns about Rich pull her down.

Long-distance calls weren't working for her but they were working for Julianne and André. They spoke on the phone for hours every night. If Julianne wasn't talking about André, she was asking questions about the Book of Mormon and the Church.

Alex was concerned Julianne's interest in the Church was mostly because of André. But after sharing her concerns with her friend, Julianne told Alex she was reading the scriptures because she liked what they were teaching her. Julianne had grown up in a religious home, and had been taught to pray as a little girl and attended Sunday School most of her life.

"It's funny," Julianne told her, "all my life I've learned about Jesus Christ and about the commandments, but it hasn't been until we started talking and I've been reading the Book of Mormon that it finally seems to all make sense. I've never before felt the way I feel now when I read the scriptures. What do you think that means?"

Alex smiled at her friend, and told her how she'd felt when she first noticed the Spirit actually working in her life.

"You mean, the Holy Ghost is giving me those feelings?" Julianne's eyebrows lifted in surprise.

"That's right, and after a person is baptized, he or she gets to have the Holy Ghost as a constant companion."

"You get to feel that way all the time?"

"Well, yeah, mostly when I'm doing spiritual stuff like praying and scriptures and being at church. But there have been times when we've been talking, you know, when you ask me questions, and I've felt the Spirit."

"I have, too! I just didn't know it."

"It means that the things you are learning about are true, Julianne."

"So what do I do now?"

"You follow your heart and keep studying and praying. The Lord will guide you and help you."

Julianne nodded in understanding, but her face had a worried look on it.

"Is something wrong?" Alex asked.

"No, not really," she said. "It's just that Mums and Pop would have a hard time if I became a Mormon. They haven't had much good to say about my uncle's family, you know, Sydney's family, joining your church."

"Everything will work out," Alex said, reaching out and resting her hand on her friend's shoulder. "Believe me, I've been in your shoes."

"Thank you, Alex."

"For what?"

"Oh, I don't know, for everything. But mostly for being such a good friend."

At first Alex had been surprised by Julianne's interest in the gospel, questioning her sincerity, but now she realized Julianne was receiving spiritual guidance and was indeed being prompted to seek after the truth. Alex learned a very important lesson that day. Never again would she try and decide who was ready for the gospel. Even the most unlikely person, someone she would never dream of, could be waiting, literally yearning, to find the truth and receive the gospel message.

And she knew the Lord expected her to help provide as many opportunities for others to hear his message as she could.

In the train, on the way from Amsterdam to Cologne, Germany, Julianne and Alex got into one of their many gospel discussions.

Julianne was sharing her feelings about the account of the Lord's visit to the Americas after his crucifixion when J.J. decided to get in on the conversation.

"You talkin' 'bout your Mormon book?" he asked.

"Yes," Julianne answered. "I've been reading it."

"I didn't know Mormons believed in Christ." He directed his question to Alex but it was Julianne who answered.

"J.J., of course Mormons believe in Christ. In fact, the name of their church is The Church of Jesus Christ of Latter-Day Saints. This whole book," she held up her copy of the Book of Mormon, "testifies of Christ and was written by the early inhabitants of ancient America."

"My mama always wanted me to go to church, but I wasn't much into all that singin' and prayin' and stuff."

"Let me ask you something, J.J.," Julianne said. "Do you feel it's important to teach others about the importance of good health and fitness?"

"Sure I do. Otherwise I wouldn't be here."

"Why do you feel it's so important?"

"Because, man, when you take care of yourself, your whole life is better—less illness, more energy, better attitude, stronger body, lookin' good . . . all kinds of reasons."

"That's why your mother wanted you to go to church and that's why you should read the Book of Mormon, because it will improve your life."

He looked at her out of the corner of his eye, his eyebrow raised. "Really?" He looked over at Alex, giving her a questioning glance.

"Really," both Alex and Julianne said in unison.

"It says all of this in that book of yours?"

"It sure does," Julianne said. "And if you want you can have this one." She shoved the book into his hands.

"No, that's okay." He handed it back.

"J.J., it's a gift. I want to give it to you," Julianne returned it. "Alex has more copies. I can get another one from her." She glanced at Alex. "Right?" Alex nodded.

"All right," he said, accepting the book. "I guess I could take a look at it. Sure would surprise my mama if she knew I even owned a religious book."

He excused himself to find the dining car, promising to bring them each back a bottle of Evian.

Julianne had surprised her. Alex was also grateful she'd been prompted to bring extra copies of the Book of Mormon along on the trip with her.

* * *

After a quick overnight stop for a small conference in Cologne, Germany, and a look at the Kölner Dom—a cathedral as beautiful as any Alex had seen during her entire trip, and the most famous in all of Germany—the group then traveled to Boppard, Germany, where they boarded a boat for a cruise down the Rhine River.

Once again Alex felt she was in a fairy tale as they floated down the peaceful river. On either side of the Rhine, beautiful castles dotted the lush green cliffs above its shores. Relaxing in the warm afternoon sun, Alex felt as though she were transported back in time. She could almost imagine medieval knights and round tables, kings and queens, damsels in distress.

A lump rose in her throat as she thought about Rich, who at one time seemed like her knight in shining armor. But he wasn't there to rescue her anymore.

"Mind if I sit next to you?"

It was Nicko.

"Oh, hi. I'd like that." Alex moved over, making room for him on the bench.

He took his seat and caught a waiter as he passed by, ordering them each a glass of cold apple juice.

"How was everything in Brussels?" she asked. He'd stayed on after the conference to do some business with his sister there. Alex had been hoping to meet Sophia but between his sister's meetings and Alex's demands, they were never able to get together.

"Wonderful, thank you. Sophia had good news."

"Oh?"

"She's engaged to be married."

"Who's the lucky guy?"

"His name is Michael Thainestone. He's one of our affiliates in

Manhattan and a very good friend of mine. In fact, he's helping me put this deal together for the fitness facility we're building. We've all known each other a long time. I knew this would happen sooner or later, and I'm very happy for both of them."

"That's wonderful."

"Thank you. So, how are you, Alexis? We haven't spoken much lately."

"I'm fine. I'm enjoying the trip a lot. Thank you for scheduling in sightseeing and excursions like this."

"It is important to me that you and all of the team enjoy yourselves."

"This cruise is unbelievable. I was just imagining what it must have been like to live during the time the castles were inhabited."

"Look," Nickolas pointed up ahead. "That is the famous Lorelei Rock."

Ahead of them on the right bank of the Rhine, about 425 feet above the river, was an enormous, towering rock peak.

"Why is it famous?"

"The Rhine River has always been and still is, one of Europe's most important waterways. Long ago a tunnel was bored through the rock, which created a mysterious echo. Legend has it that a beautiful siren would lure sailors to their destruction by the music of her voice."

All of Europe seemed to be filled with stories of enchantment, mystery, legend, and fables. Famous sights were abundant in an atmosphere as rich as the decades past. Walking the streets, seeing all the ruins, was like a storybook coming to life before her very eyes.

The waiter brought their drinks, and Nickolas and Alex chatted comfortably, enjoying the scenery and the beauty of the day. Nickolas was attentive, caring, and kind. She loved the way he looked her straight in the eye when she spoke, as if every word she said was the most important thing in the world to him.

"Excuse me, sir," their waiter said. "You have a phone call."

"Thank you," Nickolas said. He turned to Alex, took her hand in his, and kissed her knuckles lingeringly. "Don't go away. I will be right back."

"I'll be here," she said, then watched him walk away, his two bodyguards leaving their posts and following behind. She didn't think she could ever grow used to having those men around her constantly, or maybe it was the fact that Nickolas needed to have armed guards around him at all times that she could never get used to.

For a moment she allowed her thoughts and feelings for Nickolas to surface. He didn't make her heart flutter, her scalp tingle, or chills go down her spine like Rich had, but she was growing fond of Nickolas. Not for his gifts or his constant flattering, but because he was caring, warm, affectionate, and generous. She liked how he made her laugh, how he accepted her the way she was, and how he was honest with his feelings.

"You better be careful, girl," J.J. said as he took a seat next to her. "That man's a big roller."

"I know," she said lightly, not wanting to validate that he needed to be concerned. "There's nothing going on between us. We're just friends."

"For some reason, I don't see a 'just friends' look in his eye."

"J.J., don't be ridiculous!"

"Hey, girl, it's your life, but I just think you ought to know who you're dealing with."

Alex folded her arms and looked away. J.J.'s warning wasn't necessary.

"The man has had affairs with hundreds of women and dozens of flings with models, actresses, and political figures. He has Mafia connections, too. Why do you think he has bodyguards?"

As if it wasn't enough to have J.J. become her surrogate father, Gabi sat down and joined in the conversation and assumed the role of surrogate mother.

"J.J.'s right, Alex."

"You guys don't understand. I don't have romantic feelings for him and he doesn't have them for me. We are just friends. Besides," she looked at each of them, "I have a hard time believing that he's as terrible as you say. He's been nothing but a kind, considerate, perfect gentleman."

"Hey," J.J. said, "for a pretty girl I could put on an Academy Award-winning performance, too."

"There's much more to him than you can even begin to understand," Gabi said.

"So, are you saying that I shouldn't even be his friend?"

"No, not at all," Gabi was quick to respond.

"We're just saying this guy's not the same underneath the surface. Let's just say," J.J. paused and looked around him, "I wouldn't want to get on his bad side."

"Do not forget, Alexis, I work for Signor Diamante. I know what he is like," Gabi said. "He is not always charming, like you see him now. He is a very powerful man. He knows what he wants and he always gets it."

The boat blew a loud whistle as it passed under a bridge, and Alex waited until it was quiet again.

"Gabi, J.J., I appreciate your concern, I really do, but I don't see how he can hurt me. There is nothing going on between us."

"Maybe for you," J.J. said, "but I still say he's got that look in his eye."

"What look, J.J.?" She was getting tired of the conversation.

"The look a lion gets, just before he attacks a gazelle."

She laughed at his absurdity. "I assure you, I am no gazelle and Nicko is definitely not a lion. He's a very powerful and wealthy man, that's true. But he's also lonely. He just happens to trust me and consider me a friend."

All three stopped talking as Nickolas emerged from the ship's cabin.

Wanting to lighten up the atmosphere, Alex asked Gabi, "Is your mother sure she wants you to bring all of us over for dinner tonight?"

Gabi didn't answer for a moment, as she watched Nickolas come toward them. Then she said, "Yes, she's probably already got a pot of sauerkraut on the stove. You like sauerkraut, don't you?"

"As long as there's no eel on the table, I'll be happy," J.J. said.

"I think I'll go find the others," Gabi said.

"Yeah, me too," J.J. followed her.

Alex watched as they greeted Nickolas. He was warm and friendly to them. She knew she wasn't wrong about him. There was probably a bit of truth in Gabi and J.J.'s advice, but it wasn't necessary in her case. They were just friends. That's all she wanted. And she was certain that was all Nickolas wanted.

Chapter 30

Dinner with Gabi's parents was unbelievable. Not only was there a giant-sized bowl of sauerkraut and bratwurst, there was a banquet table loaded with food. There was a platter of a dozen varieties of delicious breads, and another platter with a large assortment of cheeses, and a yet another platter with various types of lunch meats and sausages ranging anywhere from identifiable ham and beef cuts, to a scary-looking *blutwurst*. Alex later found out it was blood sausage and was grateful she hadn't tried it.

The meal went well and except for Gabi's parents being completely flabbergasted that *neither* Alex *nor* Julianne were interested in drinking beer, the evening was enjoyable—especially the enormous selection of desserts and chocolates following the meal. Alex thought she'd had enough chocolate to last her a lifetime while in Rome, but one taste of the creamy confection she'd chosen and she was hooked again. She knew she'd berate herself and regret it the next morning but she couldn't help herself. It was just too good.

At the hotel that night Alex slept in a bed as soft as clouds, down-filled comforter clouds. She decided she liked Germany. A lot.

The next morning, her phone rang early. It was Julianne.

"You still want to go sightseeing?"

"Yes. I'd like to locate the temple while I'm here and see some of the historic buildings in the city."

"I just got a call from J.J. He's decided to stay with Ricky. Gabi and Wes are going down to the gym where Gabi works this morning."

"Okay. What are J.J. and Ricky going to do?"

"I'm not sure. J.J. said something about Ricky not feeling well."

"He didn't eat some of that *blutwurst,* did he?"

"I don't know."

"I think I'll check on them before we go."

"Okay," Julianne said. "I'll come by your room in half an hour."

Alex wondered what was wrong with Ricky. She'd thought he hadn't seemed like himself last night at dinner. She decided to call his room before she jumped in the shower.

She was surprised when J.J. answered the phone in Ricky's room. "Hey, J.J., what's going on?"

"Ricky's really sick, man. I don't know what's wrong. He's in the bathroom right now heaving up his guts. He's all achy and has a fever."

"You probably ought to get away from him in case it's something you can catch."

"Nah, I never get sick. I could kiss someone sick right on the mouth and I still wouldn't get it."

"Well, don't go testing your immune system on Ricky."

"No way, man."

"Is there anything you need? Julianne and I are going out for a while."

"Room service is taking good care o' me. Give us a call when you get back."

"You're a good friend, J.J."

* * *

Alex and Julianne had a ball finding their way around Frankfurt. They stopped in the heart of the historic area and saw stunning churches, wonderful old buildings of historic importance, and quaint gingerbread cottages. At the train station they bought a fat German pretzel and apple juice and enjoyed it on their way to Friedrichsdorf, where the temple was located.

Julianne caught Alex up on everything André was doing and told her about their plans to meet in Salzburg to spend some time together. Hearing the name Salzburg reminded Alex of the German couple she'd met while having lunch with Rich. An uncontrollable ache pierced her heart as she longed to share these beautiful sights and moments with Rich.

Even though she was taking plenty of pictures and her charm bracelet was jingling with the many charms she'd purchased and that

Nickolas had given her, she knew she'd never be able to convey the wonder of Europe to someone who'd never been there.

With the help of some townspeople who spoke broken English, Alex and Julianne were able to find the temple. Alex got goose-bumps as they got closer and the statue of Moroni appeared above red-clay roofs.

The temple was smaller and not as ornate as the Salt Lake Temple, but there was still a heavenly beauty about its clean, simple lines and quiet dignity. The two friends walked around the grounds taking pictures of each other and the building before turning back for the train station. As they rounded the corner near the visitor's center, they ran into a pair of elders.

Introductions were made and they found out the elders were on their way back to the city. Moments later they were on the train, sailing through the German countryside together.

"Which hotel are you staying in?" Elder Brendle, from Oregon, asked.

"We're at the Palmengarten Hotel."

"That's a nice place," he said. "Our *wohnung*, I mean, apartment, isn't far from there."

"Is there anything nearby there we should go see?" Julianne asked.

"The hotel you're staying in is named after the famous Palmengarten greenhouse, Germany's largest indoor garden, which is right there in the neighborhood. It's huge and has all kinds of tropical and botanical garden displays."

"And," his companion, Elder Gubler, from St. George, Utah, said, "the city park is right across the street and is a fun place to walk through. You can see what Germans like to do in their free time."

They were excited to learn that Julianne wasn't a member but was reading the Book of Mormon and was interested in the gospel. The two elders talked about the people they were teaching in Frankfurt.

"We're teaching a family from Sri Lanka, a man from Ethiopia, a woman from Turkey, and another family from Italy," Elder Brendle said.

"But no Germans," Elder Gubler added with a laugh.

Then Alex had an idea. "Would it be difficult to get some copies of the Book of Mormon in different languages from you, elders?"

"It depends on what language you need. Oh, this is our stop." Elder Brendle grabbed his backpack and slung it onto his shoulder.

The girls got out with them since they were taking the same route back to their hotel.

"I would like to get one in Spanish, one in Italian, and one in German."

"We should have one in German at the apartment," Elder Gubler said. "And I know we have one in Italian, but I'm not sure about Spanish. But if we don't have one, our zone leaders probably do."

"We can check, then run them over to the hotel for you," Elder Brendle offered.

"That would be great." Alex caught Julianne's eye, who knew exactly what she was up to. It was fun to have "a partner in crime," or in this case, a partner in sharing the gospel.

They returned to their hotel rooms, only to learn that Ricky was feeling worse. J.J. was worried about him.

"He can't keep anything down, not even liquid. I'm afraid he's going to dehydrate if we don't get something in his stomach," he told Alex over the phone.

"Maybe we should call Gabi's mom and ask her what to do. Or we could call down to the health club and see if Nicko is there. I'm sure he could help us."

"Let me talk to Ricky and see what he wants to do. I'll call you right back."

While Alex and Julianne were waiting for J.J.'s call, the front desk buzzed them. The missionaries were downstairs.

"I'm really worried about Ricky," Julianne said on their way down the elevator. "He's going to have to cancel his presentation tomorrow."

"He won't feel much like traveling either."

The elders greeted them with smiles and presented them with a copy of each version of the Book of Mormon requested.

Instead of accepting payment for the books, they were happy to exchange them for some of Alex's English copies. The elders were able to pass them out as much as those in any other language.

"You wouldn't happen to know where the nearest hospital is, would you, elders?" Julianne asked. "One of our friends is quite ill, and we might need to take him in."

"We'd be happy to give your friend a blessing, if he'd like one," Elder Gubler offered.

A blessing! Why hadn't she thought of that? "That's a wonderful idea," Alex exclaimed. "Come upstairs with us and we'll ask."

It didn't take much persuasion to convince Ricky to give it a try. He felt so crummy he was open to anything that would help him. Judging by J.J.'s expression, Alex could tell he thought it was a little hokey, but Alex knew it would help Ricky. In fact, she realized now, there had been several reasons, divine reasons, why they'd run into those elders that day.

Humbly and sincerely, the elders anointed Ricky's head with oil then sealed the anointing with their priesthood power. Then they proceeded to give him a blessing. Ricky was promised that he would recover quickly and completely and that he would be able to carry on with his obligations. Acting as a mouthpiece for the Lord, Elder Gubler told Ricky, boldly and plainly, that "he was a treasured son of our Heavenly Father and that he had a great work to do upon the earth."

The Spirit was strong during the blessing. Alex was sure every person in the room felt it.

The elders stayed only a moment longer, just long enough to sign their testimonies inside a Book of Mormon for Ricky, then they hurried off to a teaching appointment. Alex thanked them several times for their help and promised to drop them a line and let them know how everything turned out with Ricky, and with the copies of the Book of Mormon they had given her.

Ricky fell into a much-needed sleep, and J.J. went to his room to shower before dinner. Alex was anxious to add this entry to the journal she'd been keeping during the tour and realized that the journal had become more than just a travel log of sights and tours. It had become a record of personal growth and spiritual experiences, and of the many reasons she believed the Lord had prompted her to come on this trip.

She said a quick prayer, thanking the Lord for guiding the missionaries to them. She hoped the experience was one none of them would forget.

* * *

Gabi was visibly upset when she and Wes returned from the health club where she worked in the downtown shopping area in

Frankfurt. J.J., Julianne, and Alex were downstairs at the restaurant trying to figure out how to cover for Ricky tomorrow at the fitness convention.

"What's the matter?" Julianne asked when they joined them at their table.

Gabi and Wes looked at each other before Wes answered. "Gabi's upset because Signor Diamante fired a bunch of people this afternoon. He didn't like how they were running his club."

Alex was dumbfounded. Nickolas wouldn't just do something like that for no reason.

"What do you mean, 'fired a bunch of people'?" J.J. asked

"Uwe has managed that club now for three years, and he's done a wonderful job. I don't see how Signor Diamante could do that to him," Gabi sniffed into her tissue.

"Do you know anything about the new manager he's bringing in?"

"Gerhardt? No, nothing."

"Gabi," Alex said, "don't you think you're being a little hard on Signor Diamante," she caught herself before she called him Nicko. "I'm sure Uwe was a wonderful manager, but there could be a dozen reasons why Signor Diamante felt it was time to make changes."

"She's right, you know," Julianne said. "It was most likely a business decision. Not enough profit, too much overhead, complaints or problems you may not have known about."

"But he fired Uwe, the assistant manager, and three other workers all at the same time."

"Wow," Julianne said. "That's a lot of employees to fire at once."

"I still say there must have been a good reason," Alex said.

Gabi looked at her with red-rimmed eyes and said nothing. J.J. changed the subject by bringing up the urgency of Ricky's condition and the fitness convention, and the topic was dropped.

Alex maintained Nickolas knew what he was doing. He was a shrewd, successful businessman. Occasionally things like this happened, however unfortunate it was. But she couldn't help but think it seemed very extreme, even for him.

* * *

"Hi, Jamie. How are you?" Alex held the phone against her ear while she removed her shoes. Her feet ached from being on them all day.

"Alex, I'm so glad you called. Steve and I were just wondering how you were doing. How was Frankfurt?"

She told them about the temple, about Ricky and the blessing, his speedy recovery enabling him to do his workshop at the fitness convention, and about the naked man she and Julianne had seen at the park when they went for a walk.

"You mean to tell me it's perfectly acceptable to sit on a blanket stark naked in public and read a book?"

"I guess so, because no one else seemed to notice or even care."

"I'm shocked," Jamie said.

"We were, too."

They laughed for a moment about the incident.

"So, where are you now?" Jamie asked.

"We're in Heidelberg right now and heading to Lucerne, Switzerland, tomorrow. What's going on at home?"

"Not too much, actually. Mom's still in New York but very miserable."

"Does she miss Dr. Rawlins?"

"Does she ever," Jamie answered. "I guess absence really does make the heart grow fonder."

"Not in Rich's case."

"Yeah, well, I guess that's not true for everyone," Jamie said, "but I wouldn't give up on him yet."

"I'm trying not to, but it would help if he showed some concern," Alex grumbled.

"Hey," Jamie said excitedly, "Don Beckstead got baptized."

"Oh, I'm so glad. I feel bad I missed it."

"It was a very nice service. There wasn't a dry eye in the place."

As far as Alex was concerned, Don Beckstead's baptism was a miracle. Not only was it still hard to believe that a man in Jamie and Steve's branch had been one of the elders to teach their father the gospel and baptize him, but also that this same missionary had fallen into complete inactivity after his mission. It was only when Judith had brought a photo album with her during her visit to Island Park, that Jamie had recognized Don Beckstead in a picture with their father and the connection was made. The news of their father's death had upset Don enough to make him reevaluate his life and the worth of his family. And here he was, back in the Church, with a goal to take his wife and daughter to the temple. How wonderful and powerful the gospel was, Alex thought. And as a result of their father's conversion, Jamie and now Alex had joined the Church.

"We haven't heard from Rich, though," Jamie said. "He's back in Park City but he rarely ever calls anymore. Steve is going to Salt Lake to talk to a counselor at the University of Utah about law school and is planning on going to Park City while he's there."

"I hope he does. Maybe he can find out what's really going on with Rich."

"We're pretty worried about him. I feel bad he's not around, especially with the baby here and everything."

"And how is my beautiful niece doing?"

"She's such a sweetie. I only get up with her once a night now, and she's so happy all the time. It's hard to believe she's the same baby we used to have to disco dance to sleep at night."

Alex laughed at the memory.

"So, fill me in on everything else," Jamie asked.

Alex told her sister about the tour, the workshops, what the gyms in Europe were like, and about the copies of the Book of Mormon she'd given to Julianne and J.J. as well as the one the missionaries had left for Ricky. She hadn't found the right time to present one to Wes and Gabi, nor give Nicko his, but there was still time. In a way this trip to Europe had become a two-fold mission for her, one of a health and fitness nature, and one of a spiritual nature.

Even though she worried about Rich, and missed him and her family terribly, she was surprised she wasn't more homesick. Maybe she was too busy with the traveling and conferences, or just having too much fun. Or maybe the Lord was sustaining her because she had so many special people she wanted to introduce to the gospel.

Whatever it was, she was grateful for it. Once again, the Lord had answered her prayers. She'd wondered how she would ever get through this trip, and just as the Lord had promised, he'd been by her side and helped her every step of the way.

* * *

How the trip kept getting better with each new city, Alex didn't know. But it did. She thought Heidelberg, Germany was beautiful, but then, on their way through the Black Forest into Freiburg, she couldn't get over how thickly forested and lush the countryside was. At Freiburg, she bought a famous Black Forest cuckoo clock for her mother.

But it didn't stop there. On their way into Switzerland, she found herself glued to the train windows, marveling at the sights. Never before had she seen such beauty. Constantly she had to bury her thoughts of and longings for Rich, wishing so badly that he were there to experience the same things firsthand with her.

Alex decided that Lucerne, Switzerland, a picturesque city nestled in a protective valley next to Lake Lucerne, surrounded by lofty mountains, redefined the word beautiful. She'd never seen anything so green, lush, and breathtaking in her life.

Then they went to Interlaken, Switzerland, which was even more charming and beautiful. But Alex had to change her mind again when they took another side tour and headed for the tiny city of Fussen, nestled in Bavaria. In her wildest dreams she had never expected anything to be so perfect. The gorgeous mountains, mirror-like lakes, clusters of villages with clay roofs and overflowing flower boxes stole her breath away.

Accommodations were made for the Supertour instructors at a lovely little bed and breakfast in the country called the Alpenschlössle hotel. They were the only guests at the small eight-bedroom inn.

Alex was thrilled to find a comfortable bed, complete with the down comforters and pillows she'd grown to love and expect. There was also a basket of fruit, and beyond her sliding glass door, a full moon.

Alex left her unpacking for later, and went out onto the terrace that adjoined several other rooms. Standing in the moonlight, she drank in the beauty around her. It was almost too much to absorb. The sweet smell of flowers from the flower boxes decorating the railing and windows filled her lungs. All through Germany and Switzerland she'd been impressed by the abundance of flowers and how meticulously clean the towns and streets were. Not even a gum wrapper was in sight.

A gentle breeze tickled the leaves on the trees. Crickets filled the night with their song. She was so enraptured by the magic of the night that she jumped when Nickolas appeared beside her.

"I'm sorry, Alexis. I didn't mean to frighten you."

"That's okay. I think this incredible atmosphere had me bewitched. I didn't even hear you."

"It is bewitching, isn't it?"

"The trip keeps getting better and better. Just when I've seen something I think is the most beautiful thing I've ever seen, we go to another city and it's even more incredible."

"And tomorrow you will again feel that way, and the next day, and the next. Because you are indeed in the most beautiful country God created. Truly, this is heaven on earth."

She looked up at Nickolas, his face bathed in moonlight, and listened as he told her of some of the cities still ahead and the mysteries and treasures they held.

Warmth filled her, a fondness and sincere caring for this man. He treated her with the dignity and respect of royalty. He had never been anything but kind, thoughtful, and caring to her. With him she felt special. He made her feel as though she were the most important person in the world. He took care of her, protected her, honored her.

"I have something for you," she said. "Wait here. It's in my room."

She hoped her timing was right, prayed fervently in her heart that she would do and say the right things, and returned with the Book of Mormon for him.

"You have given me so many wonderful gifts, Nicko. I wasn't sure how I could ever thank you, until now." She searched his face in the faint moonlight, trying to get a sense of how he would respond, all the while praying constantly that the Lord would prepare and soften his heart. Then she handed him the book.

"This is the most precious thing in my life," she explained. "I have nothing of greater worth I could give you than this." Their eyes connected and for a moment Alex felt a tangible connection of their spirits.

He turned the book over in his hands and looked at it, noticing it was in Italian.

"This is your Book of Mormon?" His voice reflected more than curiosity or surprise. He seemed genuinely moved by her gift.

"Yes. And along with my testimony, it means more to me than anything money could buy."

He turned it over in his hands one more time. "Then I thank you most sincerely. I am honored you would share this with me." He bowed his head respectfully.

"Nicko, you've shown me wonders and sights I never knew existed in this world. I've felt like my eyes have truly been opened for the first time. But inside this book are even greater wonders that unlock the mysteries of God. To know that he lives and that he loves us is a truth that has changed my life. And that his Son died for me, so I might return to live with him and be with my family for eternity, has made all the difference in the world to me." Alex had thought it would be awkward to share her feelings with Nicko, but it wasn't. He seemed sincerely interested.

"You believe this? That you can live with God and your family forever?" he said doubtfully.

"Yes, I do, if we do everything in our power here on earth to be worthy," Alex spoke with conviction.

"You believe that we will see people who have died, actually be with them again?" This time, the doubt was still evident in his voice, but Alex thought she heard a note of hopefulness as well.

"Oh, yes, Nicko. I look forward to the day I can see my father again and feel his arms around me."

"I will see my mother and father, too?"

"Yes. You will see them. But if you live the commandments and stay true and faithful, you can also live together as a family for eternity." Alex felt the strength of the Spirit adding power to her words.

"My mother," he said softly, "was a very religious woman. Even on her deathbed she told me that family and a belief in God were all that was important on this earth. That is why I have felt a need to search for myself. Her words were said with such power and conviction that it has changed my life."

Alex looked at him, a man of great power and wealth, opening his heart and soul to her. He was trying to make changes, but change was difficult and sometimes slow.

Nickolas was silent for a moment. "This idea, that I will see my family again, I have never known this before." He looked down at the book again. "Are you sure of this?"

"Yes, with all my heart, I am sure."

"You must realize that I am a man who works with facts and figures. All my decisions are made in my head, not with my heart. This is difficult for me to accept such ideas without proof."

"I understand," she said. "I know exactly how you feel. But, Nicko, you can know for yourself the same truths I know. There is a promise in the Book of Mormon." She opened the book and turned to the chapter of Moroni. "I have marked it. When you are ready all you need to do is read this, and listen with your heart and your mind, and the Spirit will take care of the rest."

"The Spirit?"

"Yes, the Spirit of the Holy Ghost. He bears witness of truth."

"Oh," Nickolas nodded. "I see." He looked down at the book he held in his hands. "Thank you, *cara mia*. Right now my life doesn't have much religion in it. But when I am ready, I will remember these things you have said."

He put down the book and drew her to him, holding her tightly to his chest. Kissing the top of her head, he stroked her hair with his hand.

"I am so amazed by you, my Alexis. I have never met anyone like you at all. You are beautiful and brilliant, yet there is so much more to you. A depth, an understanding. It is, I think, serenity. The feeling I get that you truly know who you are and where you are going. And I feel inspired just being around you."

She didn't know what to say. Gabi made him out to be ruthless and cruel, but Alex didn't see that side of him. He was a dear man. A man who needed the gospel to fill his empty life. Nickolas truly epitomized the truth that money couldn't buy happiness. Nickolas had all the money a person could ever want, all the material things a person could buy, yet still he was hollow and alone. Yes, the gospel could fill him with truth and knowledge and purpose. With the gospel he could be very instrumental in furthering the kingdom of God on the earth.

He was a businessman, yes, but he was also a man with other needs, spiritual needs. She hoped she could help him find the truth.

Chapter 31

Nickolas was right. The next morning they went to the beautiful castle of Neuschwanstein, built by crazy King Ludwig, the same castle Walt Disney used as a model for his famous Sleeping Beauty castle. And indeed it was a fairy tale castle. Alex could think of dozens of words to describe the castle, the setting, the countryside, and the weather, but they still couldn't adequately express what she was experiencing. Nothing short of "perfect" could describe it.

Swarms of tourists crowded them as they took the tour through the castle, but Nickolas and Alex found a perch overlooking the lake below that was surrounded by brilliant green mountains and crowned with a startling blue sky, and stopped to admire the view. Atop another hill was another castle, smaller, but stunning in its own way. It was called *Hohenschwangau*, the summer residence for King Ludwig and his family.

"This is really incredible," Alex told him. "I feel like I've slipped through time."

"I looked forward to bringing you here. I knew you would love it."

"Nicko, you've gone out of your way to make this whole trip a wonderful experience. I know I speak for the others when I tell you how much we appreciate all the planning and time that went into arranging the tour."

"Don't give me too much credit," he said. "I did have some motives for the project, you know. It has helped promote my ProStar products, and the conferences have been very profitable. Plus it gave me an excuse to spend time with you."

Alex remembered the card on the roses. He'd told her up front that was his reason. She hadn't believed he was serious at first.

"I've been giving a lot of thought to your offers," she said. "I think it would be very exciting to launch a new line of fitness apparel and footwear in North America. You're up against some competition, but I've had a chance to use your products throughout the tour and I feel they are every bit as good, if not superior to Nike, Reebok, and Avia. I guess what I'm saying is, I need to discuss it with my business manager, but I would be proud to be your spokesperson."

Nickolas grabbed her and swung her off her feet. "Alexis, you have made me so happy."

Without warning, he surprised her with a kiss—long enough to be noticeable, short enough to be innocent.

Once she got her breath back, she said, "I'm not quite ready to make a decision about the move to New York. A lot depends on what happens when I get home."

"I am a patient man. You must feel good about this decision. Take all the time you need, Alexis. I am willing to wait for you, because you, my charming Alexis, are definitely worth waiting for."

He stroked her cheek with his finger, his eyes intense and warm.

She probably should have realized the feeling behind that look, the deeper meaning behind his words. But she chose not to.

* * *

Alex was able to call home and talk to her family that night. She missed them terribly and worried about everything they were going through, feeling guilty that she wasn't there to help them.

Her worries became realities as she talked to Jamie, who shared the bad news with her.

"What do you mean the state might not approve the adoption?" Alex couldn't believe what Jamie was telling her.

"That's what they said after they completed their evaluation of us. As of right now, Steve is jobless, the fire wiped us out, and financially we might not break even. Rich and Steve had just purchased a whole new fleet of snowmobiles a couple of months ago and a ton of other stuff, and the debt is much higher than what the insurance settlement will be."

"But to take Andrea Nicole away . . . The fire wasn't your fault. You shouldn't be punished for that."

"I know," Jamie's voice trembled. "I'm trying so hard to have faith that this will work out. I just can't imagine not having her. She is part of me now. And I know without a doubt that she is supposed to be here with us. The Lord has made that known to me many times, in many different ways. They just can't take her from me."

"Is there anything I can do?" Alex felt helpless so far away.

"Just pray for us. All any of us can do is wait."

"Did Steve get back from Salt Lake?"

"Not yet, but he called me earlier. He saw Rich."

Alex's heart clenched. "How was he?"

"He's spending all of his time painting. Elena's been in Boston for the past week, so he's finally had time to work in the studio instead of gallivanting around with her."

"Did he say anything about his plans?"

"Actually he did. He's going to take a break after he finishes the painting he's working on. He wants to come back to Island Park and help get things straightened around. Steve said he thinks some of the newness of this art show has worn off, and Rich has his head out of the clouds."

"That's good news. Did he say anything . . . you know, about me?"

"He asked Steve how you're doing and about your trip. He mentioned you talked on the phone."

"We did. It wasn't the greatest conversation we'd ever had."

"Steve said Rich acted funny when your name came up."

"Funny, like funny ha-ha, or funny peculiar."

"Weird is more like it. Steve said he was acting, sort of, I don't know, dejected. Like he was all picked on and lonely and stuff."

"What! He was the one who was so anxious to get me on that plane and acted like he was happy to be free."

"I know. Steve told Rich basically the same thing. He let Rich know he thought he'd made a mistake to basically end the relationship then let you just fly off into the sunset like that. But Rich just pouted and said something stupid like, 'It's too late anyway, now that she's with what's-his-name.'"

There was no doubt in her mind, he had read the card. Now what did she do?

"So," Jamie said, "we all want to know who 'what's-his-name is'?"

Alex explained about Nickolas and the card, aware that she was playing down its message when she knew full well, Nickolas had meant every word.

"What do you think I should do?" Alex asked her sister.

"Let him stew in his own juices for a while."

"But what about Elena?"

"Rich told Steve he was getting tired of her. She bosses him around too much and acts like she owns him. I think he's jumped through one too many hoops for her."

"I hope you're right. Do you think I should call him?"

"Yeah, I guess. But it serves him right to be miserable for a while. I'm still mad at him for treating you like he did and taking off on us when we needed him the most."

"I don't blame you." It wasn't like Rich to abandon his friends like that. "How did Steve's visit to the University go?"

"The guy was really nice and very encouraging. He told Steve there are a lot of people who go back to school at his age and that he's not too old to go to law school. Of course, this doesn't mean we'd end up in Salt Lake. Still, I can't believe we might go back to school. It's going to be hard."

"I know you guys will make the right decision. And, Jamie, try not to worry about the adoption too much. I don't think the Lord would give Andrea Nicole to you just to take her away."

"I know you're right. I have to keep reminding myself though."

"Hang in there, sis. Next time you talk to mom, tell her I'll call her soon."

"I will. Dr. Rawlins is going crazy without her."

Alex hung up from her conversation with Jamie and quickly dialed Rich's number. Her heart thudded in her chest. She had to talk to him, had to straighten out his thinking about Nickolas, but for some reason she was *so* nervous.

After four rings the answering machine picked up. She almost slammed down the receiver but decided instead to leave a message.

"Hi, Rich, it's me, Alex. I just talked to Jamie and wanted to call you and tell you how happy I am that you're painting again. I can't wait to see what you've done when I get home.

"Uh, I also wanted to tell you that there is nothing going on over here. I'm assuming you read the card that came with the roses I got at the airport, and I felt I needed to let you know that there is nothing going on between Nicko and me. He's a friend, but that's all."

Unexpectedly, emotion clogged her throat. "No one could ever take your place, Rich. I know I need to get over you, because you need your space. But I just can't. I know commitment is hard for you and that I could scare you off by saying this, but you're the only man I want to be with. I'd give anything to be sharing this experience here with you. That's the only way it could be better."

The machine told her she had five seconds left.

"Oh, one more thing—I love you, Rich."

* * *

It was evening when Nickolas called to invite her on a stroll up the hill to see the castle lit up like a birthday cake. She hoped a little fresh air would clear her mind.

While Nickolas made a couple of phone calls to his office in Rome, Alex decided to stop by Julianne's room to tell her she was going out. When she knocked on the door there was no answer. She knocked a little louder and the door cracked open; Julianne hadn't closed it all the way.

Inside the room Julianne was nowhere to be seen, but Alex gasped when she saw empty chip bags, candy and chocolate wrappers, cookie boxes, and foods she didn't even recognize, scattered all over the bed.

The sound of coughing followed by the toilet flushing behind the closed bathroom door made a connection in Alex's mind she didn't want to make, and in a split second she made a decision she didn't want to make but knew she had to.

After a minute or so the bathroom door opened. Julianne's face registered shock at the sight of Alex in her room. A flash of anger crossed Julianne's eyes, then her countenance relaxed. "Hey," she said, "you missed the party."

"Oh, you had a party?"

"Sure, the whole team was over here."

Alex knew full well the rest of them had gone out to dinner.

"Looks like you guys had a lot of fun."

"A little too much fun," Julianne said with a laugh. "I knew I shouldn't have eaten all that chocolate. You know how it upsets my system." She started gathering the trash and putting it in the garbage can.

"Julianne . . ." Alex said a quick prayer to help her say and do the right thing, ". . . I know what you've been doing."

"What do you mean?"

"I know you've been in the bathroom, throwing up."

"Oh that? Actually, you're right. I told you my stomach was upset from too much chocolate."

"I also know that the rest of the group went out to dinner. They aren't even here right now."

"They came over before dinner," she insisted.

"Julianne." Alex walked toward her.

"It's true." The volume in her voice grew. "They grabbed some snacks, then left."

"Please don't lie to me, Julianne. You don't need to. I know. I've been there."

"I don't know what you're talking about. This is making me uncomfortable, Alexis," Julianne said as she turned her back toward Alex and dumped an almost empty bag of chips in the garbage.

"I'm sorry, but I am not about to ignore what's going on here."

"Nothing is going on!" She threw the trash can across the room, spilling its contents everywhere.

"I want to help you," Alex said gently.

"Help me what? There's nothing wrong! Can't you hear me?" Julianne kept her back toward Alex and rested her head in her hands.

Alex should have anticipated something like this. Julianne had told her at the beginning she had hang-ups about food. Alex had noticed how she ate nothing during the day, living only on coffee and plain lettuce salads with no dressing. Then how she spent a lot of time alone in her room. Where all the junk food came from, Alex didn't know. Room service most likely. Julianne probably told them she was having a party in her room. Since they didn't stay in one place longer than a night or two, no one at the hotel would suspect and even if they did, they wouldn't report anything. It wasn't their place to criticize their guests.

Keeping her cool, Alex stood directly in front of her and said, "Julianne, I am your friend. You can trust me. I know you've been bingeing and purging."

"What? You got that idea just because I have a few empty wrappers lying around?"

"A few? This place looks like a vending machine exploded in here."

Expecting fireworks, Alex steeled herself for the impact, but instead of anger, Julianne looked at her with fear in her tear-filled eyes. Taking her friend into her arms, Alex held her while Julianne released an ocean of tears.

"I know, Juli, I know," she tried to soothe and reassure her friend. "It's going to be okay."

"I thought I could do it on my own," Julianne sobbed. "I've tried and tried."

"I know. Me too."

"But I can't do it alone."

"We'll get you some help." Alex patted her gently. "Don't worry, everything's going to be fine."

"I don't want André to know."

"Okay, okay. We'll worry about him later. For now, let's just take care of you."

* * *

"Is it going to be a problem for the tour to have Julianne go home?" Alex asked Nickolas as they walked up the paved path toward the castle.

"No, of course not. We can make adjustments and work around it. The most important thing is to get her home so she can get well."

"I'm going to miss her. We've become such good friends."

"You played an important part in helping her confront her problem."

After Julianne had settled down and unloaded the story of her bulimia, she and Alex had had a good talk. Alex could've kicked herself for not catching on after the first time they'd talked about eating disorders back in Rome, but she was grateful she'd been prompted to go to Julianne's room that night.

"I'm just grateful we found out before it was too late," Alex said. "Bulimics can suffer from dehydration, diseased teeth and gums, and even seizures and stomach rupturing. But worst of all, eating disorders are potentially life threatening. Julianne could be fine these last two weeks of the tour, but then again, her body could have become so depleted she would have suffered something serious before she got home. The problem's not going to go away by itself. She'll need professional treatment to help her get better."

"What a coincidence it is that you were with us, to recognize the problem, and help turn her around so she would be willing to accept help." Nickolas took her hand and squeezed it firmly.

Alex knew it wasn't a coincidence. The Lord had guided her every step of the way.

"She was talking to her parents on the phone when I left. Her admitting she had an eating disorder is the first step in the right direction. They're going to make the arrangements for her so she can get the care she needs as soon as she gets home."

Nickolas shook his head. "I just had no idea. I mean, she's thin but she's so active, I guess I thought she was healthy."

"It's going to be hard, but she'll be okay. I have a lot of faith in her."

"She's very lucky to have a friend like you."

"She's done a lot to help me, too," Alex said. Julianne had been there for her many times when she was down or worried about Rich and her family.

"Did she tell her friend André?"

"She didn't want to, but he called and she just blurted it all out to him."

"Did he take it okay?"

"He was wonderful. He told her he was proud of her and that he would join her in London soon. He wanted to be near her to help any way he could."

They stopped and took a seat on a cement bench where they had full view of the illuminated castle.

Alex didn't mind when Nickolas cradled his arm around her. She was drained and was grateful to lean upon him and let him be strong for her.

"I've been so impressed by you throughout this entire tour, Alexis. You've shown me so many wonderful qualities that I never knew you had. I admire you a great deal."

She leaned away from him so she could look at his face in the dim light. "I admire you too, Nicko."

"You're unlike any other woman I've every known." He reached into his pocket and pulled something out. "There's something I want to give you."

He gave her a small, black velvet box. Assuming that it was a charm of the castle for her bracelet, Alex protested, "Nicko, you shouldn't have done this. My bracelet is going to be so full when I go home I'll need a separate piece of luggage to take it in."

"Go ahead," he said, "Open it."

She lifted the lid and nearly passed out right there. Inside was the largest diamond ring she'd ever seen. Elizabeth Taylor didn't own anything this big. The crown jewels couldn't have a diamond of this size. Good heavens, it looked like an ice block set in gold.

"Nickolas. What—? How—? Why—?"

"Alexis, I am as surprised as you are that I've done this. I'm not one to do spontaneous things like this, but you are everything I've ever wanted in a woman, and now that I've found you, I don't want to lose you."

He pulled her into his arms and held her close. "I know we don't know each other very well, but that's what engagements are for, aren't they?"

"Engagements?" she said, barely getting the word out.

"We can be engaged as long as you want—one year, two years, even five years if we need to. Whatever it takes."

Alex was speechless.

"Will you, darling? Will you marry me? I'll make you the happiest girl in the world. I'll do anything for you."

"Oh, Nicko." She couldn't say another word. She just started crying. And she couldn't stop.

Chapter 32

She wasn't exactly sure why she was crying. Maybe it was because she was so surprised. Or it could have been because she was so confused. She loved Rich so much, but he just didn't seem to need her in his life anymore. Perhaps it was sadness that their future really did seem to be over. Maybe it was all of those emotions happening at once, or maybe it was just the plain fact that the wrong man was asking her to marry him.

"I don't know what to say." She couldn't take her eyes off the ring. It was the most incredible thing she'd ever seen.

"Don't say anything. Just think about it. I know this comes as a surprise to you, and you need some time to get used to the idea. But, Alexis, I want you to know that I've searched many years for a woman I could share my life with. Until I met you I never thought I would find anyone like you. You remind me of my mother—intelligent, beautiful, warm, and generous. And you have a strong set of values that I admire. Your honesty and integrity have proven to me that my money and power would never sway your feelings. I know those things have never been important to you. You are also my friend. We get along very well, and our personalities complement each other. We would make a wonderful team, Alexis."

For a moment Alex pictured what marriage to Nickolas would be like. Yachts, chalets, villas, Mediterranean cruises, traveling, and much, much more. But then she also pictured the armed guards, the Mafia, the angry employees, and who knew what else.

Before she could reply, he took her in his arms and held her close. "All I ask is that you think about it. That's all. You don't have to answer me right away. Please, just say you will think about it."

"I . . . I . . . I'll think about it."

He hugged her tightly then kissed her beneath the stars, in the soft glow of the castle, a fairy tale castle, one that dreams were made of. But this wasn't a dream. This was very real.

* * *

Having the ring in her possession made her nervous. She didn't dare put it in her suitcase for fear her luggage might get lost. She put it in her purse, then took it back out, afraid it wasn't safe there, either. She couldn't wear it, although she tried it on several times.

She didn't mean to, but thoughts of being married to Nickolas played out in her mind occasionally. It was easy to be attracted to Nickolas. He was a very handsome, charming man. He had been nothing but a gentleman with her. There was just one problem. One very big problem. She didn't love him. Like an idiot, she still loved Rich.

Should she give up the opportunity to be with Nicko and gamble on Rich?

Rich's actions reinforced time and time again that he wasn't interested. She reached out for him, he didn't reach back. She tried to talk to him, he didn't respond. The bottom line was, he didn't want to make a commitment to her. There was nothing else she could do. She couldn't force him to marry her.

So maybe Rich wasn't the man for her. But in all honesty she knew Nicko wasn't the man for her either. She could never marry someone who wasn't a member of the Church.

But she had promised Nicko she would think about his proposal, so, for the time being, she kept the ring, she thought about him, and she prayed and searched her scriptures for the right thing to do. Until she knew, she kept the ring on a chain around her neck, tucked away inside her shirt, next to her heart.

* * *

"I feel so stupid. I can't believe all this is happening," Julianne said as she closed her suitcase and clicked it shut.

"There's nothing stupid about what you've done. You forget, you're talking to someone who's been there, okay?"

"Okay." Julianne gave her a big smile. "It's been fun, hasn't it? I'm sure going to miss you." She hugged Alex.

"I want you to call and write. Let me know how you're doing."

"I will."

"And, who knows, maybe I'll get to London sometime."

"That would be fantastic."

"How did the phone call with André go?"

"He was very understanding. I don't think he fully understands about bulimia, but he was very supportive." Julianne zipped up her garment bag. "You know," she looked at Alex and gave half a laugh, "I can't believe how much better I feel just getting all of this out in the open."

Alex remembered how difficult it was for her to admit to her family that she had an eating disorder and needed help. But that was the first, crucial step in recovery.

"I know I have a lot of work ahead of me, but I feel stronger already."

"I'm very proud of you," Alex said.

"Thanks," Julianne said.

Alex helped Julianne stack her luggage by the door.

"Alex." Julianne fiddled with the name tag on one of the bags. "I don't know how to thank you."

"Hey, you would have done the same for me."

"But I don't just mean the eating disorder stuff. I mean the Book of Mormon and all of that. Learning about who Jesus really is, and what he means in my life. You know . . . the gospel."

"You're welcome. I certainly can't take any credit except for dragging you to church in Paris. I did that much. The Spirit did the rest."

"You didn't drag me. I wanted to go. And now, so much has happened. André said he would be with me when I met with the missionaries."

"I'm proud of you. It takes a lot of courage to do what you're doing."

"I've had a good example."

"I expect you to keep me posted weekly on your progress."

"With my treatment?"

"Of course, with your treatment, but also with André and your meetings with the missionaries."

"André's wonderful, isn't he? I feel so good about him, Alex. I can't wait for my parents to meet him."

"You're going to be fine, you know that?" Alex said with a smile.

"Yeah, actually I do."

* * *

The ride to Salzburg was breathtakingly beautiful. Alex had looked forward to coming to Austria, especially to Salzburg, the entire trip. They would spend three days there, just for rest and relaxation. Salzburg would be a place to recover and re-energize for the last few weeks of the tour.

The rest came at the perfect time. Alex was still keyed up over the whole experience with Julianne. Adding to her stress, her mind constantly trampolined about the ring that hung secretly around her neck. Nickolas had stayed in Munich for business and would be joining them in Salzburg that evening. Having him out of the picture helped her think more clearly, but she still didn't have any answers. Why did some prayers seem to get an immediate response, and others seem to go unanswered forever?

"Alex, I said, are you going on *The Sound of Music* tour with us tomorrow?" J.J.'s voice interrupted her thoughts.

"Oh, sorry. Yes, I'm looking forward to it."

Wes, J.J., and Ricky sat across from her and Gabi in their private, first-class compartment on the train. This was undoubtedly the best way to see Europe. The train took her up close and personal with the countries, through countryside, cities, and farms, and even allowed them to ride and mingle with the people.

The group recapped highlights from some of the last few cities when the subject of Ricky's illness came up. Which led to a discussion about the blessing he received from the missionaries.

"What's this book you've been giving everyone?" Wes asked Alex.

"Oh," she said, unprepared but ready to do her best at presenting the gospel, "that's the Book of Mormon. We use it in my church along with the Bible. It's the story of the people who lived in the Americas before, during, and after the birth of Christ. It also gives an account of his appearance to them after he was resurrected."

"Oh," he said, turning away, his interest waning.

She wanted to let the subject drop, but she couldn't. With a deep breath she said, "I've given copies to Ricky, J.J., and Julianne."

Wes didn't answer.

"I also gave one to Nicko."

"Nicko!" they all exclaimed.

"Well, well," J.J. said. "I underestimated you, girl."

Alex shrugged and smiled, not sure how to reply to his comment. Then she said to Wes, "I would like to give one to you," she looked over at Gabi, "and to you."

She opened her travel bag and took out two copies. She handed an English copy to Wes, then handed the German version to Gabi.

"Hey, you're a nice girl and everything, Alex," Wes said, "but thanks anyway. I'm not much into religion."

"I'm not religious, either," Gabi said.

"That's okay," Alex said, "You don't have to be, but I still want to give them to you as a gift. And you don't even have to read the whole thing if you don't want to, but—" she took Gabi's book back and opened it to Moroni, "—but there's a promise in the Book of Mormon, I would appreciate it if you'd read at least that."

She had planned on giving them a little background about the Church, but she found she didn't have to. J.J. and Ricky started telling Gabi and Wes about the missionaries. Without even realizing what he was doing, Ricky basically bore his testimony about the healing power of the blessing he'd received. He'd completely recovered from his illness the following morning and was so impressed he'd decided to read parts of the Book of Mormon and was thrilled that it was about people who lived in South America—his country—long ago. People who could have been his ancestors.

The whole conversation surprised Alex. The fact that they were all actually sitting there having a religious discussion was something she never, ever would have expected. She knew it was also something that would never happen again; the setting, the feeling, and the experience could probably never be duplicated. The Lord had created a window of opportunity, and she was grateful she'd had the courage to take advantage of it.

A warmth filled Alex's chest as she listened to the conversation. Gabi didn't act too interested, but Wes asked some surprisingly probing questions about latter-day prophets and revelation. He also showed an interest in temples and revealed that he'd actually visited the temple in Cardston, Alberta, Canada.

As Alex listened to the others talking, she realized anew that sharing the gospel with others brought her a great deal of joy. She was thankful she didn't have a shy personality and wasn't easily intimidated. She knew that everyone she gave a Book of Mormon to wouldn't join the Church, but she was eager to plant as many seeds as she could. A Mormon Johnny Appleseed, that's what she was.

Even if they didn't accept the gospel right away, or ever, she felt good about at least making a contact with them about it.

The subject was changed and the books put away and forgotten, but the warmth she felt in her heart stayed with her for hours after.

* * *

A picturesque train ride past an enormous ocean-sized lake called the Bodensee, and past charming villages tucked inside the folds of lush green valleys, finally brought them to the charming city of Salzburg. A driver met them at the train station and took them to the historic part of the city where they were guests at a lovely bed and breakfast right on Mozart Platz, where the statue honoring Mozart stood.

The others decided to go exploring and get familiar with the town. Alex promised to meet them an hour later, after she took a long bath and a quick nap. She hadn't slept well the past few nights and was drained. Before she had a chance to even kick off her shoes the phone rang.

"You made it."

"Nicko, hi. Yes, we're here."

"How is your room?"

"Charming and very comfortable." She eyed the bed longingly. The minute her head hit the pillow she knew she'd be out. "Are you in town?"

"Just flying in. We'll be at the inn an hour from now."

"How was Munich?"

"Things didn't go as well as I expected. I've got some calls to make later this evening. I wondered if you are available tonight, I would like to get together."

Alex sighed inwardly. He had promised he wouldn't pressure her for an answer, but his presence was pressure enough. In all honesty, she didn't want to see him.

"I'm going out with the others for a bit, but I'll be back later."

"Call my room when you return. We can meet then."

She hesitated, trying to think of a reason why she couldn't, but came up with nothing. "Okay. I'll see you later then."

Foregoing the hot bath, Alex hung up the phone and fell directly onto the bed, letting the cool sheets and a gentle breeze from the open window lull her to sleep.

* * *

Alex awoke with a start. She shook her head, trying to separate herself from the dream and reality, yet her dream had seemed so real, leaving her with a heavy feeling in her heart. She'd dreamt of Nicko, of them together, drifting on a tiny boat in the ocean with nothing else but her diamond ring on a pedestal between them. Nicko had been yelling. He was upset because instead of bringing food and protection with them, they only had the diamond ring.

Alex still felt the frustration she'd had in the dream. She'd tried to tell him to bring food and water, but he hadn't listened to her. Now they were stranded with nothing but that diamond ring.

Getting up off the bed, Alex went into the bathroom where she splashed her face with cold water.

Dreams are so ridiculous.

She knew it was only a dream but the feeling that stayed with her seemed impossible to shake. It was an uncomfortable feeling, one that made her want to avoid Nicko. It made no sense. It was just a dream, but the feeling was very strong.

She laid a pair of shorts and a light sweater out on the bed to get dressed, but she stopped, deciding to say a prayer first. Kneeling by the side of the bed, she asked Heavenly Father to continue to guide her and direct her. And most of all, to help her know what to do.

The first thing she saw when she opened her eyes was the ring. It rested on the bed, right before her eyes, still on the chain she wore around her neck. A feeling swelled in her heart. A feeling she recognized and cherished. And she was grateful for its calming effect and assurance. She knew exactly what she had to do.

Quickly she got dressed and went to join the others downstairs, desperate for some fresh air and a distraction. She stepped out into the cobbled alleyway and headed for the meeting point, the statue of Mozart.

Around the square, Alex watched as cute German couples strolled hand in hand, window shopping and licking ice cream cones. She marveled at the abundance of bicycles and lack of automobiles. She loved the explosion of color all around her where flowers overflowed in their window boxes. As she sat in awe at the beauty around her, she spied, through church steeples, dome-topped mansions, and above red clay roofs, a glimmering white monastery, watching over the city. Everywhere around her was art, history, and beauty.

The scent of sausage cooking, and the tang of vinegar and spices tantalized her taste buds. It was getting near dinnertime and she was hungry.

The others seemed to have forgotten her. After thirty minutes, she decided to go back to the inn and ask if they'd stopped by.

Just as she turned the corner to the cobbled alley leading to the inn, she saw Nickolas. His back was turned to her; he was on his cell phone. About twenty feet beyond him were his two men. They hadn't seen her and she quickly stepped back into the shadow of a doorway.

She hadn't intended to eavesdrop, but she listened for a moment to see if he was almost finished with his conversation before approaching him.

"Antonio, you don't seem to understand. I don't care how long this business has been in their family; they are practically bankrupt. Pressure them if you have to. Offer them more money. For the right price they will sell."

Nickolas was upset. The tone in his voice had gone beyond being firm and commanding; it was cold and heartless.

"Then find a loophole," he demanded. "There is something, somewhere. Some weakness. I want that company. I have to have it and I don't care what you have to do. Just get it!"

He slammed the cell phone shut, said something in Italian, and grabbed his briefcase off the stone walkway. Without a backwards glance he strode into the inn.

Alex stayed outside, giving his men time to reposition themselves or follow him inside the inn. Meanwhile, she mulled over the scene she'd witnessed. Gabi's and J.J.'s words came back to haunt her: "He knows what he wants and he always gets it."

That was just in business, she had thought; certainly he didn't pursue people the same way he did companies. Then she recalled what he'd said on the phone moments ago: "I don't care how long the business has been in their family . . ." That was a hard businessman talking, not her kind and gentle Nicko.

She'd seen glimpses of a darker side, and had been warned by Gabi and J.J. about him, but still it surprised her. He'd never been anything but a gentleman to her, never raising his voice or getting upset. She didn't want to believe it, but she was realistic enough to know that Nicko could very possibly have a rough, dark side.

Deep down, she had to admit she had known it. Just as she'd sensed the awful spirit of those people at Sandy's apartment, those anti-Mormons with their lies, she knew. Nickolas wasn't an evil man, but his heart was in a different place than hers. He cared about building his empire, gaining money and power and material objects. He had told her that he was searching for something more, and she believed a part of him truly was, but there was something else, something she couldn't put her finger on. It was the same feeling she'd felt when she'd prayed that afternoon. Nickolas had many good qualities, but he was not the right man for her.

She jumped when he walked back outside and came her direction. Taking a deep breath, she steeled herself for the encounter. Her thoughts weren't yet clear. It wasn't fair to jump to conclusions, to judge him, but she trusted her instincts. So far they hadn't misled her.

He stopped when he saw her. "There you are, darling." Closing the gap between them, Nickolas pulled her into a hug and exclaimed how happy he was to see her.

"I've been trying to find you. Where have you been?"

His tone wasn't just inquisitive. There was a hint of annoyance in it, perhaps because he was still upset over his phone call, but Alex believed it was something else. She'd heard that tone of voice before, from an ex-boyfriend, Jordan. He'd been very possessive and jealous. That tone meant expectation and ownership.

"I was supposed to meet the rest of the group out by the statue, but they never came."

"I will wait with you? Then we can all go out to dinner. I made reservations for us."

She hoped the "us" meant the others, too.

They waited almost half an hour more, but the others never showed. Leaving a message back at the inn, Nickolas and Alex went ahead to the restaurant.

Doubts filled Alex's heart and head as they wound their way through the old city of Salzburg, past the birth house of Mozart and dozens of tiny shops displaying everything imaginable from leather to chocolate. Then Alex froze as they approached the restaurant. Peter's Keller.

She couldn't go there. Not without Rich.

Just as they were at the door, Alex heard someone calling their names. It was J.J.

"Hey, you two. We found a great place to eat. Want to come with us?"

Before Nickolas could decline, Alex jumped at the chance. She knew it was silly, but she didn't want to be alone with him, not now and especially not at *that* restaurant. She wasn't ready to talk to him. She had an answer to give him. She just wasn't sure how she was going to deliver her news, or how he would react when he heard it.

She felt safe having her friends around her during dinner, but her luck ran out after they finished eating. On the way back to their rooms, everyone split off in different directions, leaving her alone with Nickolas.

They had stopped to admire a beautiful German dress in a store window. It had a deep green skirt and a gray leather dirndl over a fluffy-sleeved, crisp, white blouse. Nickolas converted the schillings into dollars for her—four hundred and fifty dollars to be exact.

Moonlight and street lamps outlined the buildings. In the distance cheerful music played.

"Salzburg is as charming as Florence, as romantic as Venice. No?"

"It's a lovely city, even though I haven't seen that much of it."

"My mother loved Salzburg. This is, in fact, where she met my father. They were both students and very passionate about art and music. They both loved Mozart. When they found him, they found each other."

He guided her to a wooden bench, surrounded by baskets of flowers.

"I spoke with Julianne's parents this evening," he said. "She arrived safely and was happy to get home. They are handling all of this very well."

"I'm glad to know that. I plan on keeping in touch."

"Yes, you must. She's very nervous but she sounded strong, and ready to get the help she needed."

Alex nodded knowingly. Those had been her exact feelings before she went in for treatment. Nervous, even a little scared, but finally convinced she needed outside help. It had taken a lot of convincing but she'd finally trusted her family, her own instincts, and Dr. Rawlins.

"How are you doing, *mi bella?*"

"I'm fine, but I'm relieved to have a few days to relax. I was more worn out than I realized."

"Yes, it has been a strenuous trip. But fun, no?"

"A lot of fun." She knew she had to tell him. But how did she do it? *Just hurry up and get it over with.*

"Nicko?"

"Yes, *cara mia.*"

She looked at his face, his eyes, intense, studying her, waiting for her next words.

Her heart raced, her breathing grew rapid. Her mouth was as dry as sand.

"Alexis, you are troubled. What is it? You can talk to me."

"Oh, Nicko." She fought hard to keep tears back, but her voice trembled with emotion.

"It's okay." He rubbed her shoulder soothingly. "Nothing can be that bad."

It didn't help to have him so sweet and tender. Being around him was so confusing. He was like two different people inside the same body. The kind, loving Nicko, and the cold-hearted businessman, Nickolas Diamante. She cared for the man "Nicko" but not for Signor Diamante. The problem was, the two came together.

"Tell me what is on that beautiful mind of yours." He brushed her hair away from her face and stroked her cheek with his thumb.

"It's this ring you gave me." She pulled the chain from inside her sweater and displayed the ring.

"You don't like it. It's too big? Too small?"

There was no point in telling him that even though the ring was stunning, it wasn't her style. She'd never be comfortable sporting a ring of that size. "No, no. It's beautiful. That's not the problem. I am so flattered and honored that you would ask me to marry you. But I can't, Nicko. I can't marry you."

She shut her eyes, not quite ready to see his face and his reaction.

"Alexis." He put his arm around her and pulled her close. "You mustn't fret. You have all the time you need to consider this. There is no hurry to make a decision now."

"But, Nicko, that's not the problem." How did she tell him?

"Is it because I am not a Mormon? Is that why you are worried?"

"That's a very big part of it. I couldn't marry anyone who isn't a member of my church. I've seen what happens to marriages where one is and one isn't a member."

"Your parents?"

"Yes, and others."

"Then I will join your church. I have read some in your Book of Mormon. I wouldn't have a problem getting baptized."

She knew she should be touched that he was willing to get baptized, but he didn't understand; it didn't matter what he did on the outside if his heart wasn't committed to the gospel. Without a testimony he would merely be a shell of a member.

"I told you, Alexis, I will do anything for you. And I won't pressure you. Take more time. There is no hurry. I told you I am a patient man. We have all the time in the world to get to know each other, to become better acquainted—to fall in love."

She closed her eyes and prayed for help, then went on, "But, Nicko, that's not it at all."

"Alexis, you mustn't rush such a big decision. There is no hurry. Please take more time to think about it." His voice was elevating, becoming stronger, more commanding.

"Nicko—"

"Alexis, please, listen to me. I know that you have heard many things about me."

She started to object, then held her response. She was curious to know what he said next.

"I am guilty of many things—gambling, spending my time with many women, my associations with the wrong people. This is all true. But I am changing. Meeting someone like you has helped me see that I want to change my life. You are not like the other women I have known. I have never loved any of them; those were meaningless affairs. You are the type of woman a man wants to marry."

As she weighed his words carefully in her mind, a thought came to her. "I want to ask you something," she said slowly.

"Yes, of course, anything."

"Would you be faithful to me?"

"Of course," he answered, obviously offended that she would even ask such a question. "I would never leave you."

"I don't mean stay by my side. I mean, can you promise that you would never be with another woman again?"

Nicko stared at her, surprised. "Alexis, I cannot believe you would ask such a question."

"I have to know, Nicko," Alex persisted. "And if you love me as you say you do, you will be completely honest with me."

She could tell she was testing his patience. He struggled for control. After a moment he calmed himself and spoke in a measured voice. "I would be forever devoted to you, Alex. I will love you and only you."

Alex thought Nicko was deliberately misunderstanding her. "But does that mean we would have complete fidelity in our marriage?" she asked pointedly.

"What has this got to do with anything?" He jumped to his feet and threw his hands in the air, muttering to himself in Italian. "Alexis, I need a woman I can come home to, who will support me and raise my children. Who will entertain our guests and give me enjoyable companionship."

"And what does that woman receive in return?"

"Everything the world has to offer!" he fired back at her.

Allowing several seconds to pass to let him calm down, Alex finally said, "But, Nicko, don't you see? That's not enough. I want a husband who is committed to me and our marriage and no one else. I cannot live any other way."

"Alex, *cara mia,*" Nickolas said patiently, and Alex thought she detected a pleading note as well, "I have sworn my devotion to you. Why can't that be enough?"

"Because that, Nicko, means more to me than any amount of money or worldly possessions on the earth."

Nickolas looked as if he were about to speak, to try again, to convince her to see things his way. But then his entire demeanor changed as if he remembered who he was speaking to and what had attracted him to her. His shoulders slumped and he drew in a deep breath.

"I understand what you are saying," he said, almost wearily. "I don't agree, but I understand."

She fingered the chain on her necklace until she found the clasp. Undoing it, she slid off the ring and offered it toward him.

Reluctantly he took it.

Looking at the ring in his hand, he said, "I have never asked before, but I think there is also something you haven't told me. Does your heart already belong to someone else?"

She didn't answer for a moment. Then she said, "No. Yes. I don't know. Kind of." She knew she sounded like a complete dunce, but that was a difficult question and an even more difficult answer. "I love him. I'm not sure how he feels right now," she finally clarified.

Nickolas shook his head. "He was a fool to let you out of his sight. He doesn't know how precious you are, otherwise he would have never let you go. But Alexis, I would never take you for granted. I would treasure you always." He looked at her hopefully, as if to remind her that his proposal was still open.

"But I still love him." She dropped her chin and sighed heavily. How was she ever going to get on with her life?

Nickolas watched her intently. "This man, does he know how you feel?"

"Yes."

"And yet, he still does nothing?" he asked curiously, almost disbelieving.

"No."

"My heart breaks to see you so sad," he said softly. "For your sake, I wish he returned your love."

Alex was amazed. In his own way, Nicko truly did care.

"Perhaps something with him will change, *cara mia,*" he said comfortingly. "But if it doesn't . . . I would be honored to hear from you."

She smiled. Maybe he didn't realize it, but his comment actually made her feel better. There were probably thousands of women who would kill for a proposal from Nickolas Diamante, but what he had to offer still wasn't enough to turn her away from Rich, the man she truly loved.

Chapter 33

Alex couldn't believe she actually cried on *The Sound of Music* tour. But when the tour bus director turned on Julie Andrews singing, "The hills are alive, with the sound of music," as they drove through the lush countryside where the scene in the movie had actually been filmed, it was just too much.

She shouldn't have been surprised though. She'd been overemotional lately and the song just uncorked her.

Back at the square, as the afternoon wound down into evening, the five fitness-experts-turned-tourists discussed plans for the rest of the day as well as their agenda for the next day. Among other things, they planned a tour of Mozart's family home and a bus tour to the Eagles' Nest hideaway, Hitler's retreat during the war.

As the others batted around ideas, Alex's mind wandered along with her gaze. She watched a youngster tossing pennies into a fountain pool, his parents laughing at his squeals of delight with each splash of a coin. All around the square people relaxed and enjoyed the perfect weather and the clear day.

Her gaze stopped again, resting on a man with a suitcase, his back to her. He was studying a map. She shut her eyes tightly then opened them again. From behind the man reminded her of Rich. The same long legs, the same broad shoulders, dark wavy hair, and tanned skin.

Her breath caught in her throat as her heart dared her to think it was actually him. Her mind quickly squashed the idea, realizing her silliness. But she continued staring. He was far enough away that she couldn't be sure one way or the other.

Then he turned. If that wasn't Rich, then this wasn't Salzburg.

She jumped to her feet and started walking across the square.

"Hey," J.J. called, "Where you goin', girl?"

She didn't stop to answer. Her walk turned into a run. Rich! It was Rich!

Tears stung her eyes, and her throat ached and clogged with emotion as she hurried toward him.

He recognized her before she was halfway to him.

Dropping his map and shoulder bag, he headed toward her, calling her name.

They met in the middle and fell into each other's arms. They laughed and cried, and even Rich had tears in his eyes. They hugged and cried some more.

"I can't believe it's you," she said.

He kissed her forehead, hugged her, then kissed it again. "I can't believe I found you."

"What are you doing? Why are you here?"

"I've been so stupid, Alex. Will you ever be able to forgive me for how I've treated you?"

All around them people stared. Alex didn't care. Rich was here. In Salzburg. With her!

"Of course I can forgive you."

"I missed you so much." He hugged her, nearly squeezing the breath out of her.

She held on tightly, relishing the feel of his arms around her, the scent of his cologne mixed with Carmex, the familiarity of seeing him again.

"I can't believe you did this," she said.

He led her by the hand to a bench off to the side, near his luggage. "I was sitting there yesterday in that stuffy old studio in Park City, hating my painting, hating the Fewtrells, and hating myself."

She couldn't believe what she was hearing.

"It was all wrong. I didn't like what I was doing. I didn't like where I was or who I was with, and I was ashamed of who I'd become. I missed you so badly it hurt. All I wanted was to see your smile, hear your laugh. I knew the only way I could do that was to get on a plane and come find you."

"This is so wonderful. I still can't believe you're here."

"It is kind of wild, isn't it?" he said. "But I was ready to do anything to get to you. I couldn't wait a minute longer. I thought my flight would never end."

"So you just got up and left?"

"Pretty much. I was lucky to get on a flight."

"What about the Fewtrells? Do they know you're here? Won't they get upset?"

"I left a note. And who cares if they get upset? I never did sign a contract with them. My painting ability will always be there. They can't take that away from me. I don't need the Fewtrells to tell me how to sell my work or to turn me into some 'Ken' doll they can show off to their clients. You tried to tell me about them, and I just wouldn't listen. I never knew I had such a hard head until now."

"I'm so glad you came. I missed you so much."

"I'm not keeping you from something important, am I?"

"No, not at all."

"Are those four people over there looking at us for some other reason then?"

"Oh, my goodness, I forgot about those guys." She called them over and introduced them. After a few minutes of small talk and background, they informed Alex of their plans and invited Rich and Alex to visit the Mirabelle Palace with them.

Alex declined the invitation.

"We'll catch up with you later then," J.J. said, as they were leaving. "Nice meeting you, Rich."

They waved good-bye, leaving Alex and Rich alone.

"Isn't Salzburg the place that German couple told us about at lunch in Idaho Falls?" he asked.

"Yes. And it's every bit as beautiful as they said it would be."

"They said something about a restaurant."

"Yes. Peter's Keller, I know where it is. We almost went there for dinner last night, but I couldn't. Not without you."

They kissed briefly. Alex wondered how she'd survived so long without his touch.

"Are you free for dinner? Maybe we could go there tonight," he said.

"That would be wonderful. Are you tired, though? Do you need to take a nap?"

"I'm not wasting a minute sleeping when I can be with you. I can sleep later. Right now I need to hold you and tell you again how sorry I am for everything."

Alex shook her head. "What matters is that you're here and we're together."

"But I have to. You mean too much to me to treat you like I did, and not apologize for my behavior. I was scared, but I was more stupid than scared. I let you slip right through my fingers. All the way here I wondered what I would do if I were too late, what if you didn't want to see me ever again."

"I never stopped loving you, Rich. I was hurt and confused, but I always loved you."

"And I never stopped loving you, even though I probably acted like I did. You were right when you accused me of being afraid of a commitment. I was terrified. But yesterday I realized by avoiding commitment, I was losing the best thing that ever happened to me. You."

"What are you saying?"

"I'm saying I'm ready to make a commitment. Alex . . ." he slid off the bench onto one knee, ". . . I'm asking you to marry me."

Were those angels singing? A heavenly choir? Rich had just proposed. Rich was asking her to marry him. It was a dream come true, a wish that had become a reality, an answer to prayers.

She knew she should probably be angry at him for all he'd put her through, but all of that didn't matter anymore. It just didn't matter.

"Yes, Rich. I'll marry you."

He sat beside her on the bench, cementing their words with an embrace and a kiss. Rich had made a commitment. They would be together, forever.

* * *

At Peter's Keller Alex and Rich met Peter, the owner. He nearly flipped his lederhosen when he learned that not only had they met his brother and sister-in-law in Idaho, but the young couple had gotten engaged that very evening.

Peter provided them with a wonderful sparkling cider to toast the occasion. A four-piece band asked if Rich and Alex had any requests.

Alex asked them if they knew the song, "Edelweiss" from *The Sound of Music*. She was surprised that most Austrians had never even seen the movie, let alone heard of the song, but Peter had lived in the United States for a few years and learned that Americans loved the movie and the music. So it was an extra special treat when Peter himself sang the song for them. What he lacked in voice quality, he made up in sincerity.

Across their candlelit table, Rich and Alex held hands, gazing into each other's eyes. It still seemed like a dream that Rich was with her. And it felt so right. Finally, things were as they should be.

For so long she hadn't been able to see why the Lord had wanted her to go to Europe. Not until she was able to look back and see all the many reasons why—the people she'd been able to help and the many who had touched her life. But most importantly she'd grown stronger and had learned that her testimony was solid and firm and could survive even the greatest challenges.

After some beautiful Tyrolean yodeling, Peter left them alone in their romantic corner of the dimly lit restaurant.

"Tell me what happened back there in Park City. What made you change your mind so suddenly?" Alex asked.

"At first, when I got there," Rich began, "I admit I was caught up in all the attention and the glamour of being the star of the show. But that didn't last long. Even though Elena's LDS, I wasn't comfortable with the way she treats people. We went to church while we were in L.A., to a very wealthy ward. The parking lot was full of BMWs, Cadillacs, and Mercedes. I felt like it was a business meeting for her. She made sure to introduce me to certain people, and even gave out business cards in the foyer."

Rich paused before continuing. "She also put a lot of demands and pressures on me and my work. She wanted to control everything—what I wore, where I went, even what I painted. I couldn't focus or think straight, and my paintings were awful. Then she did something that finally forced me to make my final decision to get out."

"What was that?"

"She sold the portrait of you without telling me."

"Rich?!" Alex nearly shouted. "How could you let that happen? That wasn't for sale." She didn't want to ruin their evening, but darn it, she was mad!

"It's okay," Rich assured her. "I got it back and the painting is safe now. But it wasn't without a fight, believe me. She told me that if I wasn't willing to sell my artwork when there was a buyer, then she couldn't work with me."

"But you told her up front the painting wasn't for sale, didn't you?"

"Of course I did, but she was testing me. Plus, I think she resented having the reminder of you around."

"Me?"

"She kept asking me about our relationship. I think it really bothered her that I wasn't available. You were the one thing that stood in her way of having complete control over me. She sold the painting to try and get you out of my life."

Alex had known the woman was trouble from the beginning. Her instincts had told her. She was so grateful Rich had finally been able to come to the same realization before it was too late.

"Right after that Colt called. I told him about Elena, and he confessed he had been worried something like this might happen. Apparently he knew she had a reputation for being controlling, but he had no idea just how bad she could be or how far she'd go. Then he told me he would love to represent my work and that we could put together a show on our own. We didn't need her."

"I had no idea you were going through so much," Alex said sympathetically.

"Alex, it was like I wasn't the same person without you. You make me want to try harder, be better than I am. Without you I don't have the same kind of drive and determination. You bring out the best in me but at the same time, I don't feel you're trying to redesign me. I love how you radiate, how you're feminine, but strong, how self-assured, receptive, and responsive you are. You make me feel like I'm everything you want. Just being with you makes me happy." He twirled the stem of his glass thoughtfully. "To me you're perfect, just the way you are. I don't deserve you."

Alex smiled, filled with happiness. "No, you don't," she teased. "But you're just going to have to deal with it, because you've got me and this time nothing's going to get in our way."

He reached for her hand and placed a kiss on her palm.

"I have something for you." He pulled from his pocket a white satin box, tied with a red ribbon.

Alex didn't even dare hope it was what she thought it was. For the longest time she'd wanted something, anything to represent Rich's commitment to her. With trembling fingers she opened the box to find a stunning, perfect emerald-cut diamond set in a wide gold band. Not too big, not too small. Just right.

"This makes it official," he said, taking the ring and sliding it onto her finger.

"It's beautiful." She admired the flash of brilliance from the stone, the feel of cool metal on her flesh. "I love it, Rich. It's a beautiful ring."

A group of people entered the restaurant, catching Alex's eye. She recognized her friends from the tour. But they weren't alone. Nickolas was with them.

It didn't take long for them to spot her and Rich. Alex gave a quick prayer for strength and gulped for air when they headed her direction. This wasn't going to be easy.

Before she knew it, the whole group surrounded their table and within seconds discovered the diamond, sparkling on her finger.

They each took turns admiring it and congratulating the couple, then promised to talk more later. Nickolas, as always the perfect gentleman, stayed back, waiting his turn. Alex caught his eye, wondering if the look she saw was anger or pain or her imagination.

"Nicko," she said, her mouth dry as cotton, "I'd like you to meet Rich Greenwood. He just arrived this afternoon."

The two men shook hands.

"I understand there's an engagement to be celebrated?" Nickolas asked politely.

"Yes," Rich said. "I asked Alex to marry me and she said yes."

"Congratulations, Alexis. I know this makes you very happy."

She smiled at him, wondering if there was cause for concern. Was he going to say anything to Rich about his proposal?

"You are a very lucky man, Mr. Greenwood," he continued. "I did everything in my power to sweep this lady off her feet, but she was very committed to you."

Alex held her breath, hoping Rich wasn't upset by Nicko's confession. Instead, Rich said, "And I am very committed to her."

His words meant more to her than any ring he could give her. He truly had had a change of heart. Rich was committed to her!

Nickolas inclined his head. "Then you will be very happy together, I am sure."

For a moment no one knew what else to say.

Her eyes drifting beyond Nickolas, Alex noticed his two bodyguards step inside the entrance. Right behind them a beautiful woman, tall and curvy, with thick red hair cascading below her shoulders, entered.

Nickolas noticed her entrance and indicated he would join her in a moment.

"We would be honored for you to join us at our table," Nickolas said. "This truly is a happy occasion."

"Sure," Rich said. "We'd love to."

Alex wanted to refuse but decided it was the best way to show that there were no hurt feelings on either side.

"I think I'll visit the restroom real quick first," Rich said. He brushed a kiss on Alex's forehead. "I'll be right back."

Alex was glad she and Nickolas had a moment alone. This wasn't how she planned on telling him about her engagement.

Nickolas spoke first. "So, your prince came to his senses?"

Alex smiled. "Yes, he did."

"He seems very sincere, very much in love," he observed. "And you, this is what you want?"

"I want this very much. I'm sorry, Nicko. I never meant to hurt you."

"Ah, *mi bella*, I was prepared in the event you told me no. Part of me never dared believe that you would marry me. But one can always hope, *si?*"

Alex smiled at her friend, deeply appreciative of his graciousness. "*Si,*" she agreed.

"You will always be very special to me and I will never forget you," he assured her. "I am grateful for the time we had together. And you will still be our spokesperson, *si?*"

"Yes, of course," Alex said. "I am looking forward to it."

"Then you have made me happy once again. And you will let me know on the other offer?" he reminded her.

"The move to New York?"

He nodded.

Alex looked thoughtful. "Rich and I haven't gotten that far with our plans, yet. I'm inclined to say no, though."

"But you will think about it?" he pressed. "You have a year, at least, before we need your answer."

Alex nodded. "Okay, I will let you know."

"Thank you, Alexis. And if you ever need anything, anything at all, I want you to feel free to call me, anytime. Promise?" He looked at her intently.

"I promise."

"I am happy for you. I'm glad he woke up," Nicko said, smiling at her.

She laughed. "Me too, Nicko. Me too." She was grateful there was no tension in the air. This seemed to be the right time to say something to him about another concern she had.

"Nicko, I would like to return the rest of the jewelry you gave me."

"But why?" He looked astonished.

"I don't know. I guess because, well, since things didn't work out—"

"Alexis, those gifts are yours to keep," he said earnestly. "You would break my heart if you returned them. That is, unless you don't like the jewelry."

"Oh, no, Nicko, it's not that," Alex assured him. "I just feel guilty keeping such expensive gifts."

"I know I have many flaws and perhaps that is my biggest. I am much too generous to people I care about. I tend to go overboard." He lifted his hands and shrugged in a gesture of helplessness.

She agreed. He had gone overboard.

"But you would not rob me of the pleasure I receive when I am able to give something to someone that brings them joy?" Nicko smiled gently at her, placing his hands on his heart, as if to signify that he would truly be heartbroken if she didn't keep his gifts.

"No, of course not," Alex smiled back at him. He really was such a sweet, gentle man.

"Then, please, keep them," he begged. "As a remembrance of our friendship."

"Okay," she held up her bracelet, "I will enjoy this for many years. Thank you again."

"And, again, you are welcome."

He took her hand and placed one last kiss on her knuckles.

"You will join us when you are ready, *si?*"

"*Si.* As soon as Rich is back, we'll be right over," Alex said warmly.

With a final dazzling smile, he turned and walked away. As he joined the statuesque woman who was waiting for him near the door, Alex hoped that one day he would find the woman who was right for him.

* * *

From the phone in her room they placed the call to the states. Steve and Jamie would flip when they told them the news.

Finally on the fourth ring Steve answered.

"Steve, hi, it's Rich."

"Rich! I've been trying to call you. Where have you been?"

"Actually I had to take care of some urgent out-of-town business." Rich looked at Alex and winked.

"Oh, really? Where?"

Alex pressed her ear up to the receiver next to Rich's. She didn't want to miss a word of Steve's reaction.

"Austria. Salzburg, actually."

"Austria? What in the world are you doing clear over there?"

"I came to ask Alex to marry me, and she said yes."

"What?! Are you kidding me?" The volume of his voice made both Alex and Rich jump back from the receiver for a moment.

"I wouldn't kid about this," Rich said, smiling at Alex. "We're officially engaged. She's wearing the ring right now."

Steve let out a huge yee-haw, which was immediately followed by loud crying from the baby and a scolding from Jamie, until Steve told her what was going on. Then she started yipping and hollering, too.

"Rich!" It was Jamie. "Is this true? Are you two really getting married?"

"You heard it here first."

"Jamie, hi," Alex said. "Isn't this incredible? He flew all the way to Austria to ask me to marry him."

"That's so romantic," Jamie said. "I wish you were here so I could hug you."

"I know. I do, too."

Rich gave Alex a squeeze and whispered, "I'll just have to hug you instead."

Jamie raved enthusiastically. "There's so much to celebrate—you getting engaged and the letter we got today in the mail telling us that the state approved us as adoptive parents."

Alex was thrilled. "They did? That's fantastic."

"We've set a court date and everything."

"Jamie, that's great news. I'll bet you're so relieved."

"I am. I'll be so glad when we can make this adoption legal. It seems so far off."

"It will go fast. We'll be busy making wedding plans, and I'm going to need your help. And Mom's, too."

"Were you going to call and tell her your news?" Jamie asked.

"Of course," Alex responded. "I can't wait to tell her."

"Well, here, then, I'll let you talk to her."

Alex was startled. "What do you mean? Is Mom back in Island Park?" She couldn't believe it. What had happened to bring her back?

"She missed us all so much she came back this morning. Isn't that wonderful?"

Alex noticed that Jamie sounded genuinely happy, her voice contented and full of joy. With a lot of faith and patience, everything seemed to have finally worked out for them.

"Has she seen Dr. Rawlins yet?"

"Actually, yes. He's here, even as we speak."

"He's right there with her?" Alex was thrilled to learn that her mom and the good doctor were back together again. "That's wonderful."

"Here," Jamie said. "I'll get Mom for you."

Judith's voice came on the line. "Honey, is it true? Rich actually flew over and proposed?"

"He did. Isn't he wonderful?" Alex looked at him as she spoke, still in a daze that it had finally all happened. He kissed her above her eyebrow.

"I'm so happy everything worked out for you two."

"Thanks, Mom. That means a lot to me. Are you doing okay?"

"I am now that I'm back in Island Park and especially after your good news. And I guess this is as good a time as any to tell all of you my news."

Alex didn't know what her mother was going to say, but she had a feeling she was going to like it.

"What is it, Mom?" both Alex and Jamie asked simultaneously.

"I've decided to start taking the missionary lessons," Judith declared proudly.

"Mom?!" Alex cried ecstatically. "I can't believe it." Tears filled her eyes and she suspected that Jamie was having nearly the same reaction, judging by the sounds she was hearing over the phone.

Judith started to cry a little herself as she explained, "We've shared so many special, spiritual moments together, I can't deny it any longer—something is here. Something very wonderful," she sniffed softly over the phone.

"I can't tell you how happy this makes me, Mom." Alex could barely get the words out.

"Thanks, sweetie. I'm going to need all the support and help I can get."

"You can count on us, Mom," Jamie promised. Alex knew her sister had waited a long time for this moment, when her whole family would accept the truth.

"Is Dr. Rawlins excited?" Alex asked.

"Dave's known about my decision for a few days now. He's been such a great strength to me. He answers all my questions and is so patient," Judith said, her voice full of fondness as she spoke.

"He's a wonderful man," Alex agreed, grateful to the Lord for letting her mother meet someone like Dr. Rawlins. In the background, she could hear the baby crying.

"Is that the baby?"

"Yes, I think she's hungry."

"Give her a hug and kiss for me, Mom, will you?"

"Sure, honey. And give Rich our love."

"I will," Alex said. "And tell Dr. Rawlins for us."

"I will. You two hurry home. We miss you."

There was nothing more Alex wanted to do than go home. What wonderful news they'd all shared that night. The Lord had blessed them all so much. She was anxious to get back home and see her family, to share in their joy, but first, she would enjoy the rest of the tour and Europe with Rich.

Chapter 34

"Are you sure you weren't on a two-month mission instead of a fitness tour while you were here?" Rich asked as they made their way through the busy airport to their gate.

"I gave out a few copies of the Book of Mormon, that's all."

"That's all?!" Rich looked at her in astonished admiration. "You gave out eleven of them."

Although Alex had left all her copies of the Book of Mormon with other people on the tour, she had kept one to have on the plane with her . . . just in case.

"Yeah, well, some weren't very excited about them, especially Wes and Gabi."

"But two of the others promised to look up the missionaries when they got home," Rich reminded her.

"Actually, three of them," she corrected him. "You forgot Julianne. Oh, I guess four, if you count Sandy. But that was before I came to Europe."

He laughed and shook his head. "I'd better marry you before you get called on a real mission. I don't know how good of a missionary widower I'd make. I don't bake very good cookies."

"I don't need to get called on a mission," she said. "I can do just as much missionary work now. I don't need a calling for something I'd do anyway. Besides, I'd rather have you for a companion any day," she said, snuggling up beside him.

"You wouldn't get any complaints out of me either." He kissed the top of her head. "J.J.'s sure a great guy. He seemed excited about the Church. But I really enjoyed talking to Ricky."

"He enjoyed it, too, especially since you could speak Spanish with him. He said you explained a lot of things on the way to Innsbruck."

"He asked some good questions. I've lost a lot of my language but I managed to give him some answers. It was fun."

Telling Gabi, Wes, J.J., and Ricky good-bye had been very difficult. They'd become almost like family to her. She'd dreaded saying farewell to Nicko, but he'd made it easy by bringing his friend, Brigette, along with him for the last two cities. Alex found out she modeled for some of Nicko's designer friends and was very friendly, especially to Nicko.

Alex knew this wasn't the type of woman he wanted, and she prayed with all her heart that he would find a woman equal to him. He deserved someone wonderful, loving, and devoted to him. And she hoped he would read the book she'd given him. He hadn't been ready to join the Church when he'd offered to do so for her, but she knew someday he might.

"Here we are. I'll go check on our seats. I sure wish we could fly back together. You'll have to save me some of that good first-class food, while I'm back in coach eating stale tuna sandwiches."

"I feel so bad about this."

"It's okay. I'm just kidding. But the ride would be more fun together."

"Wait a minute," Alex said quickly. "Why don't you have them check to see if there are two seats together in coach? I don't mind changing. I'd rather be with you, too."

"Are you sure?"

She nodded. She'd sit strapped to one of the wings with him as long as they were together.

She couldn't believe she was going home. In many ways she hated to leave. What an incredible two months this had been. She'd been places and seen things she never dreamed existed. But even more meaningful were the wonderful people she'd met and the experiences they'd shared. She'd grown as a person and even more as a member of the Church. Her testimony had grown deeper roots and was already bearing fruit, which she gladly shared with others.

She'd learned many lessons, the most important of which had become her favorite passage in the Bible—Proverbs, chapter three, verses five and six:

Trust in the Lord with all thine heart; and lean not
unto thine own understanding. In all thy ways acknowl-
edge him, and he shall direct thy paths.

He had, without a doubt, been beside her every inch of the way
and minute of the day. And in those moments when she truly didn't
understand why or what she was doing, she continued to trust in the
Lord, until that time when he revealed his will unto her.

How had she made it all those years without the gospel?

Then to top it off she'd given Sandy a call to tell her the good
news, and Sandy had exciting news of her own to share. She'd been
meeting with the missionaries regularly, and had even gone to
church. The missionaries had introduced her to one of the ward
members, a recent convert named Erika, who had offered to take
Sandy to the Oakland visitors' center and to a stake production about
the pioneers. Erika Ainsley was a psychology professor at Berkeley
and had grown up in the East, just like Sandy. They had a lot in
common and spent a lot of time together. They even had plans to go
on a double date with some men they'd met at a regional dance in
San Jose.

Yes, a lot had happened in the last two months. Things, Alex realized, that might not have happened had she not followed the Lord's
promptings and gone on this trip to Europe.

"Well, we're set," Rich said, handing her ticket and boarding
pass to her.

"Were you able to get us seats together in coach?"

"No, they're booked solid. It all worked out though, and I think
we have your friend Nicko to thank."

"Nicko? Why?"

"We have seats together in first-class."

"First-class? Are you sure?"

"I had her check three times. I couldn't believe it either. And
remember how we thought about stopping in London so you could
visit your friend?"

"He didn't."

Rich nodded. "He did. An overnight in London, with first-class
accommodations."

Nickolas never ceased to amaze her. Sure, he had a hard business side of him, maybe even shrewd and indifferent, but he had a big heart and there was room for the gospel. A testimony would make the difference, shift his focus. And she had a lot of faith he would one day accept the gospel.

"You still have time to hit one more gift shop," he said. Rich had teased her unmercifully about the abundance of souvenirs and gifts she'd stuffed in her suitcases.

Alex shook her head. "The most important souvenir I'm bringing home is going to be sitting right next to me," she told him, at the same time lifting her left hand so the ring could catch the light. Her charm bracelet jingled with the movement.

Looking at her bracelet, Rich said, "It's going to take the whole trip home for you to tell me about each of the charms on that bracelet."

Indeed her bracelet was full, nearly every link dangling a reminder of someplace or something special.

"I hope someday I can take you to each of the places where the charms came from," Alex sighed hopefully.

"Well," Rich said, "I think that can be arranged. We haven't discussed our honeymoon yet."

Alex was speechless for a moment. "Rich, you don't mean it, do you?" she sputtered finally.

"Come back to Europe for our honeymoon? Why not?" he said.

"That would be wonderful." Alex leaned forward and kissed Rich happily on the cheek.

"Peter's expecting us in Salzburg. He wants to teach me how to yodel." Rich grinned.

Alex laughed, picturing Rich in lederhosen, on a stage with an oompah band, yodeling.

The flight attendant called for all first class passengers to board.

"Come on, sweetheart, I'm taking you home," Rich said.

"I don't care where you take me as long as we're together." Alex set down her bags. She didn't care if she was holding up the line. She was going to give Rich the hug of his life.

"Together forever," he whispered, squeezing her tightly.

And she knew this time it would be.

About the Author

Michele Ashman Bell is a busy wife and mother, but manages to find time between car pools and her children's activities to spend time each day writing.

"Aside from writing in my spare time," she says, "I spend most of my time encouraging, supporting, and driving my children to lessons, sports events, and recitals." Michele also enjoys designing and sewing costumes for her daughter Kendyl, who is a competitive ice skater.

Michele served a mission to Frankfurt, Germany, but finished her last seven months in the California San Jose Mission. At some point she would like to write a book about her experience of having two missions in one. She has held positions in both the Relief Society and Young Women organizations. Most recently she has served as Young Women president of her ward.

"Working in the Young Women organization for the past three years," Michele says, "has given me a deeper understanding of the importance and obligation to write stories that uplift, inspire, and edify readers, as well as entertain them."

As a nationally certified group fitness instructor herself, Michele enjoys writing about a character involved in the fitness industry. She also enjoys remodeling her home, spending time with her family, and traveling both inside and outside of the United States. Writing this book gave her a chance to relive a trip she took to Europe with her husband just before she began this book.

Michele and her husband Gary are the parents of three children—Weston, Kendyl, and Andrea—and are anxiously awaiting the arrival of a fourth in the spring of 1998. They currently make their home in Sandy, Utah.

In addition to a novel, *An Unexpected Love*, Michele's short fiction has also appeared in *The Friend*.

Michele welcomes readers' comments and questions. You can write to her at P.O. Box 901513, Sandy, Utah 84090.